Praise for *You Know Her*

"A crackerjack debut thriller." —Bruce Tierney, *BookPage*

"There's a killer mystery at the center of this novel that will keep you up turning pages deep into the night. Jennett mastered the pace and secrets of this thriller that you won't ever be able to forget."
—*Debutiful*

"This debut author gives a twist to the crime novel."
—Konstantin Rega, *Virginia Living*

"Meagan Jennett doesn't mind bucking stereotypes—in fact, her sensational debut novel *You Know Her* thrives because of it."
—Dawn Ius, *The Big Thrill*

"Stellar debut . . . Jennett is a writer to watch."
—*Publishers Weekly* (starred review)

"A subversive serial-killer tale that dives headfirst into a furious mind."
—*Kirkus Reviews*

"Suspenseful and surprising, equal parts lyrical and chilling, *You Know Her* draws us relentlessly—and eagerly—into the cat-and-mouse duel between a young cop and a budding serial killer. A crackling debut." —Meg Gardiner, author of the UNSUB series

Mike Kropf

Meagan Jennett

You Know Her

Meagan Jennett is an escaped bartender who traded in
crafting cocktails for crafting her own tales. Originally
from Crozet, Virginia, she now lives in Scotland, where
she is pursuing a doctorate of fine arts at the University
of Glasgow. Her work has been published in the journal
From Glasgow to Saturn and in *Skirting Around* maga-
zine. *You Know Her* is her first novel.

You Know Her

Meagan Jennett

You Know Her

MCD PICADOR FARRAR, STRAUS AND GIROUX NEW YORK

MCD
Picador
120 Broadway, New York 10271

Photograph on title page and part openers by GikaPhoto By waraphot / Shutterstock.com.

The Library of Congress has cataloged the MCD hardcover edition as follows:
Names: Jennett, Meagan, 1989– author.
Title: You know her / Meagan Jennett.
Description: First edition. | New York : MCD / Farrar, Straus and Giroux, 2023.
Identifiers: LCCN 2022055013 | ISBN 9780374607098 (hardcover)
Subjects: LCGFT: Thrillers (Fiction) | Novels.
Classification: LCC PR6110.E563 Y68 2023 | DDC 823/.92—dc23/eng/20221130
LC record available at https://lccn.loc.gov/2022055013

Paperback ISBN: 978-1-250-32190-9

Designed by Abby Kagan

To Jeffrey and Arada, whom I miss very much

You Know Her

After

(Before the End)

It is almost October.

If the bees around me are aware of this, they make no mention of it. Instead, they bob and weave in the hazy air, drunk with the heat of a summer that has stretched on weeks too long. From flower to flower they float, scooping sticky clumps of pollen onto black legs. A few have discovered my picnic basket and busied themselves with raiding the half-opened jar of blackberry jam, long tongues probing the curve of its rounded lip. One bee crawls down inside the glass, dangerously close to the gelatinous quicksand. Another collides with a nearby flower, spins, and rolls in the center of its waving head. There is something so urgent about her action, so unlike the laid-back bumbler we believe these creatures to be. And yet the flowers live for this, the violence of the bees.

Sunlight blooms through the gnarled arms of an apple tree above me. I've curled myself into her roots, and in minutes I'm half-asleep, lost in the droning symphony of wingbeats, the drowsy kiss of late-morning sun on my skin. Something pokes at me though.

Beneath the sweet stench of apple rot lies something richer, a smell I could dip a finger into; just a hint now, but building, thickening.

A new sound has joined the hum of the bees. Its buzzing is more insistent, a higher whine than the baritone of apiary wings; a flute, to foil the chorus of cellos. In another minute something lands, light and delicate on my lips.

The flute pauses.

The smallest of feet tiptoe one after another across my mouth. I purse my lips, send this traveler into the air on a puff of my breath. The flute resumes. She is above my eyes now, and if I cross them just right, I can see her.

A blowfly.

I'd been wondering how long it would take for them to show up this time.

I watch her float, land, creep across the gently blueing body lying next to me.

December

Sophie

My story begins as it so often has: I was ignoring a man at a bar. Ignoring him, truthfully, because in all the months he'd been coming to sit two feet across a hammered-copper counter from me, he'd never bothered to learn my name. Somewhere, in revenge, I'd forgotten his; plucked it out of my pocket and dropped it to the floor, to be swept away with the food scraps at the end of the night. He became, simply, Bud Light, an epithet gifted in honor of the only words he ever deigned to toss in my direction. He was brothers with Whiskey Ginger, Beer Is the Only Thing That Can Have Too Much Head, and Give Me a Smile Girl.

When I was still young and dewy, I thought these sorts of men were nothing more than a residue, akin to mold slime under the sink and confined to the seedy, late-night dives of my early cocktailing days. Odious, but easily scrubbed away with the right sort of acidity. Soon enough, I learned they exist in every bar, from sticky-floored college dens to sleek date-night spots; they are as much a part of the decor as the fruit flies. Once, I thought they were harmless and laughed at them. They climbed up out of the mold then, as maggots do, and flew into my mouth. A thousand licking tongues laid their voices like eggs in the soft places of me, hatching with every slippery compliment drifting down my thigh, every brazen joke squeezing my waist. An entire universe of mites writhing, making a home, under my skin.

I should have known better. That's what they always say. She should have been smarter, should not have walked alone at night, should not have worn that skirt, not have opened her laughing mouth to those voices. (Even if that laugh was her shield, which so often it was.) If she'd kept her mouth, her legs, her heart closed, they'd never have gotten in.

I should have known better because I knew them for what they were, though I didn't remember at first. As a girl, I'd spent long hours scrambling through tall grass and thick undergrowth in the woods behind our house. My legs, bare save for tattered shorts, were an easy target for chiggers and clover mites. I screamed the first time I saw the insects crawling up my ankles, gnawing into still-pale, spring flesh. When I showed my father, he laughed. Mites, he told me, were the price to pay for stepping out into the wild world. If I didn't want them, I'd have to cover up, have to shield myself from the fresh air. He showed me how to brush clear nail polish over the holes they'd bored. The mites were alive under my skin, he explained, but were easily suffocated by a plug of dried polish. I painted and waited, let my body become a graveyard, and after a few days the itching fell quiet. My father left before he could show me how to paint over the holes drilled by the tongues of men.

After so many years nodding to Bud Light and his ilk, smiling, listening to them whine about their small worries and laughing at their tasteless jokes, their voices all the while building and churning and burrowing under my skin, I have become a creeping thing, hidden under smooth facade. *Smile*, they tell me, and I let the mites scuttle backward along the pitted curve of my jaw, tug my mouth into a Halloween mask. Here is my skull, grinning.

There was a time when they didn't bother me so much, their voices, not after I learned how much power I wield from the cramped space behind a bar counter. You see, more often than they realize, men hand you the very rope you need to hang them.

That night, the last night of the year, was a breath caught in my throat. Our sweet little town of Bellair, home to a mere seven thousand souls, is not a party destination; our New Year's revelers leak away past the thorn-bound town line to the sheen of nearby Charlottesville or the dirt and glitter of Richmond. A few might even splurge on a trip up to Washington D.C. Some people prefer to throw their own parties, popping in to invite those of the staff they like (*Swing by after you get off! We'll still be rockin'!*). The rest stay home, fighting sleep in front of blaring television screens. Later, out on winding roads, their fluorescent jail cells hungry and waiting to be fed, cops prowl the dark like sharks, alert for weaving stragglers. A drinking holiday is no friend to a small town.

Locked in that little bar, the Blue Bell, we waited, for the pop that may or may not come, the horde that our fearless manager, Ty, was certain would burst through at any moment because, "That one time," he reminded us for the thousandth time as he stood at the end of the counter, fixing his tie, "New Year's 2015. We weren't prepared and we got our asses handed to us. Remember that, Soph?"

What I remembered was a hungover dishwasher lagging and a busboy too busy flirting with the servers to concentrate on his job, but I let Ty speak. His voice is a gnat buzzing around my head, easily ignored. Meanwhile, the brand-new boxes of champagne flutes he'd ordered special for the holiday stayed where he'd plopped them, unopened and restless under the ice well. My barback should have unpacked and cleaned them by then, but he'd gone down to look for limes twenty minutes earlier and still not returned. Most likely chitchatting somewhere. If Ty wanted to wash and polish the glasses himself, I was happy to let him do so. It certainly wasn't going to be me who did.

Someone, probably the hostess, had draped flimsy streamers about the room. They twisted through one another, glinting silver and gold in the low overhead light. Oversize balloons, tethered to chairbacks and table legs, bobbed at the end of thin strings. The servers played at catching one another unawares with a balloon to the face or rubbed hard into coiffed hair until it frizzed. After a while, they all looked like baby chicks, fuzzy hair waving in a soft crown above their heads. Squeals and laughter rang through the room when someone caught my missing barback as he was coming up from the basement, his scrawny arms laden down with bottles, heavy bags of fruit swinging from his hands. He stumbled, caught himself, flushed pink. I tried not to roll my eyes. It was hard though, with "Happy New Year" blaring from the silly holiday headband Ty had insisted I wear. I was just as ridiculous as the rest of them.

Fifteen minutes to open, Chef emerged from his kitchen to announce the specials, shoving a plate of some dead fish across my clean countertop. It skidded to a stop near my elbow, to stare glassy-eyed at the streamers sparkling above it. The servers crowded in, greedy eyes fixed on the fish, ears cocked, half-listening to the lecture they were getting on the proper pronunciation of the specific sort of pepper delicately trailing around the rim of the plate.

"Wifey," Chef sang, passing a fork in my direction. This is a game all kitchen guys like to play, a verbal slip, a promise with an edge. *Wifey*, they call you when they're in a good mood; how quickly their declaration of love becomes slamming pans and *fucking cunt* when we're three hours into a dinner shift and knee-deep in the weeds, only to melt saccharine again when they're desperate for ice water ten minutes later. I get to be Top Wifey because I control the closest water gun, and more importantly, the alcohol. I suppose that also makes me Top Cunt.

The rest of the forks were dumped in an unceremonious pile next to the plate, for the servers to scrabble and squawk over, scoop slippery bits of fish into their mouths. Within minutes, the plate was bare and Ty whisked it away, swiping a finger through the last of the sauce.

Battle plans were drawn, sections divvied up, finishing touches made. We drew in a breath promptly at five o'clock, when, gleaming and trussed, we opened the doors to what we knew would be a dead place, a waiting place, an empty bar on New Year's Eve.

Sophie

·

What I wasn't waiting for was Bud Light, who slouched in not long after we opened. He'd come for his usual, he announced, crashing down into his favorite stool. Its rickety wooden legs creaked under the violent addition of his weight and I held my breath for its collapse, but the chair stood firm. Disappointed at his luck, I passed him a bottle, put the bowl game on TV, and turned my back on him until a time when he might become more interesting.

And then the night opened its lazy mouth and drooled us all to sleep. We twiddled our thumbs through cocktail hour, the servers gathering to stand in flocks at the computers before Ty shooed them away with that absurd proverb, favored by managers everywhere: "If you have time to lean, you have time to clean, folks! Go find something to do."

They scattered, for a moment. Two to gossip and pretend to sweep the patio, another pair into the kitchen to see what they could wheedle from the sous. My barback, apparently fearful that this edict was also meant for him, shuffled some of my cocktail menus around before placing himself in the far corner with a frown on his face that I suppose he must have thought looked like concentration. The box of glassware, now tucked under that end of the bar, waited, unopened.

To his credit, he did look down at it, once, consideration curling out of his ears like smoke, before he picked up a polishing rag to fiddle with instead. There was a time in my life when I would have just unpacked it. An easy task, it would take all of two minutes—just like picking up that sock your husband left on the bedroom floor, the one he walks past without a glance; just like putting the toilet seat down because he forgot again. I've grown tired of being responsible for men. The barback is my support staff; I would not do such women's work for him.

So the box sat.

A few customers dribbled in, and dribbled out again. Bud finished one beer, then another, and another, ordered steak frites, another beer. His eyes never left the TV. When he needed me, he'd grunt or wave or find something quietly obnoxious to do until I noticed him. It might have gone on that way all night, this game we played for the few dollars he'd tip me, if the winds blowing us around hadn't shifted.

Four hours from midnight, Bud started to fiddle with his latest near-empty bottle. This could have been the signal that he would like another, or it could have been a twitch, prompted by the tackle that stopped his ball mere feet from the needed yard line. Third down. How frustrating.

While he watched spandexed college boys slam into one another, I watched the last sip of beer trickle along the smooth bottleneck and disappear down his throat. When he put it back on the counter I heard a hint of annoyance in the tap of glass on copper: a knock at my door. He nudged it an inch or so further in my direction with the tip of one callused finger. His eyes stayed fixed on the screen, on those boys who'd failed once more in their offense and were now clumped together, redrawing plans. Bud swore under his breath, tapped his fingers along the bottom of the bottle. I wondered how long it would take for him to nudge it all the way off the edge. Now he was interesting; the noose slipped over his head.

My barback, seeing something useful to do, swept the bottle from the counter to throw it away. He forgot to ask though if Bud wanted anything else, so the man's hands flapped empty. Noose tightened. I watched.

Just as the game cut to commercial and it looked like he might actually have to speak to me, a pair of thick, pink hands swatted through the heavy portieres draped over our front door.

Ty hangs these infernal curtains like clockwork every fall, right after the first frost. "To keep people warm, keep the chill out," he says. That may be true. What they do best though is trap old ladies in waves of heavy fabric, cocooning them in a sea of black felt until, buzzing, they shoot out the other side, angry bees ready to sting the first poor server who forgets to bring them water *with* a lemon. Light ice. Our hostess, a sweet thing plucked from the local high school, was used to this sort of madness by then and so sprang into action like a seasoned warrior at the first sign of hands.

Her routine was simple: gently tug the curtains aside, so as not to embarrass the poor stranger, then sing a welcome as she ushered them in and pulled the curtains closed again. She'd hold out thin arms to catch each puff or wool coat as it was peeled off a back and flung toward her, hiding the strain in her face as she heaved them up onto the rack.

Next, the required rota of questions: "Just the two of you? Great! Would you like a table or a spot at the bar? Maybe one of our high-tops? Best of both worlds, and the view of the mountains is *lovely* from the seat right here! Perfect! Will you be needing food menus tonight, or just drinks and dessert? We're running a fresh-caught rockfish special for the holiday. The chef let me try a bite earlier and it was *ah*-mazing. And of course, a free glass of champagne for everyone who rings in the new year with us!"

To be successful in this industry, you must become a very good liar, a quality I suspect we have in common with kindergarten teachers and escorts. Smile, wipe your eyes clear of any thoughts, lift your voice. The trick is to show just enough of the self below your mask, tell just enough of the truth so that your guests drop their guard.

None of us should ever be trusted.

This particular set of hands were connected to a plush, gray barrel perched atop two crisp, khaki legs. Tan docksiders, Oakleys, and a gaudy, striped bowtie completed the ensemble. I knew this man. I'd seen him hundreds of times before, at football games and frat parties and country club luncheons. He's stepbrother to Whiskey Ginger, cousin to Too Much Head. This is Jungle Juice in the Pi Kapp Basement, though now that he's grown and got his newly minted Juris Doctor, he's trying to be his daddy, so he'll declare himself Maker's Mark Old Fashioned, if you please.

If the shrinking violet behind him was as much like her momma as the pearls she wore at her throat, she'd be Pinot Grigio, but my money was on Rosé, the pink drink being the libation of choice for the ladies of the millennial American bourgeois.

I watched the hostess skip up to them and throw herself open in a wide smile as she took the proffered coats and gloves, reaching behind her to the stack of menus on her stand. But this boy, who wanted us to think he was a man, swept right past her, his hand on the small of his partner's back, steering for my bar.

Something sparked under my right shoulder blade, in the center of the knot that had pinned itself there years ago, the one I could never seem to loosen no matter what I tried. By that New Year's Eve, it had been bound for so long by teeth and tongues and the empty muscle aches of too-long hours that it would never release.

Stools scraped the hard floor; the couple sat.

Bud coughed.

"Happy New Year." I pushed drink menus toward them. The forgotten hostess trailed behind, dinner menus clutched tight to her small chest. She knew when to make herself a ghost. Still, I saw the frustration in the way she bit her bottom lip before she smiled, the curt bounce of her ponytail as she skipped back to her stand, dismissed by their disregard. The mites had made a home in her too, though she hadn't realized it yet.

"We've been out wine tasting all day," Old Fashioned announced when I asked what I could get for them. As if that was an answer I could do anything with.

Out of the corner of my eye, I saw more hands flap through the curtains, more flustered faces pushing inside. I began to wonder if the night would be busier than I had anticipated, if we'd get the dreaded late pop. It's money, right? Butts in seats are tips in pockets, that's how the wisdom goes. The truth though is that after hours dawdling through a dead night, the late pop is a punishment. Chaos spills through the door with every new guest; tempers flare, mistakes are made, and customers, more hungry and less patient at this delayed dinnertime, groan and grumble while their generosity shrinks.

More hands, more coats tossed onto a fattening rack. Servers clogged the soda station, loading trays full of water. The TV above me flashed the score; the game was almost over. I'd have to change the channel soon.

I turned back to Old Fashioned, made his statement a question: "Sounds like you had a lovely day. Was there anything in particular that you liked, that I can pour for you here? Or are you done with wine for now?"

"Something nice, I think," he began, his voice a lazy drawl. The teeth biting my shoulder let go then, and a thousand bodies rode the ooze of his voice down the stairstep processes of my vertebrae.

"Something to celebrate—we just got engaged!" she squealed, thrusting her hand over the counter toward me.

"On Christmas, technically," he said.

Up front, the hostess pulled out her notepad for a waitlist. Behind me, the ticket machine began to cough up orders.

"Oh! Wow." I never know what to do with myself when they do this. I made my face a sunbeam. "Well, congratulations. That's wonderful."

It was anything but. Engagements mean dessert and a split of champagne on the House. Engagements are bad for bartenders who depend on sales for tips. But have you forgotten already? I'm a good liar.

"Sophie," the hostess, suddenly at my side out of nowhere, whispered. She had the phone glued to her ear, a scrap of paper clutched tight in her hand. She tipped her head toward the young couple. "His dad's on the phone, says he's got the bill. I took down his credit card info." Her eyes misted. "Yes, sir, I have her right here . . . Do you need anything else from him?"

I looked down at the paper in her hand, the numbers written in the neat, looping script of a teenaged girl.

"Nope. We're good, lady. Thanks."

"Your dad's paying for us?"

"Looks like it."

Bud looked up at me, opened his mouth like he might actually try to remember my name. "I'll be with you in just a second!" I sang as I passed him. Let him hang himself.

There's a trick bartenders play when we want something. We're no different than you—we want what we can't have; like that bottle of wine our owner won't sell by the glass, that he drinks with his buddies over steak frites and flatbreads, that he never offers his staff even a taste of.

You have to size up your customers just right. In a small-town bar like this, most of them will shy away from the price of a bottle like the one I chose for my guests. Those who bite the bullet and buy it will usually finish it. But these two had been drinking all day; it was clear from the watery sheen of their eyes, the red flowers blossoming on their cheeks. No doubt Daddy would want him to buy his fiancée the best glass of wine to pair with that rock on her finger. If they liked their bartender enough, maybe they'd even save the last swallow for her. It's a different sort of noose, more delicate and difficult to place.

I set my snare, dropped the bottle on the counter in front of them, so they might imagine it was already theirs. Another couple squeezed into stools on the far side of Bud. The ticket machine whined and scraped out more orders.

"Hands!" Chef yelled for someone to come pick up food, his voice booming through the swinging kitchen doors. "Can I get hands!"

"It's red." Old Fashioned pouted. "Claire's not a huge fan of red. Do you have nice rosé? Or dry white? Something from Fox Hall? We went there earlier and liked them."

"Excuse me, miss!" Sour teeth stung the back of my throat. *Miss.* I hate that word. I'm not a child. "Hello? Can we get some water?" The man to Bud's left tapped the counter with hard fingers. Where was my barback? He should have covered that.

"Oh yes! Fox Hall," Rosé, who was apparently named Claire, agreed.

"Miss?"

The line of tickets behind me flopped over the front of the machine and began a lurching drip downward, while the bell above the door chimed again. More hands flapped in. Dirty glassware began to pile up at the end of my bar. Where was my fucking barback?

"Can we get menus, please?"

There he was, clearing tables for the servers. Why the hell was he out on the floor? Where was Ty?

"Hey, Sophie, do you mind if I pour those beers I ordered? Table eleven's getting squirrelly." One of the servers touched my elbow.

"Go for it. Just don't forget to stab the ticket."

"Hands!"

In emergencies, hospital doctors use a triage system to gauge which patients to care for. Restaurants work on much the same system. First, your dying: the man who needs water and a menu before he makes a real fuss. Then, your hurting: I cracked Bud another beer, dropped it in front of him, and pulled my tickets from the machine. Finally: your small aches and pains.

Before you do anything: Breathe. Find the calm in the eye of the storm.

Don't forget to smile, Sophie.

"White?" I addressed the couple while I poured liquor into an empty shaker. *Two counts vodka. One count Cointreau. Lime. Cranberry. A cocktail so basic I'm bored. Next.* I dropped the drink at the server station, returned to pick up the offending wine bottle, twirled it in my hands. They were so close to the snare. I could not lose this battle; I had a weapon.

I caught Claire's eye. I needed her to believe we were friends, that she could trust me.

"You're absolutely right. Virginia isn't typically known for her reds, so I don't blame you for not liking them. This one though? This one is really something special—served at the royal wedding. A gift, from the first colony to the future British Queen." That the wedding had been some years ago, that no one outside our little corner of the world cared, was not important. What this woman needed was a chance to feel important, and what her fiancé needed was the chance to give that to her. People make themselves too easy to read.

Next ticket. *Rum. Coke. Next. Double-shot vodka, chilled. Squeeze of lemon. Simple syrup. Sugared rim. Now I'm sticky. Annoying. Next. Beer. Shit.* Beer was a step away, a turned back, seconds wasted waiting for a tap to pour. Time to make moves.

"You mean . . . not *the* royal wedding. As in Kate and William?"

This is when you look to him, to welcome him into the conspiracy. The key with couples is to find a balance, so no one feels left out. And if I kept my attention locked on them, I might be able to avoid the stares from Glass of Water for just a minute longer.

They were taking too long. Someone's fingers beat my counter in an impatient tattoo. My barback bowled in behind me, a heap of dirty glassware dangling off his fingers and more clutched tight in his arms. I pressed forward, to avoid a collision. His elbow scraped my back.

"I'm going to go pour this beer." I held the ticket up, made my eyes a plea. "You think about it, and I'll be right back." Some madness pinched me then, and I pulled the cord: "Should I grab two glasses on my way back, just in case?"

"Hunter, we have to!"

"Whatever you want, Claire Bear."

All around me, the bar filled up and I felt the wild scramble of an unexpected pop take a stranglehold on the House. If I could stay calm, ignore the nerves twining up my legs, and smile just right, let sniffs and scowls and drunken laughter run down my back, then in a few hours I might have something to celebrate too. That wine did look awfully pretty in a glass.

"Cheers, y'all!"

The hours, which I had expected to be stale things, bloated and grew turgid as more customers packed into the Blue Bell. Where they had come from and why they were here this year out of all years, I didn't have the time to find out as I danced from one guest to the next, back to the kitchen to check on a plate ("Hey, Wifey, you saving a New Year's kiss for me?"), to Bud, who seemed immune to the chaos around him, and finally to the ticket machine, which never stopped spitting and whining and shooting out order after order. All the while, the knot in my shoulder frayed and sparked, that ruined scapula turned into flint; my mouth tugged up into her skeleton grin.

Twenty minutes 'til, the box of flutes was hastily ripped open, cardboard fraying and grunting at the sudden assault. Ty dug his hands in like some army soldier in a movie, pulling out each glass with careful quick movements to be handed to the barback, who ran them through the wash as fast as he could. He always worked better when the boss was around.

Cleaned, dried, filled, the glasses were shoved onto servers' trays and into the forest of empty, impatient fists that shot out at me from across the bar. The countdown began.

Ten . . . nine . . . couples paired off . . . eight . . . seven . . . six . . . servers hastily grabbed any stray glasses they could find, splashed in a bit of champagne . . . five . . . four . . . I did the same . . . three . . . Bud picked up his beer . . . two . . . one . . .

We tipped down over the trembling wire of midnight and suddenly the world felt hollow, the hours of hungry anticipation deflated and yielding nothing more than a halfhearted "Auld Lang Syne" and a kiss on the cheek from the chef, who had ambled out of his kitchen as the countdown started to tip the last of a champagne bottle into his mouth.

Celebrations finished.

January

Sophie

The ritual of closing began.

Feeling their welcome ebbing, our midnight guests swarmed the hostess at the front door. Ever-smiling, ever-cheerful in her adieus, she ducked out of their way as they swept over and around her, reaching greedily for coats, scarves, hats.

Back on the floor, servers swooped down over tables, snatching up champagne flutes and depositing them on my bar to be washed before circling back around again to swipe crumbs off sticky tabletops. Someone pulled out a bucket and broom to clear away a family of shattered flutes that lay glittering in a warm puddle on the floor. Balloons were cut off chairbacks and once again screaming giggles rent the air as they were punched into tired faces or rubbed on deflated hair. In a few minutes, those same cackling servers would be tussling for a spot at one of the computers and clogging the kitchen aisles, mouths open for any scraps of food the chef might be willing to toss their way once he took a break from banging around pots and pans, joking with his kitchen in their homegrown dialect of Spanglish, rude hand gestures peppered throughout. My barback stood in the corner, gazing off into the middle distance while he wiped a rocks glass with a polishing cloth. The stare of the war wounded. I let him stay there for a while; the shock of having to be useful for an hour can be tough. Out of the corner of my eye, I saw Ty slip down the hall to the quiet of his office, as he always did at the end of the night.

Bud, still with us, glanced over once or twice at the growing colony of dirty glassware creeping closer to his elbow before tossing a wad of cash atop his check and clambering from his stool, off to wherever he goes. Behind him, the bell above the door tinkled. Everyone on the floor flinched, Pavlov's reaction to the noise of an intruder after a very long shift.

False alarm. Blessed silence fell.

It tinkled again.

"I'm not too late, am I?" A voice I knew too well dripped around my ear and down the back of my neck. The knot beneath my shoulder blade sparked, hot and angry. "Y'all aren't closing up already?"

"Oh no, Mr. Dixon!" the hostess chirped. "The kitchen's closed, but I think Sophie's still open for a bit if you want to grab a seat at the bar. Do you need a cocktail menu?"

I could have killed her then, dear sweet thing that she was. Instead, I looked up and smiled at the man who was sliding into Bud's vacant seat.

"How's my favorite bartender?" Mark Dixon asked me, his whitened teeth flashing. His voice scuttled down my back; a thousand tongues wriggled under my skin. "Did you have a good New Year's?"

"I was at work, Mark." To make my point, I shoved the door to the dishwasher closed and turned it on. A loud rumble and hiss ground out from its squat, steel body, cutting off conversation. My barback, reading the steel in my aura, scampered down to the basement to restock.

"Last call," I said as the washer settled into its routine. "What can I get you?"

"I would hardly call this work, Sophie," Mark drawled, sliding one finger along the cool length of my bar counter.

"I'm closing, Mark."

"C'mon now! Lighten up. It's New Year's. You're always so *serious*, Sophie. Listen, pour me a drink, and why don't you make one for yourself too. Lindsey won't mind." He tossed out my boss's name with a lazy wave of his hand. "You must have something left over at the end of a night like this. Half a glass of bubbles in the fridge? Any rails you need to finish off? I'm not picky."

Disgust scuttled across my collarbone.

Over the years, I'd become Mark's favorite play toy. Some days I wondered if he could see that knot he'd helped build in my back, in a hidden place so deep that even I couldn't reach it. He certainly took a kind of pleasure at shoving a key into it and winding me up, something he got away with because Mark was A Friend of the Owner.

Not the kind of friend who thinks they know Lindsey because he stopped by their table once to ask them how their dinner was, that same kind of friend who would shriek at the hostess on a slammed night if they're not seated immediately, because *"Don't you know we know the owner?!"* No, Mark would never have to do that, because he would already be at his seat at the bar, which was his whenever he wanted it, no matter how busy we were, with a drink in his hand that he'd never have to pay for.

Mark Dixon was the kind of friend who had met Lindsey in a frat house twenty years ago at a huge state school where the official mascot was a culture appropriated and cartoonishly fierce, but the true face of the student body was a beer keg. He was the type of friend who played on Lindsey's team in charity golf tournaments, who partied with him in the Caribbean whenever they felt like taking a week off to get blackout drunk, their girlfriends du jour scurrying behind them picking up the pieces while tittering to themselves that "boys will be boys."

Mark called himself an investor in local businesses, which meant he had more money than he knew what to do with and his sole purpose in life therefore was his quest for the Next Great Barstool. In any other place he was without a doubt Tequila and Tonic, but here at the Blue Bell he was Top Shelf Whatever He Wants Whenever He Wants It Would It Kill You to Smile Sophie.

But it's hard to smile for someone who makes a habit of squeezing in just before the door locks for the night, when he knows any other customer would be turned away; who asks you to pull wrapped juices out of the fridge and cleaned bottles down off shelves; who dirties your polished glassware without a thought. If he ever brought any cash to tip me with, we might have struck a deal. As it was, his payment was his presence, something we disagreed upon the value of.

Rails and bottle scraps wouldn't do and we both knew that, so I poured two fingers of the new mezcal Lindsey had ordered to play with during the holiday season over my last block of ice, dropped in a bit of curling orange peel, and pushed the glass toward Mark, hoping that would hold him until he'd had enough of bothering me for one night. There's a smoke and a sting to mezcal that keeps a mouth closed in a certain kind of meditation. Sometimes you have to create your own peace.

It would hold him long enough for the servers to come flocking to my counter, bellies pressed tight to the edge, yammering and ready for their shift drinks. He could talk to them. In the meantime, I had sales to close out, a cash drawer to count and lock away, fruit to wrap, bottles to wipe, and trays upon trays of glassware to polish. I turned my back on Mark. That was a mistake. I hadn't yet got him in the position to hang himself.

As long as I've been behind a bar, I've kept my drawer a certain way: Biggest bills to the left, smallest on the right, everyone else in descending order in between. They must all face up, presidential chins pointing left. Any mutineers are swiftly dealt with. That way, when I pull everyone out to count at the end of the night, there's no confusion. No one's shoved into a corner or ripped in half. No one's soggy. No one's lying in wait in the wrong pocket, ready to trip up my careful count. Everything is ordered and sensible, and my bills, crisp and clean and dry, slide through my fingers one after the other with a satisfying hiss.

I opened the drawer.

One big hundo . . . one-fifty

Chair legs scraped the floor, and a thousand mouths came alive, chattering into the nape of my neck; teeth and feet scratching one by one up each delicate cervical vertebra. This is how men like Mark climb into my brain.

one-seventy . . . ninety . . . two-ten

Thick rubber footsteps squelched onto the mat beside me. His cologne, spicy and wooden, wound a veil across my face.

Concentrate. Two-thirty . . . two-forty . . . fifty . . . sixty

There was a sucking noise, and a swoosh of cold air hit my legs as he pulled the wine fridge open. Bottles tinkled as they bumped into one another, jostled by a strange hand.

"Mark, what are you doing behind my bar?"

"Just seeing what you have back here, sweetheart."

"Don't call me sweetheart."

sixty-five . . . seventy . . . seventy-five

"Doll."

The knot, which was no longer a knot but a shard of flint, flattened into a knife. Its point, searing hot, sifting through muscle and bone, and I saw it, shining and sharp, tearing through me (*infraspinatus, subscapularis*), my dignity squirming on the end of its tip. Behind me, Mark stood up, his breath catching a strand of my hair as he winced with the strain of lifting himself on knees that were not so young anymore. I heard them pop and crack in protest, and then silence. And then, tension. The space between us grew a body of its own, something solid, rigid, tense as an electric storm. I pressed tight to the register, but there was no escaping its weight. In my mind, I dared him to try to touch me while I finished counting.

two-eighty . . . eighty-five . . . ninety . . . one-two-three

He reached over me to pull the bottle of mezcal down from the shelf, curved his other arm around my waist to grab a rocks glass from the counter.

four-five-six

The splash of tequila into glass was a finger tracing my hip. His breath swept my hair again as he placed the bottle back in its place. The air prickled; a lightning storm rose from the ridges of my spine.

seveneightnine

"Hey, Sophie." His shoes squeaked as he moved back to his chair. "Do you mind peeling me a bit more of that orange before you wrap up your fruit? Or what about lime? Lime is better with tequila, isn't it?"

Mezcal isn't just any tequila, Mark. The orange sweetens the smoke. Lime would fight it. You'd think with all that money you'd have developed a palate . . .

"And did you dump the ice already?"

Three hundred.

I complained about Mark once to my manager, after the second or third time I met him, after he'd remarked on my body in a way that made me want to hide.

"What do you want me to do?" Ty had asked from his seat at our rickety table at the bar across the street, a dive called Tap House that catered to the worst of everyone's inclinations. Local legend held that the owner, a stout man named Joe, had traveled to Europe in his youth and learned that the acronym TAP stood for "Typical American Prick." And thus, a bar was born.

At first I thought the concern in Ty's eyes must have been for me, until I noticed how often they flicked up to the television hanging on the back wall. Tiger was making a comeback, and it looked like maybe the Americans had a shot at winning the Ryder Cup this year.

"Can't you talk to Lindsey? Tell him his friend's a creep?"

Ty sighed. "Look. I'm sorry if he makes you feel that way, but you have to understand, my hands are tied. I know he can come on a bit strong. Believe me, he annoys me too, but he's harmless. He hasn't touched you or anything, has he?"

"No, but—" How was I supposed to tell him that Mark had looked me up and down one afternoon and declared that I had a cute little shape, that my breasts were the perfect size: "A handful. No matter what a guy may say, Sophie, they don't want something they can't grab in one hand."

"Soph," Ty sighed, "I'm sorry. That's all I can say. Just ignore him and do your job."

His eyes slid up over my shoulder. Somewhere in Europe, Tiger sank his ball.

"Smile, Sophie."

Mark's empty glass skidded toward me. Without thinking, I reached out and caught it before it could fly off the end, put it in the dish rack. Meditation, I'd forgotten, only works for people who don't shoot down every ounce of liquor put in front of them. All the smoke, all the time and craft, slammed straight down his gullet. Two orange peels lay in tatters on the counter. I swiped them off. They were sticky in my fist.

"You got anything else? Something you're just going to throw away? You must have some leftover champagne."

"I'm closed, Mark. Why don't you go to Tap House? They should be open for a bit."

"I'd rather stay here and bother my favorite bartender."

"Well, you should maybe come up with a new plan."

As if on cue, the servers swooped one by one to my counter, tossing check-outs and tip-outs and cash for the House into a pile at one end before clambering onto stools like seagulls come to roost. Mark called to each one in turn, inviting them to drink and celebrate another year, to which they gladly agreed. Did I expect anything else? In all my time behind a bar, I've never seen a server turn down a shift drink.

They lined up on either side of him, ties pulled loose, collars unbuttoned, eyes bright with the relief of a long night ending. Someone called for a line of shots, and in a matter of seconds my clean countertop was soaked with rail whiskey, vodka, and tequila as they tipped their glasses into wide-open mouths. One of them pulled a half-drunk champagne bottle out of her purse and they passed it among themselves, pouring bubbles down throats with glee. The chef, hearing their cacophony, ambled out of the kitchen to take a swig himself. A glance to one side revealed my barback, hovering near the host stand, nervous and bouncing on the balls of his feet. I nodded. Let him be cut.

Ty was waiting for me in his office, his usual cup of coffee next to a snifter of Jameson.

"Not mixing them tonight?" I asked, nodding to the drinks.

"New Year's makes me want to taste my whiskey," he replied simply. "How much you got left to do out there?"

"Depends on how fast the servers clear out. They made a mess of my bar again. And Mark has parked his butt in a seat with them."

"He'll leave as soon as they do." As he talked, he counted the money in his hands, double-checked receipts, signed off on each one. "Are you okay locking up alone, or do you want me to stay?" The question that wasn't really a question.

"I'm fine."

"Great. Thanks, Soph." He looked up at me. "You're the best."

I know.

A Zoo Animal

S ophie."

A threat, a suffocation, an obligation, tapped the front window. I didn't look up.

"Sophie."

When I was a child, my mother took me once to the National Zoo up in D.C. Somewhere in the middle of a day spent wandering winding pathways of pebbled stone, we fell into the noisy crush of the Ape House. For the next hour, we gawked at howling gibbons, goofy orangutans, lemurs wrapped up in ringed tails longer than their own bodies. Above our heads, still free in the building, capuchin monkeys chittered and giggled, scampering through the row of trees that lined the center aisle. In a month they'd be confined to a cage after one of their number escaped through the front doors to vanish into the snarled roadways of D.C., but that afternoon they peered down at us from their branches, tiny mouths flashing into flattened grins so like the one I would learn to smear across my own face one day.

We found the main attraction by following the herds of children to a broad panel of glass, smudged from greasy faces, errant tongues and lips. There, in a dim concrete enclosure, sat the old silverback gorilla. He was hunched over, arms crossed, back turned in defiant objection to the hordes of snotty kids all wailing for him to look their way, to entertain them as his cousins had. The beast never moved, staying stubbornly turned away from even the loudest screechers. For a long time afterward, I chuckled at the memory, at this animal, like a child thinking no one can see him if he just pulled the blankets up over his face.

That was before I worked in restaurants; before I faced my own horde pressing into the front windows, hands smudging the glass, waiting for us to open so they could swarm in. Now that I am a zoo animal too, I understand the very real power of a mind that can look away, tuck those pesky intruders off in some other corner of reality for a little while.

I kept my eyes to my work, my breath on soothing the flint that sparked and burned again with every tap on the window.

"*Sophie.*" The tap became hard, knuckles on glass.

No. If I looked up, if we made eye contact, whoever it was would take that as an invitation. Everyone loves the idea of being that one customer allowed in after close. It was two a.m., the door was locked, my lights turned down. All I wanted was to sit in peace.

"Sophie!"

The bar was almost clean. One more pass with my rag and it would be gleaming, ready to be put to bed until the next day. One more pass and I could finally enjoy the glass of wine I'd worked so hard for, those hours that felt like days ago. The man outside didn't leave. His body was a blur in the shadows, snagging on the corners of my eyes. Tiny feet tiptoed down the length of my throat, the smooth slide of platysma, sternohyoid, sternocleidomastoid; those dangerous places where breath could be aroused or cut off. I felt them pause, coil through one another in the soft bowl above my collarbone. The flint under my shoulder sparked again, and I dipped my head down to relieve it.

The rapping grew harder, insistent. It moved along the front window toward my end of the bar. I bit down on my tongue; something rippled under my skin.

"Sophie, I can see you. Let me in!"

I looked up to find Mark's face inches from mine, pressed flat to the glass pane. His eyes were watery and half-crossed, his cheeks pink. So this was what the gorilla saw, all those ridiculous tourists demanding his attention. He should have laughed. I should have laughed. Finally, Mark looked like the pig he was.

Satisfied that he'd gotten my attention, he hit the window once more, hard, with the flat butt of his hand.

"I'm closed, Mark." I let each word drip off my tongue, smiling, sugary sweet.

"I have to pee!" He banged again, a dull, slapping thud that made the pane bounce. "Please! I can't hold it anymore. If you don't let me in, I'll piss out here on the sidewalk."

Fuckitall.

He stumbled in when I opened the door, mumbled a quick thanks as he waddled toward the clean bathroom, his hands pressed tight to his crotch like a toddler about to wet themselves. I heard the toilet seat flip up, tried to ignore the rest; his need had been so dire, he'd forgotten to close the door behind him.

"Hey, Sophie," he said as he emerged a few minutes later, wiping his wet hands on the sides of his pants. He pulled one of my barstools out of line, the metal legs scraping across the floor, and clambered up into it. Here it was, the question I knew he would ask, the real reason he was here.

"Yes, Mark?"

"Found anything you're ready to throw out?"

I let a rack of glasses I'd forgotten in the dishwasher be my excuse not to answer right away, kicking the metal door open to stand hidden in the swirling clouds of steam for one quiet beat as I plucked each word I would say like apples from a tree, checking for spots or imperfections in their tone. Only the right words would do. Drunk as Mark was, there was a very good chance he'd forget this conversation ever happened; if somehow he didn't, there was a very certain chance I'd hear about it from Ty.

I chose the simplest honesty. "I think you've had enough."

"What about that wine you've got stashed back there?" He nodded at Claire and Hunter's bottle, half-hidden behind the register. Now empty save for that one last pour, its glass shone dark green in the dim light, a velvet invitation to peace. As we pondered its form, something like exhaustion rose in my chest and bit the inside of my cheek.

"That's mine, Mark."

"Didn't your mother teach you how to share?"

"Yes, sir!" I made my voice a song, to confuse him. "She most certainly did. But today I feel like being selfish. I worked hard for that bottle, and a lady's got to be able to keep some things for herself, don't you agree?"

An arched eyebrow, pouted lips, these are my sword and shield in situations like this.

"Well, I won't argue with you on that, but," Mark began, his normally rich drawl grown slack with drink; it poured off his lips in a lazy drip. He had begun to slump in his barstool, his eyelids drooping, elbows digging into the countertop to keep him from landing facedown.

I let him slur to himself while I pulled glasses from the rack. The tips of my fingers reddened at their touch, but I felt no burn; years of holding scalding plates and glassware had numbed me to the sensation. You can get used to anything, given enough time.

Highballs were tipped onto their mat. Only used as water glasses, they didn't need to be polished and could instead cool and air-dry overnight. The wineglasses, rocks glasses, and snifters would have to be wiped smooth before they were put to bed. I counted the time off in my head. Another ten minutes. They had to dry a bit, otherwise they'd polish streaky. If I'd been alone, this was when I would have poured that glass of wine. Instead, it stood tucked into its corner behind the computer, out of reach unless I wanted to share.

"Sophie."

"Mark." I puttered around, trying to find anything else to occupy the time, to calm the small mob now scaling the muscular ropes of my supraspinous scaffolding. I felt Mark's eyes slip downward, the weight of his gaze a palm on the small of my back.

"Can you give me a ride home?"

My jaw cracked. "Seriously? Can't you ask someone else?"

I knew better than to ask if he'd called a cab. It was hard enough to get them to come out our way on a normal night. Winding back roads, twenty minutes from the next nearest customer, scared most cabbies away. If you did manage to snag one, it was a long wait for a high fare. On New Year's, when Charlottesville could provide them with quick turnarounds and surge pricing, they wouldn't even think about our dear Bellair. Not that I could blame them. And city folk, I can hear you thinking, *What about Uber?* Well, the day Uber or high-speed internet wants to come out to our neck of the woods, they'll be welcomed in with a parade. That promise doesn't seem to have enticed them as of yet.

No, people around here are used to driving home with one eye squinted shut, singing prayers to the Baby Jesus, Mary, and Joseph that they didn't steer themselves into a ditch or a deer. Tonight would be no exception.

"They left before I was ready." Mark swayed as he spoke; his breath swept over me, and I caught the reek of cheap booze pulled up from a dirty bar rail. I thought about leaving him. Let him walk home if he could. Maybe the cops would pick him up; a night in the drunk tank might do him some good. At the very least, it would be a story he'd love to tell his golfing buddies, a scandal he could pass around like popcorn. The truth, however, was that they'd probably just drive him home. Nothing sticks to guys like Mark. People stretched out hands to help him, cleared the path ahead, chuckled and shook their heads at his antics. Those times he did find himself in a tight spot became stories that he wound about himself like yarn, spooling them out at just the right moment. Life for Mark Dixon was a grand adventure.

He fell across the bar, his hands pressed together, pleading. "Please? I'll owe you. The best tip of your life."

I looked at him then, really looked at him; from his red cheeks to his crossed eyes, the thinning patch at his temples where he was beginning to bald. He smiled, a lopsided grin that belied the memory of a certain rakish charm and good looks, rusted by the relentless gravity of middle age.

"Fine." There was the truth. I loathed this man. I was disgusted by this man. This man helped pay my bills. "But I need to polish these glasses first, and before I do that I'm going to smoke a cigarette. Can you stay put while I do that?"

"You're my favorite bartender. You know that?"

"If you think that, here's a towel." I tossed one of the blue polishing rags his way. Keeping a customer like Mark occupied was the best way to keep him out of trouble. "Work on those snifters while I'm outside."

"Yes, ma'am!'"

There have been times in my life when I thought perhaps my gut instinct was misguided, that it was not wisdom but a nasty relic of some distinctly feminine flaw like jealousy, or the chemical properties of estrogen. Women, I have heard, are prone to flights of fancy, overthinking, silly anxieties of all forms; that it wasn't alarm bells we were hearing in our minds, but the siren call of Crazy. No one wants to be the Crazy Girl, so we put on our rose-colored glasses, make all the red flags look white.

So, there was a glimmer of time, when I walked back in and found Mark standing behind the bar, that I doubted myself. Maybe I'd been too hard on him. Maybe Ty was right and, bumbling and childish as he could be, he meant well deep in his heart. Even after I'd been rude to him, there he was polishing my glassware and putting it away for me. I took a breath, reminded myself to be kind, to smile, moved to help him.

"Thank you, Mark. I was just kidding, you don't really have to . . ." But then I saw what I knew I could not be seeing, what the low light and my own foolish self-doubt had hidden from me. "What are you doing?"

He froze, the glass in his hand half-raised. His lips were red, shining and wet. A thin dribble trailed down his chin. The bottle, my bottle, sat empty on the back bar.

I felt a roar in my chest and bit down hard to hold it back. Bile sloshed up the soft insides of my cheeks, and that knot that was a flint that was a knife grew so sharp I almost gasped. *Hold it, Sophie.* I could not explode. Not here. Not now.

"Get out," I whispered instead, my voice an icy fist. Red clouds bloomed on the edge of my vision.

"Soph, it's no big deal! I'll buy you a drink somewhere—"

"That was a two-hundred-dollar bottle, you idiot! Get out! *Please.*" Tears burned behind my eyes, but I couldn't let them fall. I wouldn't cry in front of this man and give him the ammunition he needed to laugh my anger away.

Silence thudded like a curtain between us, so thick and heavy it had a space of its own. Underneath, I heard the two-step pulse of my heart. Mark stared at me. I could see the inner calculus of his thoughts, feel the solid weight of his shock. Something about him crumpled then, and he stood before me like a kicked dog, hunched in on himself, eyes on my feet. He opened his mouth, closed it, opened it again, put the dirtied glass down on the counter.

"Can I still get a ride?"

Was he really asking that? *No!* I wanted to scream. *No, you may not, never, have a ride, have a drink, a seat, a smile, ever again.* What came out of my traitorous mouth was, "Yes, you can still have a ride. But get outside. Now."

He was leaning on my car when I stalked out a few minutes later, his breath curling into the cold night air.

"Sophie, do you hate me or something?" His voice was small.

"You're drunk, Mark." I unlocked the doors, climbed in. The car tilted as he dropped in beside me. I heard his seat belt click into place. The sour tang of something like guilt spilled through my lips. "I don't hate you. I'm tired. I had a long night, and I was really looking forward to that glass of wine."

He didn't speak as we crept out of the gravel lot behind the bar, up to the one lonely stoplight in town, glowing red above the intersection of Peach and Ellwood. I bent my gaze down the road, which unspooled to either side of us in a long, black ribbon. No sign of cops. No sign of anyone. Even Tap House was shadowed and empty. We were the last souls in a dead town, night creeping in around the edges of my car.

The light above us stood stubbornly red. I pulled out anyway. Who was going to see us?

"I'm sorry, Soph. Can I make it up to you?'"

That poisonous guilt rolled into my knot, burned; I tilted my head to one side to relieve it. A shadow skittered in front of my headlights, a fox or a cat, hard to tell in the dark; gone as soon as I caught a glimpse and never a worry to me. It's the deer you have to watch out for. They stand in the middle of the black road and wait for you to hit them, their eyes wide and shining in the headlights, watching death rush right at them.

"Did you get a New Year's kiss?"

"What?" I gripped the steering wheel. "No, and, Mark, I don't need one."

"C'mon! I feel bad. And it's good luck." His voice was wet and heavy. It sloshed over the space between us.

I built a wall. "I'm driving. And it's after midnight. Kissing time is over for the year."

"You need to loosen up."

I heard the soft brush of a coat folding in on itself, the plastic crackle and whine of the seat belt buckle straining as he leaned across the gap between us. Hot breath filled my ear, and then his tongue, his voice. "You're trouble, you know that?"

I slammed the car to a stop, tires screeching on slick asphalt.

"You need to get out." Everything crawled beneath my skin. My heart punched my chest so hard I thought it might burst straight through. Any softness I'd had for Mark, any pity, flew out of my body.

"Jesus, Soph! It's just a game!" He pressed closer, one hand skimming over my thigh. "Just relax. Haven't you ever wondered? I thought . . . sometimes I feel something between us."

The windows fogged with our breath, the night pressed closer, held the car tight in its fist.

"That's because you're a customer and I have to be nice to you." I prayed he wouldn't remember any of this in the morning.

"You're so funny." His hand wriggled under my shirt, cold fingers a brand on my bare skin, reaching, groping for the lip of my bra cup. "C'mon. Just a little game. Could be fun, if we get caught."

Once, when I was young, before I grew my own feet to stand on, I let a boy kiss me because he'd begged to. He'd been a friend, before that. Afterward, while we watched cartoons, he cried about his girlfriend, whom he'd realized as he pushed his lips to mine he really did love and could never leave. It had been a test, you see, one that in his mind he'd passed. I was never able to look at him with any respect again after that. There would always be mold over his face for me, a shadow, slimy and rotting. That was the day I learned that even to those who claimed to love me, I was a toy, a tool, a thing to be used.

I learned how disgust and shame could curdle in your belly and turn to anger. I learned that men never felt it, though they were the cause of it. And they were all the same.

I looked at Mark, his eyes shining, his lips hanging open like a pig's. "Get out now. Or I'll fucking kill you."

A Sphinx Asks a Question

Do you think he got out?

Nora

The dead girl lay at the end of the hallway. Shadows slithered across her moonlit body, fattening as they stretched around a curve, pooling in the broken crook of an arm. A few splintered off to twist through pale strands of hair that hung over her face, a macabre curtain dropped at the end of the show. Above her, a spiderweb of shattered glass crisscrossed the window; its panes smashed upon impact with her head once, twice, over and over until bits of bone sprayed out the back of her skull. As Nora Martin padded barefoot down her shadowy hallway, a breath, a breeze, a gasp, slipped through that ruined pane and wrapped itself around her ankles.

Lauren Morris, age twenty-one. Throttled. Beaten.

"She's not real," Nora whispered. "You know there's no window there. You know the hall is empty. You're in your own home, for chrissakes, and apparently now talking to yourself . . . and you need to pee before you wet your pants."

The woman in the bathroom was harder to ignore. Nora kept her knees pressed tight together as she perched on the toilet to avoid brushing the hand that hung, limp, over the lip of the tub. Even with her eyes closed, she could feel the specter's wide-open gaze into nothing; knew if she looked, she'd see the purple ghosts of fingers ringing the woman's throat in a grotesque necklace. She stood to wash her hands. A bubble escaped from between the woman's blue lips, burst with a sigh at the still surface of water that, like the ruined windowpane, was not there.

Patricia Ng, age seventy-three. Drowned.

A nagging thirst tugged Nora down the stairs to the kitchen, past the days-old detritus of a New Year's party, past the woman who hung limp from the ceiling fan. Her swollen feet tangled in the strings of a few exhausted balloons, just as they'd tangled in those sweet honeysuckle vines after a man hanged her and her partner from a creaking Virginia pine up there on the Blue Ridge.

Samantha Wyatt, age twenty-four. Hanged. Rachel Barber, age twenty-seven. Raped, hanged.

Jane Doe, age estimated early forties, was draped over the end of the couch, black blood pooling on the antique hardwood beneath her head. Her face, Nora knew, without needing to look at the woman who was definitely not there, had been beaten to oblivion by a blunt object, most likely a tire iron, after she'd stopped on the roadside to help the man who would kill her. She was the first one he murdered. The other two he'd only raped after stopping them to ask for directions to the nearest gas station. *Only.* Nora hated that word.

What she had wanted to ask him, after she got that first dispatch call to the abandoned vehicle on the side of Route 64 (the vehicle, they'd find out later, was a hot thing, burning their lead to ashes. Nora's best guess was that he'd taken Jane's when he fled, leaving the car he'd stolen behind, taking her registration and name with him), what she had wanted to ask was if he'd known that this woman he'd beaten to a pulp was a mother. When he brutalized her and left her in a ditch to die, could he feel the cracks and scars that crisscrossed her pelvis, the pain she was willing to bear for love?

A tattooed Jesus peered out from the naked curve of Jane Doe's shoulder, His hands folded together in eternal, unheard supplication.

The clock on the microwave glowed 5:36 a.m. Two hours until sunrise. She wanted to go back to bed, to Dan, who by now had probably rolled over to her side, to catch the last bit of her fading warmth. He was a starfish in his sleep, quietly colonizing the mattress with gangly-legged cuddles, the soft snores of someone safe. The ghosts didn't haunt his dreams. He couldn't hear them as they tumbled softly down the stairs on moonlit nights. He didn't see them hanging from invisible rafters above their bed. His nights remained undisturbed, his dreams blank pages. Unlike Nora, he didn't lie awake in the dark with the ache of their broken hearts beating within his own.

"Fuck it," she whispered, taking a swallow from her water glass. She wasn't going back to bed now.

Resigned to her insomnia, she stepped up on the shaky kitchen stool that Dan was always promising to fix and opened the cabinet doors. Above the fridge she kept a secret, to be indulged in only on nights like this, when her nightmares seemed to take on blood and bone and crawl out into the solid world.

This face was the hardest one, though the child never looked at her. Save for a small trickle beneath her nose, there was no blood. The babe lay curled into the far corner of the cabinet space, just as she had been when Nora found her that awful spring afternoon; shoved by her stepfather into the back of her momma's kitchen cabinet, to die alone while he tried to hide what he'd done.

This memory, this nightmare, this ghost, this little girl was listless and blue; her tiny hands pressed out in front of her as if to ward off the man who had shaken her until her brain ballooned. Or perhaps to give him a hug, to placate him the only way she knew. How early girls learn to soothe the anger of men.

Arya, her mother had named her. For strength. Arya Ward, age ten months. Shaken.

Nora closed her eyes and stretched one hand forward, searching for her green metal tin and the relief she kept hidden inside. If Dan knew about her cigarettes, he never mentioned them. She was thankful for that. How could she explain to her boyfriend that sometimes she needed to sit outside until her feet froze and her hands shook, sucking down smoke and nicotine and waiting for the sun to rise and wipe away the shadows in the hall?

"Haints," her momma told her one long-ago June morning, "are just people who died with questions in their mouths. They can't move on to heaven, sweetheart, until they get their answers."

It had been a drizzly day, chilly for late June. Tired of sitting inside listening to the maddening pit-pat of rain on the windows, they'd slipped out to the refuge of their covered front porch. Nora was in the gawky stage of her youth, all knobby knees and elbows, and so she sprawled across the rickety porch swing, legs akimbo, stretching curious fingers toward the snarled stems of the morning glory vines that coiled through the front railing. On this unseasonable day the flowers had spun themselves into fists, clamped tight against the wet and chill. Nora pulled one toward herself, determined to unspool it and see its hidden face.

"Be careful with my flowers, child," her momma had said, in the way of all mommas Nora knew, dropping the *d* at the end of the word and sewing it up instead with a sleepy *t* caught somewhere in the breath between her bottom teeth and her tongue. *Chilt*. And, like all mommas Nora knew, she didn't have to look at her daughter to know what she was up to. Instead, Emma's gray eyes were fixed on the ceiling above her, her mouth pressed into a thoughtful pout. Her hair, a mess of wild blond curls, was trapped for the moment beneath an old green bandanna, though a few stray wisps managed to poke through the edges, casting a crown about her brow when she leaned through patches of muted sunlight. Nora had often wondered which of her parents she'd inherited her own unruly locks from. There was no question about her eyes though, which were her daddy's, brown as a churning creek after a summer storm.

An aluminum pan of paint rested on the windowsill. Nora watched

Emma dip a roller down into it before lifting the paint-covered wool above her head to press to the ceiling. It hit the wood with a sticky crackle, and she wheeled it forward, smearing a streak of blue across their artificial sky.

"I won't hurt it, Momma. I just want to open it." She slipped a fingernail under one thin edge of flower petal.

"Those flowers are dangerous, baby girl."

"What?" A bolt of betrayal shot through Nora's chest. How many years had she played with this enemy on their porch? She released the half-opened bud, watched it coil slowly back in on itself.

Emma laughed. "They won't kill you. Just make you a bit sick if you eat the seeds. Real sick if you eat too many. You can touch them though. Be careful of handling the petals is all."

"Why?" Nora squinted up at her, suspicious.

"Because, child, if you hurt my flowers, I'll hurt you." Emma chuckled to herself at the joke, at her daughter's incredulous *Mom-maaa*; all the while, her arm worked in a soft back-and-forth arc across the ceiling, and the patch of blue grew. A few drops of paint fell to the canvas tarp she'd spread on the floor below. Nora counted them: one plop, two plops, three, four. She tapped her bare feet along with the beat and reached for the flower again, tugged it out of the vine muss.

"Why blue? The ceiling." Flower bud in hand, Nora tipped her gaze upward.

"To keep the haints away," her momma replied, her tone as matter-of-fact as if she were stating the weather forecast.

"They're scared of blue?"

"The wasps sure are." Her daddy pushed through the screen door, which whined in sullen protest, the wood bloated from so much heat and damp. "How's the painting going, Emma? You scared away all the haints yet? I think I spied one out in the garden this morning."

"Just because you don't believe in them doesn't mean they're not real." Her momma rolled on, leaning forward to reach the edge of the ceiling, her cheeks blooming pink as the azaleas that lined their gravel drive, and just as stubborn. Daddy reached out to catch the ladder and hold it still. His hands were dark, the rich hue of wet earth in Emma's plant pots.

"Thank you, Ron," Emma said.

On the seat below them, Nora worked the flower bud. In a few minutes, the little white fist had spun into an open trumpet in her hand. She pressed it to her face. "It doesn't smell like anything."

"Hmm?" Emma looked down. "Oh. No. Morning glories don't have much of a smell. They're pretty enough the bees find them just fine without perfume."

"And when they do, we have our fancy blue ceiling now." Ron chuckled and moved Nora's legs so he could sit next to her on the swing. "They don't like that big blue. Think it's the sky; keeps them from making their nests up under the eaves. *That's* what the blue is really good for."

He reached into his pocket for a packet of cigarettes, a bad habit he'd be the first to admit, but one he wasn't ready to give up just yet. Nora watched as he smacked the pack on his palm a few times before popping it open and choosing one, the flower in her fingers forgotten and released from her grasp.

"I wish you wouldn't smoke those around her," her momma said as she climbed down from the ladder and moved it to the next spot to begin painting again.

"And I wish you wouldn't fill her head with fairy stories, but there you have it." He winked at Nora.

"I hope I die before you, just so I can come back to haunt you at night."

"And I'll trap you in a jar and hang you from that old tree out back." He smiled, the very same grin that had stopped Emma Shifflett in her tracks fifteen years earlier, that made her blush even now while they teased each other. It was that smile too, Nora had heard whispered, that eased her grandfather's worries about his daughter marrying a Black man. Not that *he* minded, he'd said . . . but people talk.

"I'm just teasing. The blue looks nice, Emma. And I think we can safely say, there'll be no haints haunting our front porch."

But what Emma Martin didn't know, hadn't taught her daughter, was how to keep haints from haunting a person. There were some ghosts who just couldn't be shook from a heart, who wrapped strong arms about your neck and clung on, a rotted, fetid phantom that chilled even the sunniest of days. They had names and voices, stories left untold, questions unanswered. They stood in every corner, snagged in murky shadows, dripped down into the winding shell of Nora's ears in a rattling whisper that hummed just below the sturdy sounds of life.

Out on her front porch, a new front porch, white and clean and shared with Dan, Nora watched the sky begin to lighten and burst into a watercolor painting, washed again and again with each new ray of light, until there was nothing left of the deep night pigments; soon it was only gray, the crown of a winter sun peeking up over rolling mountains, which were bruised blue in the dawn and shrouded in mist.

"Babe." Dan's voice behind her made Nora jump, and she scrambled to hide the cigarette butt, long gone cold, that she held in her fingers.

"Jesus. I didn't hear you!"

He stood bleary-eyed in the doorway, wrapped in a blanket. "Sorry. Here." He reached his hand out toward her and she saw he was carrying her phone. "It's been ringing. Woke me up. I would have ignored it, but I think it's Murph."

She thanked him, and he shuffled back inside, the tail of his blanket trailing behind him. Before she could unlock her phone, it rang again.

"Murph. What's up?"

A gruff voice answered. "Took you long enough, Martin. I've called you three times now."

"I was outside. Dan just let me know you'd called."

"Hmm . . . At least one of you is a responsible adult."

She rolled her eyes during his pause.

"You working patrol today, Martin?"

"I'm scheduled to, yeah. Later."

"Well, I'll call Barb and sort that out with her and the sergeant. Get dressed, plain clothes. I want you with me today. Charlie just called. He's been at the dump since five a.m.—they found a body on their floor this morning."

Persephone Sees Herself

I did not quite know myself when I woke in the cold, clear sun of the new year. I was in my body, that much was certain; I had two arms, two legs, breasts, belly, neck; all the dull, feeble anatomy I'd been attached to all my life. There were freckles where I expected them to be, the same small nicks and scars. In the mirror, the same dark circles bruised the peach soft skin below a pair of eyes that looked like mine. I took a deep breath and felt lungs unfold as mine had, in an elegant press of tissue and muscle and spindly blood vessels. In and out, in and out, air and blood moved through the flesh of a new body that lay flush atop the body I'd always known and until then never questioned. I felt as a snake must once she begins to creep out of her old skin, like a cicada bursting out of her summer spine.

In the South, all birth requires a baptism, and in the shower I pressed my face to the water, washed the detritus of My Old Self down the drain, off to places unknown.

Afterward, at the kitchen table, I looked down at my new hands. A line of pink slashed across my palms, still raw, tender to the touch. And I remembered. The dark. A thousand screaming mites. The bite of a seat belt in my grip. Relief trickled down my spine, and I felt tiny bodies burrow under the fat pillows of spinal discs, bury themselves in hidden places; to rest, to sleep and not dream. In the stilled breath of my kitchen, in the startling newness, I felt my being shift, reach tremulous fingers out of the self-earth I'd buried my soul in. Reborn, I began to build myself anew.

Judith Slays Holofernes

It is easier to kill a man than they tell you, so long as you know what to feel for. His throat, like yours, like mine, is flanked by two identical and quite exposed branches of carotid artery. These long, thick ropes of collagen and smooth muscle contain the bustling thoroughfare of red blooming blood cells as they rush upward and away with each strong beat of heart.

Take your fingers. Press them into the hollow space just behind the curve of your jaw. Can you feel it? That beat. Strong and insistent.

You are alive.

But if someone were to tighten hands around your throat, or bind it with a seat belt, it would take all of seventeen seconds to choke that heartbeat out, until it was nothing more than flaccid silence, nothing more than cold death.

Mark didn't get out of my car. Instead, he looked at me. His eyes grew wide in the bumbling way men's do when they feel caught, like little boys scolded for tracking dirt inside the house. The air between us seemed to hold its breath for a minute, the gnawing under my skin stopped; for a breath, our two lives were suspended in the hollow tension of waiting, of wondering what he would do.

What he did was turn his hand into a mouth, rooting up under the satin line of my bra to bite my nipple hidden within, his expression melting into a mischievous grin. "Relax, Sophie. We're just having some fun . . . God, you feel good."

And then there was no space between us and nowhere to go and his face was in mine and every part of me was fixed on my left breast, which was now being mauled by a touch it hadn't approved of. In a wretched moment of panic I froze, held my breath against the onslaught of his presence, which was heavy and sticky from dive bar liquor and stolen wine. He slipped and fell forward with a jerk, his free hand landing hard on the seat back behind me, his face landing somewhere below my right ear.

"Mark, really . . ." The words punched out of my throat in ragged gasps. There was nowhere to go. My lungs emptied, vocal cords tightened and slammed into the wall of my throat, cutting off my voice.

"Give me those lips."

I went to a place inside myself and found there a mad frenzy. The thousand bodies writhing under my skin ballooned and bellowed out in disgust. They sprinted down to my toes and the tips of my fingers; they scuttled across my eyes so my vision shattered and became fractal, and suddenly I saw all of my life behind and ahead, stretched out in searing moments of shame.

"Sophie, come here, baby." My mother called to me during our first outing to the big-box store, just opened only a town away. In my four short years of life, I'd never seen anything like it. The dazzling maze of fluorescent lighting and oversize packages of snack crackers, next to piles of clothing, across from lawn chairs and barbecue grills; this was the sort of place a child might get lost in. Or stolen from.

Mom lifted me up and strapped me into the toddler seat of our cart. I'd recently grown too big for such babyish things, and so I squealed when the metal bit into my thighs. She paid my wriggles no mind.

"You get to ride today, baby. Isn't that fun?" There was a tightness to her voice that I didn't understand, and it set me on edge.

"I want to walk."

She ignored me, pushed the cart forward with a quick glance back at the two men who stood near the pile of Fruit of the Loom underwear we'd just been inspecting. The man who'd told me he liked my choice—a set patterned with cajoling rainbow animals—waved at me as Mom pushed the cart away. When I lifted my hand to wave back, she slapped it down.

"You don't ever talk to a man you don't know again, Sophie. Not unless I tell you it's okay. All right?"

Mark still had his seat belt on; the nylon was smooth under my hands. I ran one shaking palm down his chest to the buckle, while he sighed, pleased with himself, and pressed his wet lips to the corner of my mouth.

It was August, the first week of sixth grade. We sat cross-legged on the dirty floor of our school gym, which was boiling hot and humid despite the opened doors; a fan that was as tall as me spun uselessly in a nearby corner. Sweat trickled in thin trails down our chests, past newly budding breasts that were painful to the touch and the entirely wrong shape to our eyes; not curved like the women in magazines, but shabby little triangles of fat and stretch marks. My mother had bought me a training bra, and I wore it with a mix of pride and shame that was new to me then but would become the skin I slipped on every day.

The woman in front of us paced the floor, impatient and angry. She had better things to do, and the heat was melting her too. She made us stand, our palms against our scrawny legs. I became suddenly conscious of the hair that had sprouted there, only a few weeks before; dark, like my father's. *Do your fingertips hang lower than your shorts?* we were asked. I pressed mine into the thick khaki fabric, shoving the hem down as far as I could. My body was growing out of time with itself, and so I could not be sure if I was a slut or if my arms had simply stretched a bit too long over summer. She moved down the line, measuring the length between shorts hem and kneecaps. Four inches was the rule. Nothing more. The tall girls watched her with fear, their lips moving in quiet prayer to anyone who might listen. That was the day we learned our bodies could betray us. That was the day we learned to hate ourselves.

Next, our teacher showed us how to wrap our hands gently around the base of our throats, to check that our shirt collars weren't lower than our wrists. And so we choked ourselves into womanhood. Stinking and bleeding and hairy, but silent. Modest.

Mark's eyes were closed. He pressed his face to mine. I realized I was afraid of him, and that made me angry. The disgust I'd carried around in my belly all my waking life began to slosh again, to curdle, to sour the back of my throat. Why do men push? Until you have no choice but to submit and then burn in the shame of being a plaything. Until you use your anger at their silly weaknesses like a weapon, a beak tearing out of your mouth that later, when he's looking at you like a kicked puppy, you feel guilty for using. I hated Mark for that, and the hatred sat hard and cold at the root of me. Memories wrapped themselves like a cord around us in the dark.

"Just one kiss," I heard my friend beg, long before Mark would dare the same. "We don't have to tell anyone."

My boyfriend punched the wall inches from my face when I caught him cheating. "You're crazy!" he shouted, slamming his fist through plaster. "Look what you made me do," he growled later, as he cupped his bleeding fist to his chest while I ran a cloth through warm water, to help him clean up, to try to wash away the creeping guilt that was making a home somewhere in my veins. "I'm sorry" my small reply.

Do something! The skittering, scrabbling voices jabbered deep in the labyrinthine hollows behind my eyes. *Do something! Now!*

Mark's mouth was on me. His tongue, his hands, his smell, the heavy weight of it all covered me. Someone was screaming. My hands, acting on an instinct I'd never dared to touch, grabbed his seat belt and wrapped it around his throat once . . . twice . . .

"In one long yellow string I wound three times her little throat around."

"Sophie?"

"Robert Browning, actually. 'Porphyria's Lover.'"

Before I could think to change my mind, I pulled my feet up and shoved one hard into Mark's chest, the other smashed straight into his groin.

I held my roommate after a man she thought was her friend assaulted her, after the cops told her she was lying, after the school refused to change her schedule until finally, after months of sharing a classroom with her attacker, she dropped out. I cried during a wine-drunk night with another friend who got pregnant the first time she had sex, who went to the clinic alone because she was ashamed to tell anyone and he couldn't be bothered to go with her to hold her hand while she bled out the contents of her womb. I sat in stunned silence the morning I opened the papers to see another friend staring back at me, murdered by someone she had thought loved her. I've heard hell hath no fury like a woman scorned, but I've not read yet of a man being killed simply for saying no. Women's tears, however, could fill an ocean.

Mark began to realize something was wrong and reached out for me. It was a childish motion, like a baby reaching for its mother. I felt something pause in me, something question and crack. I leaned back toward my door, pulled the noose tighter.

"Sophie!" A gasp, wheezing and sputtering against the nylon. Each inward breath was a gift to my tiring hands. Tighter, tighter, he would help me hang himself.

"Can you believe they had us read that poem in high school, Mark? He strangled her! Now she's just another beautiful Dead Girl.

How fucked up is that?" We'd practiced afterward, all of us girls; wound our hair about our throats to see if we too could be transformed into our own death. None of us reached three loops. Porphyria must have had very long hair.

"Soph . . ."

A few days into my first restaurant job, one of the line cooks followed me into the walk-in. When I asked to move out past him, he blocked the door. It was a game he and the crew played, trapping the girls in tight corners, hallways, pressing their groins to our bellies as we reached for sugar, ketchup, olives for the bar; whispering wishes into our ears. If we balked at their touch, they laughed. It was just a game! All a game. Women are so *sensitive*.

Mark was wriggling, wretching, gagging. His face in the dark of my car was turning black. Our breath burst out into clouds and hung sparkling between us.

The man next to me at the bar paid for my beer without asking. When I went to the bathroom half an hour later, he followed me. "I thought you understood," he said, when I turned to find him leaning against the closed door.

"I like your tattoo," a customer said to me, his gaze locked on my thigh, when I asked him what I could get for him to drink. "Why aren't you smiling?" another asked every time I walked past his regular seat at the end of the bar. "She's a crazy cunt," a friend whined about his ex. "Shit, I always forget you're a girl," he laughed later over shared beers. "You're so cool, Sophie." "You're basically our mom." "You're my sister." "You're a bitch." "You're a whore." "Look what you made me do." "You wanted me. I saw the way you looked at me." "You'd tell me, right, if I made you uncomfortable?" "Ay, mami!" "You're beautiful." "I love you so much it scares me." "I'm not ready yet. You deserve better. Give me a few years." "Nice legs, sweetheart." "Don't be a tease." "I'm extremely intrigued by you." "Hey! I was talking to you." "You intimidate me." "Slut!" "So you think you're better than me?" "Bitch." "Look what you made me do." "She's not as innocent as she wants us to think." "Women lie." "Never accept a drink from someone you don't know." "Never leave your drink out of sight." "Never walk alone at night." "Never run with headphones in." "Don't wear your hair in a ponytail—it makes you easier to grab." "Pretend to be talking to a friend or family member on the phone, so he won't attack you." "What did you expect, wearing that?" "If you've got it, flaunt it." "If you weren't a girl, I'd punch you right now." "Look what you made me do." "I'm going to marry you someday." "You're crazy." "Look what you made me do." "You're crazy." "You're crazy you're crazy you're crazy you're crazy you're crazy you'recrazyyou'recrazyyou'recrazyyou'recrazyyou'recrazycrazycrazycrazy."

Am I?

"'And thus we sit together now,
And all night long we have not stirred.
And yet God has not said a word . . .'

Look what you made me do, Mark . . . *Look* what you made me do."

Three things happen to a body when it's throttled. First is the sudden, violent interruption of movement between heart and brain. The carotids have two brothers, the blue and quiet jugular veins, who slide down the throat, herding weary blood cells back to the breath and throbbing life of a beating heart. Nothing more than rubbery tubes, a paltry four pounds of pressure is enough to pinch these brothers shut. If you have a bit more leverage, and really want to feel a heart surge against you, just a hair more force will do. Eleven pounds of grip will crack the muscular strength of his carotid arteries. To put life into a grander perspective: eleven pounds of grip is the strength of a ten-year-old girl. A grown man's handshake averages over one hundred. How delicate we are.

There's a pileup now as blood cells, trapped, clog into vessel walls.

If they don't find a way out soon, there'll be a real emergency. Thousands back up into the aorta, who until recently had spent her life arcing gracefully over this beating heart, with hardly a care in the world; now, uncomfortable with the sudden build of pressure, she shoots a frantic message across her network of sparking, electric nerves, screaming at the vessels in his skull to dilate (*Now!*) before everything bursts. She's a military commander under siege, ordering her men back to regroup.

Here, the victim may experience a rush of euphoria as his vessels fling themselves wide. It's been described as a feel of sudden release, even weightlessness. Some people find this orgasmic and tie up their own necks during sex to achieve it. Male corpses that have been strangled are sometimes found to have erections.

In a desperate attempt to slow the rush of blood still squishing into occluded vessels, his heart rate plummets. Slow the tide, if you cannot stem it. If our victim has been drinking though, as Mark had, he'll have no such luck. Red blood cells are sponges for alcohol; they fatten with it like microscopic beer bellies. His brain had signaled hours ago for his vessels to dilate, to make space for these bumbling, swollen cells. I saw it in the flush on his cheeks, the shine in his eyes, and it was making him easier to kill. While he dumped liquor down his throat and his vessels ballooned to keep up, his heart had been forced to beat at twice its normal pace; to keep him awake, to keep him alive. Now, threatened again, it was a wild, fluttering rush.

There was a moment in the dark, in the ragged cough of his breath, that I thought about letting him go. He might not remember, and even if he did, what sort of man was going to report a woman for choking him? While he was kissing her. He'd be too ashamed to say anything; he might even leave me alone. If I played my cards right, I could probably convince him it had been his idea. Men are so certain of their own lives that they never stop to consider that the women they've spent decades cornering might one day fight back.

I felt my arms shake; my hands were getting tired. I stared at Mark from across the vibrating bridge of his taut seat belt, and my spirits renewed.

So this was power. This was what it felt like to have the world in my grasp. This was what it felt like to be a man. I took a breath and heaved the belt tighter.

I wonder, could he feel the vessels in his eyes burst then, one by one, like fireworks in the night? Did he feel us transmuting, lifting together into a new plane of life?

It takes seventeen seconds of applied pressure to choke a man out cold. The real test comes in the minutes after. You have to be strong. He will fight you at first. Even after he loses consciousness, his body will jump and quiver. Your hands will cramp and tremble. He'll choke out air like a smoker running a marathon; his eyelids will flutter; his back will spasm. Stay still. Stay strong. You mustn't give up, no matter how your fingers ache and your arms shudder under the strain. Have faith and conviction and it can be done.

And you, here in my heart, in my tale with me, don't look away. How many times have you watched women scream? For fun, for ghost stories, podcasts, pornography, prime-time HBO? You gobble our pain down like candy, always hungry for the next handful, the next story, the more salacious the better. Well, now it was his turn.

Don't you dare look away.

Headlights flashed in my rearview mirror.

Shit.

A car pulled up beside me, window down. In the darkness, I made out two shadowed faces peering across at me. Strangers, thank God.

"Y'all okay?" A woman's voice. Sweet and tangy, Carolina barbecue.

"Yes, ma'am! My phone fell down to the baseboards and I decided it was better to pull over and grab it than to try to reach for it while I was driving. My friend here's no help." I nodded toward Mark's slumped form.

The woman chuckled. "Looks like someone's had too much fun."

"You could say that."

"He's lucky to have you around to look after him! All right then, sweetheart." I heard the car shift back into drive. "Be safe. And happy New Year!"

Nora

It was loud inside the County Waste Center. Much louder than Nora had imagined, standing outside the massive metal-and-concrete beast of a building only a few moments before. All around her, the sounds of muted conversations, camera whines and clicks, pencils scratching, skittered like rats through the cavernous space.

"M'lady." Murph handed her a pair of blue booties from a box on the floor. She took them without a word, pulled them on over her worn black sneakers.

Across the room stood a row of open-faced stalls, each one piled high with shining trash bags in white, black, some a garish green. A few had torn, spilling rotten guts that filled the air with a fetid stink that not even the cold air could tamp down. Nora wondered how people could work in a place like this. Did they forget the smell of rancid food and baby diapers, old blood and vomit and shower drain sludge? She crinkled her nose and thanked God that it wasn't summer.

"Glad I don't work here," Murph muttered, echoing her thoughts. "Where's Val? Let's get this walk done, so we can get back out into fresh air."

"I think she's over there." Nora pointed to the trash pile furthest to the right, where a group of forensic investigators were crouched down, taking photographs and notes, crawling over the scene like enormous, gangly flies. Nora had always found them to be just as disturbing, the sort of personality that peered so closely into death. At least she stood at some remove from it all, out of the lab, away from the autopsy table. They, meanwhile, made a two-footed descent into the mysteries and horrors most people avoided.

Standing over the investigators was a tall woman, her face set into well-worn lines, arms crossed tight over her chest. Seeing her, Murph nodded. "Top-notch detective work, Martin. You'll be ready to take my desk soon."

"Just as soon as I get rid of the old man clogging up my space." She smirked.

"Believe me, kid, I'm ready for my retirement party. Whenever you want to throw it." He set off toward the tall woman. "Morning, beautiful!"

Val looked up from the trash bags. "Murph, you've got to stop calling me that. My husband will be jealous."

"Well, then Jim shouldn't have married such a stunning woman."

Val waved him away. Turning to Nora, she said, "I'm sorry you have to put up with him, sweetheart. But it's good to see you again. You a detective now, or still patrol?"

"Still uniform."

"Not for much longer though," Murph said. "I've been working on the powers that be, and I have a feeling that Martin'll take my spot soon enough. I figure I just have to keep annoying Barb. Only person on this earth Wright is afraid of is his secretary. And there's nothing that woman hates more than a change in her plan. If I keep stealing Martin to tag along with me, Wright'll have to slide her over to my department just to keep Barb from quitting in protest."

"You sly thing." Val laughed.

"I call it being proactive. They've had months now, and they still haven't hired someone to fill Martin's seat so she can fill mine. So I'll force their hand. But enough of me complaining. Let's get down to business. Shall we go for a walk?"

They let Val set the course, a slow arc around the crime scene. As the lead investigator, it was her job to liaise between her crew and other teams, be they detectives, patrol officers, or the medical examiner's crew come to pick up a body. The work required sharp eyes, a quick mind, and a certain ability to assert herself that Nora admired. She never let the boys bully her. Even Murph kept his ribbing to a minimum around Val.

"So who found him?" Murph asked. His breath plumed in the chill air as they neared a set of outer doors.

Val pointed past them to a gray garbage truck, parked just outside. Tall red letters painted on the side announced it as part of Webb Disposal, the largest trash collector in the area. In the rearview mirror, Nora saw the driver huddled in his seat, his face ashen.

"We'll talk to him in a minute," Murph said, heading off Nora's question. "Let's get this scene nailed down first, and then we can let Val do her job. I know she's dying to get rid of me."

"You said it." Val smirked. "Poor man was about to pull away when the center staff stopped him. Claims he had no idea about the corpse he'd been chauffeuring. From my understanding, he dumps his truckload and the guys push it up into these piles. It was when they were shifting bags around that they found our friend."

She stopped. They were back where they'd started. "Meet John Doe."

He was blue in the particular way of corpses, as if he'd just climbed out of a pool that was too cold. Only the blackened tips of his fingers betrayed anything sinister. The collar of his crumpled peacoat was popped over his neck; not an unusual fashion in this town. From where she stood, nothing seemed out of place. There was no visible blood, no mutilation. Nothing to say that this man had done anything other than fall asleep in a trash bin and be slowly crushed to death under piles of half-eaten food scraps.

Murph squatted down next to him, his sharp eyes sweeping across the body before he turned over his shoulder, looking back toward the truck, his gaze following its path to the trash stall.

"What do you need from us, Val?" he asked.

"Well, in my opinion, this isn't our crime scene."

"I agree."

"So I'd like to get him into the ME's van as soon as possible. It's cold out, which works for us, but that trash is going to compromise any possible evidence. The less time he spends lying in it, the better. I talked to Charlie before you got here, and apparently the driver says one of his pickup spots is the big dumpster that services the restaurants down on Peach Street in Bellair. Lord knows food waste brings all kinds of crawling beasties with it. I wouldn't be surprised to find a few fruit fly maggots wriggling around in there."

"Lovely." Murph pursed his lips. "Well, no decisions should be made without the input of my protégé here . . . Martin, what do you think?"

Nora nodded. "I agree with y'all. This might be where he ended up, but it doesn't feel like it's where he died. I can go talk to the driver, Murph, if you want to find Charlie? Let's get out of Val's hair."

"Taking initiative. Good girl. That's what I like to see." He rose on creaking knees and clapped her on the back. "Val, just holler, please, when the ME gets here. I want to get a better look at that body before anyone takes it away."

"Of course. See y'all in a bit."

Nora picked up two steaming cups of coffee from a white tent standing just outside the tape line and walked to the garbage truck, to talk to the man still hunkered inside the cab.

"Mr. Pugh!" She greeted him through his passenger-side window, holding the cups in the air as offering. "Do you mind if I join you?"

Without a word, he disappeared, his body flattening against the front seats as he reached for the handle on her side. The heavy door whined as he shoved it open. Nora stretched one of the steaming cups to him, which he took with a mumbled thanks before leaning back into his seat. She heaved herself in.

"Good morning, Mr. Pugh." Nora was certain to keep her tone warm and inviting, though that was hard to do with the chill of the day, which had rattled up her throat and made her voice sound small.

"How do you know my name?" His eyes were a punch. He held the coffee close to his chest but did not move to drink it, as if he didn't quite trust her.

She pressed her lips to a smile. *Be soft, be soft.* "I'm sorry, I should have introduced myself." She reached out a hand to shake. "I'm Officer Martin. I'm here to help investigate the man who fell out of your truck this morning. I got your name from my partner. I hope that's all right."

He stared down at the coffee he was holding, stubbornly silent. Nora tucked away her annoyance and smiled, pulling her hand back safely to her side. Her daddy's voice came strolling, gentle, over her shoulder. *This is not about you, baby girl. Men like him, someone made them feel small. Maybe he's scared—look at the morning he's had. He'll try to take it out on you, but don't let him get a rise out of you. What do we learn in church? Turn the other cheek.*

But, Daddy, she'd insisted so many times, *why would we do that?*

Because the best revenge against a small man is letting him see his slaps have no effect on you.

She took a breath, reminded herself that she was the one with a badge and a gun here. "Now, Mr. Pugh, I understand this morning's events must have been very shocking to you, and I apologize for taking your time like this, but before I can let you go home, I need to ask you a few questions."

"You accusing me of something?"

"No, sir."

The truck shifted, and somewhere behind them, Nora heard the flash and whine of a camera. The forensics crew must be in its body. She imagined them creeping about like beetles, poking and prodding, peeking into every corner.

"Well, I already talked to an officer," he grumbled, staring at his driver's side mirror, where he must have been able to see the investigators climbing in and out of his truck. "What are they doing? And why don't you just ask the other officer what I said? I thought you were just coming here to tell me I could leave."

The cup of coffee in her hands was still too hot to drink, so instead she fiddled with it, popping off the edge of its plastic cover to let the steam escape. "Mr. Pugh, I'd really love to hear the story from you."

"You'd be better off asking the guys on the floor. They saw it, not me." He kept his gaze locked on the mirror. He would not look at her.

Stay soft. He's a small man. She felt herself tightening. "Yes, sir, we're talking to them too, but I also want to hear your perspective. There might be something you noticed that they didn't."

"What about that other man you were walking around with? The older one. Where's he? I'll talk to him."

She had been prepared for this reality, but it made her jaw clench all the same. Over the years, Nora had learned, more often than she liked, that the truth was a ceiling she bumped her head on, and some days she was so frustrated with it she wanted to scream. She could fight this, she could make herself large enough to fill this truck, so big that this puny man would have to look at her. She could threaten him with obstructing, with resisting, all the words that men who wore her uniform flung around when they felt like making themselves feel powerful. It would probably work too, for a while. But in the end what good would it do to get in a pissing match with this man? So she thanked Mr. Pugh for his time and dropped out of the truck to go find Murph.

"He wants to talk to you." She found him sharing a cigarette with Charlie, the patrol on duty when the call for a body came in, and one of the few guys at the station who didn't make Nora feel like she had something in her teeth when he talked to her.

Murph looked at her face and understood, and that was why Nora knew she would miss him when he retired.

"It's all right, kid. I got it." He patted her shoulder, thanked Charlie for the cigarette, and lumbered off in the direction of the truck.

"Everything okay, Martin?" Charlie asked.

"Yeah. Everything's fine." She sighed and looked over to see Murph sliding into the cab of the truck. He said something, and Mr. Pugh laughed, the gruff mask of his face melting into boyish awe at the detective sitting next to him. "You got another cigarette I can have?"

"I didn't know you smoked." Murph stood back at her side, a fresh cup of coffee in one hand, a fresh cigarette in the other.

"Only when I need to. How's my new best friend?"

"Doesn't know much. Probably going to head down to the bar to tell all his buddies about the nasty woman cop who insinuated he had something to do with a murder."

"I didn't—"

"I know, kiddo. Come on, finish that smoke. I think I saw the ME guys drive in, and I want to see that body when they lift it."

"I was just about to come find you," Val said when she saw them walking toward the scene. Two men stood off to one side. Next to them was a gurney, an open body bag on top of it. Nora had never liked the sight of those things. They reminded her of enormous mouths waiting to gobble people up.

"You got everything you need?" Murph asked.

"Yep. Can't do much more until he's out of here. Let's get him up, boys!"

The men moved toward the body like carrion, quietly swooping down to pick bits of errant trash off his back or tug a bag out from under his face.

"Careful," Val reminded them from the sidelines.

They nodded and continued their macabre work. Nora watched as one tucked his hands under the dead man's chest, while the other fished through piles of trash until he found what she hoped were his legs. They were silent as they worked, methodical and precise. When they lifted the corpse, it was with a slow and deliberate motion. Nothing dropped. Nothing shook loose. They carried him as gently as a mother did her newborn.

"Christ, he's got no pants." Murph blew out a sharp punch of air. "There goes his ID. No pants, no wallet. But look, Nora, look at how limp his body is. What does that tell you?"

"Nothing." Val leaned back over her shoulder.

"Don't listen to her, she doesn't know what she's talking about." He winked at Nora. "Now think. What do you know about bodies? What happens to them after death?"

Like Murph, Nora rolled ideas around in her mind, batting them back and forth, investigating every angle, until she was ready to make a guess. "They freeze. Rigor mortis sets in after a few hours . . . But this guy's been here for a few hours already."

"Exactly."

"That's not precise, Murph." Val watched the men walk the corpse over to the stretcher. He was heavy, and they strained under his weight. "Turn him on his back, please, before you zip him up."

They nodded and continued their quiet tussle with the dead man.

"Rigor lasts about thirty-six hours," Nora continued, enjoying the puzzle. "I'd say he's too pale to be fresh, but he's white and it's winter, so he could just be pale . . . except we can see blood." She pointed. "That purple in his fingertips. It's congealed; it's had time to pool like that."

"You got it, Martin. So, put it together. What does this tell us?"

"He's been dead for a few days."

"Bingo! Of course"—he bowed low to Val—"the ME will have to confirm it, but I'd say our friend here's been dead about a week. The cold is a wonderful preservative, but it won't slow rigor. I think he's already passed through it."

Val pursed her lips, but she didn't argue. Over on the stretcher, the men managed to flip the corpse.

"Oh God." Nora put a hand to her mouth. She wasn't sure what she'd expected to see, but it wasn't this.

The man stared open-eyed at the ceiling above them. His mouth, which had been hidden as he lay face-first in the garbage, was a gaping, bloody hole. It was normal for a corpse's tongue to protrude from its mouth, the force of sudden muscle tension, excited nerves, putrefaction. But this man had no tongue. A thick, black bruise wound about his neck, which, now they could see it clearly, was bent and stretched. Nora had seen this before, in hanging suicides, but dead people didn't throw themselves in garbage bins. His groin had been mauled as well, shredded almost as if by a wild animal, though she knew of no animals that would attack that way.

Murph stepped forward, his head cocked to one side.

"Murph?"

"I think I know our vic, kid. Unless I'm very much mistaken, that's Mark Dixon."

A Harpy Metes Out Justice

He was heavy, but I am strong. A decade of hauling fat beer kegs around walk-in coolers, of heaving cases of wine and liquor up to my countertop, has taught me to breathe, to lift from my legs, to believe in my small power and shove this man through the square door of a front-loading dumpster. It wasn't easy. It took me the better part of an hour, sweat chilling on my forehead, hot breath piling around me like a nimbus in the moonlit night. When I heard the soft crush of his body landing on trash bags, I felt all the weight of myself gather and release, a wash of something clear spilling down my back. It tasted like salt, like blood or tears, like relief, in my mouth.

In his death, I found a fierce new awareness of myself. *I am nothing more than a body*, I thought. Like him, like Mark. We are both flesh and blood and bone, the sharp electric sparks of a few coated wires, the rush of breath in paper lungs. Without that, I was as cold as him. My eyes would stare just as blankly into the dark, into some space I could not see. But he was dead and I was not, and in those hours I was more alive than I'd ever been before.

I took off his pants because I saw a footprint in his groin, where the bottom of my shoe had pinned him to the car door, and because I knew he kept his wallet in his back pocket. I felt my shoulders relax. In a moment of giddy celebration, I castrated him, flung that into the woods for an animal to find. I cut out his tongue because I was tired of listening to him; tired of listening to all of them, their small worries, their fragile egos. I made him quiet. The tension in my jaw dissipated, and I let the crooked arms of the creek bank trees pull screams from my throat, toss them away into the black morning breeze. The moon's silver face was sunk below the mountain ridge by the time I completed the rite I had made for ourselves, the sacrifice, the mutilation, the scouring of disgust from my soul. Finally, I could breathe. Finally, I could look at the moon, at the velvet black sky, and feel myself free.

The hour before dawn in this mountain place is a sabbat, thick and wild; no living soul should be out in it, unless you're prepared to meet such feral things as me.

In the end, I threw him in the trash, because that's what he was.

As for my car, tequila cleans as well as bleach, and no one's going to ask a bartender why their car smells like booze.

A Sphinx

His body was found. Then, they came.

I wasn't expecting a *they*.

Him, I knew. Murph was a Tuesday-afternoon golfer, Sunday-morning Baptist, and anytime Rum and Coke at the Blue Bell. He was a friend of Lindsey's in the sense that they knew each other and their paths crossed enough for them to consider themselves something more than passing familiar. From different generations and social strata, but brothers by virtue of their birth into the card-carrying heritage of the Ol' Boys' Club; a patchwork amalgamation of John Deere hats and polo shirts, cut from the same cloth and sewn onto disparate branches of a quilt pattern as gnarled and sweeping as an oak tree.

Murph strutted in like a goose in the farmyard, his belly gone to seed as it does for so many men his age, held out in front of him like an announcement. I watched it bump gently into the host stand, where the hostess stood, wide-eyed. She never quite knew what to do with herself around Murph, and he exploited this teenaged confusion to his own amusement, flashing his badge and watching her flush. He knew she was as innocent as a spring bunny; he just wanted to play with his food a bit.

Behind him was the real interest. I'd never seen her before. She wasn't from here, that much was certain. It wasn't her face—which was unfamiliar to me—so much as the way she held herself, curling down inward against the strength in her spine, which was straight and strong. People in this town are cursed with an inflated sense of their own self-importance, and there she was, pulling her presence in against the strength of her stance, making herself small. This woman knew what it was to wear a mask, to zip and button and lock herself away. Did she feel the mites too? Did they nip at her while she trailed Murph like a shadow, stepping out of his way if he changed direction without warning? Did his blustering make her wince somewhere under that face she pulled down over her own?

Her eyes were the only part of her she could not tuck away. They saw more than she realized, I could sense it even then. I would have to be careful with her. She knew what it was to be me, and that was dangerous.

I checked my face, made sure it was tied tight, wouldn't slip while we spoke. The conversation went like this:

Yes, I saw him that night.

He stole a glass of wine from behind my bar.

No, it's not the first time he's pulled that move. Lindsey's buddies all like to remind me that they're "friends with the owner" and he won't mind if they pour themselves just one drink. Which . . . fine, whatever. Except this time he poured himself *my* drink. But Mark's like that, you know? He's one of those men who takes what he wants and maybe apologizes later. I really wouldn't be surprised if he pushed the wrong person and got more than he bargained for.

After? I think he went to Tap House.

They were still open when I was closing up. The serving staff was heading that way, and I know they invited him. You should ask them. I can give you their names.

Yep. That was the last time I saw Mark, walking out that door.

(That's not entirely a lie. It was, in fact, the last time I'd *witnessed* him walk out the front door.)

Hmmm . . . and I know he got a ride into town from David Flickinger and his girlfriend, Mattie. Maybe they took him home too?

Sorry I don't have more for you! It was a pretty normal night here, all things considered.

Can I get you anything, before you leave?

A Sphinx Questions Herself

Maybe I said too much. I was nervous.

Lucky for me, Murph was the only detective on the scene. The woman—Officer Martin, I was told—was just a shadow. This wasn't her case; I wouldn't have to trick her for long. Alone, Murph would be easy to deceive. Men never really listen to me.

An Outsider

Nora didn't go to the funeral. It didn't feel right. Bellair wasn't hers yet; her few months of residency barely registered on their Southern psyches. Her accent was theirs, a soft roll of farm fields and slippery consonants; she'd grown up riding around in the beds of the same rusted-out farm trucks, downed the same peach 'shine at the same bonfire parties. Her history pooled with theirs in the Venn diagram of all old central Virginians, a murky tangle that smelled faintly of gunpowder and was painful to touch. But she was not theirs. Her roots grew out of red clay ten miles away, over the crest of a hazy, blue mountain ridge. They were Piedmont people and she was from the Valley, and that meant something in this moment, when the town was folded in on itself in grief.

She felt suddenly conscious of the space of her body in a way that was all too familiar. Rolling through town in the Ford sedan she now shared with Murph, Nora wondered if she'd ever find a home she clicked into without feeling questions pick at her like carrion birds. The thought grew thick, and she felt it bump up against Murph's mind as he sat, unusually quiet, in the driver's seat.

"Why don't you stay in the car, kid?" he said as they turned into the crunching gravel of the church parking lot. His voice was low, probing around the edges of his worries. She could feel him holding each word in his palm, testing them, tentative, and she grew anxious for him in a way that made her feel uncomfortable, waited for him to pour words into her silence. "It's not that they wouldn't appreciate you coming but . . . I think your presence might complicate things. They'll put on too much of a show if you're there."

"Murph." On instinct Nora reached out a hand, then took it away. "I'm not offended. I know how small towns work. I grew up in one too."

"Really? I thought you grew up in a cave. Isn't that what they have over there on the other side of the mountain?" Worries lifted, his cheek returned.

"Nah, the caves are all up in Luray. I grew up in a shack, very different. The cannibal rednecks who raised me even let me out once a month to mingle with the other feral children."

"I'm gonna tell your momma you said that."

"She'll laugh and probably tell you half her family fits that description if we're being honest. Leave the keys with me though, will you?"

"Why, so you can steal my car?"

"I've got to pay my bills somehow."

"I worry about you some days, Martin." He shook his head.

Headlights flashed in the rearview, and Nora glanced back to see a parade of cars rolling into the lot; mourners in eco-friendly hatchbacks, muscular trucks, sleek sports cars, muddy farm beaters in all shapes and sizes. Here they'd come, flocked to the church to gather, gossip, gawk, and weep in turn. A gaggle of women had knotted near the front steps, catching one another in spindly arms. Their scarves flapped in the breeze, jewel-toned birds straining away from the field of black dresses. A few wore hats, wide-brimmed and dark, which they clutched to their heads as the wind played at lifting them. It was a picture as old as time: women in black, a town besieged. Their tears and memories were suddenly on display, and every emotion had a weight, to be polished and placed carefully on the scale of public opinion.

A man climbed the steps, his face haggard and swollen with crying. *Lindsey*, Nora thought. This was the man who'd been Mark's best friend. The women absorbed him in their thin arms and pressed pale cheeks to his own, their lips moving in whispered greeting and sympathy. From her seat behind the windshield, they looked to Nora like fish gaping for breath in a tank. They shoved handkerchiefs at him and squeezed his arms, and together the group pressed forward into the church.

"Was Mark really that popular?" Nora asked.

"He was one of the boys," Murph stated simply. "Anyways, I'd better get in there before they close the doors. Should be about an hour. You sure you're okay out here?"

"I'm fine."

"I've learned to be scared when women say that." He patted her shoulder. "Here's the keys if you need to turn the heat on."

He heaved himself out of the car; it shifted its weight, rocked a few times as he slammed the door closed, and then was still. Nora took a deep breath, blew out a cloud into the quiet air.

She waited, watching the last mourners scrabble across the gravel lot, suit jackets and skirt hems flapping as they ducked inside just before the doors closed. The world grew still, she alone breathing among the gathered congregation of cars. Mist rose up off the creek just beyond the parking lot. Faces rippled across it; arms stretched up, broke apart in the sunlight. Nora blinked them away.

At her feet was her beaten-up messenger bag. She reached down into it and pulled out the autopsy photos. The corpse, the man, the Good Ol' Boy who stared back at her looked surprised, as if he'd turned a blind corner and accidentally bumped into his death. Could it have been such a shock? It didn't fit in her mind that something so brutal, so personal, could be so wholly unexpected. Maybe though, for a man like Mark, the kind who seemed to slip through life like an eel, it was.

She knew those men. They grew in every soil, across every mountain ridge. They existed in perpetual childishness, dancing through the traps and snares that life set, never looking down, never needing to because there was always a net of arms ready to catch them if they fell and soft words to wipe away regrets before they grew solid enough to be reckoned with. Nora felt a burn in her cheeks, acidic and angry. It shocked her as she stared at the photo, the hard fist that gathered in her heart. She didn't like it, didn't want to feel that way about a dead man.

Fingers pinched at the edge of her memories. There had been another death, not so long ago. Another one of those slippery men. Only this time, he was still a boy, sitting across a table from her and Murph, looking at photos of the girl he'd beaten to death against his windowsill.

"You did this." The question transmuted into accusation when it dropped out of Nora's mouth. She could feel the girl already, stalking the edges of her thoughts.

"She drove me crazy."

That was all they'd get before his lawyer swooped across the conversation. The next time she saw the boy, he was surrounded by weeping women, Marys at the foot of this shameful cross, each adorned in flowery scarves and pastels, perfect makeup, perfect hair. They glared at her, who could never be them, and cried for this boy, man, murderer, assured him that everything would be okay, that he'd get his life back. His father placed a firm hand on the back of his son's neck, his silence building a fortress around them all.

Nora wiped away the memories, focused her attention on the man in front of her, who, despite his sins, was now dead and cold. Whoever he may have been in life, he hadn't deserved that. His face in the pictures was pale, and just as blue as it'd been on the scene. His neck was bent, misshapen. The medical examiner confirmed he'd been strangled, not that there had been much doubt. It must have been awful. His killer had yanked so hard they'd crushed his windpipe, cracked his neck so it hung loose, like a baby bird's. His groin had been attacked with a small, sharp object. Someone slammed it into him again and again. A pounding anger. Hot and driving. Immediate. She'd seen this before. It was how men killed things they hated.

What spooked her most was his mouth. Before this, he must have been handsome. His jawline, even broken as it was, was square and sharp. His eyes had been blue, and Nora guessed they must have sparkled when he found some mischief to play. That was just a rumor now, a whisper hovering above the terror of his final face, which had been rent wide enough to allow his attacker to reach in and cut out his tongue. Not an easy feat after you've strangled someone. Not an easy feat when they've died with their teeth ground together.

And why his tongue? His groin made sense; she'd seen that sort of emasculation in case studies. It was an animal instinct humans had yet to outgrow, erasing someone by removing any chance of progeny, of life beyond themselves. But his tongue? At least he hadn't felt it. According to the report, he'd been dead before any of the mutilation happened.

She needed fresh air. Chilly as the car was, it felt too close, as if she'd catch a fever if she sat there with this dead face for too long. A bench squatted in the grass a few yards away, facing a rocky elbow of creek and the orchards just beyond. That would be her haven, Nora decided, until Murph returned.

Music drifted toward her from the church as she took her seat on the cold wood; murmured hymns mingled with the tinny sounds of an electric keyboard, probably played by someone's teenager. She couldn't quite make out the song but thought it might have been "Amazing Grace." Something wholly inappropriate and not at all fitting the sketch of Mark she'd made in recent days. Mark hadn't been a man saved. He'd been a man still having too much fun, making too much of a mess. And someone had punished him for it.

Sighing, Nora stretched her legs out in front of her, felt her knees crack and pop, the residue of a high school athletic career. In front of her, the creek curved in a shallow bend around the back of the church. It had frozen in the recent cold, the only sign of life a soft trickle of water burbling under the slick surface, a veil of mist moving across it. In the spring, this bend would be full of bees and blooming color; rich with blackberries and honeysuckle, coiled creeper vines. Now, it was just a desiccated brown, sapped of life.

Across the way and about fifty feet north, a gnarled willow clung to the bank, draping skeletal arms down over the ice. They swayed in the wind that rushed off the feet of the nearby mountainside, sending woody stems scratching through one another. Behind it stood a field of apple trees. Bare, they looked dead, their wood a ghastly gray, branches thin and twisted in on themselves. It was hard to believe that in just a few weeks, they'd send out their first sharp leaves.

"I always hated the orchards in the winter."

Nora turned toward the voice that slid around the bench and came to rest at her side.

"There was never a good place to hide," the woman said, lifting her shoulders in a small shrug, a smile playing about her mouth. Her eyes were dark and intelligent, and there was something behind them that Nora had noticed the first time she'd met Sophie Braam, a certain recognition, a handshake welcoming her into conspiracy.

"Mornin', Ms. Braam. What brings you here?"

"Please, call me Sophie. And probably the same thing as you—Mark Dixon. I thought I'd catch what I could of his funeral service before I had to run to work. Lindsey's hosting a memorial; cocktails and hors d'oeuvres." Her voice was smooth. She was used to talking to people.

"Yes, I know," Nora said. "Murph and I are headed there after."

"To see who looks guilty?" Sophie arched an elegant eyebrow, and there it was again, that gleam. She laughed, something bright, like a creek tumbling over rocks in the summer, and touched Nora's arm. "I've watched my fair share of *Criminal Minds*, Detective."

"Officer. Still officer," Nora corrected her, feeling heat creep up her throat.

"*Officer.* Apologies. Anyway, I know how it works. It's perfect, really. The whole town—or anyone who cared about Mark, at least—in one room together. Mix in alcohol and a few tears, and who knows what you'll see? Is it true that criminals return to the scene of the crime?"

"We don't know where the scene of the crime was."

"Well, you know what I mean. Everyone will be there. If I ever killed a man, I think I'd like to come to his funeral, to see what they say about me."

Sophie smiled, and Nora felt some secret knowledge sweep across her chest. Sophie, she was very certain, was a creature of hidden places. There was something there, a certain thickness to the space she held in the world, a mind that scuttled around things, awake and alive more so than most people. Nora, who had been starved for friendship since she came here, wanted very much to reach out and take that offered handshake.

"I think I would have made a good detective myself," Sophie continued. "Bartenders have to be just as observant, just as vigilant, you know. And just as tough too, I'd imagine. Man's world and all that."

"I hadn't thought about bartending as being a man's world."

"Stop by at the end of the night sometime, when we're closed and the kitchen are talking about the new server's ass. Or the chef is jabbering on about whatever has pissed him off that day. A bunch of babies. Sometimes I wish they'd just shut up, you know?"

Nora had to give her that. "So why aren't you a detective then?"

"Three reasons. One"—Sophie lifted a finger up into the air—"I don't like cops. No offense, but your buddies down at the"—she pulled her face into a mockery of stern authority—"*Alcoholic Beverage*

Control offices like to hassle us a bit too much. What does a liquor inspector need a gun for anyway?"

Nora held up her hands. "Don't ask me." She was relieved that Sophie hadn't turned the answer like a spotlight onto her. The day she'd told her father she was joining the police academy, he'd gone on a long walk. Well-meaning strangers brought it up more often than was comfortable. How could *she*, they'd ask, want to be a part of *them*?

"Two," Sophie continued, unaware, or too polite to mention Nora's furrowed brow, "if I'm going to be stuck working for the Ol' Boys' Club, I'd rather be paid the money I make in tips than whatever salary they toss your way."

"Fair," Nora conceded.

"And three, I've got the family business to think about."

She swept her arm in a wide arc, taking in the gnarled apple trees. "The orchard's not what it used to be. When my grandfather died, we sold most of our trees to another orchard out of Charlottesville. Most of the ones left to us are dying or on their way out, but I'd like to bring it back up. Technically it belongs to my grandmother, but she talked to her lawyer and I got to move into the farmhouse before she lost her whole mind. Dementia." She flashed Nora a smile to cushion the pity that would come.

"I'm sorry to hear that."

"It's fine. Been a few years now since she recognized me. Anyways, working at a bar has helped me build relationships with some of the local wineries and breweries, and I think we might be able to make our little Bellair Orchards into something special again. There's not much money in fruit on its own anymore, but if you can press it into a bottle or a can, you're rich. Or at least comfortable. Beats making cocktails.

"Speaking of"—she leaned toward Nora, eyes alight—"do you know how we get the apples to grow every year?"

"Pray?" It was the first word that came to her in the shadow of the church.

"Close . . ." She paused for effect. "We *scream*."

"Uh."

Sophie laughed again, that warm chuckle that pulled a person in close. "It's called 'wassailing'—an old practice, much older than that nonsense." She waved back at the church, where someone inside was singing off-key. "In late January, when things under the earth are beginning to twitch, we stand outside and scream. It's supposed to scare the bad fairies away or something, welcome the apples into a fresh world. Stories my gram used to tell me and my cousins when we were kids."

"My momma had the same tales." Nora shared Sophie's grin. "Does it work?"

"Better than praying."

Sophie

There was a memorial at the bar.

Of course there was a memorial.

The hostess stood at the door, wide-eyed and waiting for those who spilled out of the church, a weeping, choking mess of billowing black. Together, we watched the wind buffeting them as they made their way down the icy street.

I grew a gravity I had never known I could. There, standing in my corner of that dim little place, I felt my feet sink into the earth beneath our foundations. My arms grew long enough to wrap the entire town in their embrace, pull them in, and in, and inward again, until we, all of us little bodies, burned in the same room. Their faces tear-streaked, my own a mask to be painted upon. I pulled them in and became a sun, a star, a guttering black hole, watching quietly from the corner. Like them, I was dressed in mourner's black. It is the color I wear to work every day. It is the color I murdered Mark in.

Lindsey stumbled to my counter, and I handed him the drink I hadn't realized I would dare to make, though I had it ready when he arrived. The very same mezcal Mark had slammed in his last hours alive, poured over one big rock, sparkling smoke with a twist of lemon. He thanked me and sank back into the nest of hugs that waited for him. The cops moved through the mourners like beetles, listening, scrabbling together stories, tears, whispered guilts, tucking everything away for later examination. I watched them all with a smile hidden deep in the pocket of my heart. I had done this. *I am haunting them*, I thought. *I have created a nightmare. I am a ghost.*

"You all right, Soph?" Ty appeared from around a corner. "This is crazy, huh?"

"Crazy," I agreed.

He patted my back. I felt something shiver under the clap of his hand. "Let's take a shot."

He waved the servers over and lined up five gleaming shot glasses. Without asking, he filled each with Fernet, the libation of choice for restaurant lifers when one of our own is taken. I might have been insulted at the insinuation that Mark was one of our own, I suppose, but now he was. He was more a part of me than any of those lifting glasses to lips knew.

Ty shooed away the servers, poured us another shot. "Manager's privilege . . . To Mark."

And so I set the first brick of my newly baptized life, with a communion.

February

Nora

For weeks, they scoured everything. No one who lived life as Mark had, so vividly out in the open, who had so many tight ties in this town, who was never quiet about anything; no one who lived that way should have been such a mystery. But he was.

"I need the gossip, Nora. Anything you hear out on patrols. Who he was fucking, who he was fighting, who owed him money," Murph said, one afternoon three weeks after Mark's stinking corpse had been found. They stood out behind the station, her shivering with a cup of coffee in her frozen hands, and him sucking cigarette smoke into his lungs.

"Mark was . . . a bachelor. That's the nice way to put it. I've heard more than one story about him playing games with married women. We need to find out who. A jealous husband is my number one." He took a drag. "Let's check as well with the state PD. I'm sure you got this over the mountain too, we're not far from Route 29. I liked Mark, but I'm not blind to the kind of partying he enjoyed."

Nora nodded. She knew exactly what he meant. They were sitting in the middle of two big highways that made up the bulk of the interstate drug corridor, traveling in through Florida, up to D.C. and then the rest of the country. For a sleepy little area tucked into rolling mountains, Bellair and the surrounding towns had more than their fair share of illicit, and violent, crime.

Murph bent down to stub out his cigarette. It hissed on the cold ground, and steam rose up in a spiral. "People like Mark don't just end up dumped in a trash can. He must have really pissed someone off."

Sophie

My favorite time of any shift is the time of cutting fruit. There's a calm to the slide of a knife through citrus skin; a meditation to the pop and penetration, the quiet spray of juice that follows.

In those moments, I am become a lighthouse in a world that's shaking itself awake. Out on the floor, servers chatter to one another as they glide between tables, setting water glasses and saltshakers, lighting candles, laying out app plates and tight rolls of silverware. They fling bawdy jokes at one another, gossip about hookups and hangovers, tease one another like children on the playground. Ty watches them from one corner of the bar, making notes on who was late, who looks like they want to be the closer, if it's worth it to open up the patio in this weather. If he gets bored he'll amble out onto the floor to mess with Amber, who likes her tables just so. A roll of silver moved just a few degrees off-center, a water glass tipped upside down: these things send her buzzing. She makes herself too easy to tease.

In his kitchen, the chef sings to himself. He's always too loud and a hair off-key, his warm-up for later in the night when he'll be shouting. The soft squelch of low-boy doors opening and closing fills the space behind his voice. The sous and the dish greet each other by trading insults, curses rolling around on the greasy floor beneath them.

At her stand, the hostess murmurs her litany of reservations, double-checking times and table numbers, untangling each possible conflict, preparing for the onslaught to come. My barback, if he finds I have nothing for him to do, will drift over to help her. Most nights I have nothing much for him before service, so he spends his time painstakingly polishing silverware one piece at a time before rolling them into starched linens. His movements are painfully slow and measured. I want to reassure him that there won't be a test, but I'm not sure he'd get the joke. The hostess giggled though, when I whispered it to her one slow afternoon.

In this scurrying space, I meditate. A bright globe of fruit rolled from my hand onto a clean cutting board becomes an observation on the meeting of nail and tooth and flesh. Let it breathe, let it rock itself into stillness; my lemon, my lime, on brunch shift my orange, sits before me in gentle confirmation of sacrifice. To hold it, to keep it still, I pierce it. A sigh lifts up as skin and pith relent to metal tip. Knick made, victim immobilized, the blade sinks down through rounded body until the fruit falls away from itself in two shining halves. They sway on their backs like a pair of summer turtles turned over in their shells.

One sharp slice across the exposed belly of fruit tugs open a thin mouth, to plug around the lip of a cocktail glass. My wedges don't tumble into their drinks. One half done, I slit the other. Clean. Smooth. The first drops of juice wet my hands. Sometimes I hit seeds, buried in them like bones. A quick twist of the wrist is enough to nudge them out of my way.

Scored, each half is flipped onto its bleeding face. They stretch flat and long away from my body, a pool of juice spreading beneath them. Two quick lines down the soft arc of their backs birth three perfect cocktail wedges from each half—a piecemeal dome constructed of pulp and rind and sticky juice. I scoop each one up with my knife and pour them into the waiting dish. A bed of ice below keeps the slices firm and bright, fat smiles ready to greet thirsty customers.

Their scent hangs in the air after the cutting, like dew on a chill morning. By the time the process is done, my hands are coated in juice. I hate to wash it away. Sticky as it may be, it's lovely, something bright and clean and calm in the mess of dinner rush. I make sure to dab a bit on the pulse of my throat before running my hands under the faucet.

The second man was easier.

His neck, plump and slightly overripe like a lime on its last good day, popped when I drove my blade into it. His eyes popped too, in shock and betrayal and pain. The normal modes of convention weren't being followed. This was not supposed to be happening.

Charybdis

It's hard to understand the assault of customer service unless you've made a living of it. One summer slinging ice cream cones across a sun-stung boardwalk stand, or that part-time gig at the local dive that doubles as your underage drinking spot, doesn't quite cut it. Those are honeymoon jobs, where the cash is hot in your hand and everyone loves you because you're just so sweet. It's easy to be sweet when there's a light at the end of the tunnel.

There's a light, so you can ignore the way that man grabbed your wrist when you went to clear his plate. Yes, he hasn't touched it in ten minutes, but he's still got two fries left, *miss*, so stop rushing him, will you? Or maybe it's his wife, who hates you because she used to be you; who, now that she's not so taut anymore, notices the way her husband's eyes wander over bodies that aren't hers. Before she leaves, she'll make sure to call your manager over and complain about the smile you've plastered on your face, how you giggled about something (something that must have been her) with the busboy. Or maybe she'll say nothing at all but insist on paying the bill and leave without tipping anything on top of that $2.13 you make per hour; $0.00 once the support staff are tipped out and the taxes get paid.

There's a light, so you can laugh when that man, who's been taking up that table in your section for hours now, hoarding it like some fairy-tale dragon on a pile of gold, presses his mouth to your ear and slips his room key in your back pocket. "For when you get off," he says, his fingers in your belt loops a hook that you can't wriggle free from until you smile.

Do you see now?

But really, how can you? Until you have a lifetime's worth of grime under your fingernails and knots in your back and aches in your feet; until you've swallowed your pride and your intellect so many times your stomach is bloated and sour with their rotting corpses, how can you understand?

It's a bit like being a woman.

Which is why, as soon as I saw the chance to step behind a bar, I took it. I can't stop the looks, the snide questions about my recipes, the late-night pickup lines and cash waved in my face, mine if I play dance, monkey, dance . . . But they can't touch me anymore. They can't reach me. That bit of metal and wood is an ocean and I am Charybdis, and they can't throw an arm across the expanse without falling down into my pit. It is small, yes, but it is everything.

I was on my way back from the bank, my purse heavy with rolls of coins for the register, thinking about that bar. The main drag of Bel-lair, Peach Street, is a bent arm of road, and shooting off the end of its elbow to wrap around the back of those street-front businesses is an unkempt track called Garland Avenue, used mainly for delivery trucks, smokers, and restaurant employees who need a bit of breathing space. It's also the preferred route of work entry for staff. As the kitchen boys love to joke, it's more fun to slide into the bitch from behind. How original. I suppose it was fitting then that as I was walking back from the bank that day, I was thinking about breasts.

The trick to working holidays is to make them fun for yourself; everything should be a game. Otherwise, the oversize egos and under-size tips will drive you mad. Which is why, as I stepped down Garland, careful to watch for hidden ice slicks, I was thinking I'd convince Ty to order us some coupes for the pink Valentine's Day champagne; coupes, you see, have a delicious secret.

Start with the basics: fermentation of wine, of cheese, of beer, is nothing more than a carefully controlled spoilage, perfected over thousands of years of human trial and error. It's believed by some that the first beer was brewed by accident when ancient Egyptians noticed there was something funny about the runoff from their bread baking, a happy discovery that may have influenced their zeal for agriculture, and consequently the world as we know it. If the myth is true, then we owe our eternal gratitude to that microscopic fungi we call yeast. More specifically, to yeast's appetite. That ethanol that paints a rosy bloom on cheeks and loosens tongues is the natural waste product of hordes of minuscule mouths gorging themselves on sugar.

We can slow them down, drag out the process so the delicate spoil doesn't become a putrid rot; trap them in a barrel or bottle so their feast takes years instead of weeks. Only death will stop them. This is what the monks who made champagne knew.

The wine, a dusky Pinot Noir if you want to be traditional, or a buttery Chardonnay for a blanc de blanc, is bottled with an extra spoonful of sugar before being shelved. For three years, the bottles sit, alone in the dark, touched only every so often to be gently turned in their beds. Inside the glass, all is well for a time; the extra dose of sugar a boon to the yeast, who munch through it with no thought to the future. Meanwhile, the ethanol they've belched out starts to poison their home. And so, they begin to die.

This is where things get interesting. The yeast, out of sugar and starving, has no choice but to eat the corpses of their sisters. Autolysis, it's called. The destruction of oneself. This cannibalism is what gives champagne its bready flavor and full mouthfeel. It's also what causes the bubbles.

Yeast isn't the only microbe that eats itself. You do too, though for most of your life this destruction is the more ordered and well-mannered autophagy. *Self-biting*, rather than *self-eating*. In death, the rules bend. Mark's body, wilted and blue at the bottom of that dumpster, was a frenzy of microscopic mouths.

I can hear you. This is fascinating, but where's the game? Here's my answer: It's a myth that sparkling wines are best served in a flute. That long glass flank, while beautiful and easy for dainty hands to hold, does nothing more than showcase the bubbles. That wine in your glass is the result of centuries of hard work and chemistry and unaccountable deaths and should be understood and respected as such. In a flute, it's pretty but one-dimensional. Allowed to bloom in the wide bowl of a coupe, it becomes a multisensory symphony of taste and sound and smell. Those yeast who've survived the famine can gulp the fresh air and sing.

If my humor bent in a sophomoric direction, I might not have cared, might instead have delighted in a bar full of couples all dressed to the nines, lifting the traditional phallic flutes to their lips. There's something especially delicious about the irony of that scene. My glee is more sophisticated though. Bar lore holds that Marie Antoinette's breasts were so lovely, her husband, King Louis XVI, modeled his stemware after them. The phallus is overdone. Let them sip bubbles from bosoms; what a good joke that would be.

I had decided this, chuckling to myself, when the man who would become my second man made himself known.

"You got a nice smile, girl. Can I get one?"

It didn't compute at first, this sharp intrusion into my sacred quiet. This wasn't right; he didn't fit. This place here in the weeds and gravel, which smelled slightly of trash and iron-muddy water, this behind-place, is our church, where we who pin smiles to our faces, raw from where we peeled off our pride, can exist as we are. There between stinking garbage cans, splintering stacks of pallets, beat-up chairs and milk crates; there is where all the misfits of our Vera

Bradley–toting and Vineyard Vines–wearing, pastel paisley world can sit and take a breath, take a break from eyes, whistles, hands.

And there he was, in that sacred peace, intruding. I felt my hackles rise up, the creeping lift of hundreds of arrector pili caught between the toes of a thousand tiny feet.

On its western flank, Garland Avenue is hemmed in by the creek. The other side is punctured by several blocks' worth of alley heads, interstitial trailways like veins slicing between smiling Peach Street storefronts and bars. They are dark places, and narrow, each capped at the eastern end with a tall wooden fence or cramped mudroom, to keep our trash out of the main street, to shield the better public from our smoke breaks and outfit changes, our unsmiling faces. The Blue Bell shared our alley with the hair salon next door and the bookshop above them. He stood between me and the alley, which was still a good ten steps away. If I made it, escape from this man was only a short climb up the back stairway and into the restaurant.

Into work.

Before my break was over.

The thought stirred something in the curve of my jaw; just there, tucked behind the rounded point of my mandible. Feet crept through bony canals, shivered themselves into the plush pillows of my tonsils. A sour sting in the back of my mouth. An itch. I felt all the taut fibers of my shoulder blades contract. This had been my space, my time. And he had pressed into it, expecting and demanding my attention. My hands clenched into fists. I had a choice.

The door was right there, a few steps away.

The back windows were closed faces, curtains drawn over them to keep out the cold. Steam guttered from the kitchen vent. The heating unit, hard at work on this frozen day, rumbled and chugged. No one could see us here; no one could hear us. It was winter; the dark was coming earlier, the alley already drowning in soft shadows.

If I was attacked here, now, no one would know. No one would help.

"Hey! I was talking to you!" A yell, short and sharp; the sound of feet on gravel, ice crunching underfoot. Then a growl, spit on the frozen ground: "Bitch."

An idea that I had tried to bat away escaped my hands and flapped, frantic, between my ears: Why should I have to go back to being harassed at work to avoid being harassed on my break?

I watched as my hand grew a mind of its own, slipped down into my purse to fish for the gloves that were buried somewhere under the stacks of pens and check-out slips, the packet of cigarettes I kept to placate the line cooks on slammed nights to ensure that they always loved their Sophie, who took such wonderful care of them. They were simple, cotton things, those gloves; truth be told they didn't do much for the cold, but they were just right for covering fingerprints.

When I turned back to him, I made sure my body was a welcome, held up the pack of cigarettes for good measure. He followed me under the back stairwell.

Men don't like women with empty mouths. Sew them shut, stuff them full, before she fills it with a voice. Maybe that's why I didn't speak a word when I broke the contract he'd signed my name to. Not that I needed to. So certain was he of his own beating heart that he followed me under those stairs of his own accord. All I needed to do was what they've always demanded. *Smile, girl. You've got such a pretty smile.*

I stabbed him in the alleyway again and again and again, while not twenty yards from us, people continued about their day. When the shock wore off and he thought to cry out, I stabbed him in the cheek, the soft hollow under his chin, the cup that held his tongue. My knife shuddered as it collided with the arched ribbing of his palate. When I yanked it out, his screams burbled out of his throat in a gurgling rush of blood and mewling whimpers. One more thrust to his throat silenced his pain. Shut up shut up *shut up.*

I drove him into the space below the stairs, turned him facedown to keep his blood away from me. It splashed on my shoes, but that was no matter. As long as my work shirt stayed clean, stayed black, no one would notice anything amiss. It splashed on the discarded boxes, and I moved more under him with my toe. Let the cardboard soak him up; it was easily thrown away.

He sank. I stabbed him again, this time in the nape of his neck. My knife hit bone and gristle, and I twisted until they slid away, nothing more than lemon seeds. He collapsed to the filthy ground, and I let myself fall on top of him. Blood pooled under us while I waited for him to deflate. Men, I was learning, had soft spots. They were no less flesh and bone than I, or you.

It was over almost as soon as it began: the sudden plunge into tight flesh, gasping and bucking and then, release. Stillness, quiet, flooded the open air around us. I didn't move. For a long stretch of breath, I sat on his back, riding out the electric twitches and jerks of his body beneath me, his nerves short-circuiting one by one. It would have been funny if I hadn't felt so exposed, the absurd flailing of a body suddenly finding itself unplugged. But the flimsy shelter of the cave beneath a few rickety wooden stairs was no hiding place, no safe space to catch my breath and settle for a moment into this, my second slaughter.

Seconds ticked by, heavy as hours and just as solid as they hit the air with each soft click of my wristwatch. I crouched over him, like an animal, mouth opened wide to quiet the ragged sounds of my breath scraping against chapped lips. Steam rose up in front of me, from the blood that he'd spat to the chill ground. All it would take was one employee on a smoke break. What would I say?

In the end, I didn't need an answer. No one came. The alleyway stayed frozen and silent, gently steaming. The only sounds the distant caw of crows, the quiet burble of the creek, the wheeling thrum of my heart.

Worries poked into my thoughts like fingers. *You can't leave him here! You don't have time—where are you going to take him? And the blood! What if someone sees you with these boxes? Where else did it splash? What are you going to do?*

What are you going to do? What are you going to do, Sophie? Pay attention! Look at me!!

There he was. Facedown on the icy ground, broken, no longer bleeding. I saw the stark truth of him: he was pathetic, this ugly man who demanded of me, who thought I owed him something. My cheeks stung with bile, and I kicked him, hard. And then I went to the place that was always there, buried just behind my eyes, where I knew I could find peace when the world around me was too thick with noise and faces and the scratch of too many voices on the chalk-board of my brain. It's quiet there, calm. I can take a breath and put my feet on the ground, make a decision.

There was nothing to be done then, in the fading light of that bare winter sun. The man would have to stay where he was for now. Empty boxes and broken pallets became my best friends. I shoved my attacker deep under the stairs and built a fort about his stiffening corpse. His legs fit into an old wine case; his head found a strange hat in a discarded silverware rack. All the vomited debris of the bar was re-tooled as a grotesque sort of couture, and he was my mannequin.

A half-dead blackberry bush growing under the stairs became my ally in silence. Fitting, really: my last name, Braam, is Dutch for "blackberry." The thorny spill of her arms would keep me safe, give me time to figure out what to do.

Later, the last customers gone, the sun dead in the sky, I handed Ty my check-out and told him I needed a break from cleaning, that I had cramps and needed some fresh air. Men never question anything having to do with menstruation—all I had to do was root around in my purse like I was looking for a tampon and they fell over themselves to get away from me; so I knew I was safe, for a few minutes. I stopped in the bathroom first, to complete the ruse. Then, I unboxed my man.

I pinned them together, but even so, my hands weren't big enough to wrap easily around his wrists; they slipped and struggled. Once or twice, one of his arms flopped out, heavy, and I had to scramble to gather it back up into this strange bouquet I'd made.

He was heavy, his body unwieldy. The zipper of his coat tore through clumps of dead grass and hissed as it slid across gravel. I had to squat down low and pull, one firm step, then another, another, one more, as fast as I could, while my eyes and ears swept the alley for signs of life. Despite the cold, I felt sweat break out on my forehead. My breath swept out of my mouth like smoke.

When I bumped into the cracked milk crate at the far corner of the alley, I almost dropped him. The splinters of plastic were so like fingers in my back, I had a vision of myself as a child playing Stick 'Em Up on the playground. The world around us stayed still; my heart tiptoed back down my throat.

The last steps were simple. Stay quiet, stay calm. I rolled him to one side while I moved crates, heaved pallets, shoved the broken chair over to the opposite corner. No one coming out here to smoke would accidentally put their feet on my man. Then came the necessary work. I checked his pockets for ID, his body for any noticeable scraps of myself. I picked off some cotton fluff from my gloves, wiped away a drop of sweat, teased out a strand of hair that had fallen down onto his coat. The rest, I would have to trust, would be ruined by the elements. He had no ID, and I began to suspect he had no home. No one would miss him. That gave me time.

His tongue was easier to take than Mark's, exposed as it was through the tear in his throat. I shoved it into my pocket and then covered him up under a pile of old boxes, broken trash, forgotten scraps.

The gravel that was too smooth from our crawl, I set to scattering. His blood had frozen the boxes solid. I gathered them up into a trash bag, tossed them into the dumpster. The rest I found splashed on the ground, I broke up with a few good, hard stomps, before kicking ice chips as red as jewels around the alley. Let them melt into nothing.

It started to snow just as I finished, soft kisses sinking onto my hair, my cheeks, my neck. *Breathe*, they said. *Breathe*. I closed my eyes, felt each cold touch soothe away a bit of the dangerous flush from my skin. A giggle bubbled up in my throat, something like relief and giddy freedom. I caught it before it could erupt, but it swept upward and flared as a gleam in my eyes. I was powerful. I had a secret, two secrets, one of whom would soon be slowly eating himself in the unseen depths of the far corner.

When I walked into the bar a few minutes later and Ty told me the snowflakes looked pretty against my dark hair, my whole body smiled.

Nora

The air crusted over, and by February it had grown fangs. Sheltered as it was from deep snows by the firm décolletage of the rolling Blue Ridge, Bellair couldn't avoid the chill; winter seeped down over the mountainside, poured into ditches and creek beds, painted delicate lace patterns on morning windowpanes. The icy air built a weight in February, a body that slipped under Nora's skin and spooled around every length of bone, rattled the stolid soldiers of her teeth until they chattered. She began to feel those night faces press into her flesh again, the frost on her front porch shimmering evidence of their sighs in the dark. They poked her awake in the morning, these horrible deaths that far too often she bore witness to; their bodies were flimsy things, easily broken in the weak sunlight and gone as soon as her eyes cracked open. *Here.*

You are here. Be here.

Here. She felt her heart beat, strong and insistent. She was here, in her crooked rolling chair. Here, where all the dark winter days that had dragged on since she and Murph had found Mark's body were gathered on the chipped vinyl of this little desk that was hers; here under skittering fluorescent light, in this cold cinder-block-and-brick building. There was nothing. The trick of throwing him in the trash had obliterated so much, left so many questions coiling around his corpse. They'd pulled in old business partners, girlfriends, even his aging mother, to see if anyone knew anything at all. All they got was a picture of a man who partied maybe more than he should have at his age, whose restlessness belied a certain pathetic loneliness. The closest they came to a real lead was the day Murph brought in Lindsey. Mark owed him money, a lot. But the man was so distraught at his friend's death it was hard to see that he could have been responsible for it. And he had an airtight alibi to boot. A week of skiing up at Wintergreen. It was only an hour's drive away, true. But there were enough photos, enough people to vouch for his presence.

"He was supposed to meet us there," Lindsey said, his voice wet with tears. "When he didn't show, we assumed he'd just got a wild hair and went down to Ocracoke. He did that sometimes. Just escaped, didn't tell anyone."

So Mark's file sat hollow, became a deep well that swallowed him whole, and Nora had spent too many days now standing at the edge of it, peering over into the dark.

"Never put your hands where you can't see, child." Nora heard her momma's voice as she dipped into that well. "You don't know what might be waiting there, ready to bite you."

Of course, Emma had meant snakes.

But no matter how deep Nora prodded, how many times she swirled her hands through the questions curling in on themselves at the edges of so many official reports and interview notes, she found nothing save for a sort of itch at the tips of her fingers; her answer still only a thought, with no teeth yet to bite.

Her desk mocked her. She spent too much time sitting there now. They all did. Blown indoors by the bitter cold, the officers molted the straight backs and sleek musculature of their summer uniforms, revealing underneath the soft bodies of house cats; so transformed, they draped themselves over desks and chairs, hands glued to phones glued to eyes that glazed over in boredom. Mouths hung slack. This was where the trouble started, Nora knew. Men were no good bored.

They soured in their seats, like wine left too long on a dusty shelf and turned to vinegar.

Winter meant days huddled in their patrol car, stolidly freezing while doing their best to ignore the backache that came from too many sedentary hours, the only entertainment the rather tedious chore of watching housewives in hatchbacks spin out on black ice. A domestic dispute down on the Sanderses' farm was a relief, something hard and exciting to shake life from those frigid doldrums. Another tractor-trailer stuck under the railroad bridge would free a man from a day chained to a desk, writing up notes. Panhandlers on Peach Street may have been nothing more than an annoyance in summer, but in that frozen season, anything was an excuse to get up, get out, get the blood moving again.

Nora grabbed that call. She knew she was the best one to ask a mother why she had her kids outside begging with her on an icy street corner when they should have been warm and fed in school. The boys would have made their questions an accusation, put the woman's back up. Nora, who knew something of being soft, could turn the concern in her voice into a blanket, welcome that woman and her babies inside.

This was their life in the winter: long, drooling days punctuated with bursts of anger or boiled-over frustration. All the mildewed debris of human behavior wrapped up in a cold so sharp it made your eyes water and your nose sting. By February she began to feel her soul slide down to the toes of her sensible shoes and sink into the dirty floor beneath her feet.

And always, behind the parking tickets and offense reports and grant proposals, was Mark Dixon staring at her, his own questions plopping out of his blueing mouth like wet snow off a roof. Whatever evidence there was had stayed silent. Mark was a haint without a tongue; his questions were left slowly puddling on her desk until thoughts of him had soaked through all her other paperwork.

It annoyed her, though she'd never admit it. Mark was Murph's; his docket, his responsibility. He was still the homicide detective in-house, not her. Not yet. The fact relieved and frustrated her, a constant itch that sat under her skin, uncomfortable, incurable. Always poking and taunting her.

The boys could smell this, her frustration, her stuckness. They'd tolerated her well enough when she was new, a cold shoulder here or whisper of "diversity hire" there, but for the most part a gruff sort of tolerance was what they'd offered her back in August. She'd taken it for what it was, the small-town territorial games that small people liked to play. But when it became clear that she was staying on, that she was Murph's chosen protégé, and that meant she must think she was better than them, then the real trouble started.

At first it was hissed conversations floating out of the break room. "Satterwhite's been waiting for that spot to open up for years now, put in good hard work, and Sarge is just going to hand it to *her*?"

"It's liberal PC bullshit. Gotta make the taxpayers happy so they stop threatening to slash our funding. Like we're rolling in it over here. I'm so tired of this. What the fuck do they know about police work? I don't tell politicians how to do their job." His voice dropped half an octave in mock pretension. *"Why didn't you just shoot him in the leg, Officer? A few bad apples ruin the whole bunch."*

"Better watch out, I bet she'll be taking notes, looking for problems she won't find."

"What's she gonna do if a fight breaks out?"

"Cry, probably. Maybe it's a good thing they're trying to tie her to a detective's desk. I don't want to get shot because my partner's PMSing."

"Can you trust her? When shit hits the fan, whose side is she on?"

Nora bit the insides of her cheeks, decided she didn't really want that cup of coffee. The whispers though tangled around her ankles like vines, trailing her in the hallways, scraping against her bare skin.

One morning she walked in on Charlie scooping away a box of super-large tampons and a bottle of Midol that someone had left sitting in front of her locker.

"It's just a shitty joke, Nora," he tried to explain, though to her or himself, she wasn't sure. "Don't let these assholes get to you. Murph and I've got your back."

But Charlie wasn't working the day Davis stuck a rebel flag on his locker and loudly declared that since his son's school didn't seem to understand the difference between heritage and hate, and so had banned the wearing of Confederate symbols, he'd be proudly displaying it here.

"All those little fags get to keep their flag," he said, slapping his sticker onto the blue metal door. The paint was the same color as its hateful bars, Nora noticed. It might have been stenciled right on. Davis continued his diatribe. "Doesn't seem right, censoring some people's history and not others', and in a public school too. Wouldn't you agree?" he sneered, pressing down the bubbles in the sticker until it lay smooth. "Unless I'm mistaken, all of us here swore an oath to protect the Constitution. Does their free speech matter more than my son's?"

What she'd wanted to say to him then, what she bit her tongue over instead, was that maybe that flag had given up its constitutional rights when it declared war against its own nation.

Nora spent that afternoon sitting in the emergency room with a girl who'd been raped in a school stairwell. She couldn't help but wonder if the boy who did it called that heritage too, the heritage of the powerful asserting themselves. Her heart grew a fist. The next time she looked at Mark Dixon's file, it punched her rib cage.

When it was clear that their more overt tactics wouldn't work, they simply started stealing calls from her.

"No, you stay right where you are, *Nora*." Her name in their mouths sounded like an oil smear on a counter, too smooth for comfort, and with a certain viscidity that was hard to scrub away. "Murph might need you, you know. It'll be easier if Bowles takes this call. Then we won't have to scramble to cover if you get pulled."

She could have argued, she could have reported them and made a stink, but what good would that have done? Then she would be what they wanted her to be—angry. And angry was a weak place for her to be. Angry was what she'd been fighting against her whole career, in back alleys and the break room and every contested space between; men were always goading her, poking her, daring her to sink into the emotions they could use as a cudgel against her. So she bit her lip and clenched her jaw and reminded herself that they were nothing more than hungry dogs snapping at their own bellies; trying to quell their jealousy by taking bites out of the air. She would not give them something to chew on. Her jaw though was beginning to ache, and the migraines she thought she'd left behind in puberty were threatening to come roaring back, their thorny fingers too often now testing, pricking the darkness behind Nora's eyes.

"You okay, baby girl?" Barb asked first, and then, later, her momma. To both of them Nora replied with a nod and a smile: "Yes, ma'am. Just tired is all."

Barb had to accept that answer. Her momma didn't. So, while Nora was sitting out on her parents' tired front porch, her daddy came to find her.

"Momma need help in the kitchen?" she asked, sitting up. She knew she should be in there, helping stir or chop and nodding along to whatever local gossip Emma had collected over the past few weeks, but her heart wasn't in it. Instead, she'd retreated outside, to the sunset, to the sleeping vines scraping worn gray wood. Winter here was quiet, the only sound the distant hiss of cars on the highway, a mile off and easily ignored. The rest was ice and silence, and even her most restless thoughts found space to still in the cool blue evening.

"Nah," Ron said, lowering himself down onto the porch swing. "Scoot your tush."

Nora did. "She sent you out here though."

"She's worried about you, and so am I."

Nora knew the words that fell out of her mouth were a lie, knew that her daddy would know that too, but she said them anyway. "I'm fine, Daddy."

The sounds of Dan's and Emma's laughter bubbled up from somewhere inside the house, light and warm as fresh biscuits, and just as filling to a soul. The sound sparked a light in Nora's heart, smoothed some of the wrinkles in her brow. She wondered what they were giggling about, guessed it was probably one of their TV shows. Her momma loved that fluff as much as Dan. They were peas in a pod, those two, had been since the day Nora brought the boy home for dinner a decade earlier. She was glad of it, Dan fitting so easily into their family.

Her daddy's voice rolled out of the growing darkness, pulled her back down to the creaking porch swing. "Nora Jean Martin, I've known you since the day you were born, and I know when something's on your mind."

Nora curled her fingers into her momma's morning glory. The plant was dull in the winter, dry; a leaf splintered off beneath her thumb. "Can I have a cigarette?"

"I quit. Two weeks ago. Doctor says my blood pressure's getting too high."

"Dammit."

He laughed. "I agree. But I'd rather be here than in the ground, especially so my daughter can tell me what's got her up a tree."

Nora sighed. To argue was useless, and she thought maybe he was exactly who she should be talking to. So she told him, about the breakroom whispers and dispatch politics; about Davis, about the snarling disdain he'd flung toward her, how they'd all watched, that no one stepped in to stop him. She told him how alone she felt. Even with Charlie and Murph, and Dan at home. It felt like whining, this venting; she felt childish and stubborn and was angry for it, resented her team for pulling her down to this level, even if she knew she was right to be so upset.

"I know what you're going to say," she said, crushing another leaf between her fingers, her frustration biting her cheeks. "That I shouldn't let it bother me. That I should ignore them and keep moving forward. Turn the other cheek. But, Dad, my life is tough enough at work. I'm the worst part of most people's day. Every day. Or if I'm not, I'm holding their hand during it. I expect the spit and the slurs from drunk assholes. The guys are supposed to be on my side."

Ron thought for a moment before he answered. Around them, the blue evening deepened into black; Nora watched the faraway gleam of headlights slide up a distant hill, disappear. Finally, with a sigh, he said, "I'm sorry, Nora."

She looked up at him, into his eyes, which were her own.

"I'm sorry that I've taught you to make your problems small. A father is supposed to protect his children, and your momma and I made a decision when you and your brother were young that we were going to teach you to hold your heads up, that there was nothing wrong with you, that you could be who you wanted to be and do what you wanted to do. We didn't want to build a cage around you before you even got out there. But in doing that, in some ways, I think we set you up for getting hurt . . . You ever talk to your momma about her family, Nora?"

Another set of headlights climbed the hill, dipped away. "I know she had some problems with her granddaddy."

"He never spoke to her again after she married me. Built a fence between his property and her parents', that's how mad he was. Never spoke to them again either. Mad his son let Emma marry someone like me. It's terrible, the cruelty of small minds. What a waste. What a loss. He missed out on you and your brother's entire childhoods because he chose to live with a spiteful heart. And I know that broke your momma's heart. She spent years trying to hide tears from me, didn't want me to know she was crying over a racist. But he was her family—of course she was upset. And that made me mad, for her." He sighed, and suddenly Nora felt the weight of her parents' lives in a way she never had before.

"The truth is, you've got a layer of complicated right there in your face, you can't hide it, can't run from it. And you shouldn't. So fuck 'em."

"Dad!" All her life, Nora had never heard her daddy swear.

"No, seriously, fuck 'em. That man tortured your momma for years, and for what? And this man Davis? He can't pretend his flag is just about family heritage anymore. That earth is being dug up, painful questions getting asked—things people like him have been able to avoid, they can't now. And that's made him mad? Good. Let him go scratch his mad place. That's what 'turn the other cheek' means some days—let him see his temper tantrum is just noise. He can't hurt you; don't give him that power.

"Your momma and I, we worry about you, Nora. We worry about your brother too, but you're on the front lines in a way that he's not. I think about, what if you get in trouble on a call? Someone decides to pull a gun on you or grabs you, and I know, you're trained"—he held up his hands—"but you're still smaller than a lot of guys out there, and when they're drunk, or high, and angry, they're strong. What if you get into that situation and your teammates don't have your back? That scares me. Keeps me up at night. So you be better than Davis. Get onto that detective desk as fast as you can. And in the meantime, you keep your head up, and do your job as well as I know you can, and everyone will see how small he and his buddies really are. You do that, the right people will notice, and they're the only ones who matter."

"Fuck 'em."

"Fuck 'em. And now, don't ever let me hear you use that language again." He patted her knee. "Should we go in and see if Dan needs rescuing? You know how your momma gets about cooking."

———

It had been six months since the move, and maybe the right people had noticed, but what did that matter if the wrong ones were still snarling?

Her transfer had been sudden but easier than expected. Dan, tired of climbing up over the mountain every day, had pushed for it first. They'd been talking about buying a house of their own—why not look and see what was available across the county line?

"Remember last winter, Nor?" Dan said over dinner one night, his fork twisting through his favorite spaghetti with ketchup, a childhood delicacy they would have to hide from friends if they moved to more civilized parts of the state. "There were more than a few nights I drove home from the hospital with my heart in my mouth. Ice is always bad up on the mountain, and fog. And if I'm driving tired, which I almost always am—"

"I don't want to hear that!" Nora had covered her ears. She'd seen enough cars plowed into ditches after drivers fell asleep at the wheel.

Dan took a bite, red splotches of ketchup dripping onto his chin. "Well . . . it's an accident waiting to happen. That's all I'm saying. I'd rather not die after twelve hours of being puked and bled on. There are better ways to spend your last day."

He wasn't wrong.

"I don't know if I can find a job though, Dan," she'd said. "It's a tough time. Everyone's cutting back. And I'm about to get the move I've been working for—detective. Darrow hasn't confirmed it yet, but I can feel it coming. Wood's moving down to North Carolina in the fall."

He hardly looked up as he said, "You'll get there again. You're good at what you do, Nor. Even I can see that. Look, I'm sure there's tons of jobs for you over on my side. Hell, the university has its own little squad. They haul in all the freshmen with alcohol poisoning. Maybe you can start with them; then we'd practically be working together."

"Yes, the epitome of my career is babysitting drunk rich kids just so I can wave to my boyfriend while he's at work."

Dan stuck out his tongue, took another bite of his spaghetti. "Just think about it. Summer's the best time to move. Do you really want to stay here?"

They both knew the answer to that.

The valley they had both grown up in, which had nurtured them and loved them and taught them the sort of cleverness known only to those who grow up in such places, was withering. Things had begun to snag down there, their wide bowl between mountain ridges growing breathless with the weight that had laid itself down over her rolling green sometime in Nora's childhood. The earth was still alive, the dirt smelled just as fresh, crops popped up on time, cattle grazed in sunny fields, and the woods were a veritable riot of wildlife. But it wasn't the earth that was dying around them; it was the people. The people in the valley were rotting.

It wasn't their fault. Generations of crushed dreams had a way of breaking spines, cracking souls like concrete. Nora had felt it growing up, watching herself grow strong and limber, while the paint peeled off the hardwood of her drooping home. The humidity, her momma had insisted one morning as she dragged a comb through Nora's hair while her daughter winced. Though she tried her best, Emma never really got the knack of her child's texture.

But then the roof of the bowling alley caved in one night after a wicked thunderstorm. Its carcass became a way station, parking lot glittering with broken bottles; the long teeth of discarded needles; minivans full of kids, waiting for the weekly parent swap. The general store went next, boarded up and abandoned. On her childhood road, old houses fell silent, their sagging porches giving way to a jungle of weedy grass and vines, while five miles up the interstate, cheap new apartments were slapped together and trees were torn down. The place that had once been a treasure began to feel worthless.

As the town began to sag and sink into the ground, the people did too. They laughed, and they loved one another, and they floated what lives they could out of the sinking, but Nora couldn't help but notice a sort of fraying at the edges, a resignation born of always being used as a Ping-Pong ball in a fight much bigger than them. This was their life: *Thank God you live in such a beautiful place. Try to ignore the smell of chicken shit from the factory across the highway.*

By the time she was grown, the only places left were the leaving places. Giant chain stores popped up, quick-stop restaurants where no one asked your name. Target had moved in across the road from Walmart. A Starbucks opened not long after. A force bigger than any of them was steamrolling through, and Nora watched as the heart of the valley she loved so much crumbled and died.

At first Nora hoped she might heal some of it, the crumbling. So she'd sweated through the academy to wear a badge that earned her more disrespect than thanks, but that was what she'd signed up for, she reminded herself. Real change was never easy, and no one had asked for her help. After six years, she began to give up on that dream. She'd been spat on, cursed and wheedled at; shot at by rednecks with grudges against big government and chips on their shoulders as heavy as any family name. She'd picked up children selling themselves and being sold in damp basements. She'd questioned men with gray teeth, rotted to the root, who made a point of looking at her body curving under the cut of her women's-issue uniform so often that her sergeant had suggested she try a men's set of trousers. The suggestion made Nora feel dirty for something she couldn't change, and the pants didn't really fit, but she wore them anyway, showered the slime of those eyes off her after every shift.

She'd gotten to know the town drunk, who was harmless, really, and just needed a reminder every once in a while not to piss in the Walmart parking lot. "I understand it's a dump, Kevin, I really do, but Mrs. Brown called us again and, you know, she doesn't want her kids to see you . . . urinating. Does that sound fair?" He'd giggled at that and said something quite rude about Mrs. Brown that Nora pretended not to hear. This was her gift. She knew when to play along and when not to, how to talk down tempers before they flared, smooth and soften even the most bruised egos—psyches damaged by two tours in Iraq, mothers cradling pill bottles instead of babies, people so down on their luck they were desperate.

Every day she had pulled on an ill-fitting uniform and sat for lonely hours in an uncomfortable car, pounded the same beats over and over again until she was so bored she thought she might cry; all for the shot at that desk with a window, the chance to cut that chain from around her ankle. Detectives were the ones who really got to bring justice to the world, that was what she told herself. She'd been so close, but then she'd started to feel the crumbling begin in her too. This place was fading, and it would drag her with it if she held on too tight. If she wanted to grow, she needed to leave.

"I'll look around," she said, watching Dan slurp up the last of his ketchup, one long noodle sliding in through puckered lips.

"I love you, babe." He leaned around their small plastic table and kissed her on the cheek.

And that was it. She'd put out feelers and almost immediately someone had grabbed her hand.

"So, you're going over the mountain," Sergeant Darrow said when she came to tell him. "Well, I can't say I'm surprised. You're built for better things than chasing drunks and junkies. Don't forget about us though. You're always welcome at a desk back here, if you find you want it."

She'd thanked him and shook his hand, the firm squeeze her daddy had taught her that always took men by surprise. A month later she was packing up the truck with Dan for a move that in the end wasn't so far but felt like a world away.

Her words felt a little slower here, her manners a little less polished. There was no Walmart or Applebee's. Target wasn't where you went to buy fancy underwear. Gas cost twice as much. Lawns were manicured, not littered with the rusted topiary of broken-down cars.

There was order here, and care. The stubborn pride of the slowly dying could only be found out on the forgotten edges, and they'd be pushed out soon enough, the corners tidied up behind them. Nora felt out of place, as she'd known she would; but Out of Place was a place she was used to, and so she adjusted. She would figure things out. At their core, people were all the same.

On her second day she met Murph, who promptly welcomed her and dragged her off to his end of the station.

"You'll be with me, kid," he'd said, by way of introduction. "I know I'm going to have to share you with patrol for a while, but your old boss Darrow and I go way back, and he put in a good word for you. Said you'd been about to scoot over to detective, so I thought I'd snap you up before Boggs did—he's the other detective in the station. You don't want to work with him. Boggs does the boring stuff. The little bit of cyber foolery we get around here, which is why he's hardly here anyways." He leaned in close. "Works a lot with the guys out of Charlottesville. A bunch of stiffs. You stay with me, kid. The real meat and potatoes lands on my desk.

"You have perfect timing too. I'm hoping to bust out of this joint soon. I know I look like a spry young man, but it's just good genes." He waited for her to laugh. When she didn't, he continued. "I thought I'd train you up to take my place. Truth is, I've been looking for someone for a while, and none of these dolts around here is worthy of the position. Nice enough guys, except I guess the usual few meatheads, but . . . well, let's say I've got my hopes pinned on you."

"No pressure then."

"I like you already, Martin."

The sergeant, a stern man named John Wright, made it known that he'd okayed the situation but that he expected no slack on her end. "I'll be honest with you, Martin, I'm glad to have you on. You came with great recs. But we're short-staffed right now and funds are tight. I know Murph wants you all to himself, but my hands are tied for the time being. You go with him, you train when you can, but you come in to work prepared to be on your A game every day. If he wants to pull you, he has to talk to me and my secretary, Barb."

Barb waved from her desk.

"Yes, sir. I really appreciate everything you're doing for me. I won't let you down."

Now, staring at the piles of questions on her desk, Nora felt as if she was letting everyone down. There was the folder with photos of Mark Dixon's corpse. There were the witness statements, the forensic files, the endless strings tied on one end to Mark's body, flapping loose in the dark. He was like a marionette, cut from his control; the crux that tied all these strings together was gone; a gaping black hole, swallowing her attention.

"Let an old man give you some advice," Murph said the third or fourth time he'd found her shoving files into her bag to take home. "Take a break. Let your mind sit. It's like doing a puzzle—if you get stuck, walk away and come back with fresh eyes. Besides . . . this isn't your job. Not yet. Let me earn my retirement; otherwise I might feel guilty."

But questions didn't trail behind him like shadows. Unlike her, Murph didn't feel the need to prove himself every day he came to work; she wondered if he ever had. As she packed up that night, Nora shoved Mark's file into her bag again.

The cold kissed her cheeks when she walked out to her car, froze her tears so they glistened like jewels on her eyelashes.

The New Kid

She would never forget the blood; how, even days after their initial search of the tiny brick ranch, they were still finding drops of it flung far across the room, splashed into the deepest corners, dripping down behind furniture as if the room itself were bleeding in mourning. Nora could barely walk without kicking a yellow placard marking a bit of brain or bone, myriad pieces of the woman who'd been beaten to death by hands she knew, in the safety of her own home.

It had been an especially bad summer for cicadas, that first summer Nora spent in Bellair. Six weeks into her new life, and she still felt like one of them, clumsy and unwieldy, out of place. But while the bugs didn't seem to care what was thought of them, dive-bombing cars and people with a certain, admirable aplomb before sending screaming hisses out into the humid air, Nora noticed every strained smile and testing, too-firm handshake, every look that made her feel like she'd forgotten to put on deodorant or fix her hair.

Out of the men she met those first weeks in the new station, Murph was the only one who didn't treat her like an intruder. As soon as she was settled, knew enough of the roads and her coworkers to be useful, he began to tug her along with him. She followed him like his shadow, like his pet dog, to every meeting, every interview; staying quiet, watching, learning.

"There won't be a test, kid," he joked with her one day, after noting the lines drawn on her forehead. "Relax. Trust yourself. Wright brought you here for a reason."

This bleeding ranch was their first real call as a team since she'd started shadowing him. They sat in the car outside for a minute, before going in; Nora, catching her breath, Murph, warning her about the things a stomach could do in the face of violence. "It's totally normal, Martin. The guys here all act so tough, but I've seen every single one of them run out through the tape to hurl. Hell, I've done it myself a few times. You just go if you need to, no need to ask me."

"I'm not that green," Nora said, "but thank you." Without looking, she knew there were faces, pressing out from the heavy dark of the trees just beyond the house; hands, waiting to reach for her ankles as soon as she stepped outside. Yes, she had seen death.

"I know you're not. I just didn't want you to feel you had to be tough."

Why? she'd wanted to ask, but didn't know him well enough to break that barrier yet. *Because I'm a woman? Or because I'm Black?* A cicada slammed into the hood of the cruiser with a hard thwack, tumbled off toward the ground, hissing.

"Shit. They're terrible this summer," Murph said. He was uncomfortable with silences, she was learning, always needed to fill them up with small talk or the radio. "They this bad over the mountain?"

"Oh yeah."

"Assholes." He shook his head. "Well, should we get going? I think Charlie has this one. Have you met him yet?"

"I have not."

"I think you'll like him." Murph patted her on the back and swung himself out of the car. It rocked with the shift of his weight. Nora let it settle and then, eyes turned toward the silent house before her, climbed out herself.

———

There was a yard, summer-scorched lawn and a few scrubby plants. There were two Adirondack chairs, elbow to elbow facing a blackened firepit. A pair of beer bottles lay beached, belly-up in the grass. Forgotten in the midst of a drunken heart-to-heart, Nora wondered, or abandoned in a fight?

The house was like every other on the street; it squatted on the corner, its eyes closed. It was the sort of small box she and Dan had moved into while he was finishing nursing school, perfect for a young couple testing out what it meant to be an adult. Where there should have been life though—music, laughter, breakfast smells—there was only a thick quilt of quiet lying heavy on the little home. In the shimmering, buzzing summer air, that silence was ice on the back of Nora's neck.

"Mornin', Charlie!" Murph heaved up an arm in his quick-stepped waddle to the house.

Nora followed his line of sight to an officer, standing with arms crossed over his chest just across the tape line. The man looked up, waved back. His mouth was knotted as tight as his arms. Never a good sign, Nora knew.

"Murph." The man, who Nora guessed was Charlie, reached out to her partner for a handshake before turning to her.

"Nora tells me y'all haven't met yet?"

"Can't say we have," Charlie said, taking her hand in his own. His grip was firm but not cutting, an invitation rather than a challenge.

"She's from *the Valley*," Murph whispered with a conspiratorial wink. "Moved to the right side of the mountain about six weeks ago. I've decided to take her under my wing."

The knot in Charlie's mouth unraveled. "Good luck," he chuckled, catching Nora's eyes with his own, which were warm and blue and unexpected. Charlie, she saw, would be a friend. The loneliness she'd felt since moving here lifted an inch, big enough for a hand to slide under and take her own.

"Why haven't you two met yet anyways?" Murph asked.

Charlie rubbed the back of his head, glanced over his shoulder toward the dead house. "I've been working with the county guys a lot lately. A string of burglaries right on the line."

"You're cheating on me with another detective, and a county one at that?" Murph feigned shock.

Charlie smiled. "I didn't want to tell you this way . . . but yes."

"Good thing I've got my new protégé here, huh, kid?"

When Murph clapped her on the back, she tried to smile, but the joke was a jacket that didn't quite fit yet. This was not a space she was used to being in, and she still questioned if she belonged. Her plain-clothes felt out of place, as did the idea that she had any clue how to run this show, how to look at a scene like a detective and not a patrol officer. There was a wedge growing between her old life and her new that was uncomfortable. If Murph understood the tight wire she walked on, he paid it no mind. She was his pupil, she'd come with excellent recommendations—that was all anyone needed to know or care about. Quite often, Nora wished she could be more like him.

"All right, Charlie." Murph's voice pulled her out of her reverie. "Let's see what we've got."

The little red house made no sound as they squeezed themselves into it, though Nora felt something like a scrim in the open doorway, which tore as they pressed through and fluttered around them in the oppressive heat. Charlie walked them down the hall, which held its breath, quieting their footsteps.

"Her momma found her," he explained as they walked. "They were supposed to go shopping in Charlottesville today, but when she came to pick Lauren up, she found . . ." But there was no need for him to continue, they all saw what Lauren Morris's momma had found.

Under the hall window, which at first Nora thought had been left open and later realized was not opened but smashed, lay the girl, hair covering her face, which was broken and no longer a face. The smell of iron hung in the hazy air. Blood. And something underneath it, a more primal emotion. Piss and fear.

Later, on the front porch, driven by some instinct she had forgotten about, Nora looked up to the ceiling and saw that it was not painted blue.

The first time she saw the girl's face in the night, cicadas had burst from the open scream of her mouth.

Sophie

I tried to move him once, after my shift was over and I was sure the town had gone to sleep. By then, he had frozen quite solid and it was all I could do to peel him from the back of the pizza box he must have fallen onto when I rolled him into the corner. He was too stiff for me to get into a position to roll, and the ground was too slick for me to make any good effort to pull him away. So he stayed.

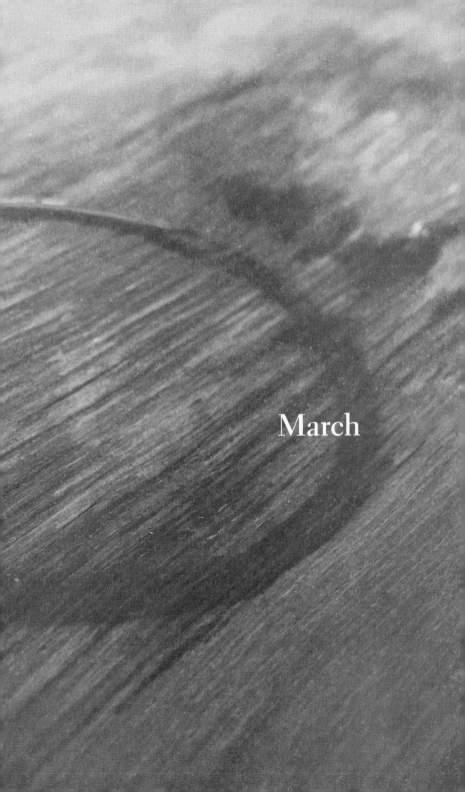

March

Datura

In the creaking damp of still-dark spring, I felt a thought billow into the hollow space behind my rib cage. It took on form and weight and climbed the bars of my bones to settle into a chattering squat behind my ears, where it began to spool out a story in the fine threads of my hair. Listening to it, I dreamed of a distant future, still murky, but solid if I pressed a finger out into the shadows. Twice now, I had seen my face reflected as fear in someone's eyes. The knife was powerful, and with it I shed this woman skin for something sharp and cold and strong. But the knife could be traced; the knife could be broken or lost in a fight; the knife made too much of a mess. I needed something else. And besides, the blood was too fast, the death over too soon. I peered inside the well of myself and found that one day I would want to watch life slip away with breaths rather than gasping gushes of blood. It would take time, but I had that. It would take patience and care and planning, and I had those to spare. A witch in the woods is not born overnight; we are grown.

And so, I invited a friend into my house. The picture on my computer showed her as she would be one day, a full white bell trumpeting up out of a thicket of green. Her seedpod round and dressed in thorns. Her name was Datura; she is sister to my Morning Glory, the old crone of flower medicine, the choice of witches and wisewomen for centuries. And I had a plan for her.

She came to me asleep, swaddled in paper and cardboard, spongy plastic pillows that floated across my kitchen counter when I tugged them out, swiped them out of the way with the back of my hand. They billowed up, wafted down to the old wood floor while I ripped a mouth into her cradle, poured her out of her paper gullet into my palm. She yawned in the soft sibilants of a hundred tiny seed sighs, then, silence. Then, my sweeping breath; then, my heartbeat; the only noises in my still house. I am the only noise in my house. I am a ghost; in this howling emptiness, I have begun to haunt myself.

I made her a bath. Lukewarm water, clear and clean. It was her dreaming place, this liminal space where she might start to feel the thought of a world around her. Until then, she had been living in puffs of air. To put her feet in the earth, I had to first plant her in a womb. We too learn to swim before we breathe dry air. Each tiny seed pilled the water's surface soundlessly as I dropped them in, one by one, spiraling down to lie on the glass bottom of my bowl. They would sleep for the night in still, cold silence, shivering together. What was it like, I wondered, to lie at the bottom of a pool and feel your body dream of unfurling?

I think I know something of it now.

In the twilit dawn, I gathered her from the water, now shining, still asleep but trembling. I pressed her body, one seed, one seed, one seed, into the pot I'd readied for her. By the end, my fingertips were black with the damp soil. I wanted to eat my hands, pull the dirt down into me. Instead, I washed it off down my sink.

I had a home for her in a southern bay window, snuggled in between the winter tomatoes and my wild, snarled jasmine, which breathed scent onto my face as I bent beside her. This had been my grandmother's favorite window. Bright and warm, with a view of the apple trees and, shining in the distance, the soft curve of the creek. She would sleep here for a bit longer, my witch. And in full spring, when she yawned and stretched a thin arm up into the air, my garden would be ready for her. Would I use her then? Would I dare? I did not know.

Patience, the mouths inside me whispered. *The best dreams need time to grow.*

An Anatomist

March descended. In slapping rain and heavy plops of wet snow, in a cold that bit the tip of my nose and made my eyes water. March is the worst month in this pocket of Virginia. February is brutal, the air so cold it feels like a solid thing, cracking at its seams and ready at any moment to impale you. But February at least is honest. March is cruel. March holds spring out with one hand, peeling back the clouds to let the sun shine for an hour or two, long enough to think the weather might be turning, before she snatches it away, spilling winter back out of her mouth. In this miserable damp, I felt myself become a creature swollen and creaking, the wet dripping down to pool in the bulbous bases of my bones. Heavy and cold, I grew still as my witch, dreaming in cold water.

I wanted to tear off my skin, swallow myself, fling away the quilt of this horrid unmoving before I grew too stagnant to draw breath. My grandmother would have known what to do with such discomfort. Before she lost her mind, she had been a masseuse, and spent her days gently peeling bunched coils of connective tissue off one another, smoothing anxious tension, opening bodies up like flower buds.

They carry us, you know, our grandmothers; nestled deep within the fetal bodies of our mothers is an infinitesimal colony of eggs, asleep for another decade. You and I were held, as all the generations before us, tight in the matryoshka embrace of our maternal ancestors, absorbing their pain, their joys, their fears. That March, wet and miserable, hampered by the sodden gray of the not-quite-spring, I sank back into the atoms of myself, which had been birthed twice before and were now emerging for a third time. While flowers yawned beneath the cold earth and stretched the first of tiny fisted leaves to prick through the hoarfrost, I explored the new world that was blooming in the dark places of my heart.

"You could kill a man," my grandmother said to me one long September afternoon. We were sitting out on her front porch watching the apples grow. They were still hard green globes, too young and bitter to eat. With another month, cooler nights, they'd swell and bloom a hearty crimson or dusky blush, perhaps a soft butter yellow. My shoulders were bare, and my grandmother's hands were wrapped around them, slowly working through the knots already bound under my teenaged flesh.

"What?"

A bee landed on the butterfly bush planted at the bottom of the porch steps. Heavy and clumsy, it clung to the thin stalk of flower that bobbed under its weight.

"Pay attention, child. This is important." Her hands contracted, kneading my muscles like bread dough. I felt something like relief drip down my neck. "You should know this. All you young girls should. Running around the way y'all do. Turn around, Sophie. Look."

I did, and she took my arm in her hands, twisted it.

"Look at how you fold," she said, pressing into the crook of my elbow, forcing my arm to collapse, each half closing in on itself. "Have you ever wondered why you're put together this way?"

I couldn't say that I had. Somewhere in middle school, my body had become a foreign thing, always too much and never enough. In those years I was acutely aware of it, the space it took up in the world, the uncomfortable currency it was beginning to hold, but I never liked to think of it. If I made my body a living, breathing thing, I'd have to feel guilty for hating it.

She pinched the inside of my elbow, hard, and I winced. "That's why. Your body covers what it needs to protect. Nerves, vessels, the guts that keep you alive. Now, if you were to hit a man hard enough here"—she reached down to tap the back of my knee—"or stab him here"—she lifted my arm to press sharp fingers into my armpit—"you'd hurt him pretty bad. Kill him, even, if you got him just right.

"And if you really want to do some damage, slam him here." With one quick motion, she pressed her fingers up under my jaw. I gasped in shock, but I didn't pull away; instead I sat still as a rabbit in a trap, listening to the wild pounding of my heart. My grandmother had a way of making mortality feel so alive.

Unperturbed, she continued. "Hell, one good whack to the back of the skull can down a person if your aim's good enough. Feel."

She pressed her fingers into my neck, to the place where it met my skull. "See that? Right here, there's a lip in the bone and your vertebrae scoot up under it. That space is what lets your head move. But God, in all His infinite wisdom, forgot to cover that tiny tip of your brain stem. It's hard to reach unless you know where to find it, but if a man's on top of you, you get your fingers up in here, baby, and shove.

"Never be afraid of being small, Sophie. That's your secret weapon. Men don't pay attention to small things. Use yourself, however you're able."

As the sun plunged into the winter ground and the trees fell dormant outside her house, my grandmother pulled me under the soft sweep of her wings and taught me how to understand a body.

136

Start with your root, she taught me, the scaffolding of you, the delicate architecture of bone. I closed my eyes and watched the trails of her fingers light up somewhere in the murky dark of my mind.

Here, the Long bones—your thighs, your arms. They're dense, to carry the weight of you, to hold a man or a child. Her fingers felt like raindrops as she touched down on my Short bones—the pebbles of your wrists and ankles, she explained. They can get clumped together and must be worked apart, to make space for your nerves and vessels. If someone grabs you, you take his wrist and squeeze as hard as you can, find the nerves, show him pain. Here are your Flat bones; she touched the crown of my head. They hold all of you in the puzzle of them. And last, her fingers tripped down my back, your Irregular bones. They form the spiked string of your spine, balance on the stirrup inside your ear. This is the hidden structure of you, not brittle but alive, always rebuilding, protecting, carrying.

She showed me my muscles. Here is how a body builds itself up, from the powerful gluteal family, the quadriceps, adductors, pectorals, abdominals, the rolling bellies of the gastrocnemius and biceps. Here are your erectors, ropes of tissue that pull you upright, binding themselves to the backs of ribs, to shoulders, to the serrated processes of vertebrae. Your fingers, your toes, the twitching anatomy of your face. This is you, this is how you move, how you breathe.

Here, binding the puzzle pieces together, these are tendons and ligaments. Here is how they twist into hard cables, how they stretch apart into all the webbed connective tissue of your muscles, tying you together in tight, glittering white.

Under her tutelage I learned how a body clicked into place and how it could be pulled apart. If I was a boy, perhaps my grandfather would have taught me about the shining machinery of cars. But my grandmother knew a different sort of guts, and she brought my hands to them. She taught me how to melt a knot with patience and persistence, how to read the stories printed under flesh. To sit still and listen, to feel the thrum of my own small strength. And always underneath, the warning, the lesson: *This is how you damage some-one if you need to. A body is an open book, baby, if you only know how to turn the page.*

By that muddy, miserable spring, my grandmother was no longer her-self. Confined to a wheelchair in a nursing home, her once steady hands were a constant tremor and roil as the dementia slowly ate its way through her brain. *I don't know. I don't know. I don't know.* All day long she whispers a rosary for St. Anthony, pleading that he might help her find her misplaced mind. *I don't know.* I held her hands, as I did every Saturday morning, and thought about the man in the alleyway.

He lay there still, melting under a pile of boxes and crates and crushed pallets. I'd taken to sitting with him on the nights I closed alone, smoking a cigarette or drinking a beer, tipping a bit off the top for him each time. In death he's become something better than him-self; he feels almost like a friend, like we are the same, me in this body and he facedown in the trash. I never look at him. After my first failed attempt, I've decided I don't want to disturb the boxes. Some-times though I try to peek through them, to see if I might catch a glimpse of him seeping into the earth, becoming a part of something bigger. Perhaps this was his purpose. And mine to give it.

The flies haven't found him yet. It's too cold. Too wet. Though I suspect some larger predators may have smelled him. One morning I walked by to find the boxes torn out on one end. Let them come, I thought, even as I propped the plastic back up. Let them carry him away. Less for me to worry about.

A Woman in Black

There was a third. So quiet I doubt anyone noticed; so quiet I sometimes forget him too, though in some ways he changed everything. He is the one who reached in and pulled the ghost up out of my mouth.

It was a day like every other in early March. Trees, clothed through the bone-cold February in a coat of slick rime, melted in the pelting rain to become black things, twisted and stark against the pearl-gray sky. Hard buds poked out of the ends of their branches. In a few weeks, they'd be green with new life; in the raw air of early spring, they slept naked and shivering. The sun, when he did break through, was a weak thing, the smallest brush of yellow against a cheek; nothing more than a thought, forgotten as soon as he swept past. In the alleyway, my cat-caller lay dripping.

Like him, I felt too damp to move, and so I let myself become aquatic. Waterlogged, I pulled the bar together, cut fruit, speared olives, shook the cayenne salt down into a dish for my Bloody Mary rims. From somewhere under the surface, I watched the servers flit through the room, the hostess tidy her stand. The chef stumped out of the kitchen, muttering to himself. He scooped ice into a plastic pitcher, shot soda water into it from my gun. Everything was muted, separate. My skin felt like ants, bobbing on the surface of still water. Beneath it, I wondered.

I had killed two men. And I felt nothing save a vague sense of being pleased with myself, like the cat who finds the canary cage unattended. The satisfaction was filling but fleeting, and in the dim wet of that half spring I began to feel questions pricking under my skin. Could I do it again? How many times could I play this game without getting caught? The witch in my house had been pressed into the dirt. If she grew, when she bloomed, would I be brave enough to use her? Or would she sit, a pretty decoration, deadly but defanged, on my summer porch?

The better half of my mind was a constant alarm. I had been justified, it assured me. Mark was a mold slime; the catcaller attacked me. I was a victim, I was a martyr; I slid my knife through an orange, watched the juice spread across the cutting board. I was bored. I didn't want to wait for a flower to bloom.

Pans banged, someone in the kitchen swore; I opened my fridge to find all the stocking-up had not been done by my barback the night before. A breeze skimmed across the surface of the pond inside me. They were all the same, men. Useless. The ants bobbing along the surface twitched.

Brunch that day was a dead affair. A few sodden customers tripped in somewhere around eleven o'clock, soaked and ruffled like birds caught in a bath fountain. They fell onto couches tucked into the far corner of the floor and ordered hot toddies. Drinks delivered, I promptly forgot about them until an hour later when they left, wrapped tight in cumbersome coats, damp umbrellas yanked out of a bucket near the door. The servers watched them go with something like longing on their faces, hungry for the tips that wouldn't come today.

By two o'clock, cabin fever had set in and the servers dissolved into a jittery mix of coffee, pilfered rail shots, and cold french fries. A ripple of giggles erupted from the kitchen when the chef screamed, *For the love of God, you scavengers, get out!* The last hour was a Sisyphean exercise in patience, polishing one glass at a time, wiping down bottles, toothbrushing beer taps, anything but daring to look at the clock to see how much time hadn't passed. Rain lashed the windows; an errant tree branch scratched back and forth along the tin roof. At quarter 'til, the servers gave up and collapsed down onto the couches in a flurry of loosened ties and untucked shirts. The chef scowled, yelled at me to yell at them, but what did I care?

His voice aroused the things under my skin. They looked up at me, picking, biting, pinching.

"Come on, *manager*. What if a customer walks in and sees that?" His face was red, sweaty and bloated from too many hours spent in a cramped, airless room, grunting and moaning that we were not Burger King, the customers could not, in fact, *have it their way* no matter how much they insisted. I was manager in name only on Sunday mornings, the title bestowed upon me when Ty got tired of babysitting hungover staff. All men are the same.

"Then Ty can yell at them when he comes in at three. Front of the House. Not your responsibility."

He answered with a chorus of slamming pans, a few scattered *fuck*s dusted throughout the steaming kitchen air. I let him rage. He'd be seated at the bar in an hour, ready to gulp down his daily shot of whiskey and lecture me on the best Italian wines. They are all the fucking same.

A flame snagged on the corner of my eye. Through the rain-soaked window I saw it, hovering behind the trees, my freedom marked in a blaze—brick red, bobbing along the train tracks that ran over the northern bounds of Peach Street, just visible from the far end of my bar. An idea tiptoed under my jaw and into my ear. Another crept out from under my aching shoulder blade. I felt my fingers tingle and clench. This was what we'd been waiting for.

The flame was moving slowly, the driving rain not seeming to be a deterrent to his mid-afternoon ramble. Ty was due in ten minutes. My hands found an anchor in the polishing rag; my feet bound themselves to the rubber mat below. I sank under the surface of my pond, crouched at the edge; I became a pair of eyes in the reeds, waiting, watching the bobbing flame drift west toward the mountains.

The train tracks skirt the southern edge of my property, so I drove home, left my car in the driveway to be a question answered should anyone think to ask. (*Sophie? She was home then. Hiding from the weather like we all were.*) My heart beat a drum up into my throat, a frog's deep rumblings in my pond. I crept into the trees.

It's a misconception that the woods feel open in winter, though an understandable one. Bare branches should be empty hands, holding nothing but air and sky, leaving those who walk beneath them exposed. In truth, it's in the warm green of summer that you can reach an arm or leg or soul out into the tangled heart of this place and know you've billowed and stretched into something greater than yourself. Summer, with its canopies, its shoots and mushrooms and curling ferns, is a world bursting. To walk in the woods in June is to feel your soul flung wide.

In March, in the sodden dripping of late winter, the trees feel close. Tight. Everything is falling downward. Branches crack under the wet weight of heavy snows; even the best paths become treacherous mud slicks that pull a walker down to the earth, to soft pits of leaves where legs sink into mucky traps. The wind cuts through trunks like a razor, until all the treetops clatter against one another, creaking and hissing, the ancient language of a dead time. Only the daffodils grow there, in the winter woods. Sunny faces shining through the endless brown; at night they are moonstruck, pale will-o'-wisps.

He hadn't gotten very far by the time I cut out of the woods. Barely a mile further up the tracks, though it had been a full hour since I had spotted him. Weighed down by wind or rain or his own scattered thoughts, he meandered along the line of sodden wood and metal. His hair, soaked and hanging lank, was as red as it had been when he slipped across my windowpane, and I had a sudden thought of the vests hunters don in the fall. That blaze orange warning to keep safe, to signal they aren't a deer, aren't a body to be penetrated, though they sit just as still as the deer, and I know are as easily penetrated.

Behind him, my soul no longer stagnant but awake and creeping out into movement, I picked my way through scrubby trees and water-logged ferns, the shells of blackberry arms and burned ropes of poison ivy that spilled down to the sopping ground. At a bend in the track, I stepped out from the cover of trees, to stand full-face in the driving rain.

When I was young and the night was a hungry mouth, my grandmother would fill it with stories, spun through long fingers and cigarette smoke. Her voice husky with flame, she'd regale me with visions of mountain witches creeping through windowpanes, ghostly women rising up out of creek beds and their lovers wandering lonesome fields at dawn. She warned me too, about the family banshee. A woman to be respected and feared, who clung to the rigging of a long-ago ship and now made her home coiled in the twisted branches of our apple trees, who made herself known in a cold gasp of wind on your neck, a painting dropped suddenly off the wall. She was a coyote in the dark night, howling. Waiting.

Would they see her, someone watching from far away? When they looked at me, could they see the nightmare that had laid its writhing body atop my skin, walked with my legs, saw with my eyes? When they told the story of the boy on the tracks, would they swear they saw his death trailing behind him in the shape of a woman?

Rain poured down my face in rivers, dripping down past the collar of my shirt, running its tongue along the cold flesh of my chest, stomach, hips. The wind slipped sharp fingers under my hair, tugging it out of its braid until it whipped about my forehead and lashed itself to my face in dark ropes. I sank under the calm surface of my pond. Underneath my skin was a frenzy, but there in the wild air, I was still.

The gravel below my feet was thick. It crumbled and rolled with each step, and so I had to dig in and drive forward one foot after another. He was tiptoeing across the ties, his steps light with rambling thoughts. Once or twice he slipped, his worn canvas shoes finding no grip on the rain-slick wood beneath them.

He was young, I could see. A twig of a creature, tall and lanky, what my grandmother would have called a string bean. He had a body built for swinging up into passing train cars or clinging spider-like to their sides. Where he was going and why, I never had the chance to ask.

I got within three feet of him before he heard me and turned. He had hazel eyes.

Everything froze. The wind, the rain, the beat of my heart, dropped for one long, shocked moment while we stared at each other out on the tracks on a rain-soaked Sunday afternoon in early March, in the fetal days of spring.

I've read that if you meet a predator out on a walk that you should never run; that it's the running, something about the quick motion, the visible fear, that incites the instinct to chase. Would he have survived then, if he hadn't looked down and seen the knife in my hand? If he hadn't lifted his own open palms and backed away with a laugh, his brow knotted in a tight question? If his voice hadn't cracked when he asked what I was doing? If if *if*. If she hadn't worn that skirt. If she hadn't had so much to drink. If she hadn't made him angry.

If only he hadn't looked at me.

I made the first stab while he stared, the air between us a question and a challenge, something alive. I stabbed him with the same knife I had used in the alley, that only that morning I'd used to cut lemons and oranges, that I'd lent to the line cook when his peeler fell between the lowboy and the wall. The blade was short; it hit his canvas jacket with a soft punch, didn't do much more than nick his skin below.

"What the hell, lady?!"

I needed to get his jacket off. His arms were long, and using them he made himself a wall I couldn't reach past. But there was no turning back now. He'd seen my face. I needed to get his jacket off.

All men are the same. My skin scurried and screamed and bit into itself. He tried to run, but I grabbed hold of his hood and held tight. If he wanted to free himself, he'd have to take off his jacket. He hollered and twisted and stepped down onto the metal of the rail lines. We fell together.

Our heads cracked against each other; breath flew from my chest in a gasp. Everything in me was clanging. I reached for his zipper; he grabbed my wrist. We grappled between the train ties. *He's afraid of you.* He had my wrists—*all men are the same*—but I managed to pull one knee up and dig it, hard, into his groin. He yelled and dropped me, and I managed to rip open his jacket front before he could stop me, and then my grandmother's voice was in my head:

"If you get a man under his armpit"—smoke blooms from her mouth as she speaks—"you have a straight shot."

The places we fold. Arm, ancient root *ar,* "to fit together." This here, in that soft pit of flesh tucked up at the trunk of you, this is your life held safe only by that puzzle piece of armor, humerus, biceps, triceps, ribs, protecting so much of what keeps you alive. But there in that hole, that *arm-pit,* that chink in your fitting, is the soft underbelly of the dragon that is you. Axillary artery, brachial nerve, thoracic vein, all the pulsing, electric life fitted into one tight space. A good hit to those alone will kill a man. Bite a bit deeper and you hit heart and lungs. Watch him deflate.

He grabbed my hair, pulled me back. But in his defense, he'd opened up the space I needed. *If. If. If. If.* I punched. His gasp let me know I'd hit his lungs. The heat of his body poured out over my hands, soft, curling into the air. My fingers were red.

He held on to my hair, which by then had fallen like a shroud over him, while I lowered him onto the tracks, into a depth I could not follow; the ghost of him rose behind his eyes, which were no longer hazel, but darkening. He trembled. His breath was a shallow thing, mist curling over a creek in the morning.

Hush.

The ground beneath us began to tremble. Fat raindrops wobbled and bounced off the ties. In the distance, a mile behind us, a train was screaming.

Bellair occupies a space of particular danger. The looming mountains, which protect us from so much of the catastrophe of the natural world, become weapons when the train rumbles through. Cumbersome and unwieldy, with an engine too small to propel her up the steep mountainside, she cannot slow as she passes through our town. This tension has birthed a decades-long fight, our safety pitted against company dollars. To appease us, they've given their leviathan a mouth, so as she nears our borders she wails out a warning: *I am coming! Stay away. Stay safe. I am coming!*

In my shock, I froze, and he managed in one last terror-stricken fit to pull me down with him, his hand snarled tight in my hair, his grip tightening with the chill of incoming death. I tried to push myself up, but he was too strong, the ties slippery with rain and blood.

The tracks began to rattle beneath us. I felt my teeth chattering, my brain bouncing in my skull. *Get up! Get up!* My skin scuttled through the layers of itself. *Get up!*

With a shout, I pulled myself free and rolled away from the tracks into the thickets of grass and bramble and thorn that guarded the ragged space between wild and train. He had followed me, tugged upward in the sudden jerk of my hair, but somewhere in my escape, he'd caught on the railing and was now flopped over it, silent and still.

The train screamed again. I saw her face appear in the near distance. She was screaming and wailing and warning. *Stay away! Stay safe! Stay away!*

Later, when they found his mangled body, they would call it a tragic accident. There would be town meetings and worried mothers and then, after a month, all would go back to normal. He was no one. A kid far from home and anyone who cared about him.

I can't help but wonder though what the engineer thought when he flew past me, face twisted in shock and horror at the body he could not avoid, and the figure crouched in the thickets beside the tracks, dressed in black and covered in blood. Did he cross himself afterward? Did he pray? Did he know that he was looking at Death?

The boy's tongue was the only one I did not collect. There was no tongue to take.

A Tired Soul

I know we used to do it when we were younger, but why do kids still do dumb shit like walk on the tracks?" Dan held his tea mug close to his chest, steam curling over his face, which was pale after long hours spent out in the cold and rain, helping the volunteer crew pick up pieces of the boy. A grim job on a grim afternoon—the body had been dragged for almost a quarter mile under the scorching stomach of the train.

Nora sighed. "Because they're kids."

That was the truth of it, but something else stuck with her, something she couldn't shake. The engineer, when he finally calmed down enough to speak without winding himself into a panic attack, swore he'd seen someone else on the tracks.

"Were they walking with him? Another kid?"

The man let his eyes slide down to a corner of the drab room they were sitting in, which Nora had tried to make more friendly with a smile, but there was no hiding the fact that the cinder-block square was built for interrogations. It was not the sort of space anyone wanted to find themselves in. He pulled his flimsy Styrofoam coffee cup an inch closer to his chest and took in a deep breath.

"You're going to think I'm crazy."

"Try me," Nora said, making her voice a blanket. "I promise you, Mr. Decker, I've seen just about everything."

"It wasn't human."

"You mean, it was an animal you saw? A bear maybe?" It was a bit early for bear, but Nora had seen it before. The animals, dazed and hungry after months of hibernation, could sometimes wander through territory they'd normally avoid.

"No." He looked up at her then, his eyes wide. "It was . . . I can't explain this without sounding nuts."

Nora waited for him to continue, her breaths a slow count of time.

"Its eyes were black. And it had hair, long, I think. Dark, but that could have been because of the rain. It looked like a human, a woman maybe, crouched off in the grass at the edge of the woods. But it looked up at me as I passed, and I didn't get a good look because I had just hit that boy and . . ."

He began to tremble and seize, his breaths fast. Nora reached out and put a hand on his, still clutching the coffee.

"You're doing great, Mr. Decker. I can't imagine how you must be feeling. Did you notice anything else? You said this thing looked not human?"

"I've never seen anything less so in my life."

"Can you explain what you mean by that?"

He took another breath and crossed himself, whispering prayers that Nora felt like pleas sweeping across her cheeks. Something over her shoulder hissed; in the corner, a wisp of shadow coiled and sank down to the floor. She focused her eyes on the man who was shaking in the seat across from hers.

"Covered in blood, its face. Pale, bone white, but covered in blood. And its eyes, I said they were black, but that's not quite right . . . It was like looking at a skull. Just as I passed by, it opened its mouth, and it might have screamed, but I couldn't hear it over my own and the brakes screeching against the ties. It was a demon, I swear it." He crossed himself again, and Nora could see his thoughts building a shield in front of him: *I'm not crazy. I'm not crazy. Please, believe me.*

She squeezed his hand. "I believe you." That was all people needed, really, to be heard.

"It was a nightmare."

"Yes. I imagine it was."

She excused herself, went to find Murph, left Mr. Decker still holding his cup and staring off into the middle distance, his whole body trembling.

Later, in the long grass, she found stories. Broken twigs. Fern arms flattened and bent around one another. Just at the edge of the tree line she found the ghost of a footprint. It was half-filled with rain and had shed any defining patterns, but it was still there, a mucky crater in the red clay.

"No demon then," she whispered to herself, crouching down to look at the print. It might have been the boy's; they could test it against his shoes, if they found them. But something swooped in her heart when she put her own foot next to it to take a picture. The print, what had survived the rain, looked to be the same size as hers. There were very few men with feet that small.

A girlfriend? Too shocked or terrified to come forward? Itinerant kids liked to travel in pairs for safety, for company. Whoever they were, they knew something.

"Nice catch, Martin," Murph said when she showed him the photo. "But I think you can file that away. The boy's death was an accident. No need to spend taxpayer money on a search for a 'demon' who's probably long gone by now. Those kids know how to make themselves scarce."

"You're not even going to look into it?" Her heart clenched.

"You'll learn, Martin, this happens more often than I'd like. Kids on the tracks, heads in the clouds. Or worse, suicide. Let's give him the benefit of the doubt and say he just tripped and couldn't get up before the train hit him."

"But the engineer saw—"

"The engineer saw someone in the grass, which you have now possibly confirmed, though with the rain damage, we have no way of knowing how fresh that footprint might be. We also cannot afford tracking dogs, unless you're volunteering to foot the bill yourself?"

When she didn't answer, he continued. "What the engineer saw was a nightmare. What he did not see was a murder. We won't close it, but right now I can't afford to spend more time on it unless I hear something else. We've got enough on our plates as it is. Put it away."

"You okay, Nor?" Dan said, later, after. "You want me to make you a cup of tea? I keep forgetting you were out there too. Not used to working on the same side of the mountain yet, I guess."

"No, you stay there. I'll make one myself."

She brought her mug and a blanket to the couch and curled into Dan's open arms, let him hold her, didn't complain when he turned on the crap reality TV he used as a balm. It was a habit he'd picked up, from years of seeing people during the worst moments of their lives, something she was surprised she'd never taken to herself, only watching when he turned it on first. That day though she let herself sink into the screen, trying her best to forget the shiver that ran up her spine at the sight of that footprint in the mud, the proof of a demon crouching in the thicket.

Sophie

I heard nothing.

I heard whispers of a demon on the tracks. Housewives pulled their children close; hunters warned one another not to get drunk out there in the woods, tempting as it was during long, cold hours; teenagers passed rumors around about vengeful Confederate spirits, spurned lovers. For the second time, I had stepped outside of myself. For the second time, I became a ghost, a nightmare prowling the town.

They set up a memorial for the boy, a lonely white cross planted in the grass where he died. I visit that too, now. Watch it glowing in the velvet dark. I feel the moon and the stars, raw on my skin out here in the open, in this place where I unhinged my jaw and let an animal burst from my belly.

Who are you? the stars ask.

The creeping things under my skin answer with hard silence.

Thorns stick in my legs when I push back through to the trees, tear at my flesh. All new life demands blood. I feel myself draining down into the ground.

Nora

A hair was found. Tight in the grip of what had once been the boy's left fist, they found a single, long dark hair. It was probably nothing, Nora knew. It could have been anyone's. Maybe he'd plucked it off his jacket before impact, maybe it had been on the tracks and he'd grabbed it in his scramble to escape. Maybe it belonged to a demon who watched the train rush past, her mouth an open grave.

It could have been anything. They didn't have money for dogs. The boy was dead. The footprint was waterlogged. The boy was no one.

She tucked the hair away into a baggie, sent it off to the medical examiner, just in case.

A Woman

In the dark, in the small hours of the night, the girl at the end of the hallway rose. Her legs were weak, spindly, nothing more than a gathering of mist and nightmares. Her head wobbled on its ruined neck as she stumbled toward the room where Nora slept. The haint had been doing this for some nights now, restless and disturbed by something in the ether that felt sharp, and wild, and wrong.

If Nora had opened her eyes then, had seen the shimmering, anxious hum standing at the foot of her bed, she would have seen the questions tumbling from the girl's gossamer mouth, felt them thread their way through her own, as they had threaded their way through centuries of women's mouths. *Why do you hate us? Why do you destroy us? Beat us up, shut us up, break everything in our hearts? What did we do? What did we do?*

Had she woken, Nora would have felt the sharp seed just beneath her tongue, the one that had been pricking her lately, the one that asked her own question in reply: *Why don't I see Mark in the night, in my house? Why don't I weep for him? Why is a part of me . . . glad?*

The girl had no answers.

In the black-gray hour before dawn, Dan woke. Something cold had grazed over his chest, a line of goose pimples raised along the backs of his arms. The blanket was gone. He turned to Nora and found her as he had so many mornings now, sweaty and tangled in the covers, her brow crinkled, jaw clenched tight.

"Thief." He rolled over and kissed her shoulder, tugging a corner of the blanket back over himself before he wrapped an arm tight about her.

The girl in the corner watched, shivering. When the morning pressed its face through the window, she gasped, burst into a thousand motes of sunlit dust.

A Selkie

The air broke by the end of March, the final fever of winter splintering; a few fingers of warm light poured through the sweeping canopy overhead. The woods came alive, heavy damp blown away on a soft blast of mountain breeze. The earth is crawling with hidden things, and so in her, I don't have to lay quite so still, I don't have to be so stagnant. I fell into myself, a phantom, a wraith crawling with teeth, a thousand scrambling legs biting the soft underside of my flesh.

The Blue Bell has bifold windows, and by the end of the month, Ty had pushed them open for dinner service, to let in a soft breath of wind that was fresh and alive, to blow away the last chilblains of a damp winter. The rosy dusk, now laced with the first hints of spring flowers, swept over warm candles whose tiny flames danced in the purple night. Behind us, the creek broke through its winter sleep, shaking off the last of the icy teeth lining its bank. Now, in the soft spring nights, it burbled and skipped, cold and clear, not yet muddied with summer storms. The peepers sang themselves to life as they do every year at this time, stretching thin voices in the dark, calling to one another, happy to be alive. A tale as old as tales. We are, all of us, reborn in the spring.

Standing behind my bar, counting inventory, tossing away those liquors that had grown stale over winter, I asked myself what this new, shivering life meant for me. The buzz was always there now, spreading like smoke beneath my mask of skin, separating dura mater from skull, fascia from muscle and bone. I was lifting, slithering inside of myself, becoming a new sort of creature altogether.

"You feeling all right, Soph?" Ty asked, one slow afternoon. The sun coming through the windows was warm, the first real hint of that promised summer heat, and I had draped myself over the counter to bask in it. For just a moment, really, just enough to feel the me inside myself stir to life.

The question, a snap of fingers at my ears, a slap. Normally such a thing would have roused me enough to stand, to look alert. But that day I was a snake, shedding and slow, and so I looked at him and smiled.

"Oookay," he said, backing away with raised hands, a question or a joke, it was hard to tell with Ty, pricking the black points of his eyes.

I have read stories of women who peel their flesh off to live in the human world. I think I must be one of them, this itching, biting annoyance the touch of a skin that never really belonged to me; my own someplace far away, drying on a rock beside the sea. So I had dug into the shadowed depths of myself, found the truth of this space I moved within, and now it dared me to let it out. My teeth have grown long, my claws sharp. I feel myself separating from this scrim I had grown to protect me. The taste of men's fear in my mouth was the antidote to the sting of new growing skin. I would throw my false flesh away, pull the fullness of me back over my creeping soul.

April

Sophie

To hunt a man you have to be smart, because sooner or later, someone will be hunting you. I thought about this while I prepped my bar, while I passed beer after beer to Bud, while I wiped and shined and polished the shimmering glass-and-metal cage I had built myself into. Every scene, every interaction, became a learning place. Who are men? How do they work? How do they see the world and themselves in it? I had been lucky so far. But luck would get boring. I wanted fire to play with. They'll tell you this is a feeling that women who grow up without fathers express often. That missing the grounding influence of the masculine in our lives has flipped us sideways somehow, has us always balancing on tiptoes, peering over the cliff's edge. For fun, to feel alive, to see if anyone bothers to reach a hand out and stop us.

Maybe I wanted that, to be stopped. I think I wanted to be pushed, to be set aflame, to make a game with the darkness settling between the ivory bars of my rib cage. Notice me. Care about what I'm doing. This is the chant I've been singing since childhood.

The first mites moved in then, after he left. Their tongues slid up under my skin and grew feet and buried themselves somewhere I could not reach. They weren't the same mites though, as the ones who would come later. These scurried into the soft pericardium of my heart, made themselves something hard and bitter and angry. But they did not make me feel naked in the world, as their brothers would. Betrayed and twisted, they became my shield, my friends, so that when I was twenty-five and he wrote me a letter, I read it with bile in my mouth.

I've found Jesus and a therapist. I would like to see you, to make something of this relationship.

And so I went. Sat across from him at a shiny steel table, sticky with ice cream residue. I let him talk at me for an hour, about his new life, the forgiveness he'd found from God. And once again, I felt the old stirring, the disappointment. But I was older now, inured to heartbreak, and so those first mites mingled with the new, and I felt a revulsion for this man who wanted me to call him Dad.

Near the end of that day, he spread his arms wide and, turning his face up to the cold, industrial ceiling, revealed to me that his favorite Bible verse was Luke 23:34, when Jesus, looking down from the cross at all those who would beat him and spit on him and hang him like this, implores to the Deity, *Father, forgive them; for they know not what they do.*

"Isn't that incredible?" he asked me, eyes shining.

I leaned across the table and told him I'd always found the more poignant line to be, *Father, Father, why have You forsaken me?*

What would he think of me now, if he could see me? I do not know, I do not care. I never heard from him again after that day. Men are all the same.

All the same, therefore easy to study. So I watched, and I learned, while the witch in my house pricked thin leaves up through the dirt and the knife on my bar lay gleaming, and under my skin things crawled. I made myself a student.

Lifting boxes up to my counter became a test. How many times out of ten would one of the boys insist on helping me? How many seconds would that take? I counted. One . . . two . . . seven . . . here he comes. The keg. If it needed changing, how often did Ty shoo me out of the cooler, heave a new barrel into place himself? If I was reaching for something in the kitchen, a pan for syrup or a plate for salt, did the chef let me struggle, or did he grab it down for me? I was cheating, of course. I live in the South. Had I run this experiment in a place where men's small gallantries were unusual or unacceptable, perhaps I would have tried a different tack. A predator knows how to play their prey's weaknesses against them.

I made friends with my body. The delicate boning and lighter muscles, all the frail architecture I had so long disparaged, I saw then was no flaw but a boon. Every day men trapped women in a net of their own kindness, feigning brokenness or love, to lure them. I would have to rely on no such lie. I simply had to be myself, the bare truth of myself as Small, as Doll, was all the trap I needed. When has a man ever been afraid to climb into a car with a woman?

There in the bar in the bright new spring, I knew the time for chance encounters was over. It was time to begin the work of hunting.

Sophie

There are few holidays more important to the denizens of this little swatch of the Piedmont than the spring steeplechases. Race day, always the last Saturday in April, is our high holy day, full-throated and alive in the bursting spring, a rite that reaches near-zealous levels of devotion in certain sectors. It is a day characterized by the sheer gratuitous embrace by the better classes of their own carnal natures, a day to see and be seen, to down whiskey and champagne and the tastiest gossip. It is not a day to be missed. And so, every April, to the hallowed grounds of old Montleigh farm, they flock.

The earliest arrivals are the university students, hopeful that if they squeak through the gates early enough, their underage buddies might be able to fly under the radar of the still bleary-eyed security. Alcohol isn't banned, but an SUV packed like a clown car with kids is sure to raise some eyebrows and earn a more thorough shakedown at the gate. Once safely inside, they spill out to begin their panto-mime of the Southern genteel class. The boys dress in their Faulk-nerian best, sports coats and bow ties, button-down shirts tucked in. By midmorning they'll have shed the coat and ties, the heat by then grown heavy, trickling down their foreheads. The girls, meanwhile, who never wear jackets even in the bitterest winter, open themselves to the sun like flowers blooming—sun-kissed necks and shoulders, bare arms glowing. While their boys lugged coolers of piss beer and boxed wine, whatever else they'd managed to sneak past security, out into the open, they dipped slim hands down dress fronts to liberate an army of airplane bottles. They'll spend the rest of the day nose-deep in Solo cups, barely surfacing long enough to smile for pictures. By midafternoon, if they aren't cross-eyed on the ground, it's a day ill-used.

The crowd changes at the homestretch, where parking spots are expensive and reserved far in advance. Up here, near the grandstand and pressed close to the finish line, this is the place to see and be seen. The mood is merry. Women greet one another with airy kisses while the men wrestle with handshakes. All are donned in their Sunday best, an assortment of paisley pastels and printed animals, sports coats, wide-brimmed hats and aviators, chunky jewelry, striped bow ties, gleaming silver flasks that flash in the sun. It's a party at everyone's house, and if you're here, you're invited.

No one ever actually watches the horses.

That would be absurd.

I took a note from the hunters. If you want to be forgotten in a place designed for you to be seen, you have to construct a blind over your face. A box in a tree at the edge of a field, a ladder leaning against a scraggly oak, leaves that look just a hair too perfect, branches stacked too neat. There sits death, perfectly normal and unassuming. I would be too, perfectly normal and unassuming, my quarry's eyes passing right over me while I watched, and waited and found my shot.

I covered myself in calm, painted it over my breath, the heavy pulse of heartbeat in my throat, so when I drove through the gates and smiled to the security guard, he only nodded, waved me through with hardly a glance. Down I drove, into the cool cleavage of grassy hills, still wet with dew, the edge of night's chill not quite burned away, and so a few lazy ropes of mist slithered over the field in front of me. They'd be gone in an hour, once the sun stood up straight. As I nosed my car up to the winding fence line hemming the back stretch of track, I wondered what that sun would see, when he looked at me.

Parked, the car sighed and stilled, and there, on that expectant rim of a new world, I sat and gathered myself. While cars squeezed on either side of me, while people hauled coolers and folding chairs out of trunks and greeted one another in cheerful hellos, I built my blind. Bit by bit, I pulled myself together. Here is the smile, smooth as honey; here is the laugh, a bell; here are feet moving, always moving, so you don't get caught in a trap. For one anxious moment, the weight of my plan pressed down on my chest, demanding a certain awe. Worries tugged at a corner of my heart. I closed my eyes, imagined her held in two calm hands.

A question slithered around my arms and down into the curve of my belly, where it grew wings, flapped once, twice. Was I really going to do this? I looked out through the window and up, following the path of seersucker, suit jackets, swishing skirts, and I felt those wings rise up in my throat. Yes. I was going to do this. Yes. They deserved it. Yes. It would be fun. *All men are the same. Do not doubt yourself.*

I am no hysterical woman. Don't let them say that I was.

The grass was long, and cold on my feet. The red clay beneath it clammy, like something dead. My feet slid in my sandals, and I had to dig in and force out my first few steps. *Are you sure?* I heard with each push forward, breathy voices doing summersaults under my skin, testing, diving, poking me. *Do you want this?* With each determined step, I answered. *Yes.*

The field had filled up while I sat in my car, remembering that I had lungs and a heart that beat, nerves that scratched worries on my bones. By the time I pulled the mantle of my still self around me, the wide, sloping hill was ablaze. Windshields glittered a Morse code of flashing sun on glass, an SOS that no one was reading. Tents popped up further on, white and blue, black, a few obnoxious orange or red. Gathered around them, still sleepy-eyed and slow moving, knots of people held out hands for the first mimosa of the day, a shot of warm Fireball, anything to shake the dew off and pull their spirits up out of their chest. I weaved through them all, watching, listening, taking careful note.

We used to keep the Blue Bell open for race day—a bucket to catch all of Lindsey's friends for one last cocktail and a mountain of fries on their way home; a chance to breathe and escape the first round of cops swooping down over weaving drivers on the road. Sober them up enough, was the thought, and they might even stay for dinner. It would be good money, we were promised. Who tips better than cross-eyed drunks?

A lot of people, it turns out. Still, we tried for a few years, before accepting that the idea was a disaster. Exhausted and sunburned, revelers would stagger in and promptly fall asleep, drool spreading out from under their faces pressed into the polished wood tables. Danger for a bar. If a cop walked in and found a room of sleeping drunks, we'd be shut down. Those few who did stay awake weren't worth the trouble. It's impossible to take someone's order if they can barely open their mouth to speak, and try arguing with someone who forgot how hungry he was twenty minutes ago, when he asked for two bowls of fries and a burger, which also came with fries. We comped more checks, cleaned up more vomit, poked more people awake than our wages were worth, even with the tips.

The final straw was my man Mark Dixon, who passed out in the bathroom one afternoon after a particularly raucous race day. I was the one who found him, who had to pull his pants back up his legs, wipe the urine off the floor, pat the cocaine off his nose with a wet paper towel, and toss the last lingering shreds of my respect into the trash along with it. Later that night, Lindsey sent me a thank-you text. "Mark is a good guy. I hope we can forget this and move on."

Move on we did. Seeing in the failed business opportunity a chance to pretend he cared about his staff, Lindsey made race day a holiday. He'd buy a space and set up a tent and invite his staff and friends to come drink themselves silly. It was optional, in theory. And we came, as much for the free liquor as to see one another dressed in any color other than black. I would be expected to show face there; it would be noticed if I didn't. To be invisible, you can't act out of line. It was best to get my hellos out of the way early, before they got too drunk to remember they'd seen me, should anyone ask.

"Well look who showed up!" Ty held arms wide when he saw me, a bottle of Maker's Mark dangling from one fist. The whiskey, a warm honey brown, sparkled in the sun. "Here, let me get you a drink. What do you want?"

The setup was the same as every year. Lindsey stationed his Land Rover up against the fence, prime viewing, just a few yards away from the finish line. The trunk was popped open, revealing the usual display of top-shelf liquor and wine. Sitting on the ground below were coolers of beer, a blend of bottles from all the best local breweries, a few Coors Lights mixed in for posterity. One row back was Ty's truck, a makeshift buffet set out on the dropped tailgate. The rest of the bed was forfeit to a flock of the servers, who must have arrived just before me. They perched on the side rails, Solo cups and smartphones in hand, taking selfies and giggling.

"They got here maybe twenty minutes ago," Ty said, following my gaze.

"How long do you think before one of them falls off?" I asked.

He laughed, as if the question were a joke.

And so it began. Spring in Virginia is the warm of cheeks flushed, a sudden sharp spread of blood under cool flesh. As the sun strode higher into the sky, that cool morning swelled and broke into a perfect sunny day. Somewhere around noon, a bugle sounded, and riders from the local fox hunt club blazed past in bright red coats, a pack of baying hounds swarming the grass below. There were dog races and donkey races; a stick pony show for the children; somewhere in between, kilted men marching by as they blew on bagpipes, their faces red and distorted with the rolling breath of music. And then, finally, the horses came.

They ripped by in slashes of bright silks, snorting and kicking clods of dirt up into the humid air. One flew over the fence and landed in Ty's cup, sending the servers into a cascade of giggles; Amber almost fell off the truck she was laughing so hard. Lindsey stumbled back and forth between his Land Rover and us, dragging us all into bear-armed hugs, pressing his flask to our mouths. By midafternoon, Ty's jacket, a simple navy linen, was off, and he was in rolled-up shirtsleeves, sport sunglasses wrapped around his head. The servers clung on to one another, barely upright, every one of them flushed and glassy-eyed. The rule of the day was excess, and they were executing it brilliantly.

I could have stayed there. It would have been so easy to let myself be carried away in the drink and music, to sit on the truck bed and tilt my face to the sun until my hands stopped shaking and the mites that were squirming in my chest fell asleep.

The questions would have haunted me though: *Who am I? Can I do this?*

So I poured the beer handed to me into the grass and sipped my whiskey slow, taking just enough to quell the jittering ends of my nerves. I was breaking apart, all of me was moving and twitching, and I began to be afraid that pieces of me would start rippling up and out of my ears. A mite wriggled out from under my tongue, tried to slip out between my teeth. I drowned it with a shot.

It was time to go. I'd waited as long as I could, long enough for everyone to get liquored up, to see me as a friend. If I wanted to make a move, it was now or never. I shared one more swallow from Ty's cup and drifted away, into the bacchanalia.

All the affected decorum of the morning had shattered, and into its place stumbled a rollicking mess of humanity. Everyone's movements grew a little too wild, a little too big. Eyes brightened like new pennies while cheeks flushed and laughter grew just a hint of an edge. Someone sloshed warm beer down my dress; sticky hands fell onto my shoulders, my waist, my back. I became a railing for strangers to cling to, to keep from falling down. My body, no stranger to strangers' touch, recoiled. The peace of my blind cracked, and the self beneath my face scrambled to pull back. Take a breath. Quiet the mouths laughing in my ears; stay calm, take careful aim.

"Sophie?"

So lost had I been in my own thoughts that I hadn't seen the woman until I walked straight into her.

"Oh, I'm sorry, I . . . Officer Martin?" I felt my pulse rise. What was she doing here? Every crawling thing in me fell to the ground.

Away from work, she looked like a whole person instead of a storm cloud, brewing thoughts cleared away for the afternoon. A bow-tied man stood an arm's distance behind her, his face fashioned into a bemused sort of smile. Just behind them stood a tent where a small crowd of people were shoving ham biscuits into their mouths, pouring drinks, laughing.

"I didn't recognize you!" I forced a smile, an answer. Of course she would be here; everyone was. *Stay calm, stay smooth. You are wearing a mask.*

She shrugged. "I'm a whole new person out of uniform."

"I know how you feel. No one ever recognizes me when I'm out of work clothes either. Always feels weird to be wearing anything other than black."

I saw it there, the barest hint of a question rippling across her face. I pulled my breath in—had I said something wrong? But then she smiled.

The man behind her, who had by then tilted his head to one side, stepped forward. "Hi. I'm Dan. You're a friend of Nor's?"

Officer Martin flushed. "Dan, Sophie . . . boyfriend, bartender," she said.

The man, who was Dan, reached out and took my hand in his. "Lovely to meet you, Sophie. Bartender? Where do you work?" His grip was lazy. I was afraid I might break it if I squeezed.

"The Blue Bell."

"We haven't been there yet. Is it any good?"

I pulled on the face I wore to work on busy nights. "I think so. But you should never trust a bartender. We lie."

He laughed. "Well, we'll have to come visit you sometime, judge for ourselves. Next time we get the same day off, Nor?"

"Dan's a nurse at the hospital," she explained. "Between both our schedules, we rarely have a whole day free together. This is the first one in . . . how many weeks?"

"Too many," he said.

"Too many," she agreed. "Anyway, I wouldn't usually be caught dead at an event like this, but his work friends buy a block of tickets every year and rotate who gets off. And since we were both free . . . here we are."

"Here you are." *Smile.* I pulled the mask on tighter, checked the edges, made sure none of me was spilling out. "Well . . . don't let me distract you from your day." Someone bumped into me, hot beer spilled down the backs of my legs. Beneath my skin, mouths opened. The sun had crept over the zenith of sky and begun his slow drip down toward the tree line.

"Oh nonsense," she said. "Come have a drink with us. We've got plenty."

"Yeah, Sophie." Dan pressed in. "A glass of wine? Some snacks?"

I held up a hand. "Oh no. Thank you, that's very generous, but I don't want to intrude on you, Officer—"

"You're not intruding. And please, call me Nora."

Call me Nora. Call me Nora. There it was, there was everything I needed to know. If she hadn't said that, I might have considered staying just for a while, to fish for whatever I could about Mark, to see what she knew. That statement told me enough. She may have had questions, but in truth, they had no inkling who had killed Mark. She considered me safe enough to address as a friend. *Sophie. Nora.*

"I have to go find Ty. I left him back at the paddock watching the horses, and Lord knows if I don't rescue him soon, he'll go home with one girl or another." The lie fell easily from my mouth.

"That doesn't sound so bad," Dan chuckled.

"You haven't seen the girls he takes home when he's drunk." Low-hanging fruit, I know, but it made Dan guffaw. Trap set, we were friends now in his eyes.

"Well here, take this at least." Nora pressed a warm biscuit into my hand.

I thanked them again. "Let me know when you want to come down to the bar. I'll make a reservation for you. Best seat in the house."

"Deal," Dan said, and sent me on my way.

My hands were trembling again. I wanted to look back over my shoulder as I walked away, to see if they were watching, but I steeled myself against the impulse. I needed to be careful with her.

The New Kid

If anyone had asked Nora just what she was doing there in that field, wearing the only sundress she owned while sipping someone's cheap rosé and pretending to laugh at jokes she didn't find particularly funny, she would have been hard-pressed to give an answer she felt was the truth.

The truth, when she pressed a finger to it hovering just at the edge of her thoughts, was that this was the last place she wanted to spend her day; that she'd come here because Dan wanted to, because he'd paid his dues at the hospital for years and now he'd been offered the golden ticket to go out and play for a day instead of waiting on tenterhooks for the waves of alcohol-poisoned patients to stumble through the doors. He'd earned it. She was happy for him and glad to have a day to let her hair down. That was what she told herself as she watched him press back into the center of a circle of his work pals, his tie loosened, his hat turned backward; that was what she told herself as she avoided looking too closely at the old plantation house that crowned the far end of the field, white columns gleaming in the afternoon sun.

It was a dead thing now, a carcass; only used for weddings and holiday parties, a backdrop to countless selfies. It made her uncomfortable all the same. For Dan though, for one day, she could ignore it.

She watched Sophie walk away. The woman looked as uncomfortable as she felt, sidestepping stumbling drunks, her steps quick and curt. Neither one of them, it seemed, fit into this boisterous place. Not for the first time, she began to wonder if Sophie Braam might become a friend.

"Nor! Hey, Nora, whatcha doing, baby?" Dan's hand on hers. "You feeling okay?"

"Huh? Oh yeah, just thinking."

"You do that too much." He kissed her cheek.

She smiled. "I know."

Sophie

The day, which had felt so alive in the morning, began to drag as afternoon wore on. Exposed now to the full sun, the field became an oven we all baked inside. I felt sweat trickle down my chest as I slogged through the thick grass. More poured down the backs of my arms, my legs.

Keep focused, I heard voices scratch into my ear. *Don't get sloppy now.*

I turned my head at the sound of something metal banging against itself, and there he was.

He was tall, at least six feet or so. Legs splayed wide in a triangle as he hunched over the beer keg. From my spot in the grass, I watched him for a minute as he pumped the handle up and down to no avail before giving up, letting the nozzle fall against the keg with a clang.

He looked over to his friends, who were gathered around a nearby SUV, where two duck-booted girls were practicing some kind of dance in between taking swallows from a shared bottle of champagne. Bubbles fizzed over their faces, to the squealing glee of everyone involved.

Go, now.

"Need help?" I asked, walking over to him.

He jumped as if scared, and then turned to me.

"You know how to work this thing? It hates me."

His eyes were hidden behind a pair of sunglasses, but I felt them trawl up my body all the same. His lips were cracked, sunburned. His cheeks bloomed with the first blush of drunken red.

"I'm a bartender," I said simply, reaching down to grab the pump and hose from him. "I know my way around a beer keg."

"A lady who knows what she's doing!"

It was an invitation held out between us; I said nothing. It was too easy, it felt cheap.

Instead, I reached out a hand. "Give me your cup."

Our fingertips touched. His were sticky, whether from beer or sweat, I couldn't tell. I felt tiny feet on my neck and turned away before he noticed them scuttle into my eye.

"You forgot to press the coupler down," I said. In a quick second, the keg was fixed, and with a few short, sharp pumps, I had his cup filled and frothing.

"My hero," he said.

"A girl likes to feel useful every once in a while." I winked, taking a proprietary sip. I knew he would watch my throat, and though I'd done it on purpose, I burst into something like shame. I tamped it down with a firm hand. A deep breath. He watched my chest rise and fall.

I nodded as I handed his cup back to him, toward the girls who were now having a handstand contest in the grass, their skirts gathered up between legs by responsible friends, who ducked from wild-legged kicks. The boys circled around them like wolves, pretending to care about this display of acrobatics, though we all knew what they were really watching for.

"What's that about?"

He grinned. "Cheerleaders. Showing off."

"Your beer is shit," I said, taking it from him again for another swallow. Men love it when you lay claim to them in small ways. They think it's cute.

"Hey, what did Natty ever do to you?" he asked with a chuckle, taking the cup back from my outstretched hand.

"Nothing. That's the problem."

He snorted.

I took the cup from his hand a final time, poured it on the ground. "I've got better stuff in my car. I was just heading there to get it. Come with me? Help me carry it back up, you win a prize."

"What sort of prize?"

"You'll have to wait and see."

The thing about these sorts of outdoor events is that in the bright sun, the cool breeze, the perfect harmony of a half-drunk day, everyone is your friend.

But didn't your momma tell you? You should never get in a car with a stranger.

He was clumsy and drunk, tripping behind me as we wended our way down the shallow slope of the back field toward my car, a fold of my dress clutched in his hand like a child following its mother. When I got tired of his fumbling, I reached back, took his sweaty palm in my own. Every few yards, I'd slow my step; a heartbeat, a breath, a seemingly unplanned opening for the backs of his knuckles to slide against my thigh. A trick I've learned about handling men is to make yourself something soft, something lovely. Push all other thoughts from his mind. So I stepped, and sometimes slowed, and let his hand graze against the bare flesh of my leg, let him feel my careless permission to touch me.

The world changed as we moved further away from the melee of the main field. The grass was taller, less groomed. It snared our ankles, choking our steps. More than once I had to stop to pivot and he bumped into me. I bit my lip, swallowed the mites that roared in my cheeks. We, all of us, were disgusted with the touching, his sticky palm on my hamstring.

The people back here were sparse, cloistered in cars, single-minded in their errands. No one left the party unless they had something specific to do: drugs or sex or the alcohol run. We passed a knot of what looked to be freshmen, squatting behind an open car door, passing something between them. Smoke curled up into the air with their giggles, broke apart in the open sky. A soft gasp came from further down the field; I didn't look to see its source. The boy behind me squeezed my hand, let himself press against me. I felt like a twenty-year-old again, in a way that made me angry. The mites bit into my jaw, coiled down my throat in a sharp drag of something like bile. *Only a little longer,* I told the multitudes of myself in that long afternoon. *We're almost there.*

I let him kiss me in my car. His chapped lips scraped across mine. His hands, still sticky, roamed over my arms, my legs. I held my breath and gathered myself into my skull as far as I could when I felt him push a hand under my skirt, tug away my panties with the deft twist of two probing fingers.

"You're so wet," he whispered, wolfish mouth pressed against my ear. His breath was loud.

You think I'm lying, that this is too fast. No one is so easily lured. But I once watched my friend coil into a boy's arms at a club. Within the clock span of two songs, they'd vanished to a dark hallway. She was back with her hand threaded through mine a few short minutes later, the glow of sex hot on her cheeks. It can be done. All men are animals.

I made a sound that might have been a moan to his ears, closed my eyes, and lied that his fumbling felt good. I have known since I was a teenager that my body is a liar, that she'd rather play possum than fight back. So I let him touch me, swallowed him whole in a trap of his own making.

When I heard him tug his pants zipper, I stopped him.

"You know what?" I said, catching his eyes, which without his sunglasses I saw were wide and blue, "I've got a better idea. This place is about to close down anyways, and I don't want to be caught in traffic trying to get out. I know somewhere better. Private."

He looked back up toward the tents, and I felt my heart pound as I watched him weigh his options. He was drunk when I found him, but the walk, his arousal, they had sobered him enough and I saw the teetering seesaw of his mind: Stay with the party, or leave with me? Never once did he weigh his safety. That was not a question he was used to asking. His only worry was the potential for fun.

"I left my phone up in the tent. I should go get it."

I squeezed his hand. "You can use mine if you need it. Otherwise, your buddies'll ask where you're going and it'll be a huge deal and you'll forget or get sidetracked. Besides"—against my better dignity, I placed a hand on his thigh—"I don't have good service out where I am. Your phone would be useless."

"Country girl, huh?" He was melting, he was putty. He was trapped.

"Born and raised."

"Should I be scared?"

"If anyone's going to be scared, statistically, it should be me." I winked, and he laughed, and then I drove us out of the field and away.

Persephone

It was peaceful, when it was done.

After only a few short moments, his eyes began to glaze over; the result, I have read, of the potassium in his bloodstream breaking down. By morning his blue gaze would have clouded, as milky white as the mists that crawled up out of the nearby creek to drape over us both as we lay on the damp ground. Red splotches marred the whites of his eyes, and more edged around the soft rims of his corneas. There was no bleeding nose; no blood dribbled out from lips. He was simply quiet, a man staring into the clouds that are sinking down over his eyes.

I sat with him through that first long evening, as the sun rolled down the mountain ridge behind us. The little town of Bellair fell into a stupor, sated with a day spent in the heat and booze and excitement of the races.

For the first time, the blowflies came. Did you know they're female? The males are rather docile creatures, satisfied with flower petals. Harmless. It's the females, pregnant and hungry, who consume us, bury their eggs in our flesh. Stirred back to life by the new spring warmth, they introduced themselves to me that day as friends, partners in this grand game I was playing.

In the long golden hours of that evening, I studied them. The earliest few buzzed in about an hour after his death, blown in on a soft breeze sliding down the creek. He was still warm when they touched tongues down onto his cheeks. They were clumsy things, zipping up and down, bumping into me and one another as they tasted, tested, explored this death beneath the apple trees. They tiptoed up into his nose and slipped between his lips. What would they learn down there, in the subterranean places of him? What secrets would they find? I stretched my body next to his and pressed my cheek to his shoulder, listening for the small eurekas of their discoveries. A few flies flitted onto my own throat, to examine the heaving pulse of my carotids. I swiped them away, sent them back to their feast.

His skin took on the barest tint of blue about the edges of his mouth, the corners of his eyes, his fingernails, as if the real color of him were starting to creep through now that life wasn't there to burn him to a flush. I've read that our bodies are as much as 70 percent water; I like to think then that this slow slide into blue was a return to his natural self. If I hadn't known any better, I'd have said then that he was still alive, that any moment he'd shake off the blue tinge and sit up, blinking in the warm light of the setting sun.

By nightfall he'd grown stiff. His eyes, lazily awake to the shifting light above us, snapped open with a suddenness that made me wonder if he really had come back to life, and I picked up his tie, ready to wind it around him again. But he lay still, now wide-eyed, watching eternity race toward him. It was only a muscle reflex, that was all; the rigid reflex of early decay. To be sure, I reached out and gently touched one of his eyes, a trick I learned from a drunk veterinarian. The blink response is the last to go.

Nothing. Around us, in the deepening shadows, the tree frogs began to sing.

You're asking why he didn't stop me. When he realized what was happening, why didn't he buck me off, punch and scratch and roll away? I'm a small thing after all, easily defeated. The answer is simple: a man underneath you isn't thinking of such things.

And it was his idea.

Choking would be a fun game, he thought. He'd seen it in a video. And I was a townie. I must be more fun than those stuck-up, milquetoast girls at school. Townies knew where the good drugs were, the best parties, the games to play when all the lights went out.

"Choke me," he said.

So I did.

I kept my knife within reach, just in case.

I watched through the deepening hours as blood pooled in his limbs, a congealed purple and black settling in those parts of him that touched the ground. Bit by bit, his blue flush thinned to pale white. His skin took on a waxy appearance, like apples at the grocery store, the kind my grandmother used to scoff at.

"Something unusual about that," she'd say, sweeping a hand over the piles of fruit, pulling one out to spin it around, drop it back. "Unnatural, that shine."

Unnatural. That is what he became then, in the dark, in the long hours of the night. He became just a body. Pale and waxy. Whatever it was that had made him a man was gone.

Before he froze, I reached into his mouth and took his voice. His lips, chapped, scraped against the back of my hand and I felt disgust ripple through me. Mute, he melted into a scream; whether the result of my surgery or the minuscule tugs of dozens of tiny muscles pulling themselves into fists, I do not know. Rigor mortis had begun to settle in. We scream, did you know, after death. The last act of a skull looking at the face of nothingness, or maybe God, is to fall into silent awe.

I would have liked to stay, to watch him contract inch by inch, to feel the squeeze of each organ and muscle as they spasmed. I wanted to watch his back arch in a kind of ecstasy as powerful trapezii, erectors, gluteal muscles clenched and yanked him open. To bear witness to the mortification of his own flesh, brought on by nothing more than a few proteins trapped inside an anaerobic chamber.

Each twitch of his muscles disturbed the flies, and they lifted into the air, annoyed and gently buzzing. Still, more and more of them came, and within a few hours, I could no longer sweep them away. The flies, confused by the smell of two bodies, had begun biting me.

Night fell over us. The air grew spines and was no longer pleasant on my flesh, which had grown clammy with the gathering dew. I knew if I didn't leave soon, I'd catch a chill. I was alive. It was time to leave. To stay alive and let him be.

He died below the apple trees skirting the crumbling edge of the creek, and when it was dark enough to move without being seen, I rolled him there. It was easier than I expected, the rigor holding him stiff. He was not a flopping doll, to be clumsily tumbled end over end, but a board. Heavy, but simpler to manage. I dug my heels into the clay and drove us forward. Flies blossomed from his skin, danced a halo around my head, touched down like lace over my hands.

There was a hollow there, in that bend of the creek just across from the old Baptist church. It had probably once been a fox den or groundhog hole. Caved in and open on one side, half-hidden by the twisted trunk and roots of an old willow tree, it was the perfect hiding place for a precocious child avoiding chores on long summer days. This pocket in the earth was a library, an art studio, a quiet place to sit with my thoughts. It was high enough up that the creek below hardly ever flooded it, but I could easily dip a foot down into the cool eddies of water. On the hottest afternoons, I'd sit with one foot dragging in the creek, watching the play of sunlight shining through the curtain of willow leaves onto the earthen wall of my little hole. No one ever saw me, not even on Sundays, when the church across the way belched out her congregants. I've learned that people very rarely look deeper than they need to. What they saw, if they let their eyes sweep over the creek, was a drooping tree, a bramble-choked bank, water sliding through long grass and dancing over rocks, and beyond, the apple trees. Never a girl in a hole, never a foot waving through water. So that is where he would stay. This place, unkempt and wild, would hide my secrets as it always had.

In a few panting minutes, I'd pulled him deep into the hollow. To be careful, because I could not quiet the nagging worry in my brain, I piled leaves and dirt over him, extra cover should any eyes happen to wander by. The animals would come in a day or two and do the rest. In a few weeks, there'd be nothing to find.

I saved the last swig of whiskey for my walk back through the apple orchard. The trees were in full bloom by then, blowsy flowers glowing white in the full moonlight. The song of crickets and tree frogs swelled to fill the air around me. I saw a bat skitter overhead. Somewhere in the distance, a pack of coyotes yipped and cried out into the silver night. I let my skin slough off, joined them.

A Tired Woman

It was always the flies that Nora noticed first. Even before she ducked under the taut yellow tape that edged the boundary between the civilian world and her own, their voices swept across her skin like fingers on harp strings, plucking nervous notes, raising a chorus of goose pimples as thousands of filmy wings hummed their way into the space of her ears, a puff of tinny sound coating the air. It was impossible to keep them away, to ignore them. Any efforts were quickly thwarted; their song was incessant, their hunger ravenous and unstoppable. Disturbed by a step, the timbre of a voice, the flies rose; a strange, diaphanous beast that burst at face height into a spray of wings and hums and pinprick bodies before falling back down upon their feast table. Voracious as death, their indiscriminate tongues lapped at whatever flesh they settled on, alive or otherwise.

She was fascinated by them, their shimmer and flash, their soft billowing flight. She was disgusted by them, their frenzied whispers, their mad, scurrying steps on bloated bodies and sticky blood. The thought of them sent a ripple sliding down her spine, no doubt a buried genetic dream of contagion somewhere under a wide, blue sky.

"Carrion beetles," she said, brushing a fly off her forehead as she looked to the ground, nudged a bulkier insect with her toe. It pitched sideways, scuttled around a bit of gravel.

Murph followed the line of her gaze. "What does that mean?"

"Whoever's back here's been dead awhile."

Bugs had their secrets, Nora knew. Working on a farm meant her daddy had befriended even the creepiest of crawlies, and so when she was a girl, he taught her how to listen to the oracle of beating wings, shivering incisors. Each species had its own voice, its own time. First came the blowflies, bottle green and frantic. They arrived at the earliest muted agonies of a body not yet realizing its own decay, their music tinny and annoying, but easily swept away. Next came the flesh flies, family *Sarcophagidae*. Parasitic, brutal, they delighted in all manner of putrescence. Their arrival heralded a wave of other immigrants: maggots, beetles, scavengers of all kinds. If you needed the bones picked clean, you couldn't find better friends. At Ron's side, Nora learned the names of each of these ghoulish psychopomps; she learned their patterns, to read them, to befriend them as he had, to decode the teeming language of insects.

She crouched down for a better look. The bugs, maybe half an inch in length, scooted along the ground in a stiff stop-motion that sent chills up the back of her neck. It was like watching a ghost in a horror movie, all backward and upside down, crawling on broken legs. Not right. Natural, maybe, but not right. She swallowed a yawn and stood back up.

"You gonna make it, kid?"

"Just tired."

"You're too young to be tired." His words a prick under her skin.

She bit back the retort she wanted to make, the one that would have been rude, would have been disrespectful. Instead, she focused her eyes on a beetle now scuttling over the gravel before her. "Well, I spent all day out in the sun yesterday with Dan, then got called in late last night to cover the graveyard shift for Cruz."

Nora rose, pressed her hands to her face in an attempt to wipe away the headache she felt building just behind her eyes. She hadn't been sleeping well the past few nights. Restless, tossing and turning to the touch of fingers that melted into thin air as soon as she was too awake to fall back into sleep, her head had begun to clamp down on itself in an exhausted tantrum. She'd have to take an Excedrin when she got home, or she'd be fighting a migraine all night.

Murph chuckled. "Those dang horse races. An old man forgets. We've all been there—keep your hands in your pockets and no one will see you shaking; if you need to puke, run around the corner. I can't believe they called you in when they knew you'd been out partying."

"We're short-staffed, as you very well know." Her patience for personal questions was thin that morning, rubbed raw by the sun and the long, stale night. "And I didn't have much. Stopped drinking around two or three in the afternoon, because I had a feeling this might happen. I saw Cruz attached to the back end of a beer bong not long after Dan and I got there."

"You're so responsible, Martin."

"Fuck off."

She hated that it was true. That she'd been wise enough to curtail her fun on a day that should have been her own to do with as she pleased. She should have been in bed with Dan right then, dying from a hangover and grumbling about who was going to get up and make the recovery breakfast for them both. Instead, she'd had to crawl out of bed at an ungodly hour and drag on her uniform for a night of driving bored down dark roads, her only company the crackle of her radio and the M&M's she kept in her cupholder.

"Don't get your panties in a twist. You know they only take advantage of you because you let them, right?" Murph asked.

"And what would you have me do? I don't exactly fit into the boys' club."

"Well, fuck 'em. I've been here a long time, Martin, and I can tell you, they're just jealous. Look at you! Pretty woman waltzes in from over the mountain, gets to work with me. I'd be jealous too. And, maybe more importantly, they can't just open the door and piss on the side of the road when they're partnered with you."

"What does that have— We hardly ever share a car anyways."

"My point, young grasshopper, is that they can't just be guys when you're in the locker room."

"Oh, believe me, I don't think they've held back in my presence." Nora felt her eyes flash.

"Hey now." Murph held his palms up, as if to calm an animal. "I'm on your side, Martin. And I think I know a thing or two more than you about young guys, so consider this advice from an old fart: You need to butter 'em up a bit. Be sweet. I'm cringing saying this, but maybe try being a bit more womanly. We men are simple creatures— give them compliments, puff up their egos just a hair. They're intimidated by you, so they don't trust you. You catch more flies with honey than vinegar, your momma ever tell you that?"

And there it was again, a man telling her to cover up, to dull herself. Making her feel dirty for something she couldn't change; only this time it wasn't eyes rounding the curves of her body, it was her mentor, whom she respected, telling her to sell herself short. *For the boys.* Nora knew he didn't mean for them to, but the words stung. She had known when she started at the academy that she was choosing to move into the world of men, that there would be days she could not be herself, that there would be frustrations and annoyances, that she would, without being asked, become the station mother. She was prepared for that. What she wasn't prepared for was the icing-out. Women did that. Women kicked you out of the group; women turned their backs and gossiped. She had never fit in with women.

Men, she'd thought, were simpler. She'd learned instead that men had their own ways, more subtle, less studied, but clear and hard all the same. She watched Murph take a drag of his cigarette, the end burning bright in the gray morning. The same brand her father had smoked, the kind passed around in the barbershop he and his buddies sat in long after close. Nora remembered going there with her momma after hours to pick him up. There the men were, sprawled about the silver shop interior, beers and cigarettes in hand, the air a hazy smoke filled with laughter and off-color jokes. They always stopped what they were doing when Emma walked in. No matter how many times she went there to grab a beer herself and pick up her husband for dinner, there was always an edge to the scene, some-where under the surface, that Nora could never quite put a finger on. She wondered if this was the price to be paid, for wandering into the world of men.

Later, she wondered if they too didn't feel accosted, if they didn't fear a blond woman standing in the door. The lines and politics of her world were so blurred, Nora often couldn't keep the threads straight. They tangled about one another, looped back and through, sometimes spun out in their own directions entirely. Always was the tension, the feel of straddling a fence or standing on a tightrope, wait-ing for the fall, for someone to push her off.

She wanted to ask Murph why he didn't just stand up for her. A complaint from her mouth was weakness in their eyes, something they could nail her on; a stern word from him though would be re-spected. Why couldn't he do that? Why was he so afraid to rock the boat? Did he care? *Bullshit*, she wanted to say. *And fuck you.*

She'd been raised better than that though. So instead she bit the inside of her cheek, which was burning with the frustrations she'd been swallowing for years, and said, "Yeah, okay, sure. Easy."

Murph laughed and patted her shoulder. "You'll be okay. Don't let those boys beat you up! Now, let's get back to business. Walk me through this scene. What have we got, Detective-Officer Martin?"

She fell down into the speech she knew, simple and direct. "Elderly gentleman called in around seven this morning. He'd been out walk-ing his dog. He said he likes to walk early, even on Sundays, because it's quiet and he doesn't have to worry about meeting other dogs or runners."

"Makes sense," Murph interjected.

"What? Oh. Yeah, it does." She was still angry, distracted by his lecture. And she'd been at this scene for hours already, talking to the witness, calling in Murph and the forensics crew, doing her own quick sweep of the area. Her tired brain could only handle one job at a time, patrol or detective or angry. She took a breath, chose calm control.

"He said they don't come back here often. The smells, trash and stuff, they distract the dog and he doesn't like to have to struggle with it."

"What kind of dog?"

"Some kind of doodle thing."

"Of course. Like everyone around here. I don't understand the draw myself. Give me a good old hound any day—"

"Murph." *Christ, must he have an opinion about everything?*

"Right. So . . . the dog, whatever, smelled something and tugged his owner back here?"

Nora calmed herself, took a page from her daddy's book. Murph probably didn't realize how much he had frustrated her. "Not quite. He saw a deer just as they were leaving their yard and ran off. They live just off Grandview, maybe a half mile away? Man chased him but couldn't keep up. He thought the dog might come here if he gave up going after the deer."

"The restaurants, yeah." He nodded.

"Right. So he follows it down here, and when he finds it, it's got what looks like human remains in its mouth. Fingers, to be exact."

"Good morning!" Murph let out a low whistle. "Bet that woke him right up?"

"You could say so, yeah."

"Have you looked?"

"Enough to close down the scene. I peeked down under the pile of junk there and saw a bit of a jacket and what I think might be a knit hat. Haven't moved anything though. Checked out the remains too. Definitely human. Shredded. I have a feeling they've been . . . uh . . . feeding . . . other animals for some time now. The shredding plus the beetles seems to indicate they've been here for a few weeks at least. There'd be other bugs if this was fresh and only ripped up by the dog."

"You scare me sometimes, kid. Good. We'll let the specs go in and tear everything apart, see if you're right . . . Shall we then? I think I see Val over there."

Nora rubbed her eyes. Normally, her job would be done by now. She'd taken witness statements and contact information; she'd cordoned off the scene and called in the professionals. It was time for her to clock out and go home. And today she really wanted that, to go home. She was cranky and tired and was having a hard time caring about anything.

"Come on," Murph prodded her. "You want to get out of that uniform, you have to make them see you as my partner. Let's go. You can sleep when you're dead."

"I hate you, you know that?"

"Of course I do. And that fire under your ass is what'll make you a better detective. You're welcome."

He winked and turned on his heel to slouch toward Val, who was standing under a blue pop-up tent, so like the one Nora had been relaxing under not even a full day earlier. She blew a puff of air out of her cheeks and followed him, smoothing the frown from her face.

Nora

The clouds, which had been holding their breath in their bellies all morning, started spitting as soon as Nora and Murph walked back out from under the tent, leaving Val to discuss plans with her crew.

"Lovely." He peered up at the sky, which hung low and gray, a fat tongue sweeping down to lick the buildings below. "Hey, Val!" he called back over his shoulder. "I think you're gonna want to move that tent over the fence. Rain's rolling in."

She peered up from her notes, and then at the roof of the tent. Nora saw her mouth something that could have been *crap* but was probably *fuck*, and then there was a flurry of movement as she directed her team to lift the tent and run it down to the end of the alley without disturbing the scene.

The two detectives swept off to one side to let them pass. Murph pulled out a cigarette.

"Really?" Nora asked.

"It'll be a few minutes, and we're not close to the body. Don't be such a square, Martin." He took a drag. "Now, tell me about these beetles. How do you know about them?"

"My daddy worked on a farm. Death happens; he'd go clean it up. Sometimes he wouldn't find an animal for days, and he had to make a decision to haul it away or leave it in the field. Flies are okay, even sometimes maggots, depending on what else you see, but by the time the beetles came, it'd be easier to leave the thing than try to move it. It'd just fall apart, make a bigger mess."

"I see . . . You're a strange bird, you know that? Full of surprises. Don't let Val hear you though; she'll try to steal you for her squad. Always remember: I found you first."

Nora smirked.

Murph took another pull of the cigarette before stamping it out, shoving it back into the pack for later.

"So, here's my other question," he said, smoke billowing out of his nostrils, making his voice something pinched and small. "This is a test: If he's been here so long, why didn't anyone notice? No smell? No one saw him before now?"

"Well, someone definitely *saw* him before now."

"Okay, smartass. Answer my questions. Think."

Nora looked around the alley. The gravel was chunky, pitted and pocked in places, overgrown in others. This wasn't an alley that saw a lot of traffic, at least not the kind with wheels. She followed the rutted track up until her eyes snagged on the rough railing of a crooked wooden stair. The space underneath was overgrown, dry grass and the stubborn trunk of one thorny blackberry bush. The rest of the space was crammed with broken-down boxes, splintered pallets; a few empty kegs lay like wounded soldiers up along one wall.

"Who are we behind?" Murph asked. "I always lose my way back here."

"The Blue Bell," Nora said, pointing to the kegs, "and on the other side is a bookstore, and I think a hair salon? Cutz."

"I'm forever inspired by the creativity of their name." He blew out a puff of smoke. "Okay, so what do you see?"

"I see a place that has a lot of nooks and crannies to hide. And a lot of junk to hide someone behind. It's close to the road—that fence isn't much of a shield from prying ears, or even eyes if someone were to peek through a crack, but if you picked the right time of day . . ."

She looked up, saw faces pressed into a window above, gossipy women whispering to one another. They saw her looking, waved. Nora lifted her hand in robotic response and bit her lip, thinking. "Or time of *year*. If I'm right, and our victim's been here for at least a few weeks, it could have been winter when they were left out here. We had some bitter days in February, even March. No one would have been outside to hear anything; everyone was hunkered down. The smell would be easy enough to cover. The cold would do most of the work for you. It would keep the bugs out too. And if anyone noticed, they'd probably think the odor was coming from that dumpster over there. It would really only smell for a day or two, in that weather. Gone before anyone took the time to wonder if it wasn't just rancid trash."

She glanced off to her left, where not fifty yards away squatted a fat green dumpster. A question slipped into her mind: Was that the dumpster that had swallowed Mark Dixon? The thought gave her chills. She looked back up at the shop staff, still crowded around the tiny window. Had any of them seen anything?

Murph followed her line of sight. "Vultures. All right, let's go see if Val will let us squeeze in under that tent, and then we'll get a better idea of what we're working with."

And so it began, the ritual of investigation. The forensics crew scattered when the two detectives ducked under the tent, flying off to photograph the rest of the alley, to grab tools and baggies and notebooks out of Val's beat-up old Tahoe. She watched them go and then turned to Nora and Murph.

"We haven't moved much. Just enough to uncover him. Yes, I think it's a male. Hard to tell with the amount of decomp. We'll have to get a look at his skeleton or hair samples to be sure, but he's got men's clothing on, and his boots are big enough. Squat down; take a look. We still have a while before the ME gets here."

"My old knees can't handle that in this rain," Murph said.

So Nora dropped onto tired knees of her own, and with tired eyes she gazed at the little death before her. The man lay folded against the fence, his back arched, arms tight to his chest, his legs crumpled and twisted through each other. What she thought was his face was pressed down into the grit and gravel of the back alley. His clothes, worn by the weather, were tattered. Bits of jacket fell away when she reached out to touch it with a gloved hand. What was left of his hair lay in lank strings, and it was hard to tell what color or texture it had been while he was alive. Everything about him seemed melted, blurred. Here was a creature falling back down into the earth.

Nora looked up and saw another body, curled into the wall, her wispy blond hair hiding a face frozen in pain. As she watched, the girl stood, climbed out from behind a soggy wine box to trail around the edges of the alley, rustling, listening, curious. And something else . . . satisfied? The feeling made Nora shiver.

The weight of it all pressed in on her—the haints, the body, the long drag of exhausted hours, and Nora found she had too many feelings to hold in the embrace of her ribs. Her heart dove in a wild, sharp swoop, and she turned away, took a breath to gather herself.

To put her feet back on the ground, she pulled a question out of her pocket. "We haven't had any calls for missing persons in the last few weeks, have we?"

"None," Murph said.

Nora turned back to the corpse. "Who are you?"

He was silent. Whoever he had been, they would have to find out for themselves.

"That must be where the dog got him." Murph bent down next to her, pointed to a spot on the man's hand, where two fingers were missing. What flesh was there hung in ragged flaps around the wound. It was gray, bloodless. There was no stench; his death had long since passed. The image struck Nora as something very sad. What kind of person could go missing unnoticed? Who deserved to rot out here, in the brutal air?

A beetle pushed up through his jawbone, flopped across his ruined face and disappeared into his hair. Nora shivered.

Behind her, she heard the forensics crew sweeping through the alley. Like bloodhounds, they sniffed everything, all senses attuned to clues others might miss. A spot of blood, a bit of bone, a tiny scrap of cloth caught on a sharp edge. They tiptoed through the gravel, whispering to one another, pointing and moving on or stooping to drop down a yellow numbered placard. There wasn't much to be found, not after so long, and soon Nora could feel them crowding around the back of the tent. Their whispers scratched over her, urgent, impatient to swoop back over the corpse before her.

She stood. "Shall we let them have their crime scene back?"

"Let's go regroup," Murph agreed, meaning he wanted to finish his cigarette.

The alley, softened by rain and misty cloud, the hushed whispering of investigators, had become a pocket world, sealed off from the punch of bigger things. The arrival of the ME van felt like a scream.

Stoic and efficient, they marched in, the stretcher jostling on the gravel. Val rushed to meet them in a flurry of hands and honeyed smiles that dissolved into stern orders as to just how to lift the poor creature up out of the dirt. The men nodded their assurance and cleared out the tent.

They had to move slowly. The body had been outside for so long that what was left of him clacked and waved in the breeze that ripped down the alley throat. If they weren't careful, he would spill right out of their hands. Nora saw them flinch and for a moment turn their eyes away from the corpse they cradled.

A soft sigh of air punched out of him as he was laid onto the stretcher, the last memory of life slipping out of the pouches it had been trapped in for weeks. Or perhaps relief, Nora thought, at finally being seen. She stepped closer to the stretcher as they rolled it toward the van and snapped her eyes shut. Behind her, she heard the girl hiss.

His mouth, whether by design or decay, was stretched open in a wide, cavernous wail. Deep inside, where there should have been a tongue, was nothing more than empty, ruined palate, the smallest vertebrae slinking up toward his melted brain.

She looked at Murph, caught his eyes with her own. "His tongue."

He bit his lip, looked back down to the man who lay, twisted and small, before them.

"Go home, Martin."

"What?"

"Go home." Murph pulled out another cigarette, lit it. "I'm serious. You've been working all night, taken good care of this scene. Let me take over."

"Murph. It could be nothing—it could be animals! He's been out here long enough, lots of reasons he might be missing a tongue."

"Martin." He blew out a puff of smoke. "I know you don't really think it's an animal that took this man's tongue."

"Well, no, but . . ." Nora stung. She was buzzing. Another body, another man without a tongue.

"Kid, if you want to take over from me, I need to know you know when to take a break. You're not going to burn yourself out, not on my watch. You've done what you can here today. Go home and rest. I'll catch you up tomorrow."

"Tonight."

He sighed. "Fine. Now, go bother your boyfriend or something."

She looked over her shoulder once, after she tore off her booties, just before she left the scene. Murph was bent over the body, his face pale and drawn.

Nora

Dan was on the couch when she got home, wrapped up tight in his blanket and looking for all the world like a giant pupal beetle. Nora went to take a shower.

"I think I'm dying," he said, when she got out.

She sat down on the couch next to him, laid his head in her lap. "I think you just need some Pedialyte and sleep."

"Not before I see if Kyle and Lisa make up."

"What?" She looked to the TV, where two women were seated across a table from each other, filmy pink florals and a crisp white tablecloth eating up the hard space between them; two wineglasses sparkled in the California sun. "Oh. Probably not. Do they ever?"

"That's the drama of it, babe. It's practically Shakespearean."

"Sure."

She stroked his hair until he fell asleep, snoring lightly. On the TV screen, a group of women screeched at one another. Someone threw a drink. Nora felt her mind become foggy, pull the curtain down behind her half-closed eyes.

A Friend

Well, look who it is! To what do I owe this pleasure?" Sophie Braam grinned, sliding a glass of water across the bar to Nora, who was climbing rather more unsteadily than she would have liked onto one of the plush barstools that lined the counter. As she did so, a slip of a girl, quiet as a whisper and just as small, pressed a menu against her fingertips. Nora turned to thank her, but the girl had already scampered back to her stand at the door.

"It's not you." Sophie plucked Nora's unasked question out of the ether. "Poor thing broke up with her boyfriend this morning." She leaned forward, one elbow on the bar, bringing them into friendly conspiracy. "At church too. Rumor is she found him in the back of the chapel after service, kissing someone else. Big scandal."

"Sounds like it." Nora turned over her shoulder to look at the girl, who had pulled out her phone and was typing something furiously, wiping tears from her eyes.

"Young love," Sophie sighed. "Everything stings more at that age."

"Yes, I remember my own. *Lord.* Shawn Joyner. So cute. So . . . wrong." Nora chuckled. "Man, it hurt when it ended. But then I met Dan."

"Where is Dan, by the way? Work?"

"He wishes, that would be better than what he's dealing with. No, Dan's got a bad case of the Sunday scaries—"

"Excuse me, he's got the what?" Sophie lifted an eyebrow in a delicate arch.

Nora leaned into the back of her stool. "You've never heard of the Sunday scaries?"

"Uh. No. Can't say that I have."

"He's hungover. Had a bit too much fun yesterday."

"Didn't we all. We're slow, as you can see." Sophie swept her arm in a long arc, taking in the mostly empty room, the pair of servers hanging over chairbacks like overgrown sloths, eyes dead with boredom. When she brought her gaze back to Nora, her dark eyes became darts, probing. "But you look alive."

"I had to work this morning," Nora said.

"I thought you had it off?"

"I did, but I got called in. Which, I had a feeling I might, so I cut myself off early yesterday. Right around the time I saw you, actually."

"Damn. That sucks. Don't tell me you were out in the alley earlier then? They call you in for that?" Sophie ducked down below the bar. Nora heard a tinkle of glass, the scrape of jars and bottles sliding past one another.

"Not for that specifically, but yes, I was the one who took the call."

"Shit. That gives me the creeps. To think, he's been out there all this time, and no one noticed. Y'all have any idea who he was?"

Sophie rose, and Nora had the sudden impression that she was being studied. She wiped her tired eyes with the back of her hand. "Well, no. There wasn't much left of him, to be honest. But Murph thinks he might have been a man named Trent Gibson. Homeless. Stayed around here sometimes."

"Oh yes, I know Trent." Sophie, who'd been pouring something into a tin, looked up to meet Nora's eyes with her own. It might have been a trick of the candlelight, bouncing off her silver shaker, but

Nora thought she saw a gleam in Sophie's gaze that felt . . . *wrong*. That was the only word she could think of. It appeared out of some dark depth of her, like a lamp bobbing at the far end of a tunnel, breaking at the liquid surface of her eye in a quick glimmer, gone as soon as it appeared. She held Nora's look for a minute, then turned her head back down to her work, rolling the edge of a glass in a dish of salt, her hands careful and soft on its stem.

"You do?"

"Oh yeah, I've known Trent a long time. Everyone that works around here does. He used to follow us girls to our cars after work, ask if he could buckle us in."

"Uh . . ."

"Yeah. But we figured he was harmless. Now that I think of it though, I haven't seen him in a few weeks. I guess I assumed he'd just found somewhere warm to go for the winter—one year he made it all the way out to California—Oakland, he told me. Came back with a tan and everything. Itinerant lifestyle. You never know where they end up. I envied him a little."

"Being cold and wet and hungry?" Nora said.

"Okay, I envied him in theory." Sophie placed the drink on the bar in front of Nora. "Cheers."

"What's this?"

"Your consolation prize, for being the responsible one—a new recipe I've been playing with."

The front end was wonderfully salty, a bite that slapped Nora's face a bit, made her sit up straighter in her chair. A wash of fresh citrus, lemon or grapefruit, Nora thought, smoothed through the middle, brightening the salt, lifting its fist away from her tongue. It was a pleasant feeling of standing alone at the hem of a sunny ocean, watching foam wash up over her feet. At the bottom was something musky that she couldn't quite put her finger on. Pickles or olives, a flavor with a weight, a cool tide pool hidden from the baked shoreline. She closed her eyes, felt herself sink into the cushioned stool.

"So, should I put it on my summer list?" Sophie's voice was glittering sunlight on her cocktail ocean.

Nora took another sip before she answered. "I'm no lush, but I vote yes. A nice warm night out on the patio . . . this would be perfect. Does it have a name?"

"Hey, Future Wifey!" An aproned man stepped around the corner that Nora realized must lead to the kitchen. His face was flushed red, a gleam of sweat shining on his balding brow.

"Excuse me," Sophie said, the sunlight in her voice dimming.

Nora watched them. Sophie standing with her arms crossed, a levy against the angry torrent of the man now waving a ticket around in front of her face. He punched it once, with a hard finger, to make his point. Nora thought she heard the words *manager* and *Lindsey* spat from his mouth. He pointed to the girl at the front stand, still crying over her phone, and then to the two servers, who had suddenly found something on the floor very interesting. Through it all, Sophie stayed quiet, nodding occasionally but otherwise as still as a cat in the grass. Nora knew that look; she had often pulled such a costume over herself. It was the look of a woman who knew how to burrow deep inside her own mind, let the hollow cocoon of her skin harden into a punching bag.

After a few minutes, the man stopped and walked into the kitchen, apparently satisfied with whatever answer she had given. Sophie was on her way back to the bar when she was intercepted, this time by one of the two servers on the floor. The girl dragged her over to a computer, her eyes wide, hands wringing through themselves. Some feet away, a family glowered from their table. Sophie's hands flew from her sides, spidering in quick steps across the computer face. She printed something out, handed it to the flustered server, and walked over to the table, her mask a sweet smile now, a nod of deepest concern for another man, this one seated at the table, who spent a few minutes scolding her for whatever small injustice had been meted out to him during his dinner.

Nora took another swallow of her drink, let the ocean pull her back to its wide shore.

"Sorry about that," Sophie said a few minutes later, as she skirted back behind the bar. To Nora she had the look of a half-deflated balloon, stretched and strained and puckered, but the gleam in her eye had returned, now something harder and brighter; the sort of steel women found hidden in their backbones. Nora had seen it before, flashing in her siren lights or gleaming under the fluorescent screen of a hospital room. That sort of steel was the end of a rope, the very same rope she'd been feeling the frayed tip of herself lately.

"No worries at all. Looked like you had your hands full."

Sophie took a sip from a plastic cup she had tucked into the rail. "Perks of being the responsible one, right? Getting shit on by everyone and not getting paid any extra for it. Love it. Thank you, Ty."

"What happened?"

Sophie shoved her cup down into the liquor well and blew out a puff of frustration. "It's just a slow night. Servers are bored silly, and I can really only nag them so much to do their jobs before they start calling me a bitch. And, to be honest, on a slow Sunday night, there's not much to do. We're stocked; we've done as much cleaning as we can with customers on the floor. It's easier to let them sit and gossip than pick at them to look busy. So, then they make stupid mistakes because they're bored, and I get yelled at by the kitchen because somehow that has anything to do with me. And my hostess, well, she really shouldn't be on her phone, but to be honest, I'm just glad she showed up at all tonight, so I'm not going to yell at her about it, even if Chef thinks I should.

"This isn't even my job. But Ty blows off whenever he wants to, or in today's case, is hungover. I'm the only one who's been here long enough to be trusted to handle the floor, so I get to be 'acting manager' on nights like this. They love to make a big deal of it, like getting the computer codes and the door keys is some huge achievement. But will I get paid for it? Nope." She took a breath. "Sorry. Jesus. *I'm the* bartender. I should be the one listening to you bitch, not the other way around."

"No, I know exactly how you feel." Nora sighed. "They've got me straddling two desks at work, so I'm getting it from all sides. Guys think I took their job, and Murph, God love him, he talks my ear off some days. Half the time I'm patrol, but then I'm getting dragged over to homicide, which is where I'd rather be, where I was hired to be, if I'm honest. I know they can't afford to put me there full-time right now; Murph's got decades of experience, and we're short-staffed, and our funding keeps getting cut, and it's just not the right timing. But I'm really getting worn thin..

"And then today, having to come in on my day off, which I knew, I *knew* I wouldn't get off, because I saw Cruz wasted yesterday . . . Yeah, I know how you feel. Bitch away."

"You working tomorrow?" Sophie asked, her voice open, an invitation.

"No, thank God. Why?"

"I'll be off in"—Sophie checked her watch—"about an hour. Not much to clean up tonight. You want to come over to my house? I've got a few bottles here past their prime, was just going to bring them home and drink them myself, but I'm happy to share. Been a long time since I've had a girls' night. Unless you're tired. I know you've had a day. You're welcome to sleep on my couch, by the way."

Nora thought about it. It had been a long day, but it would always be a long day. Dan was passed out for the night, and if she went home, what would she do? Just watch crap television alone? She caught Sophie's eye, and for just a glimmer of a moment she thought she saw something roiling under the surface of the woman's face. Almost a buzzing. Sophie smiled, and Nora realized she just must have been excited to make a friend, if they could call themselves friends now. She felt it too, the jitters at finding a mind she clicked with. Nora didn't have too many female friends, so each one she found felt like a gift, not something to be tossed away.

She smiled back. "No, that sounds nice. I mean, I am tired, but I took a nap earlier. Let's do it. Before you close up though, maybe I should eat something, and—sorry to be a pain, can I get some more water? This was great"—she tapped the rim of her cocktail glass—"but one more and I'll be on my ass. What do you call it, anyway?"

Sophie leaned across the bar, her eyes a joke shared, a warm handshake. "Men's Tears."

An Anatomist

Fruit, juices, ice, syrups, brine: these are the things that make up the spine of a bar. I build it up each day. First, the base, the sacral ice, bucket after bucket poured into the shining gullet of my waiting well. The trick to a bar is to keep everything cool; the fruit turning as slowly as possible, the juice kept from going sour, the liquor chilled and frosty in your shot glass. A bar is in a constant state of battle, against rot and decay, the puffed clouds of fruit flies burrowing into anything warm and dark. We must have perfect preservation, though this comes at the cost of my fingertips. After years of this work, I no longer have any qualms about plunging my hands into a bucket of ice, to fish out a beer bottle or search for the scoop. The pain goes away after a while.

Scale the steps of this spine with me, build up the rest. There are your juices, freshly squeezed or poured from a Minute Maid carton; each in its own bottle, a green storm pour for lime, red for cranberry, yellow for lemon. The simple syrup we keep in a squeeze bottle, along with her sisters the various berry cordials; grapefruit and pineapple stay in their cans, shut away in the humming dark of the refrigerator. Beside them on the floor, only used for middle-aged housewives and millennial women who want to seem daring, sits the cervical piece of this spine: the jar of brine.

It's simple enough. First, build an ocean: salt and water. Can you taste it? The grit in your mouth when a wave sucks you down.

I use a thirty-two-ounce glass jar, the size of two pint glasses and just big enough that I won't run out on a busy night, but not so big the solution skunks before I can use it. Why don't you use the juice from the olive jar? I hear you asking. That would be the simplest solution. But those jars are as big as two of my heads and can take weeks to go through. Hand after hand after hand diving in, pulling out fistfuls of olives, leaving behind skin and dirt, the assorted droppings of cellular life. You could wear a glove, but that's hardly better. The juice still goes bad, after weeks of being exposed to air, assaulted by hands, jostled and jiggled and poured. There's no control. No care. Do I seem like that sort of person to you?

The trick to brine is balance, of salt, of water, of air. Like a knife, it has a tang, a point of still perfection. Find it. Hold it on the tip of your tongue.

Salt, water, more salt, when you think it's done, add more. Enough to float an olive or a bit of celery. Enough to crawl inside the bacteria who'd think to make a home in your aquatic terrarium; crawl inside and crack them open, until their mouths tear in half. There's no room for life in the brine, no space for yeast to gorge themselves unless you've got a stinking, gloopy mess. A brine jar is quiet; a brine jar holds its breath and dips a finger into your cocktails with its eyes half-closed.

You can store things in your brine. We in the industry like to call this Craft or Artisanal. It sounds good, right? Into my Artisanal Brine go olives, of course, for dirty martinis. Celery for Bloody Marys. Or cucumbers, capers, if your tastes bend that way; south of the Mason-Dixon we prefer okra. Pack them in salt for a few minutes; long enough to steep a cup of tea or slice some lemon wedges. This will draw out excess water, keep your green firm and fresh for that crisp snap. Stop them from polluting the brine. Blot the crust away when you're done.

Press them down into the jar, as many as you can. The trick is to keep them submerged. Air is your enemy here. Air is breath, and breath is yeast and spoilage, an over-sour curdling in the soft pockets of your cheeks.

Before I leave for the night, I drop in the tongue. This one sliced from that poor bow-tied boy while he lay beneath my apple trees. With the handle of a spoon, I prod it down to the bottom, where it sits next to my alley man's, and beneath them both, now ragged and pale, Mark's.

I decided that spring to make a new drink, a spin on that favored classic, the margarita. I call it Men's Tears. Tequila, a bit of lemon, a drop of grapefruit, a splash of my special brine. Served straight up in a chilled glass. Twist of lemon for a bit of bright zing. The name alone was enough to make it popular.

Store in a cool, dark place. Good for one month.

Nora

It almost felt like a crime, so long had it been since Nora had sat on a couch and giggled with a friend. Where had the time gone? Why had that stopped? She thought about that as she curled back into the fat arm of Sophie's overstuffed couch; their legs tangled together on the center cushion, half-drunk glasses of wine cupped in each of their hands. It wasn't that she didn't have friends. It was that life happened. Work happened. Husbands and families, the steady distilling of days until she looked up and found herself quite alone in a new town, her only company men. She hadn't realized how much she'd missed girl-friends until she met Sophie.

"It's warm in here, isn't it? Let me open a window." Sophie, who had just been laughing about something a customer said, lifted herself gingerly off the couch and moved to a bay window some feet away, where a handful of ivory-white flowers slumped out of a clay pot. She brushed them gently aside, heaved the old pane up. It cracked and wheezed, shuddering with movement; frog song rushed into the room.

"I just love the sound of peepers, don't you?" Sophie said, settling back into her end of the couch.

"This is such a beautiful house, Sophie. You're so lucky to live here," Nora sighed. She was trying to drink slow, but the wine was going to her head all the same.

"Believe me, I'm aware. Here, finish this bottle with me." Without waiting for Nora's reply, she split the last swallow of the red they'd been sharing between each of their glasses. "Cheers, lady."

It felt rude to refuse. "Cheers."

Sophie picked up the thread of their conversation. "I can't believe Mom didn't want the house, but I was glad to take it over. This little farm's been in the family for generations. Since the 1700s, I think? Something like that. Scotch-Irish riffraff, came out to the edge of the world to see what they could do. Same as everyone else around here. White-bread."

"My family too," Nora said, and then seeing the question in Sophie's eyes, she clarified, "My momma. She's got some German also, I think. But who knows. I'm a mutt."

"I guess we all are. I think that's the point, right? Our great 'melting pot.' All those immigrants, searching for the American Dream."

"They weren't all 'immigrants.'"

"No." Sophie's eyes grew bigger than her voice. "No, I guess you're right."

For a moment, the women fell quiet, the only sound in the room the songs of a thousand spring peepers, singing love songs to one another in the night. Nora wanted to open her mouth, shove her foot in. She wondered if a wedge would fall between them now, as it did sometimes when the rotted bones of this beautiful place jutted up out of their grave.

"Can I ask you a question?" Sophie said. Her eyes in the half-light of the living room were dark and steady, like the face of a deep lake in summer; no matter how still and calm it lay, there was always the promise, the threat, of something hidden beneath.

"Go for it."

"You're a cop. Why? I mean, I watch the news. I listen. Forgive me if I'm blundering, but . . . well, I'm blundering . . ." She wedged her glass into the couch, lifted her hands in defeat.

Nora took a long swallow of her wine. She'd had this question posed to her before, and she wasn't shocked it was coming up now, but it was always something tricky to answer. A question like that came with baggage; no one asked it without expectations. This budding friendship was a precious thing to Nora; she wanted to tread carefully.

"Sophie, did you know that during the Reconstruction Era, Virginia actually had one of the lowest numbers of lynchings among Southern states?"

"I did not."

"She did." She finished her wine, set the glass aside. The peeper song swelled around them. Nora waited for it to burst, to fan out to join the chorus of crickets that was rising in the background, before she continued. "It wasn't from some altruistic love of Black people. It wasn't decency or morality. It was because she was using the *courts*— judges, jails, the cops, they were arresting innocent people on trumped-up charges and then executing them. Kept Virginia looking clean while doing the same fucked-up work."

"Shit. I had no idea," Sophie said.

"Most people don't. After I made it through the academy, I called my brother—he lives up in D.C.—and you know what he said?"

Sophie waited, her eyes locked on Nora's.

"He said he was glad I got the uniform, that there was at least one cop on the road he didn't have to worry about when he comes home to visit. That broke my heart. And pissed me off. I want to live, I need to live, in a world where those sorts of conversations don't have to happen."

For the second time that night, the barometric pressure in the room seemed to drop. Nora peered across the expanse of legs and pillows between them and found that Sophie's eyes were as still and dark as ever, a lake pulled in, waiting for storm clouds. The woman pressed her lips together, cocked her head to one side.

"So you're fixing things." In other mouths, those words might have been an accusation or a joke.

Nora shrugged. "World needs fixing. Not just the cops, all of it. The violence, the deaths, the giving up I've seen in people."

Sophie was quiet for a minute, staring at the wine in her glass that she swirled first one way, then another, slow and thoughtful. When she finally looked back up, the deep well of her eyes had caught life, sunlight playing over rippled waters. "I admire that, people who do something about a problem. Too many of us complain and complain, but no one's willing to get their hands dirty. And how can anything change if we don't put our boots on the ground? Right? I like to think I'm a problem solver myself." She drained her glass. "Another?"

"Was that the problem? An empty glass?"

"According to my customers it is."

Nora laughed. "Of course. But no, thank you. I'll have some tea if you've got it. And maybe a glass of water. I should sober up before I head home."

"Oh please, you're hardly tipsy compared to half the people driving home right now." Sophie rose from the couch, took Nora's empty glass from her hand.

"That's what I worry about."

"Fair enough. Tea it is . . . So." Her voice echoed as she walked into the kitchen. Nora heard glass tap the steel bottom of a sink, the rush of water belching from a faucet. Sophie threw her thoughts over her shoulder. "Let's talk about something else . . . How did you meet Dan? I don't think you've told me that story yet."

"Oh gosh, you don't want to hear that." Nora chuckled.

"Of course I do." The teakettle was filled, dropped onto the stove.

"Only if you promise not to laugh."

"Pinky swear."

"Well," Nora began, "it's embarrassing, but our life is basically a country song. My daddy worked—still works—at a big farm over the mountain. Horses and cattle. Hay during the season. And Dan showed up one summer, just before his junior year. We went to the same high school, but he was older than me and we ran in different circles, so our paths never really crossed."

"And?"

"I worked out there mornings in the summer. He'd say hi, help me muck or pull in horses in the morning, but if I'm honest, I think he was afraid of my daddy. Never really talked to me for the first year or two."

"Every boy around here's afraid of a girl's daddy." The teapot began to burble and hiss. The hint of a whistle peeped out of its mouth.

Nora laughed. "Yeah . . . I don't know. One day, we just started talking, and we haven't stopped."

"Surely there's more to the story than that." The kettle was whining now. Sophie pulled it off the heat; Nora heard her reach into her cabinet for a cup. "Or else this sounds like an awfully boring country song. Black, green, or mint?"

"Mint, please," Nora said. She didn't know how to explain how her passing curiosity for the boy with the nice smile became something bigger. She wasn't quite sure herself. "If I had to pick a moment, I'd say it really started when he caught me trying to dump a water trough one morning. It was heavy, almost full, but one of the cows had shit in it so it needed to be cleaned. A hundred gallons of water, and there I was doing my best to rock the trough until it tipped over. I don't know if you've ever tried that?"

"I've lifted kegs, so I have some idea." Sophie walked back into the room, Nora's steaming cup of tea in her hand.

"Thanks. And, well, Dan saw me struggling and came over to help." She'd noticed the freckles on his nose for the first time that day, dusting down across his cheeks. And the tan lines on his arms, peeking out from under his shirtsleeves when he moved.

He'd helped her dump and scrub, and after, he'd sat on that peeling black fence line with her while they watched the trough fill back up, the hose spitting out water in a lazy whirl. They kissed for the first time a week or two later at that same water trough, both of them sopping wet and smiling after a hose battle of epic proportions. And that was it, they'd never looked back. What they had was a simple bond built in childhood, nothing messy, nothing complicated. It worked.

Sophie cocked an eyebrow. "Most people would say that was sweet, not embarrassing. You were the damsel in distress, and he rode in on his white horse."

Nora felt herself flush under the weight of Sophie's words, the accusation she felt waiting under her tongue. "Something like that, I guess. But . . . I mean, he knew I could have dumped that trough myself, but he wanted to be helpful. He's just like that—kind."

"I have a hard time believing any men are kind."

"No men? What about your daddy?"

Sophie laughed, a short screeching bark, then put her hand to her throat. "Excuse me, caught me off guard there." She choked up a cough. "My daddy left, a long time ago. Got bored with us, I guess. Started a new family somewhere, I don't know, I've never met them. I've only spoken to him maybe a handful of times since then, and every time I have, I walk away feeling small. Getting angry now just thinking of him, actually. He's like a fucking vampire—even when he's not in the room he manages to suck all the life out of it."

"I'm sorry to hear that."

"It is what it is. Anyways, I'm tired of talking about him. And I'm a little drunk, so . . . Look, Nora. Can I be honest with you?"

"You mean you haven't been?" Nora cocked an eyebrow, leaned back against the couch. The tea in her hands was warm; she felt good here, tucked into this house.

"You know what I mean." Sophie's eyes glittered. Just the candlelight, bouncing off the steam, Nora told herself. She couldn't ignore the hackles on her neck though, which had suddenly stood up, alert.

"Shoot."

"You see them, right? The women."

"Excuse me?"

"The dead women. I feel them. Everywhere. Hear them, tugging on my ears, whispering. Hell, I can't pass certain places in this town without a face or a memory reaching out for me. But you know what I mean, I think. They haunt you too, don't they? I've seen it in your eyes, the way you carry your shoulders. Sometimes I swear I've caught a shadow tripping behind you, climbing up your back."

When the shock wore off, Nora took a breath, said, "My momma called them haints. 'People who died with questions in their mouths,' she used to say. And yeah, I see them. Not all of them dead in the corporeal way, but dead inside somewhere, where no one can reach. It sounds cliché, right? A cop who sees ghosts. But I do. It's part of the job. They're not real, but they are, right?"

"I know exactly what you mean."

"Thankfully, I don't think most people do."

Sophie grew real still. Her voice, when she spoke, was thin, a snake slicing through cold water. "I think women do."

"You might be right about that." A chorus of voices filled Nora's heart. Not the thin, rattling ones she heard at night, but something richer. Warnings passed between friends, her momma's early lessons on the safety of her own body, the lessons from girlhood: Don't leave your drink unattended, walk with your keys between your fingers, loose hair is harder to grab than a ponytail, text me when you get home. Women did know, didn't they? They saw these ghosts every day, whether or not they recognized the steady hum in their minds as the haunting it was. Because underneath each warning, each tale, was a ghost.

Nora looked up, caught Sophie's eyes. The woman was sitting very still on the couch, watching her, gauging her reaction. Then she leaned forward, asked, "What about Mark? Does he haunt you too? Trent? Did they die with questions in their mouths?"

Nora let herself sink into the black pool she found looking back at her. "No. I don't think so. And I can't help but think that maybe they deserved what was coming to them."

"That's because all men are the same, Nora. Mark, Ty, my father—I bet even your Dan, if you really thought about it. They break things. Thoughtlessly. They're cruel. They're childish." Her mouth was set in a hard line, her eyes glittering with tears or anger, maybe both, Nora couldn't tell. Sophie, it seemed, had reached the part of drinking where everything got heavy and wet. She tossed back the last of her wine and, face scrunched in disgust, said, "They should all be thrown in the goddamn trash."

Nora sat back against her arm of the couch. She knew that anger. The sort her daddy would have warned her about, the kind that had a mouth and teeth and consumed you whole. She felt it herself some days. And if she was honest, in some ways Mark had earned that end, living as he had. But she would not feed that anger here, not tonight. She took a slow sip, heard her daddy's words roll out of her mouth: "No one is trash, Sophie, not even Mark. If I've learned one thing in my job, it's that all *people* are the same. Men do most of the killing, yes, but women can be just as cruel. Manipulative, nasty, violent in a different way. We all need the same things, want the same things. I might not talk to God as much as I should, but I know we're all sinners. And we all deserve grace."

Sophie's gaze sank back into its depths and she smiled, the stale, plastic grin of rush hour. "I think on that point, we may have to agree to disagree."

They sat on the couch for a while longer, Nora sipping her tea and Sophie swirling her wine. The air around them hung raw with the work of exposing delicate things, and Nora found she didn't quite know what she was feeling, that she was glad for the sudden quiet. Sophie's anger unnerved her; she pulled her tea mug closer, let the steam wash over her face.

Her

There's a bridge at the eastern edge of my property, stretching over the creek where it gurgles and trips around soapstone and quartz, pushing fish along a swift current, before dropping down into still pools on the other side. This is where she died.

You know her. She is me, and your mother, the woman you pass on the street. You've seen her face in the newspaper or flashing by on your TV screen, heard the whispered rumors. Her husband caught her cheating. Or maybe she caught him. He was drunk, or high, or angry, or scared. He waited out here by the creek, or he dragged her here, by her hair. Maybe he found her and her lover here, wrapped around each other among the willow roots.

You'll already have guessed. He killed her. Drowned her, stabbed her, beat her with a rock. Dumped her body here in the water under the bridge, where in this shallow grave she grew pale and cold and blue. Perhaps he weighed her down so that when the gasses finally filled her stomach, she didn't burst upward and bob down the creek toward town. Her hair, whatever color it was, would have grown black with muck and slime, tangled itself like reeds around the slick rocks squatting in the current. Eventually the fish would eat enough of her that she'd come apart, float away in bits and pieces. A hand caught in the bend just south of town, a few of her teeth fished out by curious possums or squirrels; perhaps her necklace is left behind, flashing dappled light on sunny days, impossible to tell apart from the sparkling water it was lost in.

There is some of her though that will never go away, no matter how hard they scrub. Something of her clings to the rusting underbelly of this bridge, rattling when you or I or a car crosses over, reaching silent fingers and toes up over the creaking wood to poke at ankles. Her moans too creep up through the cracks.

On especially dark and misty nights, my uncle once told me as we bumped over the creek on our way home from the county fair, she hauls herself all the way up to the road and stands there, waiting for cars to catch her in their headlights. I used to hide my eyes when we crossed that bridge, afraid to see the face I knew would be looking back at me from the sheets of mist lying over the muddy water below.

But there's nowhere to hide. She's under every bridge in this town, in every town from the salty tidewater marshes to Appalachian hollers. She's in songs and campfire stories, in police reports and ragged home-printed posters flapping off telephone poles. You watch her for horror, for fun, to learn something, to feel alive.

I'm not afraid of her anymore. I am the multitudes of her now. Hungry mouths hanging open.

If you see me, pray.

MayandJune

The New Kid

Got a new one for you." Murph tossed a file across her desk. "Brody Samuels. Disappeared at the very same races you failed to enjoy."

Nora looked up from her desk, which had of late become a confusing mishmash of folders and paperwork, scraps from candy wrappers, a permanent ring marring the corner where her daily coffee habit had become something more akin to an addiction.

"Hasn't been seen in a week, and he's supposed to be graduating from UVA on the sixteenth."

Nora looked down at the boy's face, now staring up at her from a grainy printout of a social media photo. He looked like every other Southern bro she'd ever known: worn baseball hat over sunglasses, bow tie, khaki pants and flip-flops, and painted over it all an aura of easy confidence only boys like him enjoyed. In the photo, his arm was raised, a bottle of whiskey clutched tight in his fingers. He looked a bit like Dan. *All men are the same.* The thought was a punch; she pushed it away with a question: "You think he panicked? Got nervous about graduation and ran?"

"It's possible," Murph said. "I've seen it before. Kid maybe doesn't get as good grades as they need, misses out on an internship or job, and they skip town to avoid facing Mom and Dad. Also possible he went out and had a bit too much fun. Boys his age do that. They usually show back up before a week passes, but I've seen stranger in my time, especially with these rich kids who can afford to just book it somewhere."

"He have a girlfriend? Best friend? Someone he'd be in touch with?"

"He left his phone up at the truck with his friends."

"Okay, now that's weird."

"My thoughts exactly."

"And the river's not near Montleigh, is it? He could have wandered off to piss or something, fallen in."

"Already got two of the guys out there walking it, but I don't think so. This time of year, it's still pretty shallow, and it's far enough away from the main site, he would have really had to wander. Kids don't do that when they're partying."

"Right." A thought tapped Nora behind the ear, cold fingers, a ragged whisper. That long hair clutched tight in the dead boy's hand. She looked up at Murph. "Do you think there's any connection to the others?"

Murph rocked back on his heels. "Until we find a body, it's best not to assume anything."

"Yes, but—"

"I got it, Martin." He held up a hand. "I'm keeping all options open, and I need you to as well. This case is totally different. Kid disappeared in a crowded place, broad daylight."

"Well, to be fair, we don't know if two of the other three also weren't killed in broad daylight. That kid on the tracks—"

"That kid on the tracks was most likely a horrific accident."

"He was holding a hair, which we are still waiting for results from."

"And I bet if you searched me with a fine-toothed comb you'd find a dozen of my wife's hairs on my body too. You women shed like dogs, no offense. Now, come back to this case." He punched the photo with a hard finger. "Let's work on what's in front of us. We'll keep everything in mind. Truthfully, I do think there's something odd going on here. Three decades at my desk and I've never seen anything like this before."

"You mean men dying."

"Usually it's women."

That truth squatted, thick, between them.

"So," he continued, "you got anything else pressing to do today?"

Nora looked down at her stack of papers. There were reports to sign for social workers, tickets to write up, notes she needed to organize before her monthly court date. There was a lot she should be doing right now.

"C'mon, Martin. Get up, let's go. I'll tell Sarge you're with me for your last hour of shift. You can do paperwork at home, can't you?"

"I can," Nora said, a finger of pain jabbing behind her eyes.

Murph didn't stick around to wait for her answer. He was already down the hall, popping into the sergeant's office.

Dan was gone by the time Nora pulled into their drive. His night shifts had worked while she'd been on beat, their schedules overlapping enough that they could at the very least spend one day a week lying on the couch together like a pair of slugs. Her schedule was changing though, the more Murph insisted she come under his wing. Her late nights became early mornings; her weekends, once crowded with drunk drivers and rowdy teenagers, were now more often than she'd like lonely spaces, wide-open and hollow. Lately if she saw Dan, it was for nothing more than a quick kiss in the hall on her way out the door.

He always left dinner for her though, the nights he worked, tucked safely in the fridge with a note detailing his exciting day watching Netflix or revealing his newest dad joke. Tonight's entertainment matched the dish he'd made: *Hey, Nor, what do you call a lying noodle?* She flipped over the sticky note and rolled her eyes with a smile. *An imPASTA.*

Dinner was quick and lonely, taken in front of a blaring TV screen. Made-up women flounced around on a beach somewhere in Costa Rica or perhaps Mexico, Nora wasn't sure. She watched them wrap themselves around a smooth-chested man like starfish, and she wondered if it hurt him when he pried their arms off his tan skin. After an hour, he picked one to walk down the beach with toward a lovely candlelit dinner, while the rest pouted, breasts and lips pressed up in childish distress.

She tried to pay attention. Dan would want to know who won this week, who caused the juiciest drama, who had the best crocodile tears. He lived for this brainless entertainment. Nora couldn't blame him; his working life was awash with blood and crying and vomit, the acrid stink of gallons of sanitizer. His drama, like hers, was deadly and unpredictable. Unlike her, he found an outlet in these stupid shows. Nora didn't care for them much; she heard enough of white women screeching at work. But for him she'd watch and do her best to remember. She was grateful for small favors—at least tonight wasn't something about housewives.

The day picked at her though, at a frequency floating just below the TV images. It thrust sharp fingernails up under the edge of her thoughts, tugging and yanking her attention away from the screen.

They'd found nothing when they went to speak to Brody's friends, other than the usual collegiate turmoil. He was stressed about finals and graduation; he'd broken up with a long-term girlfriend some months before and since then had engaged in a string of casual hookups. He probably partied too much, but didn't they all? Nothing was out of place in his room, no desperate journal entries betraying a troubled mind, no meds not being taken. By all accounts, Brody Samuels had been a perfectly normal twenty-two-year-old boy.

Murph insisted she be the one to speak to his parents. "This is going to be your job one day soon, Martin. Might as well get used to it now, while I'm here if you need."

But how did you explain to a mother that her child had simply vanished? That wasn't something they'd covered in the academy. How was she to tell this woman that they'd searched, and asked questions, and come up with hands filled with empty air? How could she tell a mother that he was an adult, and sometimes adults did strange things, and there was nothing more they could do until they found anything solid to hold on to? Mrs. Samuels had cried, right there on the phone. Wailed. And Nora felt her heart pierce with a grief she hoped she'd never fully understand.

"I'm sorry, ma'am. We'll keep looking. We're sending a team out to the racetrack to search for anything—we'll find him." She didn't need to ask if the other woman felt the promise as hollow as she had. Some days her job made her into a liar, and she hated that about it.

Appetite ruined, Nora retreated to the comfort of her bedroom, her dinner left half-eaten on the couch. She'd deal with it in the morning.

The woman's weeping had followed her all the way home. She heard it now, in the breeze howling through the open window. She heard something else too. They were there, shimmering on the fringes of her vision, pulling themselves up over her bed on spindly arms, tapping fingers on the back of her neck. Right now, she needed to try to sleep.

Maybe if she could just sleep, they'd go away.

Psyche Prays at Nones

The boy under the tree roots burst into a brilliant green; the result, I have read, of the hemoglobin in his blood breaking down. Most people don't turn a shade quite so reminiscent of the Wicked Witch, but it's not outside the realm of possibility. In the next weeks, I watched him molt, chartreuse melting into muddy yellow, finally brown and black, oozing into the earth that cradled him. His eyes protruded. His tongue, if he'd had one, would have flopped out. I watched his hair and fingernails grow and his skin shrink around the scaffolding of his bones. One by one, they pierced through. He became a cathedral, shafts of dim sunlight sweeping down into hallowed halls. His congregation all the swarming life of insects, come to take communion in their mouths.

Like a fox, I crawled into my den for a rest; let the summer heat tug me down to a nap in the shade or a long afternoon with my feet in the creek, reading books aloud to the man who lay moldering under the willow tree. The bees danced out to join me. They built a hive in his rib cage; by midsummer, honey dripped out the hollow sockets of his eyes.

Nora

They always called Nora in for this sort of thing. She was the only woman on staff, and they needed a woman, for these sorts of calls. The boys stood in the driveway, leaning backward the way men do when they're carrying the weight of a holster and beer belly on their hips; thumbs jammed around their belts, fingers splayed in a threat. *The gun is a twitch of my hand away, not even a full second's thought. Do you really want to move?* Their faces were grim, mouths set into stiff lines. Their eyes were covered by sleek black sunglasses that flashed in the glaring sun. Impenetrable. Inhuman. Nora would never understand how some cops couldn't see why people were unnerved by them. How would they have felt, if they saw themselves knocking at their door?

That was the problem. They couldn't see themselves, or they refused to. And that was why they brought her in.

The boys looked up when they heard her approach: two identical frowns, two buzz cuts, two shining silver badges pinned to twin chests, standing still as statues as she walked toward them, waiting for her to step close enough for them to swoop down over her like vultures on a deer carcass.

"Here's the situation . . ." They pecked with sharp beaks; their voices dug finger-claws into her arms, pinning her there under their shadows, cast by the too-bright noon sun.

Nora listened and nodded, reminded herself to breathe, a necessary chore in the new summer heat. The days, which up until then had at least been cool in their later hours, had grown a sort of skin, had begun to sweat and pant and clot up the slick branches of lungs; run salty, stinging fingers down into eyes. Each movement had a weight. So did every word, so she guarded hers for the time.

". . . called about an hour ago, after she heard shouts coming from the house next door."

"Coming from this house. The neighbor who called is next door."

"Yes, of course."

Peck peck. Peck peck peck. Are you listening? We need you now. *Listen.*

Are you listening? The haints joined in, their voices a rasp on the back of her neck. *Do you hear us in the night, painting our stories onto your skin? Listen, Nora, listen. Listen!*

The air just in front of her forehead became a crowded place, black wings cawing and flapping, pecking, memories pushing through whispers piercing through the sharp snap of the boys' eyes behind their sunglasses. Nora felt a bead of sweat trickle between her breasts and resisted the urge to press it away. She didn't want them to see her melting, to turn her body against her more than they already had.

They continued. "She won't talk to us. Locked herself in the bathroom."

So that's why I'm here, Nora thought.

The blinds in a small window off the near side of the house flicked up. A pair of eyes sharp as pennies flashed in the open space before the blinds slammed down again, cold and hard. A punch, a warning. An animal backed into a corner. Nora felt a hand squeeze out a beat of her heart. The heat, the hard quiet, this was a day like the one they found Lauren Morris. When she had still been new to this town, wide-eyed and afraid to make a mistake, and the boys who crossed their arms and stared at her now were still treating her with kid gloves, unsure of how things would shake out. That was the day Murph made it known she was under his wing, and that was the day they built up their wall. Almost a year on, and it had only grown taller. But so had Nora.

"Where is he?" She looked over her shoulder, as if she expected the man to walk forward, his hand raised like a student answering a question in class. *It's me, miss! I'm the one who beats my wife!*

The sunglasses turned to a shabby cedar leaning cockeyed over the end of the driveway. Hidden in its drooping branches sat a man, wary, watching them with hooded eyes and arms crossed tight over his chest.

"He said anything?"

"Only that he didn't do anything."

"Of course. How's he look?"

"Got a few scratches on his arm, but he says the dog bit him this morning; apparently got between the thing and its food dish. They've scabbed over, but could be more fresh than he's telling us. We'll have to get a look at her to know."

A motley flock of neighbors were gathered just beyond the property line. The quiet buzz of their curious whispers rose into the air like cicada song. There was blood in the water here, and they smelled it. Overhead, a knot of turkey vultures wheeled in the bone-white sky. There must be a dead thing, Nora thought, a dead thing in the woods behind the house.

"You want me to come with you?" one of the sunglasses asked.

"No. What's her name?"

"Mrs. Massey."

"Her first name." She made her voice a slap, hoped that shamed them into something like respect. The heat had frayed her nerves, and a headache was building behind her eyes. She was tired of being everyone's mom.

"Oh." One of the sunglasses looked to the other, who peered down at his notes.

"Tara. Tara Massey."

"All right then. I'll go talk to her." Nora left them. It was time to go do what she'd been brought in for.

The house was heavy. They were on the hem of Bellair's boundary line, where it began to bleed into wild country, where the poorer locals had been shunted when property taxes rose. She wondered how much longer this pocked dirt road would be allowed to exist. How many years before another developer rolled through and brought these people to their knees?

The thought pulled Nora down from the shoulders, coiled around her bones. More crumbling people, more rotting souls. *This should have been your inheritance, don't you know? Who are you, to reach for something more? To peer into these windows and rearrange the furniture of their lives?*

Stacks of mail were splayed out on a small side table near the front door. Nora peered down at them. Medical bills, phone bills, county tax, bank statements, credit cards, letters from the Virginia Employment Commission; stressors printed and shipped and stuffed into mailboxes, stacked onto tables, screaming quietly from the corner. They built up every day, didn't they? The guilt and shame and anger. *You are sick. This is what you owe us. Pay off your debt, watch your credit score drop anyway. That stone in the pit of your stomach? Get used to it. We own you. Beat your wife. You own her.*

Tara Massey was in the bathroom, just as the boys had said. And just as they needed her to, Nora knocked gently.

"Ma'am? Tara?"

The hard silence of shame beat against the back of the door.

Nora waited. She picked up one of the magazines splattered on the living room floor (April issue of *Women's Bow & Rifle*), and sat in the shabby La-Z-Boy to wait.

And wait.

And wait.

The vultures overhead were still wheeling; she could feel them, circling in wide arcs over the house. What was it they saw from up there? The neighbors milling around outside, murmuring and cackling, scraping feet over crushed gravel. The boys, leaning against their car, eyes shaded glossy black. And beneath it all, something dark and shivering, whispers in puddled shadows, nightmares pushing up on spindly legs.

There it was, all in clear sight of her mind, the birds circling black and silent, and below them, the catastrophe, the waiting. Everyone was waiting.

Nora sat in the middle of it. She had begun to feel stretched lately, worn like an old boot, stepped on and stomped on and run down until she felt herself fraying. She'd worked two jobs for too long— much more of this bouncing between desks and she'd fall apart. There was nothing to be done for it though. Short-staffed in the summer was a bad thing for a station. The heat meant more fights, more hungry kids out of school causing trouble they couldn't help, more one-eyed drivers spilling out of wineries after Friday-night music. Behind this, their faces dim but insistent, was a growing corps of men, howling underneath the roiling worries of her daytime mind. And they'd found *nothing*.

No, that wasn't true, she corrected herself. Not nothing. They'd found the bite of a knife on Mr. Gibson's jaw. Something small that would fit easily in the palm of her hand. Sharp, but not the best metal. It didn't slice through guts like butter; there was real force behind the blows. And it was smooth, no serrated hunting knife, no redneck good old boys' weapon.

And the hair. Only the one, wrapped up with their shakiest lead, true, but it was there. That was something. If only they'd get any tests to her soon, then she'd have something she could hold on to.

She was sure this college kid was one of them, but without a body, what could she do? He was an adult, and adults leave for all sorts of reasons. Maybe he was worried about exams, maybe he fought with a girl, maybe someone was lying, maybe he was lying somewhere with no tongue in his mouth.

One of the sunglasses, Bowles, came in. The screen door whined and slammed hard behind him as he stepped into the dank room, sat down on the couch catty-corner to her armchair. He didn't speak, but Nora noticed his foot tapping nervously. He wanted to finish this.

Not feeling like talking, she turned to look out the window.

The man beneath the cedars was standing. He'd moved to talk to one of the neighbors now, both of them laughing. The lone sunglasses outside walked over to them, took the man's hand in his own. *To gain his trust*, Nora knew. This was how men got business done. Still, she couldn't stop the thought that slipped up into her mind: What would he look like without a tongue? How many days would it take, in the coming heat, for him to blacken and burst open, a feast for maggots?

Shit.

The bathroom door cracked open, and a woman tottered out into the hallway. She was hunched in the way of someone used to hiding herself under too much weight. A baggy Tweety Bird T-shirt draped over her chest, hung down around her thighs.

"You can leave. We don't need you."

"Ma'am." Bowles stood; his shoulders filled the room. "If we find something happened between you two, if he hit you, we have to take him in. State doesn't give us a choice in the matter."

"I said I'm fine."

"Your husband's got scratches on his hand. Any idea how he came about those?"

"Damn dog bit him this morning. Idiot put his hand in her food dish, to tease her."

"Bowles," Nora began. They'd brought her in for this; they should let her lead.

He barged right through. "You sure that's what happened? You two get into squabbles quite often, the neighbors said. I've been married ten years, Mrs. Massey, I know how fights can get. You don't mean to, but maybe you reach out and scratch him while you're fighting over the TV remote, and then he hit you?"

The woman glared at him, and Nora found she had finally reached the end of that frayed rope she'd been dangling from.

"Ma'am." She put a hand up, blocking Bowles from speaking. "We're here to keep you safe. I know you love your husband, and we don't want to make anyone's life harder than it is. Looks like y'all got a lot on your plates." She waited for a nod, a smile, any sort of trust, but the woman just stared at her, an animal cornered in its own den. She heard Bowles lean forward on his toes. Before he could say anything, she continued. "Now, has anyone ever talked to you about domestic violence?"

"I'm not stupid."

"I don't believe you are. Plenty of smart women find themselves in terrible situations every day. We ladies just have to take care of each other, okay? And I can't leave before I know you're safe. If you'd rather my partner go back outside, he can do that; we can talk alone, just us girls."

Bowles became a stone, looming to her side. Nora hoped he was mad, then chided herself for being childish.

"I'm fine."

The answer she had known was coming had finally come. While she'd spoken, she'd swept her eyes over Tara Massey's face, searching for chinks in her armor. Had she splashed cold water on her face to soothe the tears, cool the bruise that would bloom there in a day, despite her best efforts? Mixed the colors her mother or sister or friend had taught her how to find on her makeup palette? Yellow to neutralize that first deep blue of a fresh contusion, green if the broken vessels are too close to the top and so the red was bright, and later, peach to brighten the dinge of an old bruise. This was the rainbow all little girls who grow up in sagging places learned by heart.

She looked as hard as she dared, but only a slight edge to the sheen in Tara's green eyes betrayed any distress in her face.

"Are you sure, Tara?" Nora asked. "I can stay here with you, for a while. Or we can find somewhere for you to go tonight—a friend's house, maybe? Or a family member?"

"We just had a spat, that's all. He was talking over my favorite show. Never shuts up, that man." She sighed. "But there was no fight. My neighbor, she likes to snoop. Thinks she's real important."

Later, as she climbed back into her car, Nora prayed she would never wake up to find this woman's face peering out from the shadows of her midnight living room.

Never shuts up.

Sometimes I wish they'd just shut up, you know?

The men had no tongues.

She scrambled for her phone, punched in Murph's number, her hands shaking, the fist in her heart hammering her chest. Above her, the vultures wheeled through the cloudless sky.

A Woman in Love

Dan took her out that night.

"My girl looked down," he'd said to Sophie when the bartender asked how their day was, his hand warm, rubbing Nora's lower back. They were seated at the far end of the bar, their legs crossed toward each other, knees touching, his feet playfully kicking at hers.

Sophie turned her attention to Nora. "Long day?"

"Long week."

"Well I think we can fix that for you, or at least help a bit. Men's Tears?"

Dan choked on his water. "Men's what?"

Nora laughed and squeezed his thigh. "It's a cocktail. Sophie's special, very secret recipe."

"If I tell you what's in it, I have to kill you."

Nora liked Sophie, but sometimes she really questioned the woman's sense of humor.

"Fair enough," Dan said, choosing to roll with the game. He glanced at Nora, winked. "Well, I don't feel like dying tonight, so let's skip that. You got a good pilsner on tap? I just want something refreshing, no bells or whistles. You, Nora?"

Nora looked down the line of taps, to the wine menu, and up to Sophie, waiting frozen for her answer. Dan tickled her sides with his fingers, and she squealed, shoved him away, her mind made up. "I think I'll have wine, Sophie. Anything red, I'm not picky. Can't do cocktails if Stupid over here's going to be trying to tickle me all night. One of your martinis puts me on my butt, and I'm going to need my wits to fight back."

Dan lifted an eyebrow, his lips pressed into a cockeyed grin. "Oh yeah?"

"You two are disgusting," Sophie said, before turning to make their drinks.

They looked at each other and laughed.

For the first time in a long time, they were kids again. Cracking jokes, coiling fingers through each other's hands, blushing and flirting and forgetting all the weight that had landed on their shoulders in the past year. They'd gotten so used to having each other as a security blanket, they'd forgotten what it was to just laugh together, to not have to introduce themselves to everyone around them, play Couple instead of just be coupled.

That night, sitting next to him at the Blue Bell, sharing drinks and plates and sometimes kisses, Nora fell in love with Dan again. He was her sweet boy, smiling next to her, their hands clasped tight together. Them against the world.

"Can I get y'all anything else?" Sophie asked some hours later, after the house lights came on and the little restaurant emptied.

Dan looked at Nora. "Want anything, babe?"

"Nah," she said. "Let's get out of Sophie's hair."

The check came and was paid by Dan. "Your daddy would murder me if he heard I took his daughter out on a date and didn't pay myself."

"Dan. We live together. I hardly think he'd care."

"Well, tonight I'm taking care of my girl." The matter was settled. He helped her down off the stool and, with twin goodbyes called to Sophie, they pushed out the door.

"Let me help you with your zipper, Nor," he said later, in the half-light of their bedroom. Nora, who'd been fussing with the thing, turned so he could reach it, tug the stubborn metal teeth open. His hands on her shoulders were soft. Her dress fell to the floor. A heartbeat later, his shirt joined it.

For the first time in a long time, their lovemaking was awake and sensuous. This was no half-asleep cuddle, two tired bodies coming together for a few quick moments before drifting off to sleep. Nora took Dan into all her heart and he pulled her close to his, and when he kissed her she cried, because she loved him and she'd missed this. He wiped her tears with his thumb and covered her with the full length of his body and, after a time, they fell into deep, dreamless sleep.

The haints prowling the room stood silent sentinel, their broken hearts bleeding in the presence of so much tenderness.

July

A Ghost Pulls Herself Together

July in Virginia is slow and sticky, her days pulled long like the taffy we used to buy down on ocean boardwalks, and just as salty sweet. She's a cinnamon month, held close in the mouth and heaving with spice, and there in the back a small, quiet sigh caught in the languid late afternoon. In July, silty creek banks flame yellow and white with forsythia, honeysuckle; the first ripened blackberries drip off thorny vines, tossing away delicate flower petals as they bulge into air as round as their bellies. They're my favorite then, in those early days; still sour and sharp, full of juice that stings the inside of cheeks.

The thunderheads build themselves up in July; iron-gray clouds, pregnant with rain and shivering electricity. The afternoon air buzzes and shifts; the whole world holds its breath, waiting for the crack.

"Most powerful thing in the world is a woman," my grandmother would say, on those long summer days when we sat out on her front porch watching those storms slide over the mountain backs. "Mother Nature. Me. You. Don't ever let anyone take that away from you. Women, we create. We birth. And we can destroy."

I wonder if she still felt that power in her hands, lying there in her lonely nursing home bed. I hope so.

The mountain bellies opened up to me in that sweltering summer, and I crawled in. Through bright May and June, I had waited, rooted in the earth and deep in myself, shedding inch by inch and breath by breath the old, soiled skin of me until I became a new thing, slick and gleaming. By July, the mites weren't under my skin anymore. I'd made an armor of them.

I swallowed the storms, opening my mouth to the lightning, dancing in the raging rain. There in the full breadth of summer, I felt the crawling things inside me begin to press long legs out, to walk with my feet into the world. I held them close at work, tying my face into a smile, tossing my laugh into the fresh breeze that swept around the bar through our open windows.

The fruit flies, floating through the haze, didn't bother me so much anymore. I took to leaving scraps of food tucked below the back feet of the ice well. A safe haven for feasting, for hiding eggs. The rest of the bar I wiped clean, polished the copper until it sparkled in the evening sunset.

The whispers grew pregnant with the humidity, rolling from one ear to the next, down the bar, around the little room, out into the crumbling town streets. It had been six months since Mark was found. Six months and two more men. Three, really, but they had already forgotten about that boy eaten by the train. That had been his own fault, after all.

The whispers billowed and grew legs, walked around Bellair with nightmares for faces. I heard their names chanted in prayer: Mark and Trent and Brody. Mark and Trent and Brody. MarkandTrentand-Brody. For a few sweet weeks, I saw men glance over their shoulders before walking out into the dark.

That had ended with full summer. The silk of a warm night was enough to wipe the fear from their minds. April was the last attack, but April was so far behind us now. Men, not used to seeing their own lives as fragile things, easily forgot the predator watching them from the long grass.

It was my fault. I had been still too long, had taken solace behind the ghost story I had built, forgotten the thrill of haunting. I felt myself beginning to crumble, to flake, to melt into the earth if I didn't move. The man below my willow tree was half-gone, his skin hanging like shredded curtains from balding bone. Mushrooms pushed up between his fingers and toes, past the thick cartilage of his nose. It was time to move again. I reached into my chest and found a lion there; I reached into my chest and set her free. I would wear a costume; I would become the terror crawling under men's skin.

Circe

My witch grew. She grew until her arms dripped over the
sides of the plastic pot I'd planted her in lifetimes ago; she grew thick
and strong, green leaves unfurling in the sun, trumpeted flower heads
ripping out of tight spring buds. In full spring, when the sun dipped
our days into delicious warmth and teeth fell out of night's yawning
mouth, I took my witch up in my arms, carried her to the same front
porch on which I'd so many times sat with my grandmother.

There I was, with my grandmother again, the same medicine held
tight in her fists, which would by late summer be hard seedpods. I
tugged her gently from her baby pot and placed her in the cauldron
belly of her new summer home. She could not go in the ground; hard
as a brick, the red clay would choke her roots. Not many things can
survive here, in this brutal earth. So I sat her on my porch, at the corner of the stairs, wound her spindly arms around the front lattice,
coiled legs through the peeling deck rail. The weaving took gentle
time. Stems, flowers, leaves, each passed hand to hand as I sewed her
through the ribs of this ancient house. Bees swooped in; butterflies
kissed sweat off my shoulders. When I finished and pulled my hands
off the splintering wood, I saw they were covered with clover mites.
Red, like blood. I crushed them with a finger, trailed the stain of their
bodies over my palms.

Draped over the other side of my porch are flowers that by looks could be her sisters, though in truth they share little. Their shape and color are the same. Elegant trumpets drooping heavy over leaves; a few turn their faces up to the sun until the day grows too hot to look at and they spin themselves asleep. They're white, though some have purple edging or darken to blue in their thin centers. They share a nickname too, these false sisters: moonflowers. One so named because she blooms only in the evening and so, cheerful, she greets the dawn with a full face, before rolling back into daydreams. You might know her by another name: Morning Glory. The other, my witch, is called Moonflower no doubt for the cold, pale color of her face. Coming home in the dark that summer, I found myself greeted by dozens of those eerie eyes, watching me from the heavy silence of an empty home.

They share something else as well, these moonflowers. Like all beautiful women, they are poisonous.

Sweet Morning Glory won't do much more than make you spin off to another planet for a few hours. Datura, my crone witch, is a creature of a more serious nature. Folded deep in the tight fists of her hands are seeds that would, if taken sparingly, have me lying gleefully in the orchard watching clouds scud by, or, swallowed too greedily, they would have me dead where I stood, before I knew what had hit me. Like the moon, she has a dark half. She is all of woman power filtered through the graceful bell of her skirt.

What makes Datura so tricky are the alkaloids she hides in her seeds. Atropine: a nerve agent that slows down your heart rate; you will be Snow White asleep in the forest. Hyoscyamine: pain relief, dry mouth, flushing, faintness, blurred vision, the root of you shaken until you let go. Scopolamine: pupils open wide until the whole world tumbles in on itself.

She is sister to Nightshade, who once, long ago, women used to drop into their own open eyes or onto their tongues. Flushed and feline, these thrumming maenads prowled candlelit parties, tiptoeing along the knife's edge of death. Could they feel the thunder building in their breasts, the lightning in their bones?

I first discovered her at work. A customer, an allergy, *no bell peppers, please.* They are the lesser cousins, you see. Bell Pepper, Tomato, Eggplant, Chili. They carry within them a consumable poison, deadly only for those unfortunate enough to be too sensitive. Most of us never know any better. In that regard, I suppose even I am like a man. Ignorant.

Men have forgotten the earth they're a part of, and so they have forgotten their grandmother. They rape us, beat us, bind us, shut us up, but they would do so no longer. The summer storms pulled me up from my sleep, to ripen with the new budding apples. The spring flowers had been beautiful but were too delicate for long work. It was the fruit that swells and bulges, bursts into fiery colors, that I chose to become. The summer was long, the summer was hot, I had grown a full flavor out there in my small orchard. Let them bite me, see how I taste.

The butterflies left after a while, but the bees bobbed along with me all through the warm afternoon. Sitting on a stair, I watched them crawl into the wide trumpets of flowers, Morning Glory or Datura, they seemed not to notice or care. The poison doesn't touch them; they are sisters too.

I watched them until the sun drowned itself behind the swollen mountain ridge and the world fell into shadow; then the moonflowers stretched open to a chorus of crickets and tree frogs, the glow of a hundred capering lightning bugs.

A Spider

This is how you catch a man in a bar:

First, consider your clothing. You want to be seen but not remembered. Faces are distinct. Bodies are easier to hide, to forget. Use yours. Jeans, a black tank top; if your taste runs to something more feminine, a plain shift dress will do. This is where you start.

Keep your makeup simple. Pick one feature, make it your lure. I have always liked my eyes, but some women find a red lip to be a better enticement. Leave your hair loose; this is how you hide. Women know this. How often did my mother yell at me to pull my hair back as a child? *I can't see your pretty face! Doesn't it drive you nuts, always hanging over your forehead like that?* No, Mother, it never did. When I was young, I hated my face and hid it behind a tangled rat's nest. Now that I've grown into it, I hide it again, though my hair is no longer an oily shroud for features growing out of sync with one another, but rather a perfumed invitation to lips, to sighs, to mystery. Or so I've been told. I wouldn't know. I'm used to it, so I cannot even smell my own hair.

So you become every woman and no woman, a forgettable fantasy, like the gossamer of a spider's web, in the open, but out of sight.

Second, find a dark place. Not the kind of dark that some would call romantic, with soft candles and banquettes curved into corners, where the bartender is paid to know the difference between a mistress and a wife. The men who write what we're told is good TV believe that women like me haunt these sorts of places. They imagine that someone like me must be vain, or tilted and tattered on one edge, that my power over men is fueled by a hatred of them because one raped me when I was a co-ed. I resent the simplicity of such a hypothesis. I have never been raped. Annoyed, poked at, talked over, catcalled, groped, ignored, yes. I have been all these things. But raped, no. That narrative that they tell themselves, you see, allows them to imagine that they are a driving force in a woman's life. Phallus first as an agent of pain, and ultimately of change. The woman-butterfly in this fantasy is reborn via the transformational power of the male member. How important they think they are.

I reject that philosophy. I want to punish men because they bore me, because they assume they own me, because they talk over me, grope me, catcall me, ignore me, poke at me, annoy me. Their voices, slithering up through the hidden places of my flesh, make me crawl.

So I didn't go where they expected me to be, where they're on the alert, those men who assume my world revolves around them. I eschewed the jazz bars; the candlelit, corner-couched date-night lounges; all the places where the barstools are well spaced and the menu prices keep the riffraff out. In those places, I am still a thing on display.

I chose a different stage. My dark place was lit by strips of LED lighting. It smelled like cheap beer and rail liquor and stuck to my feet when I walked across the concrete floor. It's the sort of bar every restaurant lifer cuts their teeth in. Where you know what your co-worker means when they say they need to go on a break for the third time in an hour and so don't ask when they come back from the bathroom wiping their nose; the kind of place where the regulars know that the furthest stall from the door is for business, and no one cares except the kitchen boys, who cackle about that one girl whose knees they all know now by sight, kissing the filthy tiled floor.

Why hasn't she asked us yet? one of them will say.

Because she knows you're a pussy! will be the obvious answer, delivered with the snap of a towel whip to legs or arms or crotch.

I knew of one such bar; a sagging place that sat slumped on the side of a lonely bend of interstate highway far enough away from my home.

That's the final rule: If you want to make hunting men a sport, consider your range.

It was rough. The sort of run-down place that locals love and tourists feel special if they find, as if they've stumbled into a National Geographic documentary. That's always the game, isn't it? Can I blend in? Will the regulars welcome me, regale me with stories, call me a friend? Will the bartender buy us a round of shots?

There was a band. Those scrawny boys you find in garages and basements, who wear jeans skinnier than my own, the front of their V-necks torn open to halfway down their wiry chests. When I walked in, they were just diving into their set of nineties grunge covers, sprinkled here and there with their own songs. Somewhere in the night, when the crowd was good and worked up, they play "Peaches" or "War Pigs," maybe "Brown Eyed Girl" for the sweet things that spun in flimsy dresses just in front of the stage, smiling and swaying like fairies in some imagined woodland meadow.

I have always loathed those girls. But they serve a purpose. Everyone watches them.

This is the sort of place where all of me can move unnoticed.

I found what I needed in the bathroom. A girl, maybe *that* girl, hunched against the far wall, mascara streaming in smudged rivers down her cheeks, hair unkempt and falling in her face. Glued to her hands was a phone, dinging and flashing in an angry tattoo. More tears fall and a wretched animal sort of sound pulls itself out of her soft throat. I felt a roar echo in my chest, a squirming ripple across the bridge of my nose.

"He's not worth it," I told her, bent over the sink, pencil pressed to my eyelid. It was dull, needed to be sharpened, and so my line of black was thick, a caterpillar crawling above the fan of lashes. I pulled it out into a wing, smudged it into smoke.

The wall behind her was covered in doodles; all the scattered sediment of forgotten nights, heartbreaks and hookups; this ritual rite of passage as old as our species, to leave your handprint, your name, your drawing, on a wall. *I was here. I lived. I fucked the bartender. Smile!* Just over her head, the jewel on her crown, was a bright red kiss print. She looked up, the jewel now brushing the top of her hair, and I saw her eyes were blue; the sort of wide, innocent eyes I'd always wished I had. Mine are brown, the color of mud and hidden things.

The phone in her hand buzzed, and I watched her eyes well up with tears again.

"Give me that." She didn't fight me when I stooped down to take the phone from her hands. She was a child, trembling, torn. I knew her face. I'd seen it a thousand times before, in my own mirror or sitting across my bar counter on a Friday night. Anger swept up the ridge of my spine, buried itself in the knot under my shoulder blade. The feet that had been out on my nose paused, pivoted, scuttled back into my eye. I was glad she was drunk, was glad she was too fixated on her own tears to see the pulse of voices crawling over me. It would have been too much then, she wasn't ready, impaled as she was by the scream reaching out of her phone.

I knew what I would find when I peered down at it. The usual trash. *Cunt. Whore. Crazy.* I deleted it all. Blocked his number before he could dig in his sharpest weapon, *I'm sorry. I love you.*

Bullshit.

Thus begins the routine that every woman knows, of caring for strangers in bathrooms. Pick your sister up off the ground and wipe her tears away. Rub her back, as much to soothe her as to remind her to stand up straight. No man gets to weigh you down. You're a goddess. Let's fix your makeup. Here, you can try my lipstick; I think it'll look good on you. Seriously, red looks good on everyone, the trick is to find the right shade. We're going to have a good time tonight, fuck that loser. Hey! No tears. Look at yourself, lady, you're *hot*. Yeah, somedays I wish I was a lesbian too (laughter), but unfortunately for me, I like dick. Yes (more laughter), we should absolutely castrate them all. Have you ever heard about the Amazons? Let me tell you about them . . .

When I was young and just wobbling out into the world in cheap high heels, I believed those words when they fell from my mouth. By that night, I knew they were a lie, snake oil women sell one another to soothe the pain in our hearts. What I wanted to do was scream at her that there was another way, that we had power in our hands, that men, once challenged, were so easily crushed. I wanted to peel the skin back from her own arms, show her the mites crawling underneath. *Can you feel them?* I'd ask. *Let me show you how to get rid of them.*

I wanted to do these things because I am tired of picking women up from disgusting bathroom floors to wipe their faces and fix their hair and tell them they're better than that trash blowing up their phone. I'm tired of the tears and the broken hearts, the pieces of which I have spent a lifetime painstakingly taping back together as best I can. I'm so tired of the certainty that, in the daylight, she'll open the door for him once more. *Just one more chance, baby. I love you.*

But she's half-drunk and I'm too angry, and I have other uses for her now.

I took her hand in mine. It was warm; mine are always cold. "Come on. This band is too good for us to waste time in here—let's go find someone to buy us a round of shots, and then we dance our asses off. Plus"—and here is how you seal the deal, listen close—"your boobs look great in that shirt. Would be a shame to waste them crying on that dirty floor."

We were sisters now, walking out of the bathroom, arms threaded through each other in a Gordian knot that she was determined no man would break. Belly up to the bar, we waited. It never takes long. Two women, alone together, are flowers ripe for bees. I made myself a statue. Body long and curving, face lit with a mirth I do not feel. I ran fingers through my hair, let it fall over my shoulder, turned to face her in my seat so I was in profile. *Here is all of me,* my body said. *Come meet it.*

"This band is pretty good, huh?" A mouth pressed to my ear, rough fingers brushed my elbow.

When I turned and looked at him, I saw my night laid out before me, all my plans falling so easily into place I felt suspicious. It should not be this simple, to be a Mary Sue.

He continued, his eyes slipping between my own and the bowed pout of my lips, which I was sure to arrange just so. "What are you drinking?"

His fingers hadn't left my elbow. I felt their pinprick touch, hot as a brand and just as heavy. He was playing with them, one callused tip sliding across the rounded bone, then two, one, two. I felt bodies clamber up my throat and into the pitted pathways behind my jaw. *Sit still. You are a lion in the long grass.*

I turned to my partner, whose arm still wound through mine. Her eyes were wide, and I saw the anticipated rejection there. I would leave her for this man, our sisterhood bond broken by the only sword that could cut our knot in half.

"We hadn't decided yet. What would you recommend?" I held her arm firm through mine as I addressed him.

"My pick is either whiskey or tequila."

His voice snagged the bartender, who pivoted in his stride like a dog hearing its name and came to stand facing us. He wouldn't wait long. The room was buzzing, the bar full. I could feel every tug and poke and computer whine dinging his nerves. We needed to make a decision, before this step became a chore, before we lost our place in line.

They were both looking at me, so I chose. "Three tequilas."

"Vodka!" my girl piped up as the bartender reached for the last shot glass. "Sorry." She made herself an apology, pressed small into the back of her stool, eyes wide. "I don't like tequila."

Rail anything is pretty bad, but rail vodka is the worst, and the girls who drink it get sloppy fast. She was a lost cause, but I could use her.

Three glasses slid toward us. A saltshaker appeared, and two limes. This was my open door. I knew what to do. I grabbed her hand and sprinkled a bit of salt down onto the soft pad between her thumb and forefinger. His hand stiffened against my elbow. When I licked the salt off her, I made sure to catch his eye.

"Cheers."

Three shots lifted to lips, three fingers pressing down on my hip, hooking into my belt loop, two limes sucked dry and tossed into empty glasses.

I was the one who suggested we do another round, in celebration of my friend's newfound freedom. She kissed my cheek after she slammed her second glass down on the counter, and then, her arm looped through mine and his fingers caught in the waist of my jeans, the three of us waddled like an awkward insect out onto the grimy dance floor.

Men make it so easy to pick them up in a bar. I'm not sure why, for all that I've studied them. These creatures, who so relish the ability to wield their attention as a weapon, withholding it when they're angry or smothering us in it when they're pleased, for all that they grow so unsure of themselves in those sticky places, where all hands feel the same and kisses come cheap. Think about it too long, and it feels pathetic, dirty almost. There's a certain animal desperation to their sudden clinging, like a dog following you around the house. Here in this confusing wild, they've found a female who lets him touch her hip, press his mouth to her hair. Maybe it's an instinct that kicks in, warns him this might be his only chance, don't let go. You could shove them, mock them, kiss another man in front of them, and they will still be there on the sidewalk in front of the bar at the end of the night, waiting because you opened the door. All for the chance dangling in front of them of a few minutes of awkward grunting.

Food, sex, shelter. Sex. This is what men want. Once you understand this, you can use it. You win. You don't have to be smart to hunt a man, but you do have to be clever.

The girl stayed with us until she found someone more interesting, better suited to her brokenhearted needs than I could ever be. Some of you will question why I didn't fill that role myself, and I can only answer that my body is a balm for no one. I've outgrown my days of being a Band-Aid, no matter who wants one. And I had other things to do. The biting voices, which had grown quiet in the first sweaty hour on the dance floor, were nagging at me again. The thing in my chest was pacing. So I let the girl grab my face and kiss me and walk back to the bar with the man I knew she would leave with once the lights came up. She tasted like cigarettes and stale lipstick.

And then we were alone, he and I, and I didn't really want him to kiss me, but I let him do it all the same, as I had so many times before. I felt the flame of my old self burn up through my rib cage, crackling and spitting, wrapping hot tongues around my bones. His fingers inched down below the waist of my jeans. I danced to ignore their feel for as long as I could, until I began to fight with myself. The intrusion of space was too much.

It was still too early to leave. He wasn't drunk enough. I didn't quite have him yet. Sweat from his hair dripped onto my face; I closed my eyes against it, curled inward on the bend of a guitar riff. Further and further, I sank into myself, until the hard center of me was a heavy ball in my chest, waiting behind lungs breathing ragged anger, behind heart hammering inside pericardium, behind diaphragm and tucked kidneys and my liver pumping alcohol out and away. All the wet, muscular workings of me held my recoil in their embrace, made a home for me to go to while my hips danced and the mites protested and he touched.

My skin waxed, my eyes glazed. Like my man in the orchard, I slipped into an unnatural space. Not a death, just tucked away; put on a shelf so I could do work. I knew how to do that, had been doing it for years already. I let him kiss me again, and when his lips scraped mine, I put my numb fingers on his hip.

We tripped back to the bar for more drinks, back to the floor for more dancing. Hours dragged. The leonine teeth and claws that were buried in my chest glared out from the bars of my rib cage, growling, eyes glowing. He felt it too, and mistook it for desire. He had become bolder through the night, shoving a hand up my shirt and tucking sly fingers into my bra, coming to know the secret planes of me. Bile rose in my throat. Once, forgetting myself, I put my hand on his, tried to push him away; in response, he folded our bodies in two, his teeth scraping the back of my neck, his other hand slithering down my thigh. A flock of birds tore out of my back, screaming. In another life, this might have felt erotic. No doubt in his life, it did.

Then we were moving, and I felt my control slipping away. My own fear and disgust might betray me, make me small and shrill and angry. He was steering us toward the dark corner booth.

"No."

My hand on his chest became a barricade.

"Come on."

I felt every bit of him heavy against me, and that beast in my chest screamed. Tiny feet skittered up over the zygomatic mountains of my cheekbones, dripped over my lips, down the straining flesh of my throat. I reminded myself to be calm, bit my lip to pull the rushing pieces of my body back together, touched each piece of me with the probing tip of my mind. *You are in control, Sophie.* Be a quiet thing. Sink down into the mud.

When you look at a man as a conquest, everything about him shifts. There are his eyes, looking at you. There is his jaw, square and rough; his throat pulsing. Alive. Step back and you see the rest of him: arms, legs, chest, well-formed or awkward, together they make up a creature that could easily overpower you if you let him. And they want to overpower you. Tear off your clothes and slam you against a wall, pull your hair, slap you, choke you, bury the life they so easily waste in the deepest parts of you.

But I've learned what it feels like to make them feel mortal. Everything in me, my anger, my shame, the disgust I feel after hours of letting his sweat drip on me, compressed into one perfect, smoldering stare.

I pressed my body close, my lips against the velvety shell of his ear. "Not here. I know a better place."

We paid the tab and tipped the bar; always 30 percent. I am no monster. And then we left. In the dark, no one saw us slip into my car.

There's a lonely back stretch of highway in Texas called the Killing Fields. Dozens of bodies, mostly women and girls, have been found in this sparse desert land since the 1970s. I wonder sometimes, when I'm driving down a particularly lonely stretch of road, how many more have never been found. How many more are lying broken and crumpled in shallow graves, their faces pressed hard into the sand, mouths full of dirt and sticks, rocks, broken teeth; their screams swallowed by the wind as it whips over the plain?

We have no such wide-open spaces here. Interstate 64 slices through a sentinel of stiff, silent pines, standing tall against the choking arms of Virginia creeper, kudzu, sweet honeysuckle. The earth in this part of the state is soft, thick with fallen needles. The air is old, and smells like something left behind long ago, a dream or a nightmare.

This length of road is dark at night. Not many people live in the bogs between the humid bowl of Richmond and my Blue Ridge. It's too hot. Storms catch in the floodplain and weigh heavy on the air. Mosquitoes run rampant. The land here is too sandy to grow much of anything, its soil poisonous to all but tobacco and peanuts. The big farms are up in Northern Virginia, or back across my Blue Ridge— rolling grass fields of horses and cattle.

It is here, in the loamy earth, that I laid him down, deep under a thicket of snarled thorns. All around us tree roots popped up in strange alien mounds. Crickets played their orchestra. Pine trees waved and creaked.

There in a shallow grave in the dreaming earth, no one will ever find him, save for the foxes and birds, all the skittering life of the forest.

A Ghost Lies Down

I lay on my shower floor when I got home, savoring the cool kiss of tile on my flushed body. The world is so different from this space on the ground. Could they feel this? Where they lay, could they feel gravity tugging them down? The earth spinning beneath them as they rot?

Did they feel small?

Nora

The report came in while Nora was on patrol, a fuzzy voice rising through radio static. Joseph Aguilar, twenty-seven, of Richmond had gone missing sometime over the weekend. The last place he'd been tracked to was a dive bar just outside the city, a seedy little place known best for its live bands and strong cocktails; the sort of place favored by broke kids and broken adults.

She wouldn't have heard the call, but she'd been bored and fiddling around with her radio dial. A bad habit, she knew, but it was almost the end of her shift and it had been such a sleepy day; she wanted to hear if there was life happening in other parts of the state. There, alone in her car listening to the voice crackling through the static, Nora felt something cold slip around her heart and squeeze.

Another one, vanished.

She called Murph on her cell. "Can you get in touch with Richmond PD? They just reported a man missing. Young guy, late twenties. Last seen in a bar off the western boundary of the city limits."

"And why would I do that?" His voice was a husky drawl. Nora could see him, slumped over his desk at work. The summer heat brought petty crime to the town just as it did every year. As one of only two detectives in Bellair, Murph took not only homicide but also all break-ins and thefts, sexual offenses. Lately, he'd been up to his neck in reports of teenagers sneaking into houses abandoned while their owners were on vacation or swiping beers from the gas station fridge. Small-town summertime larceny, predictably boring and always a pain in his ass.

"Because it matches, Murph. A man. Gone missing."

"Men go missing every day. If you're really bored, why don't you check out the national registry of missing persons."

"Yes, I know!" She was irritable today too. The heat and her schedule had her tired. She knew Murph was just being stubborn because he was in a mood, but sometimes she wished he'd just listen to her, instead of challenging her or making a quip.

"We don't have a killer here, Martin. We have two dead-end cases that are going to haunt me and one horrible accident and one kid who ran away, probably to some hippie commune in Colorado."

"But, Murph, you don't really believe—"

"I'll call 'em, Martin!" he snapped. "I'll call them. Just . . . give it a rest, will you? I agree with you, it looks like something's going on. I'm not sure what yet, and I don't want to make any assumptions that lead to stupid mistakes. Murders, disappearances, they're usually the simplest explanation. You know that."

"But you'll call?"

"I'll call. But don't get your hopes up, and don't steamroll me. This guy, Aguilar, isn't our case. We can tell them what we know, but we will not be investigating. You wouldn't like it if some other department came in and bossed you around, would you?"

"No . . ."

"All right. Good. And good ears. You drive me absolutely up a wall some days, kid, but I'd rather have a sharp knife in the drawer than a dull one. Just don't get yourself so worked up."

"Did you just tell a woman to calm down?"

"Only because I have some miles between you and me. I can still run pretty fast, when I need to."

"You better start then."

She let the conversation end on a high note, but she couldn't stop her heart from pounding or the sensation that someone was watching her from just out of reach of her tumbling thoughts.

Sophie

My grandmother's hands shook, as they always did, when I took them, and I wondered if she could feel mine shaking too. In that tomb of a nursing home, we sat, facing a dirty window that was plastered with tissue-paper cutouts, stained glass for this living grave we confine our elders to.

She rolled in her chair and rocked; her feet tapped out a soft beat before curling back in on themselves. She is shrinking. The dementia, they tell me. People become fists once their brain begins to eat itself. Before I knew better, I used to try to open her up again, stretch her out as she had once eased so many others open. She'd screamed then, and cried, clung hard to my hands like an infant.

The moving hurts her, scares her. So I hold her hands now, hold them still in my lap and listen to her whisper to the air about all the things she's lost. Her voice, once so strong and sure, is nothing more than a puff of air.

I want to tell her of the men I've killed, of the rush of blood and bone and breath fighting against my bare palms. I want to tell her that I have two bodies now, the shell that houses my own blood and bones, and the other body, the wriggling, creeping, powerful body rippling under the surface. I wish I could bring her into it too. I think she would have liked that. For all her rage, she never broke out of the box men sealed her into. I think it would have made her cry, made her laugh, to see it could be done. She was right all along, a body is an open book, one I have learned how to read.

August

A Friend

She hadn't meant it to become a habit, but somewhere in the long yawn of summer days, Nora found herself almost a regular at the Blue Bell. She insisted on *almost*, because she would not be that cop who dangled off a barstool like a Christmas ornament, drowning nerves in a rotating pool of pint glasses. But once or twice a week, sometimes with Dan and sometimes alone, she found herself on a stool, sometimes drinking, sometimes just unloading. This was simply part of small-town life, she told herself, the skin you slipped on to be classified as a local. After a few weeks the cowbell clanging over the front door became the cue for her shoulders to release, to relax. In here, they did not need to be part of her armor. In here, she had a friend.

There was still something about Sophie Braam that Nora couldn't quite put a finger on. The woman seemed to be in constant motion, almost blurry, like a figure in an old photograph, still but vibrating. It unnerved Nora, somewhere down at the base of her gut, but she pushed it away. Sophie was just intense; there was nothing wrong with that. Hadn't she herself been called intense before?

"Murph's been telling me to chill out," she revealed, one sweating night in late August.

"Why? Here, let me top that off for you, not much left in the bottle anyways," Sophie said as she leaned over the bar and poured the last mouthful of the local boutique winery's newest rosé into Nora's glass.

Nora sighed. "Thanks. God, I feel like my mother when I drink this, but it's so good."

"It's unfortunate, really." Sophie winked. "So, tell me about Murph. I interrupted you."

"Oh, he thinks I'm crazy," Nora said. "And to be honest, he's probably right . . . One of my theories about all the deaths we've had recently."

"You mean Mark and Trent?"

"Them, and this kid who went missing a few months ago, right about the time we found Mr. Gibson. Young guy. And . . . you know what? I shouldn't be talking to you about this."

There it was again, that movement behind the stillness in Sophie's skin, almost a rippling of thought down her cheek. Nora forced a laugh, to wipe away the worries that flew across her mind.

Sophie smiled, pulled out a box of fruit to cut, and said, "No, of course not." She pierced the taut skin of a lime.

A question tugged on Nora's ear as she watched the woman work. Her heart jumped up to her throat, but she caught it in time to smooth her voice when she asked, "Hey, can I see that knife for a second?"

"This?" Sophie looked up.

"If you don't mind."

"Not at all. It's nothing special, though, just a cheap thing I picked up from Walmart ages ago."

Nora reached across the bar. There was a breath, a pause, while Sophie looked down at her waiting hand. Then, with a smile, she pressed the rubber handle into Nora's palm. It was still warm from her touch.

"Sophie, does anyone else ever use your knife?" She handed it back.

"Everyone. It's a bar. I try to keep my stuff organized, but if the kitchen loses a knife and needs a quick replacement, or one of the servers wants to fiddle around back here . . . people take it." The woman shrugged.

Nora was searching for her words when, as if on cue, the man at the end of the bar rose from his seat. "Excuse me, *miss?* I've been trying to get your attention, but I guess you're too busy chitchatting with your friend."

"*Shit,*" Sophie whispered, and Nora saw her zip up her face as she turned to talk to the man, who was now hanging halfway over the counter, snapping his fingers.

"Yes, Mack?" Nora felt the knife's blade flash through Sophie's voice.

He reached into his back pocket and Nora, without thinking, moved her hand to her hip, to where, in another sort of life, another moment, she would have found a gun.

"Jumpy there, huh?" The man called Mack cackled. "Calm down, Officer. It's just cash." With a sneer, he pulled a crumpled $100 bill out of his pocket. Nora sat back, her nerves on edge. She caught Sophie's eyes with her own, saw in the other woman's face the same helpless apology she felt. This man had trapped them both.

"I want another beer." He flapped the bill in Sophie's face.

She took a breath. "Mack, I told you this half an hour ago, if you want another beer, you need to drink a glass of water first."

"C'mon. I'll give you this whole thing"—*flap flap*—"if you just make me one more drink. I know you think I don't have it, but here it is. Check it." He shoved the money into her nose again, and Nora watched Sophie scowl, felt the anger growing behind the wall she'd built in front of her eyes.

"I know you got that little pen back there, and you got a cop right here, right?" He pointed to Nora. "She can arrest me if it's phony."

"Sir, I—" Nora began, but Sophie held up a hand that stopped her like a slap. It was pale and trembling, straight like a spear.

"Thank you, Nora, but I've got this. You're off-duty. Mack, I gave you your options. And I'm closing soon, so you need to make up your mind."

"You'll close before I finish my water! Just pour me another beer." He slammed his cash down on the counter.

In Nora's world, this sort of tension stiffened your jaw, raised your heart rate, pulled your hand to the butt of your gun. In her world, decisions had to be made, and too often made too quick. She'd learned long ago that people are animals, and the winner in a confrontation isn't always the one who beats his chest the loudest, or the one who moves the fastest. Sometimes, she'd learned, when an animal has its back against the wall, it would do neither of these things. Instead, it would turn cold. Some pretended to die, like snakes or possums. But others, that more dangerous kind, simply went icy cold, bitter, locked away behind some door she couldn't find the handle to. Those were animals who had nothing to lose, who were gathering themselves deep in their core.

She'd seen it before, only once; a rabid skunk had gotten into the shed in their backyard. The poor creature went stiff when he saw her, his eyes hard as steel and just as shiny. The growl, so low in his throat Nora almost had to lean forward to hear it, was the only noise he made as he crouched there in the dark behind her daddy's lawn mower and her momma's garden hoe.

"Nora! Get away from it!" Ron had cried, when he saw her facing down the raging death in their shed. That was the only day she'd ever heard him really scared, his voice cracking as he swept her up into his arms and carried her away. "Don't ever go near an animal like that, baby girl. A wild thing doesn't run when it sees a human? It's not sane anymore. It's sick. And it'll make you sick too. You come get me, you hear? And you don't ever touch it."

"What are you gonna do with it, Daddy?"

"Put it out of its misery, sweetheart. It's suffering." And then he'd picked up the rifle he only ever used for work and went back outside to the shed. She flinched when she heard the gunshot, cried in her momma's arms.

Nora never forgot that day, the cold burn in that skunk's eyes as it looked at her, not afraid but angry. *Sick. Insane. Suffering.* She saw it sometimes in people too. Not often, but enough. Those were the animals she knew to fear most.

The man, Mack, apparently wasn't wise to such things. He rocked back in his chair, the money sitting on the counter like a taunt. "What if I sing you a poem? C'mon, ask your friend here, she'll know I'm good if I sing a poem. Isn't that what y'all do before you arrest someone for driving *intoxicated*?"

His words, slurred at the edges, were a wet paintbrush on Nora's neck. She grew a new respect for Sophie then. It was one thing to face a man like this when you were armed and had backup one call away. It was another to do it totally alone. She looked for help from the other staff, but there was none; they'd left long ago. The only sign of life in the bar other than them was an atrocious chorus spilling out the kitchen door, the chef and the dishwasher, running the last of their dishes. Ty, as she had learned was usual at the end of the night, was hidden.

She wanted to do something herself, but until the man broke a law, her hands were tied. She looked to Sophie. The woman stood, a stone.

Mack began his recital, a sliming drip of words that poured down Sophie's breasts and belly and licked along her thighs. His words wrapped tongues around her throat, which remained, to Nora's surprise, pale; no flush burned on the woman's skin even as he sang of running his hands over it. She stood there, cold and hard, a sea of calm, waiting for him to finish, and when he did, she thanked him and turned back to cutting fruit.

"I gave you a poem—where's my drink?" Mack asked.

"It wasn't a good poem." Sophie sliced another lime in half, pressed it into the juicer. Green sluiced out with a squish, into the waiting mouth of an empty plastic bottle.

"*Oh.* I didn't realize I was at the bar of a damn literary critic."

"'Night, fuckers!" The chef strolled out of the kitchen, tossing a hand into the air while he slung his backpack over his shoulder. The dishwasher crashed out just behind, his adieu a grunt while he searched for his cigarettes in his pockets.

Ty, who had finally emerged from his office, lifted a fist in reply.

"You almost done, Soph?" he asked, climbing onto a stool and pulling out his phone. It was clear that her answer, if she gave one, didn't matter. He had more important things to swipe through. The fist in Nora's chest, which had softened somewhat in the past few weeks, clenched tight once more. How could he be so nonchalant?

Another poem began.

"Sir," Nora, no longer able to watch from the sidelines, began again. "I really think you should listen to her and have a glass of water."

Sophie looked up from where she was pummeling citrus and flashed Nora a small smile. Her eyes though remained just as cold and dead as they had been minutes before. The armor, once raised, was hard to let down until the assault was over.

He rounded on her. "And just who the *fuck* do you think you are? You gonna arrest me if I don't?"

The fist punched her sternum. "Are you sure you want to try that?"

"You can fuck right off to wherever you came from, piggy. Is that the right animal? Or should I call you a coo—"

"Whoa. Hey, bro!" Ty jumped up from his stool, his chest puffed out like a banner in front of him. "That's enough, man."

"And who the hell are you?"

"I'm the manager, and I need you to leave."

"I'm trying to give her a hundred dollars!" Mack waved his bill again, his battle flag, his banner proof of being A Good Customer. Behind the bar, Nora saw Sophie was seething.

"He needs to go, Ty. Now."

Ty kept his eyes locked on Mack, held up a hand to calm Sophie. "And she doesn't want it, brother."

"I mean it, Ty." The knife in Sophie's hand flashed, and for one second, Nora wondered what it would feel like to watch it plunge into this man.

"Sophie, I know. Dude, it's time for you to go." He put a hand on Mack's shoulder, started to push him toward the door.

"I can walk on my own!" Mack said, shoving Ty's hand off. "Jesus Christ. A bunch of snowflakes in here. Thought police going to arrest me now?"

"No one's arresting you. Right, Nora?" Ty turned to her, as if to confirm this. She kept her eyes on the man, who looked like he was considering making a dive behind the bar. The liquor rail was only one good arm's length away.

The disgust in her mouth curdled, and she felt herself grow spines. "I'm thinking about it."

Ty moved to block Mack with a hand on his shoulder. "Seriously, man. It's time for you to leave."

"Fine," the man said, backing off. "Fucking *cunts*!" he spat, and slammed out through the front door, the bell jingling cheerily above him.

"Fuck." Ty ran his hands through his hair, crashed down into the stool next to Nora's. "Are you all right, ladies? Nora, I'm so sorry about that. That was totally uncalled for. He's banned. Forever. You have my word. And whatever you had, it's on the house tonight." He folded back into his seat, his face a mask of shock.

"Of course she's not okay, Ty," Sophie said, her voice poison.

Nora thanked him and assured him that, really, everything was fine, even though it was not. Later, she'd wonder what was worse—the lying to her friends or to herself.

"Well, still. It's on me tonight, okay? No one hurts my girls." Ty got up, patted Sophie on the back, and took down three shot glasses. "What'll it be?"

Later, after their cheers, after the bar closed and they said their goodbyes, Nora stood in the dark beside her car watching Sophie slide off down Peach. She thought again about that skunk in the shed, broken, in pain, shimmering with some sort of darkness that could only be felt in the bottom of your gut, where your instincts lived. Shadows seemed to trail after her, there and then not, gone before the thought formed. She reminded Nora of a haint, something poisoned and hidden, haunted.

No, she's just intense, Nora told herself. And who wouldn't be, after years of nights like that?

Sophie

A bar is a body. Each year, she trails through a lifetime. It begins in January, with the raucous celebrations, a bright burst forth into life. In the bone cold of winter, we light a fire in her, find warmth in the pour of liquor down throats, anise and cinnamon and frothy egg white curing the winter chills. By spring and summer, she's ripe with customers, spilling out of doors and onto patios, tasting each fresh cocktail recipe with eyes closed, enjoying the singular pleasure of a perfectly balanced drink on their tongue, much in the way a fencer might admire the tang of a sword, perched on a fingertip.

By August, by the time the year has split open and begins to deflate, my bar's a new sort of creature altogether. The relentless heat lulls the customers into a sleep only the iciest of aperitifs can rouse them from. In this spoiling heat, she falls into a constant state of dreaming about rot.

This is when they take over.

The first whispers flutter through in spring, floating just out of sight, soft and dreamy. By summer, they've colonized the sink drains and trash cans, any naked pour spouts, searching for anything sticky-sweet. I used to hate the fruit flies. Every year I zapped them and swatted and built soapy traps, and every year they beat me.

This year I let them come. I watched them dance on puffs of air, tiptoe around cherries, held them buzzing in my mouth if I caught one in a word or a breath. I told the customers it was a bad year.

"Just can't stop them. Global warming, you know. They get worse every year."

I threw the traps Ty made in the trash, left puddles in the bottom of the trash can for them to feed, kicked bits of fruit under the kegerator, where the air was warm and damp. I stopped even wiping the last of the juice puddles out of the counter corners. Who was I to deny my sisters a treat? Hadn't we all had the same long days in the heat?

I am a crawling thing too. We move together, the flies and I. I feel them spilling out of my mouth; like Midas I leave drippings on everything I touch. I have descended; I am transforming.

Beneath my skin I am a frenzy.

Nora

B y August, the clouds had built themselves into heavy things and begun to hang low, scraping paunched guts against the treetops; and so, torn open by late summer, they made the sky an ocean. The thunderstorms and crackling lightning of July took a new bent, became something sharper, violent. Those earlier summer storms were a tantrum, an hour's stomping respite from the fat days, swollen and dragging through doldrums.

The beast that came in August was a fiercer sort of creature, churned up far out to sea and sent slamming to shore, spitting and screaming, sending people scuttling home, to watch with wide eyes as the world broke apart. Those unlucky enough to be caught away outdoors found themselves at the mercy of a sky with no love for anything. Roads flooded in minutes; trees, their roots shallow, unable to burrow through hard clay, cracked and fell across power lines and highways; creeks gorged themselves, muddy water churning in their beds. The only choice a person had was to stop; stop your car, stop your walk, stop your gasp as rain poured down your face; just stop, and remember you were a minuscule thing, a weak heart beating within a magnificent world. Stop. And pray.

And then it was over, the thunder rumbling off to the north, crashing and splintering against the mountain spine. The storm blown out, the world still and soggy, panting, glad to be alive. They would pour themselves out by the end of the month, these storms, and then the world would be bone-dry, creek beds cracking, the ground rock-hard beneath feet; everything sucked back, sucked in, waiting for the next round to come in September, more hurricanes swirling in off deep water.

Could a person be a hurricane? Building themselves out on some far horizon, until they were turgid with wind, crackling like lightning. Nora pulled their names into her breath: Mark Dixon, John Doe, Trent Gibson, Brody Samuels, Joseph Aguilar. Their names were thin, their presence intangible. They did not flop over her couch at night or lie down beside her in bed to groan nightmares to her, but they haunted her all the same. A finger, poking in the back of her mind, pointing to something she couldn't quite see. The girls, the women, they tugged at her, emerging from the filmy morning gloom to wrap flimsy fingers around her wrist, pull her ear close to the shadows streaming from their pale lips. Their hearts forever beating in time with hers.

Listen. Listen!

"I'm listening," Nora said to the heavy electric air, but all she heard was the thump of her own life in her chest. The beat a steady *ba-dum*, proof that she was here, her feet on the ground, air in her lungs, and hands still empty; her questions fell from her fingertips like rain.

When her phone rang, she jumped.

The New Kid Bites Back

Y ou need a nipple for that glass?"

"Huh?"

"Your glass." Murph, seated beside her, nodded toward her now tepid pint of beer, sweating on the bartop. The night's storm had blown away by midmorning, leaving behind it humidity thick enough to run a finger through. "You're nursing that beer. Should I get you a nipple for it?"

"Oh, fuck off, Murph." Nora scowled. "What are we doing here anyways? It's barely lunchtime. I thought detectives only did this in books." She looked over her shoulder, as if she expected the sergeant to waltz in at any moment, but all she saw was the early crowd of graying men hunched over beers on wobbly tables and knots of lip-sticked ladies sipping glasses of Pinot and nibbling Caesar salad. The world had a muted quality, deflated after the night's deluge and sitting still until it could gather strength again. Everyone slumped. Overhead, a sluggish fan punched hot air from one corner of the room to another.

"You looked like you needed a drink." He shrugged, swallowed down the last of his own pint.

"Looked? You called me."

"Well, I could see by the tone of your voice." He cocked an eyebrow. "Besides, I can't leave without passing along my best trade secrets, one of which is beers on Monday. Isn't that right, Mike?"

The bartender nodded. "Murph on Mondays."

"I do my best thinking when I'm drinking." Murph smiled like the cat who caught the canary.

"Christ," Nora muttered. *Murph on Mondays.*

"You've ascended, little grasshopper. You're ready to wear my shoes."

"Gross."

"I'll air them out first, kid." He clapped her on the back and with a grunt heaved himself out of the chair, which creaked as it scraped backward on the concrete floor. "You stay put, I'm going out for a smoke. And"—he tapped the counter with two rough fingers—"finish that beer while I'm gone."

She watched him lurch out the door, his belly held out in front of him, bouncing off chairbacks and table corners in the tight space of the little bar, and she felt something like resentment well up in her, unexpected and unwelcome.

It was the heat, of course, the silence of unanswered questions, the long hours pulling third shifts and arguing with drunks and using her presence as a shield between her coworkers and civilians. It was the stares and snide whispers that she was still getting from some small corners at the station; it was Dan's hopeless optimism because everything in his life made sense. She was tired. It had been over a year since she'd uprooted her life, all her hard work, and here she was on her day off having drinks with the man she should have replaced months ago.

It wasn't Murph's fault; she knew that, could logically understand it. He was as ready for him to go as she was; it was clear in his increasing short temper, the growing slouch in his walk. But Bellair was as strapped as any small-town force, and their shrinking recruit pool meant they couldn't move her, couldn't afford the overtime pay for the guys who would have to cover her shifts until they found someone new.

That had all been fine for the first few months, especially understandable given the nightmare of deaths and disappearances they'd been wading through. Nora had been glad to have Murph around. Now though she was hot, she was tired, and she was wondering why she was sitting in a dive bar with him on her day off. And why he was here, today, and apparently every Monday, in the middle of his workday? The arrangement was so emblematic of their relationship, she wanted to scream. She didn't like the feeling. Frustration was sticky and uncomfortable. "A chip on your shoulder," her daddy had always said, "will just weigh you down, baby girl."

She took a swallow of her beer, put the glass on the bartop with more force than she'd meant. Well, maybe she wanted to be weighed down for once. Maybe that weight would help put her feet on the ground, so she could walk forward on her own. Maybe it would feel good to wallow and snarl and lick her wounds, wounds that were real, wounds that stung and tore and scarred over. What did her daddy, or Murph, or any man really, know or understand about her position in their world? What could they tell her that mattered? They never listened to her; they leaned on her because they knew she'd show up, on time and uncomplaining. And here she was, proving them right.

Murph was in front of the window now, smacking a pack of cigarettes against the open palm of one hand. It was so easy for him—the assurance, the smiles, the job. She knew he was working too, knew that every smile, every handshake, was a question, that afternoons spent eavesdropping in bars could be as useful as those in an interrogation room. Murph was clever, like one of those little dogs they send down into foxholes. He would let the drooling hounds around him do the footwork and then rush in to take the kill. It was what made him a good detective, that waiting, that watching, the fearless attack at the very end. She'd learned a lot from him, but she was ready to work on her own now.

So much of her life had been spent waiting, watching, holding her thoughts close to her chest. People told her to be one thing, and then another and another and another, until she found herself dizzy from trying to keep up, so she'd learned to stand still and let them project what they needed her to be onto her. And while they did that, she watched and learned. That way she kept things straight; she knew who she was and where she was going. Or she had.

But she'd grown tired of waiting. Waiting weighed on her just as much as anything, and beneath it was always the tension, the feel of walking on a wire, the threat of a fall. Maybe, what she needed to do, was jump. Maybe then she would find out she had wings.

"Earth to Martin. Come in, Martin."

Nora winced at the sound of Murph's stool scraping across the floor. He heaved himself up onto the seat and plopped down with a sigh. A ghost of cigarette stink washed over her face, the stale memories of his trip outside.

"What? Oh, sorry. I was thinking about something."

"I could see the smoke coming out your ears. You almost done with your drink?" He peered down at her glass with an approving nod. "Good. Hey, Mike! Another round. And is it all right if we take them over to that corner table there?"

Mike, who was still polishing the same glass he had been when Murph walked outside, nodded. "You want me to transfer your tab over to Katie? That's her section."

"That works for me. And in that case, can we order some mozzarella sticks too?"

"You go on over then, I'll have her bring them out when they're ready."

"Good man," Murph said as the bartender turned his back to type something into his computer. He pulled a wad of cash from his wallet and left it on the bar. "Only seems fair," he said with a shrug.

"Good man." Nora grinned.

"Who taught you how to be such a smartass?" Murph ribbed, motioning for her to lead the way to the back corner table.

Nora didn't dignify the question with an answer.

"Now," he said after he sank down into his new chair. The far corner of the room was quieter than she had expected, ambient sound drowned out by the hum of the TV screen above them, where sun-glassed poker players stared at one another around a blue table. "What's bothering you, Martin? And don't tell me nothing, because I can feel it—I've got spidey senses."

Nora took a breath, reached one toe out past the solid line of her high wire. "Murph, if I'm going to shift into your place soon—"

"No ifs. You are. I talked to Sarge yesterday, put my foot down. I'm retiring on Halloween. Felt appropriate for an old ghoul like myself."

She crossed her arms, refused to meet his joke with a smile. "Right. Well, thanks. But if you're so sure I'm ready, I need to ask why you don't trust me?"

The words sat, a heavy-bottomed question, between them. A girl, presumably Katie, skipped over and slid two fresh beers across the table at them. Foam sloshed in mock tidal waves, spilled over the lips of the glasses. "Your mozzarella sticks will be right out!" she chimed as she skipped away.

Murph folded his arms over his chest. "I'm not following you, kid."

Nora fingered the bottom of her glass. The high wire trembled under her foot and the wind snapped, but she held firm. She had to believe she had wings. "Murph, everything in my gut's telling me there's a woman's hand somewhere on this case, and you won't even consider the idea."

"Martin," Murph began, taking a deep breath. "We've gone over this. Other than one hair on an accidental—"

"The engineer said he saw a woman." Nora felt a fist clench her stomach, and she bit the inside of her cheek to will it away. *Maybe I'm just tired*, she thought, and then, recognizing the pattern in her thought, pushed it away. She was tired. She was also sure she was right.

"One hair doesn't a case make. At best, it means a woman was likely present. And need I remind you, we're still waiting for the lab to throw back any analysis on it."

"Still? It's been five months!"

"Val says it was pretty badly damaged by heat. Takes time, very delicate. And they're as crunched as we are." He shrugged. "Case wasn't a priority. So in the meantime, unless you'd like to personally interview every single person with long dark hair in whatever range you feel appropriate, we're a bit stuck."

"And the knife? I told you about Sophie's bar knife. I could buy a paring knife at any grocery store. Or hell, anyone who works at that bar could have taken it for a night. Shit, how many bars are there on Peach? In Bellair? It's the right size, the right type of blade. A woman could easily handle it."

"Handle it, sure, but have you ever stabbed someone to death? It's hard, Martin. It takes a lot of force. And a cheap knife could break, you thought about that? Never mind the most glaring question—what about Mark? Could a woman throttle a man? I'm not saying it's impossible." He held up a hand against her interruption. "I'm just saying, until we have other evidence, we've got nothing. And should I remind you, we haven't found Brody Samuels yet, or, *or*, any evidence of foul play."

"And Joseph Aguilar?"

"Not our case. And from what I've heard, there's nothing there either. Say it with me, Martin. No body . . ."

"No crime," she muttered. "It's only a matter of time, Murph. And what about their tongues?"

"What about them?"

"Every woman I know has wanted to shut men up at some point."

"Well, you've got me there . . . But I don't know, kid. People have done stranger things. I just don't think it's strong enough, and speaking of strong enough . . ."

"Yes, I know, you don't think a woman could lift those men, but, Murph, I've lifted mountains when I had to. If someone was determined, in the right state of stress and adrenaline, who's to say she couldn't?"

"Look," he began, just as a basket of mozzarella sticks was pushed across the table, two paper plates and a stack of napkins right behind it. "Thanks, Katie." He waited for her to skip away. "Now, *Nora*, I know you're frustrated, and I get it. You've been ready for a year, and believe me, my old ass has been too. No one wants me out more than me. And if this psycho hadn't shown up last winter, I would be.

"But if you want my spot, you have to play the game. And the game is not wild conspiracy theories about killer women that don't fit any of the patterns we know. Women kill for two things: love or money. Period." He tapped the table with two thick fingers to make his point. "Love or money. I know feminism has fed y'all some kumbaya shit about everyone being equal, and hell, if we're all equal, why not extend that to serial killers? But that's simply not how the real world works. You've *got* to keep your head on here, if you want Sarge to give us both what we want.

"And here's the real shocker: I actually agree with you, Martin." He laughed, and then Murph's face did something she'd never seen before. It fell. "There probably is a woman involved in this case. Something in my gut's been pushing me that way too. To be quite honest, I'm surprised women haven't just turned on us all by now. Y'all do have the upper hand. I know you don't believe me, but you do. Men are *terrified* of women. Maybe that's why we kill them.

"Look, I know you think I don't trust your judgment, that I question you too much, but I needed to know you could justify your instincts. Maybe I went about it the wrong way, but I had to get you mad enough to want to prove me wrong. A gut feeling is a good place to start, kid, but it doesn't do us any good if it doesn't turn up something we can use in court. So, you got someone you want to question?"

He had her there. "No." She crossed her arms over her chest, folded legs through each other. A grudging sort of respect had risen in her heart again. Murph could be a real dick, but he trusted her.

"Well."

"Not yet." She took a bite of a cheese stick, steam spilling across her face.

He threw his head back in a deep laugh. "We should have hired you sooner, Martin. You hold your own better than half the cowboys we got in that station."

"So I can take those files home then? Give them a look-over where I have some quiet? Come up with a list."

Murph sighed, took a swallow of his beer. "I would tell you to take a day off, but I know you won't listen to an old man."

"I—"

"Don't sweat it, kid. How about, since we both know that big brain of yours is going to keep spinning whether you're at the station or not, we go back to my desk and work on it together? Sound good?"

Nora nodded, not believing her luck and not wanting to press it.

He continued, his voice suddenly serious. "The shit thing is, I don't think we're going to get a crack in this case until we get another body. The worst part of this job isn't the not knowing; it's the waiting. And whoever this person is—man, woman, whatever—they're very good at what they do."

A chill seemed to creep into the bar then, cutting through the heat of that sweltering day. Nora pressed an ear to it, reached out a finger to try to touch it. She could feel them there, whoever they were, out in the world, hiding in the shadows. Like her, waiting, watching. How long would it take for them to get bored? How long would it take for them to make a mistake?

September

Sophie Braam

What makes women so difficult to catch, I've read, is that we're more careful than men. I've read a lot about us. We creep in the background, pull strings instead of triggers, slip poisons or pillows over a life. You've heard our names; can you see them, in your mind? Over there, leaning against the cocktail bar, a cigarette folded just so in her pout, is the Black Widow. And there, in her scrubs, bending over her patient, the Angel of Death. Or outside talking to your daughter, that most reviled creature, the Femme Fatale dancing a dangerous pas de deux with her lover, reeling in young victims like fish for him to play with. Nightmares.

Scientists will tell you that we don't exist. That we're too emotional, too caring, too weak. That we only kill when we need to, for mercy, for money, to keep us safe from men.

I guess I am rare then. I am a woman who's found I rather enjoy it, killing.

And because of that, I made a mistake.

It started like this: I was ignoring a man at the bar.

Ty draped his body across the counter like some sort of beached sea creature, feeling with tan fingers for the liquor bottle he knew was nestled just beyond his reach; he swept over the cool metal spout, once, twice; so close and so unsuccessful.

"Coming for a drink with us, Soph?" *Swipe.*

Ignoring him because the last thing I felt like doing was playing pals with the servers who were now doing cartwheels across the newly mopped patio floor, the space clear after all the tables had been tucked in and chained for the night. Giggles erupted as Amber, already tipsy from ramekin shots snuck during dinner rush, flopped over halfway through her acrobatic routine.

An early, sharp pop and a slow drag to the end of the night meant most of my bar was clean, the dishes washed and polished, the fruit neatly wrapped and packed away. I had the next two days off; they stretched before me, wide open and empty, a pit to fall into, a place to get lost. The part of me that was growing hollow, that echoed and clanged and needed to be filled, tugged at my arm, *Go home. They'll see you.* I emptied the dishwasher, the draining water loud as it was sucked out the bottom.

"You can't ignore me forever."

"Why not? I'm a pro."

"I know you are." Ty caught the tip of the spout in two tight fingers, tugged until he had it up enough from the rail that he could slide a hand around its slim neck and pull the bottle upward. "Hand me two shot glasses, will you?"

The trash. I always forgot to take the trash bag out on slow nights. I grabbed the slick black bag, twisted it in on itself, wrapping the plastic around my fists and tying tight. Air squeezed out its lungs; sweeping past my face was the sharp smell of soured fruit, bits of discarded dinner, stale beer and wine. A cloud of fruit flies rose up from the bottom of the bin.

"God, they're bad this year, huh?" Ty was behind me then, disgust written on his face for my sisters, who floated between us.

"I hadn't noticed."

"Really?" Out of the corner of my eye, I saw his head tip sideways, like a dog listening. When I was a girl, we'd had a corgi who would do that, tip her head one way, then the other with each word we said. I used to call her Air Traffic Control.

He reached around my shoulder for the shot glasses that lined the shelf. "Have a shot. Come out with us."

"Why?"

"Because"—he shoved one of the glasses into my palm—"I'm tired of being the only adult in the room after hours. And I want to catch up with my buddy, find out why she's been smiling to herself so much."

The words spilled out of my mouth on the liquor, before I had time to catch them. "Because I killed a man."

He choked on his shot, and then his head dropped back in laughter. "You're a smartass, you know that? Never fucking change."

He'd forgotten. So many months without anything to shake this town, and he'd forgotten how small his life was. He couldn't see the truth because he didn't believe it, would never believe it; such a thing simply wouldn't cross his mind. I could have laughed at the absurdity of it all. I could have confessed to everyone at this bar and they'd all think it was a joke. I held the idea in my hand, a hard, shining globe, thought about tossing it out into the aisle. Instead, I winked and said, "As long as the cops don't catch me."

And Ty laughed.

The night, late-summer velvet that smelled of fresh hay and felt like a millstone hanging around our necks, opened its mouth and swallowed us whole. I looped an arm through Ty's in a lazy bridge as we made our way to Tap House, the servers capering in front of us like children, caught in air brimming with the last cricket songs of the season.

Maybe it was that humid air, or the dervish joy of my coworkers, or that nostalgic tug from Ty that got me out the door and across the street that night. Maybe it was boredom, after weeks of silence from the police; I had an itch to grab a tree and shake it, just to see what fell out. No matter the reason, I found myself on that mid-September night doing something I never did: following my coworkers out into that dark and pulsing air.

Every town has a kitchen sink, that bar where everyone ends up at the end of the night, circling the drain. It's often too bright or too sticky, too loud; the whiskey is always warm and the wine is always off, but the nachos are second to none and the bartender is the only man you know you can trust to make your drinks. In Bellair, that bar is Tap House. And on a Tuesday, she was as full as she would be any other evening, catching the regulars at the end of their play and the lifers just off work. We slid into the drain.

That night unrolled as those nights do. A shot slammed, a beer cracked, a cigarette out front when the room grew too close. Customers and coworkers, not used to seeing me out anymore, bumped into the back of my chair to say hello. I let them bustle up to me, glassy-eyed and teetering, press their hands onto my shoulders and tell me how happy they were to *see me out for once*.

"So, Soph," Ty said, sometime late in the night.

"Sew buttons. What's up?"

"What's up is, we've been sitting here for an hour, I'd say we've got thirty minutes to last call, and you still haven't spilled the beans about your secret lover."

"I told you, I killed him."

His laugh was a bit smaller then, the gleam in his eyes sucked back. "You sure you're all right? You know, I still feel really bad about Mack the other night . . ."

I stopped paying attention to him somewhere around there, though his voice curled around my throat like a tongue or a fly on a hot day. I felt it creep down the smooth ripples of trapezius, deltoid, squeeze up under infraspinatus, through the hidden foramen, to rest there on the knot, which had begun to spark again. The bar was too much, all those laughing, jeering faces, sticky counters, overhead lights. I was crawling and they would see me. I pushed off the counter to leave.

"I know Mark could be like that too, obnoxious. To be honest though, I know he drove you nuts, but I always wondered if there wasn't something going on between . . . Oh shit." Ty put his hand over his mouth.

They say, in moments like this, that your heart stops. This is untrue. What really happens is that, flooded with adrenaline from a sudden shock, it begins to beat harder. The shakes, the tunnel vision, the sudden loss of air are all the symptoms of a brain flooded with oxygen and scrambling to keep up. My heart did not stop when Ty touched my secret; it prepared me to run. I'm lucky, I suppose, that I have years' worth of practice with such uncomfortable feelings. I made my face a mask of sadness, willed my eyes to water.

Like a deer caught in my headlights, Ty froze, then slowly put his glass back on the bar counter. "Shit. I forgot you were with him that night. Sorry. *Fuck.* I'm an asshole. Forget it, let's move on. Another round, on me—for Mark. Mike! Hey! Sophie and I need you." He turned down the length of the bar, his cheeks burning with drink and shame. I watched his fingers fidget with one another, curling about the base of his pint glass.

If only he knew.

I wondered though, if like those deer, he knew, he felt it, the weight of death sitting next to him. Could he sense me rippling beneath my skin, smell the graves I'd dug with my fingers? Did he see their faces, flashing across mine?

The next man I killed stumbled in through the door just before last call. I'd never seen him before, though his accent and the bags of

Chinese takeout slowly choking the ends of his purpling fingers implied someone who was at least comfortable in our little neck of the woods, if not native to it.

He came in like a punch. Even tipsy as I was, I felt the air stiffen at his stomping approach, my spine flinch at his big-bellied crash with the bar counter.

"Hey, have a drink with me!" he called out to anyone in the room unlucky enough to make eye contact. I was not afraid, so I lifted my gaze to his face and found two small eyes pricking over meaty jowls that shook with each bold step he took. The bags twisted tighter on his fingers, but he paid them no mind, focusing his energy on shoving his hospitality on unwitting victims.

"Hey, let me buy you a drink." His breath swept over my head, to Ty.

"No thanks, man. I'm all good."

"What about you?" A hand fell heavy on the back of my stool. "Let me buy you a drink."

It was the attack I didn't know I'd been looking for, though I gritted my teeth against it all the same. In this garish light, surrounded by people who knew my face, I could not be a viper; I had to sit still. The grave that had built itself in the center of my being yawned. My creeping armor, now flush atop my skin, touched tongues to his fingertips, tasting, testing. This one, yes, he might do. *Take a breath, Sophie. Don't let them see the pits in your eyes.*

"She's good too, brother. But thank you. Why don't you just take a seat, have a glass of water? Right, Mike?" Ty, not used to being ignored, put his hand on the counter.

This is a game men play. *Brother* and *man* and *buddy* are triggers cocked halfway. Hands on the counter, when pushed, become fists. Chests swell forward like great yacht sails, throats tighten, and jaws tense. And my voice, if I dared to think I had one, is tossed over a shoulder and carried away by the greater force of Man. But I was bored and I was restless, and the mites picked at my skin. *You should have gone home, but you didn't. Now he's fallen into your lap. Don't let this one get away.*

I had one move here. The queen always wins. Place a palm on a thigh, another on the opposite chest. Make your voice small, soothing, something soft and barely there so it has to be listened to. Like a rattlesnake. Let your body become both weapon and shield.

"Ty. I'm fine. Sir, thank you for the offer. But I was just about to leave."

I hate this game. I hate this part in the play. I want to scream at both of them, tell them to *Oh, go and just punch each other if it'll make you feel better, you enormous, idiotic babies.* I wanted to melt into a thunderstorm and tell them I'd already killed five men and no one had caught me—what was two more? But I didn't. I sat, one hand flat on Ty's thigh, the other pressed against the stranger's chest, my body a lightning rod between them both, grounding their electricity, pulling their focus to me. I needed to make myself the quiet locus of their attention. This was a game, nothing but a game, just like those times locked in a walk-in with the kitchen boys. Just a game. Teeth retched at the solid weight of male bodies under my palms. *We know what to do, let us do it.* I forced a smile.

Let Ty think he's special. Let this stranger question my touch. Swallow your pride, let it light a match in your belly. When they're not looking, burn them all down.

"Let's go, Ty."

We tossed handfuls of cash onto the counter and crawled down from our stools. His hand on my back as we walked out the door stung like a brand. I quickened my steps to escape the mouths sticking to the ends of his fingertips.

"We're going over to Billy's house. Y'all joining?" A voice slid through the darkness, a cigarette raised to a shadowed face. Red glow. Smoke.

"I'm down." Ty, still beside me, finally dropped his hand from my back. "Sophie?"

You remember their names: Bundy, Dahmer, Ramirez. And you will remember mine. You'll remember my name—Sophie Braam—because I am smart, because I have made a game of this, of killing men. You'll remember my name because I am more than a nightmare.

An Impossibility

A chef I worked with once, years ago, at another bar in another life, told me he found a paw print in his yard one morning. The print, pressed deep into the red mud near his daughter's swing set, was too big to be a coyote and didn't have claw marks, like a bear's would. The print, he was certain, was from an animal park rangers will tell you hasn't been seen in Virginia since the 1970s. Park rangers, like police, prefer to ignore things they don't understand, like mountain lions or dangerous women.

What makes the cats so deadly is their silence. They'll follow prey for miles, winding through trees, their footsteps more quiet than the breath that plumes from your mouth. And they're patient. Waiting hidden for hours, for just the right moment.

He passed me on the way back to my car, his lumbering step an earthquake that shook loose those last worries clinging to me. While the boys waved and hollered, debating with one another whether the gas station was still open and selling beers, I stood at my car in the dark, watching the man with the dangling Chinese food bags stumble away. I waved the boys ahead. "I need to change! Get out of here. I'll meet you there in a minute. Yes, I know where I'm going."

Into the dark.

The liquor boiled under my skin, so it was easy to slide it off in the warm air, in the shadows crisscrossing the crumbling back parking lot. I am small; my steps are light. I am small: "I'm so sorry about my friend back there. He's just drunk, and he gets protective of me." I am small: "Here, you've got a lot in your hands, let me get the door for you." I am small.

He was parked at the far edge of the potholed parking lot, past the reach of streetlights, in the thorny grasp of a few blackberry vines.

I am small.

Could he see me crawling, when I got close to him? See the cat ripping out of my rib cage, feel the teeth gnash under my flesh as I reached for his wrist?

I am small. Trust me. I am small. Don't look at me.

I have claws.

He fell into his back seat with a gasp, and I left him there. He had a blanket on the seat and I yanked it out from under him, threw it over his fat face, walked away. I was feeling like a man. Reckless and unbound. I could deal with him later. Tomorrow. Tonight, I had a party to go to, life to celebrate.

A Maenad

There's a certain too-bright sparkle to a group of restaurant lifers at a party. It's hard to understand if you've never seen it, never been a part of the off-kilter family that spends their days in the trenches, getting paid $2.00 per hour to smile and simper to the worst of humanity. Like deep-ocean fish, the light that emanates off a server after shift and away from the confines of concrete civilization is something neon and unnerving. Something is always just out of place. On the fish, it might be a horrifyingly large set of teeth or strange blank eyes. My coworkers, not aquatic save for their drinking habits, found other ways to glow. I saw it in the light of their eyes, slashing in my headlights as I pulled up; the odd sort of tilt to their shoulders as they walked or danced or leaned close to ferry secrets from their mouths to waiting ears; I heard it in their laughter, which had grown a sharp edge in the hour since I had last seen them. In the dark, in the night, away from customers and computers and all the mundane stresses of a life lived always on display but never really seen, they could finally let out their spines. I saw them, sharp and glistening in the night.

This is what I was born from. Days so long that even after years of working them, my feet still sometimes ached like bruises and my back broke itself over and over. Days that, after I tipped out the busser and the hostess and paid for my staff meal, I realized I'd spent money to come to work. Hands on my wrists and eyes on my thighs and mouths pulling me apart; we are, all of us, only so much meat, after all. The flesh is stripped from your bones year after year until you find yourself something dangerous, something that shines in the dark.

It's a wonder more of us don't turn to murder. Maybe, if we weren't so busy dying of suicide or alcoholism or suicide by alcoholism, we would.

That's how I saw them, that close September night when I pulled up the gravel drive to park in the grass in front of Billy's house. There they were, that bacchanal, dancing and laughing, smoking, drinking, falling, in front of the fire they'd built.

And for that one star-strewn night, I allowed myself to dissolve with them. I dropped my mask into the grass, and all the flapping, pulsing, roaring itch of me stretched out into the wide world and relaxed. I was safe. In the dancing firelight, no one would notice how I quivered.

Someone shoved a cup into my hand and I drank it down, held it out for another. Arms looped through mine, and I let them sweep me away to the kitchen, where Ty was slopping together his own concoction of cherry limeade and vodka, maybe a bit of lemonade too, oh, and can someone grab a can of soda water from the fridge? Let's give Soph some fizz. He finished it off with a handful of various assembled fruit bits and a sprig of pine from a tree outside.

"Beautiful." It tasted like bad decisions.

We drank until the sky tore at the hem and began to fade to her morning hue. The last cigarettes were lit, their red tips like so many stars fading into the dawn. In those quiet moments, those of us still awake became our own constellation, amid the peepers and the dew, and the humid air that hung still and heavy over the gray dawn, waiting for us to break apart, fall limp to the cold ground.

Perhaps, if I'd been listening, I would have heard a warning in that stillness. Instead, I found myself utterly alive and swept up in the budding birdsong, in the delight of my own secret power that was growing, that, better, I was learning to control enough so that I could sacrifice an evening to that certain tipped-over madness.

We were shining then, all of us. Dreamers, thrumming with the coming dawn. Free and in love with the world. And always, forever, more interesting than you.

I should have been listening though, to the whispers in the mists, the soft prick of the hairs on the back of my neck, that feeling in my feet of spinning too fast, of being out of control. If I had been, I would have seen it before it happened. I would have stopped. I would not have hit that car in the intersection.

Sophie

They put me in a cage.

But first, they stripped me.

They began with my shoes, the cheap flip-flops I keep in my car to relieve feet cramped and suffocating after too many hot hours closed under the leathery cover of my work clogs. They had no laces, nothing with which I could hang or harm myself, but they took them anyway. "Standard protocol." "Because." These were the answers I was given to my whys. My belt too, they asked me to pull from around my waist, place it into the waiting plastic bag. Watch, necklace, rings, each slipped off under watchful eyes, dropped into that same gaping mouth and folded away. The last thing they took from me was myself. A solemn-faced woman with a too-tight bun plopped my purse down into my lap.

"We need your ID."

I have given myself away in many ways, but this was a new sort of flaying of my identity.

"What are you going to do with it?"

She didn't answer. Merely folded her arms across her chest and stood, glowering at me. I suspect she's seen too many of Me before. We are sisters then, her and I, dealing night after night with the drunk and annoying public. But in that moment she saw me as Them, and there was nothing I could do to dispute that.

Except there was one thing. "I want to talk to Nora Martin. She's an officer here."

"No, she's not."

"She works for the Bellair PD."

"That's not us, sweetheart. ID, please."

The pit in my stomach, the animal thing that had grown teeth and claws and roared out of me, became a stone. Behind my eyes, the mites shivered; their voices grew quiet. This was a time to tiptoe, to be a solid face, a woman and nothing more. The animal inside me would need to purr.

"Sure it is. This is the jail. You're not connected?"

Silence.

"Can't I call her? I get one phone call, right?"

"No. You're drunk."

I wanted to tell her that I wasn't, that the shock of the last hour had sobered me up quite nicely. Instead, I dug into my purse, fingers searching for the tongue I'd slipped into a pocket some hours earlier. It was still there. I pulled out my ID, pushed it across the table to the woman now scowling at me.

"We don't want you to waste your one call. Turn off your phone for now. When you sober up, then you can have it back. And purse goes in here." She opened the plastic bag wide again. I almost broke then, the chorus of giggles rippling down my throat at the thought of that tongue, being put into this new sort of mouth.

The woman, who was without a doubt a Michelob Ultra when she got off, Barefoot Moscato when she was feeling fancy, scowled. "Something funny?"

"No, ma'am."

"Hands."

She pressed each finger, one by one, onto the pad on her desk while I sat frozen in the glaring fluorescent light. The ink was cold. She pushed my fingers down hard, so they bit against the plastic box of the pad. I watched the tips flush white with each press, then red with her release. White, red, white, red, on and on until each one was done. These bits of me, rolled onto a screen to be swallowed down into the nest of tubes and wires connecting its eyes to a brain somewhere far away.

Would they find a match?

The giggles that had been bubbling up became a frenzy, boiling beneath my ribs, up into my skull to rattle and churn through my meninges—dura, arachnoid, pia—all the hollow space between my ears. I'd been careful, but what if I'd left behind a scrap of myself somewhere? A fingerprint kiss on Mark's neck, a ghost on Trent's zipper? What if someone found a body out in the woods? What if what if *what if*, the questions rolled over me like a wave and suddenly I was a ship tossing on an ocean. All the *what ifs*, the small moments, the creeping worries and lip-biting and hairs standing up on my neck fell over my shoulders and I was drowning in the same small panics I'd known all my life. What if I wore that skirt, drank that drink, kissed that boy? They circled my mind like carrion birds, screaming, until I heard my grandmother say again, in her husky voice, "Sophie. Breathe."

There was nothing I could do, sitting there in a cage. So I took a breath, crawled into my chest, and began the process of pooling my soul in an untouchable place.

She waved to a man who stood off to one side. An order. "Over there."

I was a baton, passed between partners. He stepped forward, put a hand out as guide.

"Stand on that black X there. Good. Face me."

Flash.

"Turn to your right."

Flash.

They scolded me and turned me, picked at me like vultures, and I let them because I had to—what other choice was there? Everything in me coiled until I was an itching, biting, scrabbling mess of feet and bodies below my skin, while my face above stayed cold. I knew how to be in a cage. This one was uglier, meaner, the worst of any I'd been in yet, but it was not so different, at its core, from the one I'd been walking around in all my life.

The man at the intersection hadn't listened to reason when I told him he should just take my insurance information and go. He didn't care that I knew I was only tired, not drunk, *only tired*; that I didn't expect him to be stopped, because no one stopped at this one dinky red light on Peach Street until at least seven a.m. on weekdays, eight a.m. on weekends. What sort of maniac stops at a red light on a lonely road? So, really, who was in the wrong here? We should just both feel lucky that no one was hurt and move on. There was no need to call the police.

He was unbearably stubborn. "You might be fine, miss, but I won't be if I don't show my employer proof of why I'm calling out of my shift this morning."

It was then that I noticed the hospital logo on his oversize T-shirt, a few pale bleach stains along the bottom hem. His shoes were sensible, rubber-soled and close-toed. A janitor.

The orders continued, a staccato grunt. "Grab a mattress from the pile. Yep, that one over there. Bring it here. This is your cell. How long do you stay here? Until we decide you're sober enough. Once you cross that line on the floor, you belong to us."

Shit.

The cell was too bright. Too cold. Too clean. Concrete and white-painted cinder block, light so bright I felt it digging claws behind my eyes, bodies flooding into the open sinuses beneath them until my bones were soaked and dripping with the sort of malaise that can collect in only such a space. I felt all my breath gather into a tight ball at the base of my throat, tucked hidden and away, too small to find, too heavy to lift out.

Fifty feet away from me, those ogres plopped down in front of their shared TV, shoved handfuls of chips and candy into their slobbering mouths. I've heard that these people, jail guards, are the bottom rung of the law enforcement hierarchy. A kinder mind than mine would argue that's because they put in long hours dealing with the absolute worst abuse day in and day out; that to spend eight hours every day locked in a stale, fluorescent box would ruin anyone. But I don't have a kinder mind, and so I saw them for the selves they showed me—schoolyard bullies too lazy or inept to even make it through the police academy, too bitter because they knew we all knew this, and too depressed to care. Why should they? They had power here, in this concrete world where the lights never turned off so it was always horrid artificial day, where sound smacked against hard floors and the rule of law was something akin to that arm-twisting game all children play. Which one of us could hold out the longest—the one turning my bones past the point they could bend, or me, gritting my teeth against the clanging warning of a break?

Across the way from me was a man who looked like he'd been here before. He stood with his arms stretched up to the top of his door lintel, grabbing hold and sucking air down into his toes, filling the space with his striped body. An hour later, they brought in another man, handcuffed and wearing the same uniform.

"You don't have to wear one of those," I'm told when the guard walks past me. "You're small beans."

I didn't feel so small. The sudden shock of shame and panic blooming in my chest swelled until it filled the hard space of that too-bright cell. All the years I'd felt trapped, I hadn't known what trapped was, that it could grow a body and a mouth and climb up out of my nightmares to gobble me whole. *Small beans*, he'd said, so casually, as if these hours of being stripped of myself and locked away were a joke;

like a catcall on a hot afternoon, like feeling guilty for saying yes to a date you don't want to go on, but it's easier than hurting his feelings. Safer too. All the cages I've locked myself away in my whole life opened their mouths that awful morning and I felt myself tumble in. There was nothing to hold on to, no way to save myself. The only thing I could do was promise myself I'd never be put in a cage again.

I should have reached out, shown him we were no different, he and I. We both lived a life bobbing along the ocean of other people's whims, cleaning up after them, yes-ma'aming and no-sirring, making them happy. If I had been thinking and not prowling, I would have. If I had been thinking and not quivering, I could have made this all go away with a smile. Sweet smile. Honey.

He locked himself in his car. Maybe he's met women like me before; he felt the lion pacing behind my ribs. Or maybe he saw my skin ripple and my jaw clench when I asked myself if, maybe, he was a problem I could fix.

My car.

His car. Him. Someone would find him. And what would they find in my car? I'd gotten blood on my work shirt. What had I done with it? Teeth chattered at the tips of my fingers; something was screaming behind my eyes. I had a dim memory of tossing something into the woods, but I couldn't hold on to it. The lights were too bright, my thoughts couldn't get a foothold. They fell over themselves, slipped past one another; all the while, underneath, those mites, bloated now with panic, pressed their rasping tongues to my ears.

I looked down at my hands, was thankful that I'd been sure to wash the blood from under my fingernails. It was down the drain at Billy's house now. Small blessings.

"Where's my car?" I asked, the next time the guard came around, pushing the breakfast trolley before him like a horrid flight attendant.

"Breakfast."

"Let me have my phone call. I'm sober. What happened to my car?" A fist clenched my belly. My mask slipped, a mite crawled out across my skull. He would see it; the light was so bright I couldn't hide.

"You want breakfast or not?"

It is humbling how quickly a sort of madness can creep in. I couldn't see the sun, but I could feel it, climbing the sky. The minutes dragged their feet. Would I ever get out of here? What if they found him before I could escape? Did they already know? Anyone paying attention would notice that underneath the cigarette smoke and the alcohol, I smelled of death. Just a whiff, barely rotted, sickly sweet, lying quiet in the shallow pit above my collarbone, the soft cotton of my tank top. What if they find it in my car? What if they looked into my purse and saw the tongue there? What if even now they're putting together a case against me? There, in the cold and stagnant cell, I became a mite myself, scrabbling and scratching under its dead, concrete skin.

"I want my phone call, now."

"I guess you're not hungry then."

I slammed my fist against the glass of my cell as he rolled the cart away. "Fucking *asshole*."

If he heard me, he showed nothing, instead continuing his roll from one cell to the next, slopping food out onto trays or wheeling past those who, like me, dared to be anything less than deferent.

I felt the day creeping on, moving past me as I sat and stood and paced and sat again, every once in a while stopping to peer across the room at the guards all seated at their desk, eyes glued to something on the TV. They traded jokes like playing cards, ignored the man standing a few cells away, shouting that he needed to see a doctor.

Finally, when they got bored, or maybe needed my cell, or found they could no longer justify holding me, two of them walked over. They were fat, stooped in the way of men who spend a lifetime working long hours on their feet, their faces sallow from a lack of fresh air.

"I want my phone call."

"How about you blow into this for us first, and then we can think about that call?" the fatter one said, pulling a Breathalyzer out of his pocket.

"I'm sober. I'm talking to you just fine, aren't I?"

"People aren't great judges of when they are or aren't drunk." In another life, we would have shared a nod here, a chuckle; maybe he would have even winked. After all, hadn't I had the same thoughts, standing behind my bar on a Friday night?

The other one piped up: "Just do this for us, sweetheart, and we'll see what we can do for you."

Sweetheart. I closed my eyes to hide the tears of frustration and shame I felt welling in them and let the men press their pipe into my mouth.

"Blow," one of them said. *Sweetheart. Doll. Blow.*

And I did, feeling just as exposed and abused as I had so many times before, in my younger life, when I let men use me like a toy they could pull down off the shelf when they wanted to play. Deep in my chest, the part of me that I had tucked away for safekeeping curled tighter in on herself. My skin crawled. I balled my hands into fists. If only they knew.

"Point-oh-six. Almost there. Drink a few more cups of water, and we'll come back after we get these guys signed out."

"That's under the legal limit. I'm sober. And I'm not driving anyways."

"It won't take long."

"I want my phone call."

"You can have your phone back when we let you out."

———

So that was their game then. I waited their hour, drank the tepid water that dribbled out of the sink next to my toilet, curled on my mattress in the back corner of my cell. Sometime later, one of them taped a cover up over my window. "So you can pee if you need," he said. Not unfair, given I was the only woman in a room full of men, all within easy view of me. But I suspect he did it more so they wouldn't have to look at me until they were ready. I glared at the window, willed my eyes to bore holes through it.

One thought was a beacon. My car. They must have searched it and found nothing. The realization slides a hand over my skin and I am crawling. To know that a stranger has gone through my space, taking stock of it all. They do this, they say, "more for your good than ours." To avoid lawsuits, to help you, if something is stolen from the impound lot.

"I'm doing this to help you," "Believe me, I don't enjoy it"—this is what they say when they need to feel better about breaking you. This abandonment, this humiliation, this pain that I've decided to inflict, it's all "for your own good. Because I care." They must have taken lessons from my father.

They can't have found anything though, or they would have said so. I clung to that. Let them pull me apart, look at me, so long as they don't see what's hidden. His body, they wouldn't find with me. The rest—what had I thrown into the woods? Where was my knife?

They would have said something though, if they'd found anything, I was certain. So I waited, put a hand over the mouths chewing on my heart.

They burped me out at twelve thirty. I never got my phone call. After, in the back seat of my cab, the tears fall. My driver doesn't ask, and I'm glad for it. I feel something clamping down on my ankle, and the bristling urge to run, to fight, to get away. And there, just behind it, slower but just as powerful: anger. Hot, driving rage.

Nora

He was a carcass, that bloated and blackening thing stuffed into the back seat of a beat-up sedan. A carcass, not a corpse. A corpse was human. A corpse had a name and a family; a corpse had a smile. And this man who was a carcass and not a corpse had not been human to the one who killed him.

Everything was wrong. This wasn't how men died. Men weren't strangled or butchered like pigs, left naked and humiliated to rot in the trash. Their tongues were never cut out of their skulls like trophies. Men died in barroom brawls, territorial spats over girlfriends, drugs, cash. They died from beatings and bullets, the occasional sloppy stab slicing through something vital. The deaths of men in Nora's world were loud, pointless things. Their violence toward one another was a chest-beating flash in the pan, over as soon as it started and covered in blood. Even in their rage, men treated one another like humans.

The mutilation, the mortification, the disgust and anger and overkill slashing through his ruined throat was a rage they reserved for women. Men beat women like they were beating the Atlas weights of their world into the dust, threw them out like they were nothing, they meant nothing. The strangling, the butchering, the spitting and abuse, violation of their bodies even after they were dead, that was what men did to women, to disabuse themselves of the notion that they were anything less than whole. Whole. Holes. Holed people did this. Holed people ruined people as a stopgap for their own spiritual weep.

But men did not do this to men. No, Nora couldn't concede that, no matter what Murph thought.

The carcass, the corpse, the man, shimmered and flashed and a thousand beating blowfly wings swallowed Nora as she bent down to peer into his face, which had been shoved deep into the footwell at an awkward angle; his neck, broken, bowed under his chin in horrid imitation of a boomerang. Something like breath pushed out of the ruined cave of his mouth, and the rancid stench of rot reached an arm up into Nora's throat. She gagged. Turned away into the flash and whine of cameras behind her. They were scouring the parking lot, peeking into the car, their questions asked in the language of shutter speed. Nora turned back to the body.

Flash.

Disgust was torn into him, this man, this corpse, this carcass. Rage, bit again and again in deep puncture wounds. This was the language of an animal trapped, broken loose and out of control. There, and there, again and again, teeth and claws. Teeth and claws.

But only, it appeared, on the front of him. This attack was a bomb, not a fire. It didn't swallow him whole.

She found his hands, tucked tight to his chest, and tugged one up to get a better look at it. If he'd been hit from the front, surely he'd have fought it; yes, there, on the wide, cold palms, she found long slashes. And something else.

Hair. Long dark strands, wrapped around fingers, caught on the serrated grooves of shredded flesh. Hair, Nora thought on first sight, very like what they had found in a boy's hands all those long months ago. She pulled a plastic baggie out of her pocket and a pair of tweezers, her heart hammering. She was right, she knew it. These deaths didn't feel like men's deaths, because they weren't. There was no partner involved here. This was a rage only women could understand.

A reckoning too long overdue. She shivered. The thought triggered something deep in Nora's brain, something that made her feel uncomfortable, a shadow she didn't want to face. This was an anger she understood, that she kept hidden under her bed, where the only damage it might do was swipe at ankles in the night.

"Whatcha got there, lady?" Val leaned over her shoulder. In her excitement, Nora hadn't heard the woman creep toward her across the crunching gravel lot.

"Questions . . . An idea, I don't know . . . I . . . Look at this, Val." Nora held up the baggie for the other woman to see. "Hair. Long hair."

Val crouched down next to her, waving away a cloud of flies that swarmed toward her, attracted no doubt by the feel of death that always hung around this woman who spent so much time with corpses.

"You think there was a woman involved?" Val looked thoughtfully at the strands lying coiled in the bag.

"It's long."

"A lot of men have long hair too . . ." Val peered down at the carcass, moved a gloved hand up along the broken line of his throat to his wretched, gaping mouth. Blowflies scattered into the cavernous car, buzzing. "Damn, whoever did this to him slammed hard. Chipped his cervical vertebrae. Look." She teased the hole in his throat open enough for Nora to see in. "Must be how they shut him up."

"So you don't think a woman was involved?" Nora felt her heart deflating.

When Val looked back up at her, she felt the same questions skirting in the dark behind her pupils. "I'm not saying it's *not*. I'm just saying men can have long hair too. Or maybe this man was attacking her and someone else stepped in. Can't rule out self-defense until we know more."

"Until we know if this matches that other hair." Nora conceded the point and then made one of her own: "Has it even been tested yet, that one we found in March?"

Val sighed. "I think you might have to let that one go. We've still got it, but it's looking like heat from the train probably cooked any DNA we could have gotten off it. I'll do what I can; we can at least use it to visually test against these. If our friend here yanked them out in a fight, the root may very well be still attached. That can give us sex at least."

"I mean, *look* at him," Nora said. "Look at this anger. Tell me you don't believe a woman would want to do this."

Val smiled. "Oh, I believe it. But I have to follow the science."

"Yeah," Nora sighed. "Yeah, I guess you do." Val was right. That voice though had been so strong in the back of her mind. "All the same, can we get a rush on this?"

This was a woman, she was sure of it.

Murph was waiting for her in the little blue tent that followed them around to every crime scene. He waved to Nora and held out a cup of steaming coffee in offering, which she took with a quiet thanks. Charlie stood next to him, sunglasses pulled down over his eyes, his mouth set in a grim line, his own coffee half-gone.

"So, you cracked the case? Can I retire yet?" Murph asked, and as he did so, his belly pressed forward in the breeze like a balloon.

For a moment, Nora half expected him to just float away. A laugh bubbled up in her cheeks at the thought. She swallowed it. She had too many half-submerged feelings to make any sense of them, and there was no time to untangle them now, so she said simply, "Not yet . . . But we did find hair."

"Not his, I'm assuming?"

"Doesn't look like it."

Murph rocked back on his heels, tilted his face up to the cloudless sky. The sun, which should have been cooling now that the days were growing shorter and the shadows longer, was still too hot. Nora watched sweat sparkle and glisten on his forehead, felt fingers of it trail down her own. Summer had been creeping into fall for a while now, and it looked like this year would be no exception. This late though, the heat, which had been a friend only a few weeks before, was an oppressive thing, flat and listless and long overstaying its welcome.

"Charlie," he said, "catch me up to speed. When did the call come in? Who've you talked to?"

Charlie took a sip of his coffee and began. "Maybe around midmorning, just before lunch. One of the Tap House cooks, Chris Perfater, came out for a cigarette before service began."

He nodded toward a man who sat smoking on the curb some yards away. His hands were trembling, eyes unfocused, a look Nora had seen in a thousand other faces. This was not a person who was used to death.

"Yep. So, he says the car's been here a few days. No one really paid it much mind. Happens all the time, you know, people get drunk, get a ride home. They get their vehicle when they can. And this is so far back in the parking lot, no one really cared."

"Right." Murph nodded.

"Well, he was curious because it *has* been a few days, so he thought he'd take a look inside and see if he could figure out whose it was or if they should call the tow truck . . . when he noticed the smell. And the flies."

"Did he touch anything?" Murph pulled out his own pack of cigarettes, lit one. It flared under his face for a moment before curling into pale smoke.

"Says no. Says he called us straightaway."

"Smart man. So then you came out. And, Martin, when did you get here?"

"I was already in the office, so I just rode with Charlie."

Murph lowered his sunglasses so he could peer straight into Nora's eyes. "Martin, how many times have I talked to you about taking your day off, *off*?"

She flushed and bit her tongue, but she didn't look away.

"Okay," he continued, "so walk me through it, bug lady. What did you see?"

It was easy to say the words: *abandoned car, blowflies, maggots, smell*. It was all there, simple and perfect and tied up with a sterile bow. But that couldn't give the full picture of the scene. Those words—*abandoned car blowflies maggots smell*—didn't show the creeping dread that swept over Nora like a shadow as soon as she stepped out into the parking lot. How could she describe the buzz, humming below the pops and tings of metal stretching in the heat? The few flies that slipped through hidden cracks to flit around her head? The way that stench, rotten and thick, tumbled over her like a wave and she'd had to turn back and away, gather herself before she could move forward into the macabre work of unlocking the door and finding what she knew without looking would be death? Could Murph feel the insects bumping into her legs as she opened that metal casket? Thousands of them, suddenly free in the bright sun after days baking in this nightmare oven, eating and breeding and shitting and dying, and suddenly bursting out into that precious fresh air. The blanket that had been covering the carcass that had once been a man forever stained now, brown and black and putrid. Shoved into one corner were boxes of Chinese food, orange sauce sickly sweet, spilled out onto the floor, a nursery pool for hundreds of writhing, white maggots. And stuffed into the other corner, his face, the gruesome smile in the bend of his neck, where someone had torn out his tongue.

"Charlie, why don't you go back to Mr. Perfater, get his contact info, make sure he's got someone to talk to if he needs it . . . you know. All that good stuff. Nora and I should go talk to Val, and I want to get a look at this man before they move him."

Charlie tipped his head. "On it."

"Okay, kid, shall we?" Murph motioned for Nora to follow him back over to the buzzing car.

"Murph"—she tapped him on the arm—"long hair. Again."

316

"Let me see."

She showed him.

"Oh, I thought y'all were just going to stay over at the tent gossiping and let me have all the fun," Val said when they reached the car. Her team of specs was creeping closer by the minute, and Nora was certain that if they didn't get over there soon, Murph wouldn't be able to get a spot in edgewise at the car before they descended.

He looked at Nora and winked. "Antsy today, isn't she?"

"She's not the only thing with ants in its pants," Nora said, and then, realizing her thoughts had slipped out of her mouth, slapped a hand over her face.

"Martin!" Murph howled. "I didn't expect that from you! You really are ready to take over my shoes. Good."

Just as Val started talking, Nora's phone rang.

"Hey, Barb, what's up?" Nora answered, turning away and waving for Murph to keep listening to the investigator.

"Hey, Martin. Listen, are you or Murph able to leave the scene? We just got a call about a break-in at that new housing development. Mailboxes smashed, patio furniture stolen, flower beds trampled. Probably teenagers pulling pranks, but you know how those HOAs are. They'd rather waste their own tax dollars calling us than just have a community meeting."

"Yuppies," Nora muttered, swiping away a fly that was buzzing around her head.

On the other end, Barb laughed. "Don't let them hear you say that, girl."

"Never."

"Anyways . . . Sergeant wants one of you to head over there. I know y'all just got a big call over at Tap House, and Murph might want to keep it since he's more experienced. Either you or him is fine, I just need to know."

"Sounds good, Barb. I'll ask him."

"Great. Just give me a call back and let me know who's where when you decide."

"Will do, Barb. Thanks."

"I'll go," Murph said when she told him.

"Really?"

"Yeah, kid. You're ready to take a scene on your own. Charlie can stay here with you, and I'll meet you in the office when we're both wrapped up for the day."

"You sure?" She'd wanted to give him a chance to assert himself, not out of respect for his experience, but because she'd hoped to have an argument here, to stick up for her own advancement, prove she was ready. But here he was, taking even that small satisfaction out of her hands. She could have smacked him then. But she also could have hugged him.

He laughed and kicked out playfully at her. "Don't make me question my own wisdom. You're ready. Besides, you don't have a car, how you gonna get over there?"

He winked, and Nora flashed him her middle finger, but she couldn't hide her smile. She felt like she'd swallowed that sun itself, she was beaming so bright when she walked back to the car.

Sophie

I felt myself unwinding; like a snake, like a corpse, like a pupa. Peeling out into some new space that felt too wide all of a sudden, and stung when I looked at it. The world had turned me upside down and shook me out. I was becoming. My lungs ripped open and collapsed. I was becoming. The glass in my hand was polished perfectly.

In the melee of my arrest and the sunken hours after it, I forgot to move the car, and now they'd found something.

It was the hostess who noticed first. *Look*. She pointed out the window, her fingertip held a breath away from the clean glass. Her ponytail shone as it flopped over her shoulder to swing down her back. I remember what it was to have a tail like that, to shimmer and sparkle. *Look*. She was there, glimmering in the sunlight, not yet a worn and tired thing, and my barback saw that shine and let himself be pulled to her like a fish to a lure. *Look*, she said to him; eyes as round as moons, he followed the long line of her pretty hand and pressed his own onto the glass while he turned from her and looked, across the street, to the clamor that was happening there.

I didn't need to look. I knew what they could see. But when she turned to me, and I saw him look at her throat, I walked to her all the same, pressing my body between them. He moved back, his fingers leaving an oily smudge on the glass.

I hadn't moved the man's car yet. I hadn't had the chance, hadn't been able to stomach the idea of sitting in his filth. Let him rot, let him bloat, let him melt down into himself until there's nothing more for me to worry about. That had been my plan. Standing there at the window, watching the crew across the street tear it apart, I felt something like fear drip down the electric cord of my spine. Fingers poked at the pain that had long ago made a home in my shoulder.

There, still far away and small, was a trap crawling around the parking lot. Noses and eyes and tasting tongues, sweeping over my mistake like a feast. Women aren't caught, because we're more careful, but I'd acted on impulse, like a man. And look where it got me.

I felt my mind grow heavy in my head and become a panicked thing. Legs and arms shot out from all sides, slipped along the smooth slick of my fascia, blood and bone. This mind, which I had learned in recent weeks to quiet, to soothe, to unleash only when we had need, suddenly found herself scrabbling.

It was exhaustion, I told myself. That fear that I was feeling was nothing more than the fog of a too-long night, anger and frustration, shame left over like mildew covering the walls of an old, forgotten shed. I moved away from the window, found anything I could to clean.

But my mind, unfettered in the unseasonably slow day, tipped back and back and back; swimming far out into memories of the night, three nights before. It tugged each one, dripping, out of the deep waters, wiped the shadows away with a rough hand and forced myself to look at that night, three nights before, when the man who wasn't a man but a threat smacked into my space and dared me to rise to his challenge. That night, three nights before, when the boredom had dripped out the soles of my feet and I needed anything to light me on fire, and he heard my call and he came. Was that my downfall? I wanted someone to see me, and so they had.

I saw him, as I had seen him then, a great, flapping tongue between wet lips, a bulging ego pulling him forward, all this balanced on two spindly legs. There he was in the bar, bouncing off everyone, running his tongue through their ears. I saw their backs shiver, saw their dignity curl like a pill bug back into the bottom of their throats, as he rolled by, takeout Chinese food bags smiling from the gallows of his bloated fingertips.

We were outside. We were talking, that night, three nights ago. Ty was glowing, the sort of shade men turn when they do something they think is brave, buoyed by adrenaline, testosterone, a false sense of their own importance. I curled in on myself, let him think he saved me. I had the dark.

Things grew hazy there. They all trailed away to their cars parked out on the side streets, tucked down faraway corners, all the myriad places service staff are forced to walk from to keep our customers safe and happy. But I waited, and then I followed him. And he wasn't staff, and so he was parked in the lot, in the far back corner, alone in the weed-choked dark.

There he was, shifting to open his car, coiling the bulk of his body, puffing. He turned when I approached. What sort of lion had I been, then, in the dark? What color had I glowed, full of my own sort of bravado? There was the trouble. I let myself become a man. I forgot the kernel of who I am, and so I became sloppy and cocksure. I drank, I got arrested, I missed my chance to clean up, and now they had another body, a pretty fresh one. What would be the price of my mistake?

I walked back to the bar.

Where had the blood gone? Did I wipe off my hand before I closed his door? My knife? I didn't have it, had to borrow one from the kitchen for a day, until I could go get my own. I had tossed mine into the woods, along with my shirt. But which woods? There, at his car? Or further afield?

Fog closed tighter over my face. I wiped it away, and it left with my answers. The ticket machine burped out an order, a cloud of fruit flies billowed up from the tap drain, Ty chuckled when he saw me.

"You all right, Soph? Still hungover from Billy's, huh? That two-day hangover, man. She's a bitch."

"You have no idea."

He clapped me on the back and kept moving toward the hostess. "What's going on?"

There was one more thing. I pulled my purse out from the milk crate under the bar, unzipped a side pocket. It was dry and wilted, turning a bit green; but it was there, tucked away safely. At least that much, I had done right.

When I was sure I was alone, I pulled the tongue out of my purse and dropped it into the brine.

Clotho at Her Wheel

I waited for them to find anything, to ask any questions, to see me and to know, but they didn't. The days spun out into one long, bloated stretch, reaching before and behind me, silent and empty save for the near-constant hum of my mites chittering, digging, dancing in the hypogean caves of my bones, *foramen, fossa, sinus.* Their creep made me restless; I grew sharp points and snarled.

One golden afternoon, Ty bent into my fridge and asked, "Hey, Soph, what are you doing with this jar back here?"

I swiped the door shut. "That's my experiment."

He lifted two hands in surrender and backed away "Whoa! Okay, buddy. Just curious. Sorry!" His eyes when he looked at me were two questions, his smile tipped sideways, off-kilter. I tried to soothe him, paint sunshine across my face, but found I could not; I was certain that if I pulled back my lips into a grin, the clatter of my heart would bounce the teeth right out of my skull. So instead, I made my hands busy, made myself move, so he might not see the way I shivered. Might not see the mite crawl out of one ear and down the nape of my neck.

"It's a new brine. Very sensitive to light and air. Just . . . I'm the only one that can handle it, okay?"

"All right, buddy. Whatever you say."

When Murph and Nora came in I thought maybe they'd finally put the pieces together, but Murph just slammed down onto his stool and rolled into a deep belly laugh.

"I heard you met those meatheads down in the jailhouse, Sophie."

Christ.

"That would be one way to put it."

"Happens to more people than you'd guess. Don't let them scare you. You'll be fine, kiddo." He said this in a way that was supposed to make me feel better about being trapped in a cage, stripped of my identification, spit out into the world with a mark on my record that will tag along behind me for the rest of my life. It did not.

Nora, beside him, sat quiet, her eyes on my new knife lying on the clean cutting board. There were thoughts in there; I could see them, swirling. I could feel her trying to pin them down with a finger. She knows, it's on the tip of her tongue, but she won't say it yet because she can't quite see the shape of the answer herself.

"You all right, Nora?"

She looked up, her eyes dark question marks. "Yeah. I'm fine. Just a long week is all. I'm sorry to hear about your night, Sophie. That sucks. What day was it again?"

"A week ago from today. Last Tuesday." In truth, I'd been arrested early Wednesday morning, but some small instinct for self-preservation stepped in, mouthed to me that I should lie, that days don't end until you go to sleep and I hadn't yet, when I was caged.

"Right. Tuesday. Damn. So you have your court date soon?"

"Next week."

"Welcome to the system." She smiled, the ghosts gone from her face, her eyes once again warm brown, like the creek after a rainstorm.

I knew then that I'd have to work to make her see. She was so close, but that alibi, that perfect, shining alibi, was in her way. It was so useful, I could have laughed! It would be easy to stay hidden. But I was tired of being quiet, of hearing the town gossip of a man, a *man*, doing what I had done. How typical. Men taking credit for the things women do. The time had come to find a way to make a mark so big and wide they couldn't ignore it, to make my purpose known, to birth myself out into the world unafraid.

"Hey, Sophie." Murph's voice cracked into my thoughts. "Can we get two of those special margaritas you make? Been out in the heat all day, and I'm dying for something fresh and salty."

"Of course." Smile.

"Just one, actually," Nora said, her face pulled into a grimace. "Headache's been building all day. Alcohol's probably not a great idea. Can I have some water, though?"

"You got it."

I had to shove the newest tongue down into the jar before I lifted it from the fridge. Still full of water and fatter, it was more buoyant than the others, and wouldn't stay down, much like the man it had been attached to, pushy and clamoring to be seen.

Not yet, not yet. This wasn't the right way. I would make a scene, a story, a nightmare. I had what I needed, finally awake and waiting restless at home. The final piece would come to me, and when he did, I would know it.

Nora

Outside, she spoke. "Sophie's got a new knife."

"What, Martin?"

"Her knife. It's not the one she usually uses. Different-colored handle."

"Interesting." He pulled a half-smoked cigarette out of its box. "Let's be sure to have a chat with her this week."

A Very Tired Woman

It hit her in the face as soon as she walked through the door, the sound of grown women shrieking at one another. Someone was called a whore, someone else screamed, "Bitch!" and then the scene cut to a woman sitting primly in her perfect living room, recounting the whole sordid ordeal for unseen producers.

"Dan, can we turn the TV off for tonight?" Nora asked, sloughing off the layers of herself that she wore to work—jacket, shoes, stern face. Another migraine had been building in the pit behind her eyes for some hours now. Lights flashed across her vision, shimmering kaleidoscopes and writhing squiggles of line and pale color; the first wash of dizziness fell over her, and she grabbed the door handle for balance. If she didn't get into stillness soon, she'd be paying for it.

"Dan? Did you hear me?"

She walked into the living room, which was dark save for the flashing TV screen. The women were seated around a dinner table now. One of them was crying. Nora closed her eyes to gather herself, but the lights sparkled across the backs of her lids. Where was Dan? It was only eight o'clock. He should still be awake.

Christ, those idiot women, she thought. *I can't think with their jabbering.*

The remote was on the floor. She bent slow, careful not to lose her balance, and grabbed it to turn the TV off.

"Hey, I'm watching that." A lump on the couch that she'd taken for unfolded blankets turned its face up to her.

"No you aren't, you were asleep."

"I was just resting, Nor. Leave it on." He tugged the blanket up tighter over his shoulders.

"How can you even sleep with that?" A slap rose in her throat. She didn't know why she was so angry.

"With what?"

A sunburst blazed across her eyes, and Nora reached out a hand to steady herself on the couch arm. She could hear the blood rushing in her ears, her own breath ragged beside it. The floor beneath her rolled, and she felt her stomach heave.

"With that blanket! It's a million degrees outside, aren't you hot? And this stupid show. I don't get how you can fall asleep when they're screeching like that."

"Did you wake up on the wrong side of the bed this morning or something?"

"Are you kidding me?" The sunburst cracked open to a thousand wriggling worms. Nora pressed her palm to her forehead. Not now. She couldn't deal with this right now.

"Sorry, I shouldn't have said that. Come here." Dan scooted upright and opened his blanketed arms to welcome her in. "Sit with me and we can watch together. When was the last time we hung out? I feel like I only ever see you when you're asleep lately."

"Dan, I can't today." She needed water and a cool room. Maybe a shower. Darkness and quiet, just until she could get her bearings back. The floor tilted under her feet; she was going to fall over if she didn't get herself grounded soon.

"Then at least give me the remote back." He wrapped the blanket back around himself.

"Can't you just leave it off for tonight?" Nora felt the ragged edge in her voice.

"Babe. I need this today. You have no idea—"

"I have no idea? *I* have no idea? What did you have today, Dan, on a Thursday morning? A broken arm? A heart attack? Maybe some hungover college idiots come in for their dose of IV fluids?"

His face crumpled. "Come on, Nora, that's not fair."

"Fair! You know what's not fair? I spent hours today taking notes on a shit house, left by shit people who'll get away with being shit because we don't have the resources to track them. No electricity. No running water. The yard was full of trash—rusted-out junk, plastic crap, a fucking tetanus nightmare obstacle course.

"We don't know for certain, but we think they were keeping the kids and dogs in the same room because it was covered in feces, excuse me, *shit*, and packed with baby toys. Neighbors finally called us when they heard glass breaking—one of the dogs got so desperate it jumped out the fucking window. Everyone on the block swears"—she threw her hands up in mock innocence—"they had no idea this was going on. But there's no way no one noticed anything. How could you not? Someone did, because by the time we got there, they'd booked it. Had to have been tipped off. Kids, dogs, all gone. We have no idea where they went.

"Meanwhile, I've got six dead men staring at me in my dreams and dead women following me, and I've never felt more useless in my life. Doesn't help that everyone has an opinion about us—"

"Us? You mean you and me? Who has an opinion on us?"

"Not us, I mean *us*. Cops. They're either blowing smoke up my ass thinking that'll make me like them or telling me to go to hell, and I'm sick of it, Dan."

"Yeah, well, you chose that job."

She saw by the pop of his eyes that he'd said it without thinking, that he hadn't really meant it, that he was just tired too, and grumpy.

Every bad car wreck she had to stand by, he saw later in the ER. Every falling-down drunk, every battered spouse. They worked flip sides of the same coin, and it wasn't fair of either of them to hold their end up like a cudgel against the other. Those words though, true as they may have been, stung. He was supposed to be her partner.

"Excuse me?" Nora's tongue, forced all day to stay wrapped up and calm, became a lash.

He wiped a hand down his face and met her where she was. "I can't handle this today. You want to know what my day was like? First patient. Pregnant teenager. We suspect abuse, but you know what I can do about it? Zip. She won't talk. We called your buddies down, and CPS. Maybe they'll have more luck, but who knows. Later? Guy comes in with a black foot. Not green, not yellow. Black. Thing's dead. He's severely diabetic but hasn't been taking his meds right or getting up to walk when he should, and so now he's gonna lose his leg. And he hates me for that, as if I had anything to do with him being an idiot. Sorry, I shouldn't say that about my patients, but Christ almighty, I'm tired, Nora.

"And it went on like that all damn day. People screaming and yelling and taking all their problems out on us. One of the docs got spit on, right in her face, and honestly I have no idea how she kept her cool, because I would have clocked the guy. So yeah, I don't need your lectures, Nora. I've got my own shit."

She felt the words rise, tumble out of her mouth before she had a chance to pull them back. "Yeah? Well, as you said, you chose that job."

Dan rose from the couch, the blanket falling to a pile on the floor. His face had become granite, hard and cold and fierce. Nora felt a wall thrown up between them, something that sparked and flared and was bolstered by both of their stubborn, exhausted prides.

"I'm gonna go home for the night."

"You are home."

"To my parents'. I'll talk to you tomorrow," he said, his voice a flint, ready to start a fire if she pushed just a bit more.

"Fine. Do that." Nora knew the sour sting in her mouth was more pain than fear, but she couldn't back down. Her feet had grown into roots, and she wasn't ready to bend yet. Neither, she knew, was he.

He gave her one last look, his jaw pushed forward, eyes shining with anger or tears, she couldn't tell, and then grabbed his car keys from the side cabinet and slammed out the front door.

Silence.

Later, after a shower and a glass of water and an hour alone in the cool dark of her bedroom, Nora began to cry. She couldn't remember the last time she'd fought with Dan. They'd had squabbles here and there, maybe a few big blowouts back when they were both younger and hotheaded, but they just didn't fight. It wasn't in their natures. He was her support, and she his; they were partners. The truth was, she missed him. It had been too long since they'd had one good day to themselves, nothing else butting in.

She almost called him then, but then she heard that shrill cackle of some New York City socialite. In her anger, she'd forgotten to turn off the damn TV. The fist in her heart hardened, and she put away her phone. He should be the one apologizing anyway. It was his fault the fight had started in the first place, right?

She shut the TV off, climbed into bed, more alone than she'd felt in a very long time.

The haints didn't appear that night; they didn't need to. Other things were haunting Nora.

Sophie

That night, when it finally came, was a dead night. The air, which had been heavy all day, sticky and immobile, suddenly sucked backward in anticipation of the hurricane crashing against the far-away shoreline. I could feel the teeth of lightning high above us in the sky; out to the east, rain storms pounded the ground and rivers swelled. Everything was alive and crackling, waiting for the storm to break. I thought I might buzz right out of my skin.

And then, he walked in.

"You haven't seen Nora, have you?" he asked as he clambered onto one of my barstools. The place was empty, the lights lowered; it was an hour before close on that dead night. The kitchen staff had left half an hour ago. It was just me and the bar, and then him, alone in the electric dark.

"Nope. Was she meeting you here?"

"Well, no. I just thought . . . we got in a fight a few days ago, and we haven't talked yet. I guess I hoped I might find her here."

He was nervous, squirming in his seat.

"You haven't talked? You live together."

"I went home for a few days. To my parents'. I meant to call or come back home before now, but I don't know. I needed some space to get my thoughts together and figured she might too. Work's been grinding us both down. She texted me yesterday, but if I'm honest, I've been too nervous to read it. You really haven't talked to her this week?"

I folded my face so it became his mirror. I'm not sure when I started playing the Great Pretend with Dan. Not long after I met him, after I learned how utterly normal he was, a cookie-cutter mold of the same jeans and baseball hats and T-shirts that all the bland men around here wear. He's Cheap Whiskey and Lager and football on Sundays, while she's something altogether more complex. There's nothing wrong with a small life, so long as it's interesting, but there was nothing interesting about Dan. Worse, he'd drag Nora down with him into his numb mediocrity. She deserved better.

And there, in that crouching gloom, I knew I'd been given a gift. He was a bug squirming on my counter, and I saw I could shove a pin in his back, nail him to the boards.

"I haven't seen her. But maybe if you stick around, sometimes she comes in when she gets off."

"Yeah." He cast a glance around the room, as if to be sure I wasn't hiding her somewhere. "Slow night?"

"Sunday. And school just started. We always get a dip that first month after the kids go back."

"Really? Why?"

I ducked into the fridge. "People like to pretend they're responsible. School nights and all that. I'm sure you get swings too, depending on the time of year." Tucked in a back corner was my packet, safe where I left it. I'd told the servers they were my chia seeds, for energy, and if anyone touched them they'd be dead. It wasn't all a lie.

"Oh yeah . . ." He spun off about work, and I let him.

Into a shaker: Vodka, lemon, a bit of my blackberry simple syrup. Ice.

". . . of course, in my line of work, boring is good!" Chuckle. "Holidays will be here before we know it though, and they bring a lot of stress; and we just got through summer, people are always doing dumb shit in the summer."

Seeds. Shake.

"Yes, I'm aware."

Sugar the rim of a coupe glass, pour the drink back in. Duck down into the fridge for my fruit.

"You ever had to send someone our way? I wouldn't think, not in a place like this. You're too fancy."

"Oh, you'd be surprised . . . My barback got to thinking he was bartender one night. Private party, so the rules get bent, you know. Anyways, he fed some groomsman about ten vodka tonics, and we found the poor guy passed out on the patio. He's lucky he's alive."

"The barback or the groomsman?" His mouth was curved into nervous anticipation, a bowl to catch the punch line of the joke he hoped we shared, here together alone on a Sunday evening. I'm sure he thought that if I was on his side, Nora would be too.

I let him indulge his delusion. "Both."

The last thing my father said, before he left us, was that he'd be right back, that they'd work this out, they'd talk later. Always later, always soon. In men's mouths, *later, soon*—they mean *never*. They mean *not unless I want to.* They mean *stay at home and worry. Stay at home and beat yourself up.* And he had done that to Nora. I saw then that I could save her and wrench myself out of the terrible waiting I'd fallen into. I would make a flag out of him.

"Whatcha making?"

Two blackberries, impaled on a bamboo stick, laid gently across the top of the glass.

"New recipe." I slid the drink across the counter. "Something I've been playing with. My taste testers drink free."

"Oh sweet! Thanks, Sophie. No wonder Nora loves you."

"She loves my drinks at least. Cheers."

I hid my hands, so he couldn't see them trembling.

A Witch in the Woods

The first thing that happened to Dan was a sort of descent into doe-eyed wonder. He grew soft and slack; his pupils dilated. *Atropine, hyoscyamine, scopolamine.* I wound their names about my tongue like a rosary.

"Shit, Sophie. What's in this? They still test us at work sometimes. I can't take anything illegal."

I imagined what concern would feel like, let the paint of that lie wash down over the still mask of my face.

"I must have gotten my pours wrong—still working on it. You feeling okay?"

"Yeah." He rubbed his forehead, which had grown pale and clammy. "I've just been working a lot. Short-staffed. And this fight with Nora must have really taken it out of me more than I thought. I hate not talking to her, you know?"

His smile, when he looked back up at me, was a lost thing. His eyes wide, forehead wrinkled in slight concern.

"Let me get you some water." I shoved a glass at him, and he took it, his hands quaking and pale. They looked like leaves, caught in the wind before a storm.

"Fuck." He looked down at his water glass, which I knew he could not see, not with his eyes open so wide they were nothing more than black pits, swallowing the light.

A breeze skimmed through the open back window of the bar. It smelled like rain, like thunder rolling somewhere off in the near distance.

"Hey, Sophie, I'm sorry to be annoying, but do you think you could text Nora for me? I can't drive home like this." He pushed his phone across the counter at me. "Combination's 87 . . . 92 . . ."

But he was already gone, drowsy on the lip of the bar. I took his phone, tucked it into my pocket. It was best not to draw attention to him.

"Dan?"

"Huh?" He mumbled into the wood of the bar.

"Why don't you come with me? I feel bad. Must have put too much in there. I live a fifteen-minute walk away. We can wait for Nora at my place. I've got tea and food. The walk, some fresh air, it might perk you up a bit."

He crawled off the seat and let me take his hand, like a child. His eyes, when he held them up, were black, and he shied away from the light. I thought of the ladies from ages ago, who used to drop nightshade into their pupils so that in the candlelight they would appear as something not quite themselves, not quite human. Was that how he saw me now? His mind was already gone, tripped off to someplace I couldn't follow. I turned off the lights and led him out the door. Lightning crackled off to the south; a breeze wound itself around our steps.

I put him on the porch swing my grandmother had once sat on, so many lifetimes ago; had sat on, her head wreathed in a lace of smoke, as she spoke to me of the secret power of my hands. All around us, my moonflowers glowed pale, hanging loose over the porch railing, swaying gently in the breeze that had grown teeth sometime in our walk here.

Dan reached out for one. "Whoa, Sophie."

"Beautiful, aren't they?"

"Is Nora coming? She'd love these." He slumped to the porch floor and, on hands and knees, he crawled to them, planted his face deep in the flower bell. His skin in the moonlight had grown glassy. He was trembling.

"Soon. Here." I pulled him back up to the bench. It was difficult work, lifting an earthquake; my feet dug hard into the wood below me. "Watch the storm with me."

And so we sat, two puny souls lost in the great swell of wind and cloud and cracking light. And in his body, another storm raged. His mouth grew dry and swung open, so he became a dumb thing, leaning on my shoulder. His breathing slowed with his heart, which found its beat no longer strong, but soft, swishing blood back and forth. The pulse under his clammy skin grew quieter as the thunder rumbled louder and the wind tore through my hair.

Somewhere in the night, he turned to me, and I saw he was frightened. In my face he saw the storm in all its brilliance, he saw the haunting that had climbed out from beneath my skin, all the writhing, biting, screaming mess of the me that lives below placid waters. He saw me, and he knew me for what I was. And when I looked back, I saw myself reflected in the inky black of his pupils, my eyes as wide as his, pulsing with all the electric power of the storm.

I took his hand and turned us back to the rain and the wind and the crashing thunder, and for breathless time we sat and watched the sheer, wild force that surrounded us. And for the first time in months, I felt small.

"Sophie," he said, when it was done and we were alone in the empty dark. "I don't feel good. Can I have some water?"

"I'll make you some tea, like my grandmother made me. It'll fix you right up."

Chamomile. Honey. The last of the seeds. Stir.

We walked out into the orchard, his child hand growing clammy in mine. We walked until the lights of my house grew small; deep into the crooked forest we walked. The sweet stench of apple rot, stronger now, bolstered by the rain, filled the air around us. Coyote song, trilling and wild, rose from the black mountain just beyond my borders. I felt all the hairs of my arms prick. I was a wild thing too; they were calling me home.

Dan stumbled once, twice. I held his hand, curled an arm around his back to keep him upright until we were far enough away from my house that no one glancing would know he was mine.

And then I laid him down under the knobby arms of a gnarled, old tree, and together, we watched the last clouds scud across the vast, black brilliance of the night. We smiled at the stars, which were far away and cold.

He was blue by morning.

A Woman Alone

The bed felt small without Dan in it. The great stretch of his limbs always made the space feel boundless, a sea big enough to hold the net of his anatomy. Alone and awake in the night that was blasting itself apart, Nora curled into herself.

They'd never gone so long without speaking. She hated that they'd fought, that she hadn't seen him since to say she was sorry, that she was just tired and stressed and she never should have taken it out on him. She tried to remember when their schedules matched up for a day off again, when they could touch base, be friends again. Was it next Tuesday? Wednesday?

Recently the days had begun to drip into one another, the hourglass turning end over end for weeks until she could no longer tell which way was up and which way was down. Once, when she was a child, she'd fallen into a swimming pool at dusk, just as the sky and water pulled on the same gloomy shades of gold and blue. Her daddy pulled her out, carried her in his arms to the safety of their beach chairs, and Nora had sobbed with life. But there had been a moment, before he splashed in and broke the quiet world into pieces, in which she found herself quite adrift in its murk. Weightless and ripped from the bounds of gravity, she'd lost up and down, the sky and the pool floor part of the same vast space.

He told her, after, that she'd actually been swimming downward, the shimmering reflection of a pool light on the floor mistaken for the sun. It happened to pilots too, in the twilight, in the desert. Sometimes they flipped entire planes upside down without noticing; the only hint of anything wrong a vague feeling of unease.

Lightning flashed outside, and her room burst into brightness; Nora swept her eyes away from the girl shivering in the far corner. She started to count, as her mother had taught her: "One . . . two . . . three . . . four . . . five . . . six . . ." A boom of thunder cracked. "Six miles away."

She closed her eyes against the shadows prowling the walls, thought about her dead men. Six of them. At least three missing tongues.

More lightning, another crash of thunder. Four miles.

Six men. Three tongues. Long dark hairs. And what else? A knife. Chipped cervical bones, deep gashes in their flesh. A knife sharp enough to do damage, small enough to wield in tight spaces, to hide, probably. The decay, the soft tissues, they made it hard to see clearly; the marks jagged, erratic, angry. So angry, the tip had broken off this time. If only they had the rest of the knife to match it to.

Sophie has a new knife. But they'd talked to her. Talked to them all, the employees at the Blue Bell. Sophie had an alibi. A party. A night in jail. And besides, she was *Sophie.* It couldn't be her. Nora's radar couldn't be that damaged, could it? But then, men made friends all the time with their violent comrades. But she was not a man. No, it couldn't be Sophie.

Another flash and roll, this time so big it shook the bones of the house, painted jagged shadows in her room. Thunder cracked around her. The storm was directly overhead.

Nora pulled the sheets up tight to her chin, listened to the wind rip through the aging windows. A ghost, her mother had told her when she was young, Black Annie. It was not the wind howling, but that monstrous woman, prowling just outside, stealing children. Another one of her fairy stories, Nora knew, but a useful one. It kept her away from windows during lightning storms, kept her safe inside the arms of her house.

But something was creeping over the windowpane. Long, pale fingers, thin as winter breath. A face. A warning. Nora closed her eyes against it. But the fingers tugged her even as she rolled back to sleep. She couldn't shake the feeling of something harsh and dry, whispering in her ear. It was urgent, a creeping, crawling chill that spun down her neck to the rooted base of her spine, coiling in her belly, and Nora felt suddenly as if her whole spirit would shiver right out of her skin if she didn't move, didn't do something, anything.

She rolled over, eyes closed, tugging the sheets up over her face. Heat and humidity be damned, the breeze from the window would keep her cool enough and she wanted some peace, to cocoon in the dark, away from the shades still shivering in the corner.

She opened her eyes when the child's blue lips pressed against hers, and she discovered they were just as cold as they had been that day she'd pulled her out of that cramped cupboard. Nora clutched a hand to her mouth, to hold back the scream that ripped into her throat. Thunder scraped the top of the house; lightning flashed again.

"One . . ." She forced herself to breathe, rolling over gently to stare instead at the antique molding on her ceiling. "Two . . ." It needed to be sanded, a new coat of paint. Dan had promised he'd get that done. "Three . . ."

Two pairs of feet dropped down from above. Nora screamed. She screamed again when she scrambled from her bed, sheets still twisted about her waist, and almost stepped on Jane Doe, now lying prone on the floor.

"What do you want?" She couldn't stop the tears now, her voice cracked and raw. Shaking, Nora dropped down to the hardwood floor, shoved herself into the far corner of her room. They were everywhere, dripping down the walls, sprawled across her floor, dangling from the ceiling. She said their names, a rosary. Lauren Morris, Patricia Ng, Samantha Wyatt, Rachel Barber, Jane Doe, Arya Ward. They spilled over her tongue in a grotesque circus wheel, while new faces, new names edged in at the corners, faces she didn't know yet, broken lives she would touch, in time. Always in time.

Rain pounded on the roof, and in it, she heard her answer. *Listen!*

In the dark, in the night, Nora listened. Her heart broke with the listening, while around her the storm raged. She saw the knife, small, light, perfect for a woman's hand, flash through the air in front of her. Hair, long and dark, that Nora had never really paid attention to because she always had it braided or in a bun for work, swept up and away, tight off her face.

Sometimes I wish they'd just shut up, you know?

Their tongues. She'd shut them up. She'd been so cool, but that was because she knew how to be, after years of practice.

It couldn't be.

"Sophie," Nora whispered.

It could only be.

It was like someone had lifted a curtain; every bit of Nora, which had been thrumming only seconds before, fell still, and the whole world grew clear in front of her eyes. She needed proof though. There were still puzzle pieces that didn't quite fit. Sophie was small—could she lift a man like Mark? Like Trent? She always seemed to have an alibi, though that alibi always put her in proximity to the men. There was the question of evidence as well. Only four bodies, six men, and three of those bodies so badly destroyed there was hardly anything they could pull off them.

Suddenly she was up off the floor and out in the living room, her bag upended and notes strewn around her. The puzzle of months was right there, at the tips of her fingers; she just needed to put it all together. Something to show Murph, a path they could take together, movement. The answers were there, she just needed to nail them.

Something tugged at her, just on the bottom of her ear. A hiss, a finger wheedling into her heart. She checked her phone again; nothing. *Maybe I should call him*, she thought. She picked up her phone again. Put it down. The storm would break a call. She'd have to wait until morning; she could wait until morning.

Morning broke with a vengeance.

"Martin!"

The cry broke through her thoughts. Nora turned to see Barb rushing down the hall toward her.

"Another body," Barb panted. "Down in the creek behind Mechum's Auto. Charlie and Babson are already down there, roped everything off and talking to the poor people who found him."

Him.

"Is Murph in? I really need to speak to him."

"He's coming in later, sugar. Sarge wants you out there now."

"But I need to talk to Murph."

"No time, sweetheart. You'll have to find him when you get back. Or give him a call."

And so Nora found herself flung suddenly far out to sea, and the world tipped sideways again.

Nora Martin

The skeleton, for that was all that was left of the man, had caught in the waving arms of a Virginia creeper. On a normal day, the vine dipped her green fingertips through the pebble-tripping creek, but this morning she was half-submerged, drowning in the muddy waters that had swollen with the storm in the night. The man that was once a body but was now bones waved along with her, as if he'd seen Nora from some distant shore and wished to say hello. She supposed that might be true.

Charlie was out in the creek with his waders on, slogging upstream through the rushing water, poking the bank with a pole, searching for clues, holes, places to hide. The plants lay quiet, ignoring his prodding, revealing nothing. Nora let him wander while she went to find Babson, who was standing with the shop owners some ways away. The couple looked shaken and pale, their eyes wide and hands over their mouths. She couldn't blame them. No one expected to step outside for a smoke break and find themselves staring at a skeleton.

She made her voice a soft thing, but firm, as Murph had taught her.

"Hey, Martin," Charlie said to her sometime later, after she'd left the couple to review protocol with Babson and slid down the slick creek bank. Blackberry thorns tore at her slacks. A few berries, hard and red, still clung to the thin arms, and she knew without tasting that their juice would be sour.

"Hey, Charlie," Nora said, and she heard the sigh in her voice. She was glad to have him here on this day that she wasn't feeling quite herself. Thoughts of Dan rustled in the back of her mind. Where was Murph? She looked around, hoping to catch sight of his big belly bumping along the road, but he was nowhere to be seen. A mouth pressed itself to her ear, but she brushed it away. She needed to stay here, in the creek, in the sun, in the present with the skeleton who used to be a body.

"Murph let you loose today, grasshopper?"

"Not in yet, but yes, I guess so. Sarge did, at least." She swept an errant curl off her forehead. The day was turning out to be sticky and warm; this September was a long summer grown fetid.

He smiled. "You've earned it. I, for one, am glad to have you."

"You might be the only one."

He looked up at her but didn't say anything, and she took his silence for understanding. Charlie, like Murph, saw more than he let on. And, like Murph, he kept his head ducked and did his job, respected those who did the same and ignored the rest. The men, who'd been slowly coming around to her again, softening the worst of their edges, would surely not take this sudden shift in her position well. A backlash would come, she knew. So it was good to have a friend on the island she found herself planted on.

"You haven't heard from him today, have you, Charlie? I need to talk to him."

"I haven't. Everything all right?"

"Yeah . . . well. I'm not sure." She fell quiet, watching the rippling creek, the plants dancing in sun-dappled water. A beautiful scene, save for the skeleton, smiling in the middle of it all. Her silence grew a skin; she broke it. "You got anything for me?" Fingers poked the back of her mind, mouths pressed to her ears, whispering. She did her best to push them away. Sophie wasn't going anywhere. She'd talk to Murph as soon as he was in.

"I think . . . You got waders? Come look."

Nora pulled the long rubber flesh over her own and stepped out into the creek, taking Charlie's offered hand when the water slammed against her, steadying herself in the rushing current. Faces burbled up under the water, urgent. She looked away, to the man waiting for her. They walked.

The skeleton was still waving.

"Cheerful guy, huh?"

Nora dropped down to peer into the skull's ruined face. Bits of vine had tangled through its jaw, which hung broken and slack, as if in a scream, as if someone had wrenched it open and plucked out a tongue. She ducked closer, shining her flashlight into the hole. There it was, what she expected: sharp gashes, possibly a small, thin knife. Like the knife that had been used to puncture the man they'd found only a week ago. No more than four inches, smooth, not a hunting knife like they'd thought at first. The sort of knife anyone kept in their home to cut fruit. A whisper slithered through the back of her mind; in the spray from the current, she thought she saw a scream. Dan had never gone so long without talking to her before. Fingers ran up the backs of her arms, but when she reached to brush them away, they had already disappeared.

"Val coming?" Charlie asked when Nora stood back up.

"Yeah. Got stuck in traffic from Richmond. Accident on the road. You know how people fly down 64."

"I've got a few buddies who patrol for State." He nodded. "Well, let me show you what else I found, up this way."

Together, they waded through the swollen creek. More than once, Nora reached out to grab Charlie's elbow, to catch herself from falling. Her feet, lost in the murky water, slid across slick soapstone and quartz; wet hands reached up and grabbed for her ankles, faces bubbled up through the current.

"You all right, Martin?"

"I'm good, yeah. Thanks, Charlie." She blew them all away on a puff of her breath.

He led her to a bend in the creek, about a hundred yards upstream from where the bones now waved cheerily from their leafy net. A willow tree stood alone in the tall grass, its long arms dangling into the water. She hadn't recognized it at first, wasn't familiar enough with the walk from the south end of the creek. And it looked different now, in the fall, fattened from summer. This was the tree she'd watched from a bench that January day they cried Mark into the ground. The church, off to her right, stood silent, its red bricks warming in the morning sun.

"Look." Charlie pulled back a hank of thin branches.

The hole had flooded in the night, but there it was, an open mouth wide enough to comfortably fit a child, or a folded man, and deep enough to be sure they were never seen.

"I checked under here, because willow trees are monsters. Roots just bust right through everything. I figured if there was a good place to hide someone, it would be here."

"I think you figured right," Nora said. "Who owns this section of creek, do you know? We'll probably need a warrant."

She looked past the willow to the neat rows of gnarled apple trees, and felt a fist clench her stomach. A bench in bitter cold, Sophie, her eyes bright and alive. *I've got the family business to think about.* The screams. They fed them with screams in the winter. And sure enough, those scrubby trees had burst into colorful bloom. The apple buds, a few weeks ago nothing but hard, green things, had begun to swell and blush colors. In a few weeks, they'd be ready for picking.

"Well, depends what bank you're standing on," Charlie started, but he was interrupted by the buzz of Nora's phone. She looked down. Val.

"Hey, lady!" Nora held up an apologetic finger to Charlie and walked off down the creek, her eyes sweeping the field, looking for anything that might quell the pounding beat of her heart. "You almost here?"

"Ten minutes, baby girl. But first, I just got a call from the lab. They were able to get a rootball off that hair you found . . ."

"And?" Nora knew the answer, had known it for months, but she needed to hear Val say it.

"Female. Matches the saliva and skin samples we got off his body too."

"I knew it."

"And one more thing—we lifted a partial print off the car door . . . and got a match. You know anyone named Braam?"

"Shit. Shit!"

Charlie turned to her. "Nora?"

"Sophie Braam. The bartender at the Blue Bell. It's her, Charlie. And . . . Dan . . . Oh God." The realization hit her like a punch. He'd never been gone this long before. Had never just ignored her, even when he was mad, even when he needed a breath. But she'd texted him last night, broke down in the middle of the storm and her tears and sent him a message. He'd be up by now. She checked her phone. Nothing.

"Martin. Slow down." Charlie grabbed her arm. "Talk to me."

"We don't have time. Charlie, we need to get in the car and go, *now*. I *knew* it. It's her. Fuck!"

Before he could stop her, she'd climbed up the slippery creek bank and took off running to her car. He could come with her, or not, she didn't care. She knew where she needed to go and no one was going to stop her.

After

(The End)

And here we are, at the end. At the beginning.

I knew before I saw the dust that someone had figured me out. I felt it in my bones, my muscles, every minuscule, quivering part of me. We dance, did you know that? The very smallest parts of you, of me, dance to a rhythm cast wide over the earth, a webbing of life and death. Throbbing, pulsing motion. Even as I am, descended into some creature that wriggles on its own, I feel it. Perhaps I have felt it more, since I let go of the stiff backbone of Me.

It's a shame the picnic will have to be abandoned. That jam is my favorite. Blackberry. Bramble. *Braam.*

Behind me, the forest looms dark and cool. The day hasn't breathed into the underbrush yet; the trees are alive and shivering in the dewy chill. There's a path through the poison ivy that I know well, from so many years of living here among creeping, coiling things. I can run as quiet as a fox. It would take them days to find me, but I don't want to run yet. Not quite yet. First, watch. Listen.

The train is whistling, do you hear her? There in the near distance, screaming, *I am coming, I am coming! Run.*

The car is closer now, the smoke of gravel spitting high into the humid air. The bees hang around me, unaware or uncaring. A few have landed on Dan, their long, black tongues probing, tasting, testing. They leave trails of pollen dust on his blueing flesh. I could laugh. Those were my high school colors. Blue and gold. And here is Dan, wearing them.

He's not what they want though, and one by one they lift clumsy bodies off his, bang back into the drooping heads of nearby flowers. A few fly away into the wide, clear sky, and I wonder if they're taking him. In the oldest tales, it's the bees who carry our souls away; bit by tiny bit, we are brought to our fate.

A few butterflies join them; their wings, small and white, flap in a wild zigzag. My blowfly has brought friends. They've congregated now in the hollow places of him: his eyes, his nose, his mouth. I know soon the beetles will be digging through the dirt toward him. He is growing into the earth. He is more full of life than he has ever been.

The neighbor's dog is barking. Twin car doors open and slam shut. I'm hidden here, in the green, in the roots and mud and apple rot. They can't find me yet; they'll go to the house first. A good two hundred yards away, they can't see me yet. I have time. If I leave, can I make up a story? Can I tell them, in days or weeks or hours, when they find me, that we were both attacked? I feel a wild beat in my heart, like the first time I took a life, like the night I found myself pacing behind a plexiglass window. I will not go back to a cage. I won't let them poke me and prod at me, try to understand what they're not capable of. I know what they'll say about me.

They're knocking on the front door. My name bursts out into the heat. Short, sharp, a knock, an accusation. It's Nora. She knows. She'll know where to find me too, in the end.

The trees are whispering behind me. The mountains are calling. It would be easy, to slip away.

The train screams again. I can't hear their knocks anymore; they've been drowned out by the mechanic churning of dozens of wheels. The bees float in the air, humming and searching. Sun spills down through the leaves. For one last moment, everything is still in the world. Breathe. *Breathe.*

Once, when I was a girl, I got stuck on a balance beam, one-handed, my legs up in the air. I'd been doing a cartwheel when I lost momentum and stopped. I felt in that moment that I could have stayed there forever, grown roots that would wrap around the beam so I would become a tree. Or I would fall and break myself. I needed to make a decision.

In the pause for thought, in the perfect, still balance, when I felt the architecture of my body from fingertips to toes, I pushed off.

I am coming! The train is wailing. The trees are cool and dark.

They are coming. Look! Can you see them, running down from the porch? My poor flowers will die.

They are coming.

Ivy tangles around my ankles. In my rush, I forgot to look for the path. No matter, I'll deal with it later.

Who will hold my grandmother's hands when I'm gone?

There's no time. They are coming. They are coming.

Run.

Acknowledgments

This black sheep owes her eternal gratitude to her family, who, though they may not quite understand me, have always stood by my side. Mom, Abby, this book would not exist without your support. And to my grandmother, who always encouraged me to march to the beat of my own drum, I wish you could be here to share this moment with us.

Thank you to my agent, Mark Falkin. Your straight-shooting advice and guidance throughout this entire process have been invaluable. Every introvert needs a cheerleader, and Daphne Durham, you have been the best cheerleader I could ever have asked for. Thank you for all the hard work you put into this book, and for seemingly always knowing, through some sort of editor ESP, exactly when I needed a boost. Lydia Zoells, thank you for keeping me organized and on schedule. To my copy editor, Andrea Monagle, and my proofreaders, Elizabeth Schraft and Vivian Kirklin, thank you for patiently combing through this text. Brianna Fairman, thank you for stepping in to guide me through the finish line. To the entire team at MCD, I feel so incredibly lucky to have you all with me on this journey.

A great teacher is invaluable, and I have been blessed with many. Thank you to Mark Marini, who spent far too many hours for his own sanity reading my angsty teenager poetry, for being the first person to see me as a writer, and for encouraging me to continue. And to Bill Guerrant, who pushed me to believe in myself, and who is always up for a great discussion about Arthurian lore. To my mentor and supervisor, Elizabeth Reeder, sometimes your critiques feel uncomfortably like being nailed to the wall, but I wouldn't be the writer I am today without your questions. Carolyn Jess-Cooke, thank you for helping me wade through the fire that is the querying and submissions process, and for continuing to be a support throughout this journey. And to Martin Cathcart Fröden, the fearless leader of our little freewheeling workshop group—writers can be rather melancholy creatures, so thank you, especially, for encouraging our laughter.

A book, I've learned, is like a child in that it takes a community to raise one. Emma Chaiken, Sophie's first fan, thank you for the conversations, the support, the tears, the laughter; thank you for everything. Thank you to my favorite bar regular, Richard Field, for giving a voice to Murph and for lighting just enough of a fire under my ass to keep me going even when I wanted to quit. Thank you to William Tillery, my personal Ron, who gave me the gifts of discipline and fortitude, and always always laughter in the middle of it all. To my friends in the Charlottesville Writers Critique Circle, especially Chris Register, thank you for all your sharp insight. To my New York poets, Margaux Galli, Jack Tricarico, Masuma Ahmed, Sherri Donovan, and Jesse Bernstein, without your open-armed support I might still be keeping my writing hidden in my notebooks. A special thanks to Isaiah Pittman, whose late-night conversations at the Barrow Street Ale House gave birth to Sophie Braam. Kate Porter, where do I begin? It's not every day that someone decides for you that you will be friends, but I'm so glad you forcibly adopted me. Thank you for giving me honest feedback, encouragement when I needed it, and for always walking just a bit too far with me.

In closing, I want to pay my respects to the women who inspired so much of this story. While researching serial killers, one comes into contact far too often with an especially sharp sort of pain. It's a pain I'm personally familiar with, having lost women I loved to male violence. So, to all of them who haunt me, know that you are missed, you are loved, you are not forgotten.

389